# HIGH-PRIORITY ASSET

## JUNO RUSHDAN

# COLTON CHRISTMAS CONSPIRACY

## LISA CHILDS

# MILLS & BOON

First Published in Great Britain 2020
by Mills & Boon, an imprint of HarperCollins*Publishers*
1 London Bridge Street, London, SE1 9GF

*High-Priority Asset* © 2020 Juno Rushdan
*Colton Christmas Conspiracy* © 2020 Harlequin Books S.A.

Special thanks and acknowledgement are given to Lisa Childs for her contribution to *The Coltons of Kansas* series.

ISBN: 978-0-263-28056-2

1120

Printed and bound in Spain
by CPI, Barcelona

# HIGH-PRIORITY ASSET

## JUNO RUSHDAN

Thank you to my very own Brenda C. I can always count on you to drag me out of my writing cave and to be a cheerleader in my corner since the beginning of my writing career.

# Chapter One

No matter where she went or what she did, Isabel Vargas couldn't escape *him*.

Some days were better than others, but Thursdays were the worst. The one night of the week she closed her art gallery alone so her best friend and assistant, Brenda, could take a yoga class across town with the hottest instructor in Santa Monica.

The one night she relived the traumatic encounter with her ex. Remembered the bruises, his breath on the back of her neck, his angry hands on her skin. His body holding hers captive. The malevolent rasp of his voice, his vile words pouring into her ears, punctuated by one delusional phrase he kept repeating. *I love you.*

The doorbell rang. She jumped at the buzzing sound, her heart racing. Drawing in a deep breath, Isabel calmed herself. She powered down her laptop, grabbed her quilted-leather purse and turned off the lights on the upper level of the gallery. Going as slowly as possible, she hoped whoever was at the locked front door would go away.

*Please, don't be him. Please.*

The doorbell buzzed again, pitching her nerves higher. She rummaged in her handbag and pulled out the tan bottle. Tiny white pills rattled inside. Her therapist had prescribed Ativan after her last incident with *him*, which had necessitated a restraining order. Isabel refused to think or speak his name. Doing so only gave him power when she needed to reclaim it.

She'd started jogging three miles every other morning, taken up boxing, Krav Maga and city-safety classes for women. She even got a dog. A ferocious Doberman named McQueen that she'd had trained as a guard dog. Keeping him in the office had proven too confined a space and customers got antsy around him in the gallery, so he was at doggie day care on Montana Avenue.

From the railing that overlooked the ground floor, she couldn't see who was at the front door. The bell rang in frantic succession. The irritating buzzer reverberated inside her.

Isabel popped the lid, put a pill in her mouth and swallowed it dry. Twice a day, every day. It kept the benzodiazepine in her system and her on an even keel.

She took her time down the stairs, her Jimmy Choos clacking against the dark hardwood of the steps. At the bottom, she saw a man wearing a suit and tie standing out front.

Spotting her, he banged on the glass door. "Hi! I was hoping someone was still here."

She edged closer. "What do you want?"

"I know you just closed ten minutes ago."

Every Thursday, at seven on the dot, she locked the door and finished wrapping up until she was ready to leave.

"You're usually open until eight," he said, glancing at the sign. "Except Thursdays, apparently. It's my anniversary and my wife has been dying to get that painting, the waterfall by Kush." He pointed to the far-left wall behind her, but she didn't turn and look at it.

Isabel kept her eyes on the man.

He was clean-cut and appeared pleasant enough, but the same had been said about Ted Bundy. The United States had more serial killers than any other country and Isabel knew firsthand what kind of twisted soul could hide behind a dazzling smile and a good suit.

"Sorry." She lifted the flap of her purse and stuck her hand inside, fumbling over her EpiPen and grabbing hold of her pepper spray. "You'll have to come back tomorrow." No one ever died from too much paranoia.

"Oh, please. I'm only ten minutes late. Don't make my wife suffer for my poor planning." He looked exasperated and distraught.

If he was being genuine, Isabel felt for him and his wife, but it wasn't her problem. "No purchases after closing, but tomorrow, I'll give you a ten percent discount." She'd take the money out of her forty percent commission. "I'll even write a note apologizing to your wife on your behalf, telling her it was my fault the gift was a day late."

"If I don't come home with the Kush, she might finally divorce me." His voice grew more insistent. "I'd hate to lose the best woman in the world because I ran ten minutes behind. Please. Can you help me?"

Isabel pulled out her pepper spray with her left hand and pointed it in his direction—a show of force that she meant business despite the door separating them—and took out her cell phone with her right. "Leave. Now. Or I call the cops."

"Whoa, lady." He put up both hands. "I'll buy her jewelry instead." With a scowl, he backed up to the curb, then he ran across the street, hopped in his Lexus and sped off.

"Good luck," she muttered under her breath. All the jewelry stores in the area were closed too by now. She dialed the valet at the parking garage she used two blocks down. "Hi, Jim, it's Isabel."

"Ready for your car?" he asked in an always cheery voice.

"Yes."

"It'll be waiting for you by the time you get here."

"Thank you." She hung up.

Smiling, Isabel tossed the mace and phone back in her purse. She turned off the rest of the lights and grabbed the Patrón Añejo tequila from behind the front counter.

The bottle was for Jim. He didn't have to go out of his way to accommodate her, sparing her the curbside wait while he went to fetch the vehicle. She showed her appreciation with a bottle of his favorite spirit once a month. It was easier to hand him a fiver when she picked up her car, but the personal touch of getting to know someone and making them feel special was important.

Her gallery was on the one block within a quarter mile that had a red curb, prohibiting parking, thanks to the fire hydrant and bus stop. She'd kill to have a parking meter out front she could feed all day. Proprietors had authorized spots around the back of the shops, but the rear door was steel, and anyone could be waiting on the other side. Anyone of course being *him*.

The back-side parking was also isolated, away from public view and passersby who might be able to save her life by calling the cops. Lord knew she certainly couldn't depend on any help beyond someone dialing 911.

She peered through the large display window, to the left and right, cursing the angle of the alcove in front. It was a great spot to hang a backdrop and photograph people as they arrived for special events, but it also limited her view. She scanned across the street.

*Nothing.* All clear as far as she could tell.

But unease slithered through her, making her shoulder blades hitch together. She had that familiar feeling again that she was being watched. Maybe it was her pervasive paranoia, which had become her new normal. Maybe it was just another Thursday when the memories surfaced, putting her on edge. Or maybe someone was out there, watching her.

Once she got to her car, she'd be all right, she told herself.

After grabbing her keys, Isabel set the alarm, unlocked the door and stepped outside. A creepy-crawly prickle shot down her spine, but she tried to shake it off.

She turned to lock up. First, the bottom latch on the handle and then the dead bolt at the top, but the key wouldn't go in.

She summoned her patience with a deep breath that did little to relieve her tension. Trying to tamp down the hopped-up energy zipping along her nerves, she double-checked that she had the right key and tried sliding it in the slot again.

*Darn it.* For the third time, it wouldn't go in. Was the problem the key or the lock?

Bending over for a closer look, she saw what was wrong. The keyhole was jammed with something. *What the hell?*

A shadow lunged up behind her.

The hot burn of alarm flared through her chest. Isabel whirled around, sucking in a fearful breath. A man she'd never seen before had her blocked in. Five-o'clock shadow. Dark, hateful eyes. The hood of his zip-up jacket was pulled over his head.

Steel glinted in the dying sunlight. A cold knife pressed against her throat as panic slammed into her.

He shoved her backward. "Scream and I'll cut you," he said in a low, harsh voice.

Her throat constricted. Her mouth went dry. She shut her eyes against a shattering sense of chaos and the stark threat of violence.

"Give me your weekly bank deposit," he demanded.

Brenda made the deposit on Wednesdays. Sometimes Fridays. She found her voice, the words like gravel in her throat. "We never make deposits on Thursdays." Her heart thundered in her ears. She pressed her lips together as if the small gesture would keep the rest of her from falling apart.

She hadn't learned how to defend against weapons yet in her Krav Maga class. There was nothing she could do with the knife to her throat.

*Stay calm. Cooperate.*

"Don't lie to me. I want the bank deposit."

Tears stung her eyes. Something brittle inside her cracked. "I'm not lying." Her voice was steady, but she trembled with terror.

"Don't think I won't slit your throat," he said, with the blade still to her jugular.

Her whole life flashed before her eyes along with all the things she'd never done, but that she wanted to live long enough to experience.

*What am I supposed do?*

*Think, Isabel.*

"Give me your wallet," he snarled.

His caustic words brought everything into sudden clarity. It was the same phrase her Krav Maga instructor used in practice.

She pulled herself together. More or less. Her body tensed. The breath stalled in her lungs. Muscle memory from training firing up, she found her center.

"Take it." She dropped the keys and opened the flap of her purse, coiling in readiness.

As he looked down, going for her wallet, the knife lowered, easing away from her throat.

With a quick, powerful thrust, she struck his face with the heel of her right palm. A distinctive crunch and the flow of blood from his nostrils told her she'd broken his nose.

"Ah!" He cupped his face as a gurgling noise came from him. Furious eyes flashed up at her.

Isabel prepared to throw an elbow strike, to kick and claw.

But then he lunged at her like a rocket.

*Oh, God!*

# Chapter Two

He swung a backhanded punch to her face.

Absorbing the stinging blow across her cheek, anger came faster than the pain, burning acid in her belly. She struggled to regain her bearings and move into a defensive stance.

With a brutal yank on her purse strap, he snatched her bag from her shoulder and took off running.

Utter shock stilled her for a nanosecond, then white-hot rage consumed her.

That was vintage Chanel! From her father!

Isabel kicked off her heels and bolted after him barefoot. "Hey!" She sprinted down the sidewalk. "Give it back!" Noticing pedestrians across the road, she said, "He's stealing my bag!" Then she remembered what she'd been told in her self-defense classes. "Fire! Fire!" She kept chasing him, grateful she'd worn the dress with a flowing accordion bottom rather than a restricting pencil skirt. "Call 911!"

The robber picked up speed, nearing the corner, and she worried she'd lose him and the purse that her father had given her before he died.

Digging deep, Isabel pushed harder, ran faster, pumping her arms while still carrying the stupid Patrón.

She switched hands with the bottle, moving it from left to right, her high school days of softball springing to mind. Slowing for a beat, she cocked back her arm and lined up her aim. She launched the hefty glass container at him.

The Patrón bottle soared through the air and struck him in the back of the head, throwing off his step. The bottle crashed to the ground, shattering.

Her mugger didn't stop and neither did Isabel. She kept sprinting after him, determined to get back what was hers until fire bit into the sole of her foot. Gasping, she froze and looked down at the smashed bottle. She was standing in the middle of the shards.

Glass had cut her, and the spilled alcohol made the wound sting.

Isabel thought for certain her assailant would get away, flee around the corner and disappear forever.

But a guy darted across the street—tall, broad, muscular—and leaped into action. He threw a powerful tattooed arm up and into the thief's chest, stopping the perpetrator in his tracks.

Her mugger went down in a hard sprawl, dropping the knife. The Good Samaritan grabbed him by the back of his sweatshirt and hauled him up as he flailed. Somehow the mugger slipped out of his hoodie, disentangling himself, and threw her purse like he no longer wanted it.

The thief scrambled away from the bigger man as if terrified, grabbed his knife and bolted across traffic. Horns blared and cars screeched to a halt.

Isabel dragged in a ragged breath. Immediate relief flooded her, and her body released the fear and anger that held her muscles tight. She had never seen anything so heroic except in movies and TV shows.

The do-gooder picked up her purse and jogged down the block to her.

Up close, he was more of everything.

Larger. Taller. Maybe six-three. His light brown hair was cropped close. A dark T-shirt stretched over defined shoulders, sliding down a muscular torso. Jeans hung low on his tapered waist.

He wasn't attractive, not the least bit pretty. He was gorgeous in a rough-and-tumble, almost scary way, but instead of sensing danger from him, his proximity made her mouth water.

"Hey, there." The stranger handed Isabel her irreplaceable purse. "Are you all right?"

*Yes. No. Maybe.* She settled for nodding and taking a deep breath.

"Care for a little assistance?" He gestured to the glass and her bare feet.

"Uh, yes. Please." She clutched the bag to her chest. "Thank you."

He swept her up from the sidewalk and into his arms like she weighed nothing. But Isabel wasn't a skin-and-bones type of woman. She loved carbs. Jogging only burned off so much and her curvy figure showed it.

"Where to?" he asked. His mesmerizing brown eyes bored into hers, and an entirely new feeling enveloped her.

"The Kismet art gallery down the block."

Tucking her close against his body, he took long strides toward her shop. He smelled powerful and sensual and safe all at once—an arresting mix that had her relaxing in degrees. She wrapped her arm over his shoulder.

"I can't believe that jerk tried to mug you."

"Me either."

"You've got a great arm. You threw that bottle like an ace," he said, and she picked up his accent. Not West Coast. Something distinctive. She'd guess Boston, New York or Chicago. "You clocked him good. That'll teach him a lesson."

"Thanks." She smiled and pain bloomed in her cheek. "Ouch." Holding her purse, she pressed the back of her hand to her face.

"Did he hit you?"

"Yeah."

"If I'd known, I would've kicked his butt up and down Santa Monica Boulevard."

To that she wasn't sure what to say. White knights weren't her thing and she never wanted to be treated like a damsel in distress. But she had needed help and appreciated his.

"Better yet, I could've held him for you while you did. The

way you were chasing him down, man, that was something. You strike me as a fierce woman who can take care of herself."

*Fierce?* Nobody had ever described her that way, especially not her overbearing uncle, who was determined to coddle her like a child. She would've smiled at the compliment if it wouldn't have hurt. "I'm just glad you intervened. Thanks, again."

At the door, he set her down gently, and she winced. He bent, grabbed her keys and shoes from the ground and gave them to her.

Isabel unlocked the door and when she opened it, the alarm sounded.

The stranger whisked her inside. "Where's your security panel?"

She pointed to the wall behind the front desk.

He carried her to it and shifted so she could access the keypad. "Go on. I won't look."

Turning his head away, he didn't glance back.

A guy with physical prowess *and* sex appeal *and* integrity. He was a mythical creature lost in California.

Still, she held her purse at a strategic angle, shielding the keypad while she punched in the code, shutting off the alarm. One could never have too much paranoia.

He set her down in the chair at the front desk. "Do you have a medical kit?"

"Um, I think Brenda, my assistant, keeps one there." She pointed to the bottom drawer closest to him.

He opened it, pulled out the kit and took a knee in front of her.

Serious, intricate ink was tattooed on his arms, adding to his already hard-and-gritty edge.

Not so long ago, men such as him, quintessential bad boys, had been her catnip. It was always exciting and fun in the beginning, and inevitably short-lived and a major disappointment. Every bad boy had been a bad decision, but none had ever made her fear for her life.

The one time she decided to give a corporate guy a try, a respectable businessman, he ended up being her worst nightmare.

The stranger lifted her left leg and glanced at her foot.

Instinctively, Isabel adjusted her skirt, making sure she didn't flash him.

"Have no fear and don't let my appearance fool you. My mom raised me better than to look up any woman's dress. Unless I've been invited to first." His voice was suggestive, his lips twisting in a teasing grin.

Brushing off the sole of her foot, he inspected the skin, using the utmost care and a gentle touch. His tenderness caught her off guard. She wondered what other surprises this man had hidden beneath his devastating exterior.

"What's wrong with your appearance?" she asked.

"Nothing. In my humble opinion."

"I bet you're many things, but I doubt humble is one of them."

A laugh slipped past his full lips. The sound was rough and masculine, almost musical. "There are plenty who'd agree with you." His eyes flicked up, meeting hers. "I thought with the fancy gallery, you might draw certain assumptions about my tattoos, my boots."

Her gaze dropped to his worn-in riding boots. He was a biker.

Where was his helmet?

Only fools didn't wear one and there wasn't anything foolish about this man.

"I like the tattoos." She liked the whole package. "You have a certain je ne sais quoi that outshines what you're wearing."

His grin spread.

*Stop flirting.* She'd sworn off men for a year after messing with…him.

*Six months to go.*

"Or maybe stopping that guy and getting my purse back earned you a free pass in the judgment department," she added.

Another laugh, richer, deeper as their gazes locked. Warmth spread through her, tickling her ribs.

"Well, losing money and having to cancel your credit cards is always a bummer."

"It wasn't about that. My father gave me this." Memories washed over her as she clutched the bag in her lap. "The last present from him before he died when I was fourteen."

"Sorry. About your dad. Never easy losing a parent. And teenage girls need their dads a lot. My younger sister Wendy turned into a hellion after our dad passed away. Heart attack. I tried to fill in for him where I could, but…" He shrugged.

"My uncle and I are very close, and he tries to do the same. Play dad." She loved her uncle dearly for his efforts and didn't know what she'd do without him. "But it isn't the same."

He nodded; the understanding in his eyes was comforting. "You told me your assistant's name, but not yours."

"Isabel. Vargas."

"Dutch Haas."

"Is Dutch your real name?"

"No." He lowered his eyes for a beat. "It's Horatio." He cocked a brow as if waiting for her to judge.

"Don't worry. I told you that you earned a free pass." With her joke, his features lightened. "Were you named after Horatio Hornblower, or the character from *Hamlet*, or a relative?"

He waved a finger at her. "Fierce, beautiful and well-read. I think you might be the perfect woman."

Blushing uncontrollably, she hoped her toes didn't turn red.

"The only thing that'd seal the deal is if you enjoy pizza and motorcycle rides," he said.

"I have Pizzarama on speed dial and I've been on the back of one or two bikes."

"Yep," he said, with a smile that'd melt any woman into a puddle of hormones. "Perfect."

Clearing her throat, she broke the eye contact. "You never answered my question. Hornblower, Hamlet or relative?"

Lifting her other leg, he checked her right foot. "Hornblower. My mother was an English teacher."

"Why did she name your sister Wendy?"

"Believe it or not, from *Peter Pan*. My sister lucked out, right? She should've been named Titania, Desdemona or Goneril."

Isabel laughed. Instantly she regretted it as agony flared in her cheek and she winced.

"You've got some glass in your foot. Once I get it out, we need to put ice on your face." He took a closer look at her sole. "You don't happen to have a pair of tweezers, do you?"

"Other side of the desk in the manicure set."

He moved around the back of her chair and dug out the tweezers from the other drawer. Lowering down on his knee, he looked up at her. "This might hurt a little."

"Not as much as a punch to the face. I'll be okay."

His features pinched in a scowl, one hand tightening into a fist as if he wanted to beat that mugger senseless. "Do you want to call the police and file a report?"

"What's the point? I'm sure that guy is long gone, and I'd rather not waste the time." She'd prefer to get her dog and her car and go home to her condo in Malibu.

"Karma will get that dude. Trust me."

She hoped so, but she didn't want to think about the mugger anymore. "How did you get the nickname Dutch?"

"When I was little, kids in school bullied me and made fun of my name. One day I watched this old movie *Predator*, and Arnold Schwarzenegger's character was this butt-kicking tough guy named Dutch. I wanted to be like him. After I started working out, bulked up and called myself Dutch, nobody picked on me anymore." Turning his attention back to her foot, he squinted and carefully plucked out a shard of glass with the tweezers.

He had the skill of a surgeon.

"I barely felt that," she said.

"Good. The last thing I want is to cause you pain." Something in his tone rang sincere. He grabbed the antiseptic and cleaned the area. "Will you be able to walk in your shoes?"

"Yes."

"Sure? I can carry you."

Was he for real? "I can handle it." She slipped on her heels and stood. Not letting the soreness that she felt show, she schooled her expression. "Thank you. I appreciate it."

"How about we go across the street? Let me buy you a drink and we can get ice for you."

*Holy crap.* Her pulse started racing again. Was he asking her out?

Even more surprising, she wanted to go with him. Dutch was mysterious, a contradiction of the best kind. On top of that he'd saved her purse, carried her back to the gallery, tended to her foot and had been charming and vulnerable rather than creepy or aggressive.

But she was done rushing into dates and adding guys to her long list of regrets.

"Thanks, but I don't drink." She loved red wine and missed sipping a fine Brunello, but alcohol didn't mix well with her meds.

"What about dinner?" he asked, his honeyed, husky tone making heat rise in her face. "Or we can just get you some ice and keep chatting."

The offer was more tempting than she dared admit, but she had to learn from her mistakes. If she kept doing the same thing repeatedly, expecting different results, then she was more deranged than he who shalt not be named.

"The valet is waiting for me to pick up my car at the garage two blocks down." She hiked her thumb in the opposite direction from which the mugger had run. "And I've got to pick up my dog from day care."

"Okay. Just hang on." He held up both palms. "Give me two minutes. Please." Dutch backed up, darted out of the gallery and dashed across the street.

For such a big guy, he was fast. Agile.

Isabel put away the med kit and reset the alarm. Gathering her courage, she forced herself to lock up again, ignoring the hairs that rose on the back of her neck.

It was a natural response after what had occurred. She'd been through the routine of working past the residual fear of an attack before.

Getting to the dead bolt, she cursed under her breath and made a mental note to call a locksmith in the morning.

She spun around, throwing her keys in her purse and grabbing her pepper spray. Dutch was already pushing through the doors of a restaurant and hustling across the boulevard to her.

"Here you go." He handed her a plastic bag filled with ice. "Put that on your face. You'll thank me tomorrow."

His thoughtfulness warmed her from the inside out. The wall she hadn't realized she'd built around her heart softened, but it didn't crumble.

"Thank you." She took the bag from the sweetest man she'd ever met. "You didn't have do that."

"Can I walk you to your car?"

"No. I… I…" She didn't know how to explain it. "I have to go on my own." The way she would any other day. No crutches, metaphorically speaking.

"All right. But you've got no objections to me standing here and watching you walk two blocks, do you?"

Why did he have to be so irresistible? "No objections. Thanks again. For everything."

"How about we continue this conversation tomorrow over lunch? Or on your day off?"

She felt a flutter in her stomach and she shoved it away, replacing it with common sense. He was a hard man to refuse. A chivalrous bad boy. Or was that an oxymoron?

Maybe she was the moron for even considering it.

*Six months.* Then she'd take it super slow, with someone.

"Good night." Isabel tightened her grip on the pepper spray, put the ice to her cheek and walked away at a fast clip.

Dutch was a beautiful risk, but too dangerous to take with her track record.

# Chapter Three

"Is she all right?" *he* asked the private investigator he'd hired to watch Isabel when he was at work and unable to keep a close eye on her himself.

"Yes. I think so," Olga Olsen said, no doubt from her perch in the coffee shop that sat diagonal to the gallery, where Brenda picked up Isabel's morning latte—coconut milk, double shot of espresso, a sprinkle of cinnamon. "I wasn't sure if I should've interceded since you gave explicit instructions never to engage with her, but then that guy came out of nowhere and helped her."

"What are they doing inside the gallery? Is she flirting with him?" He clenched his jaw, his temperature rising.

Isabel could be such a horny minx. Batting those long dark lashes, flipping her thick, curly hair over her shoulder, throwing more sway in her walk than necessary, drawing male attention like moths to a flame.

Gritting his teeth, he couldn't wait to climb on top of her again and lose himself in her.

"It looked like she hurt her foot and he put a bandage on it or something," Olga said. "She's walking to her car now."

"Alone?" His chest tightened and he squeezed the cell phone in his hand, imagining that man carrying her to the art gallery, fawning over her. Disgust soured his stomach.

Isabel was the most beautiful creature he'd ever seen. And she was *his*.

No one could touch his property. Not a mugger and especially not riffraff who wasn't fit to lick her shoes, even if he had intervened on her behalf.

"Yes." The background noise on Olga's end changed as if she had moved outside. "She's alone."

He released a breath of relief.

*It had better stay that way.*

*Good girl, Isabel, for not letting him escort you to your car.* Such foolishness would demand punishment.

Remind her who she belonged to.

So far, he'd played along with the restraining order, the long *tease*. As if a slip of paper would keep him away from her. Every woman loved the chase, but none more than Isabel.

Deep down she knew that he'd never stop pursuing her. This game was fun, *foreplay*, building the anticipation until they were reunited. She needed time to miss him, appreciate him, to realize no one could ever love her the way he did. When she came crawling back home to him things would be different, better than they'd been in the beginning.

Only he was good enough for her, understood her standards, how to take care of her, what she really needed.

"But the man is still in front of the gallery, watching her head to the valet," Olga said.

"Stay on Isabel. If that man comes sniffing around her again, call me immediately." He'd handle it personally.

After he hung up, he checked the lunar calendar app on his phone and smiled, satisfaction seeping through him. In the meantime, he'd pay Isabel a visit later tonight.

STANDING IN FRONT of the Kismet art gallery, Dutch watched Isabel limp away and thought about Karma. How he was going to be its instrument and make sure that jerk got what he deserved.

Anger washed through him in a cold fury, the burn hard.

He stormed across the street, hurried around to the back side of the empty building that was up for rent, past his parked motorcycle, and entered from the rear rather than using the main entrance off Santa Monica Boulevard. Flying up the stairs, he took them three at a time. He threw open the door and charged into the surveillance hub the US Marshals Service had set up.

Dutch had reached his limit. He'd been yanked from the

Fugitive Apprehension Response Team out at Camp Beauregard in Louisiana and given this undercover assignment only
two days ago. Apparently, he was at the top of a short list of
potential candidates fitting the *right profile*—whatever the
hell that was supposed to mean—to accomplish the job.

But he was unprepared. Exposed.

With an eleventh-hour assignment, there hadn't been time
to create fake credentials. The best they could do was alter the
dates for his actual prior service military record and his type
of discharge, from *honorable* to *general*, which meant he'd
done a good job until he engaged in misconduct or received
nonjudicial punishment under Article 15 of the Uniform Code
of Military Justice. After that, it was easy enough to make it
appear as if he'd never been a marshal.

Not only was he forced to use his real name, but his support
team were marshals he'd never worked with before.

So far, the operation was off to a shaky start.

"Where is he?" Dutch asked Allison Chen, a slim Asian
deputy marshal from the San Diego office, supporting this
operation.

Alarm widening Allison's dark eyes, she tipped her head
toward the left.

Dutch marched across the wide space past tables with surveillance equipment and his gear—riding jacket and helmet.
In the adjoining open space, he found Deputy Marshal Jake
Prindle, assigned to the LA office. The blockhead who decided to hit a woman.

Prindle was seated in a chair, his head hung over his lap
with a compress to his nose, forearm resting on his leg. His
eyes flashed up at Dutch and he straightened.

Dutch seized him by his T-shirt and yanked him up from
the chair, ripping the cotton. "What in the hell were you thinking? You used a knife! You punched her!"

"Hey, dude."

"You call me deputy or Haas." Dutch's voice dropped low, turning menacing. "Not dude."

"The knife was authorized. It was a dull blade no sharper than a butter knife and I only held the spine to her throat. She wasn't in any real danger."

"Why'd you hit her?" Dutch wanted nothing more than to pound his fist into Prindle. Pulverize his face, finishing the job that Isabel had started. "What kind of man does that?"

What kind of well-trained marshal?

"It was a reflex. An accident." Prindle tried to wrestle free of Dutch's grasp. "She was kicking my butt. Broke my nose. Or did you miss how I'm profusely bleeding?"

A toilet flushed and water ran in the bathroom, then Will Draper joined the party. He was the US marshal in charge of the San Diego field office and acting liaison with their LA counterparts.

"Haas," Draper said, hurrying up to them. "Let the man go. Now!"

Dutch was barely able to keep it together, but he shoved Prindle against the wall and released him.

"That wasn't the plan we discussed." Dutch stalked away and paced. The floor of the makeshift command center was spacious and open, but he felt contained, crowded. Caged.

Prindle dropped into a chair and put the compress back to his nose.

"Listen," Draper said, "the LA office is in charge of their own guys and made some last-minute changes that I approved of."

"You thought it was a good idea for this idiot to put a knife to her throat and hit her?"

Dutch had watched the fake attack transpire from the window in the command center. When Prindle had pulled the knife and pressed it to her jugular, Dutch shot out of there like a bullet, hightailing it across the street.

After reading the file on Isabel and staring at her picture

for hours, he'd expected her to be a spoiled princess, too pampered to handle a broken nail. But beneath her refined beauty was a solid core of pure strength.

She had serious grit and impressive self-defense skills. He had genuine admiration for her that had turned to something more as he carried her back to the gallery and took care of the cut on her foot.

Attraction, sure, but something else, too, something intangible.

Draper shoved his hands in his pockets. "Hitting the asset was an accident."

"I want him written up for inappropriate and excessive use of force. It needs to be documented in his file." Dutch wanted it taken into consideration on Prindle's next review.

"Okay." Draper raised his palms. "Calm down."

Prindle got up, kicking back the chair and flounced out into the front room.

"Was a knife necessary?" Dutch asked.

"The knife increased the intimidation factor and the perceived threat to a necessary level. It helped you initiate contact in an impactful way."

"I didn't agree to this," Dutch snapped, shaking his head.

"You don't have to agree with or like any of this. Just do your job and follow orders. Understand, Haas? Don't forget the gravity of this situation."

How could he? The WITSEC database for the Pacific Coast region had been compromised. A crooked marshal out of the San Diego office was responsible for the breach, but sensitive data—the new identities of all the witnesses and the personal information of the marshals and their families throughout California—had fallen into the hands of Dante Emilio Vargas. The ruthless leader of the West Coast branch of the *Los Chacales* cartel. The Jackals.

As powerful and brutal as *Los Chacales* had become in recent years, they were considered the largest-growing threat to national security. To make matters worse, Vargas planned to auction the information to the highest bidder.

Now, here was Dutch, brought in to cozy up to Isabel in order to get close to her uncle and retrieve the compromised data before it was sold.

"I know what's at stake," Dutch said. "But I'm questioning the means by which we get it done."

The use of violence against her, heck, simply *using* her to get in with her uncle, struck him as wrong.

"The asset is our only way in." Draper threw his hands up in exasperation. "The one connection we have to exploit."

"She has a name," Dutch said through gritted teeth, hating how they kept throwing around the word *asset* like she wasn't a person.

His temporary boss sighed. "Do you have a better plan? One that's foolproof? And will work in the short amount of time we have?"

No, he didn't.

"Think of all the men, women and children counting on us," Draper said. "On *you*."

A lot of lives were on the line if Dutch failed. Those of witnesses, good marshals and their families. He despised the method of achieving the goal, but he'd handled more challenging assignments in Special Forces, and he'd toed the mission line.

So why did it leave a bitter taste in his mouth and have his stomach turning?

*Isabel.* She had money and the unfortunate luck of being related to Dante Emilio Vargas, but there was nothing in the file to indicate whether she knew about her uncle's illicit affairs and turned a blind eye or if she was an innocent, ignorant that he was the leader of *Los Chacales.*

Face-to-face, she was vivacious and witty and kindhearted.

Damn it, he liked her. He'd been genuinely worried about her and the emotional state that attack might've left her in. Any other woman would've taken up his offer to at least walk her to the parking garage to make sure she got in her car safely.

Not Isabel. Independent. Strong. *Fierce.*

Yeah, he really liked her.

"The FBI has much more experience with undercover work than we do," Draper said, "and that's the reason we consulted them on how to proceed. It was one of their behavioral analysts who picked you for this, decided the best avenue of approach you should take with her was a romantic one and created the threat scenario that played out with Prindle and the *asset.*"

Figures it was some profiler, a person with extensive experience assessing victims and diving into the twisted minds of murderers who'd decided this was the right course of action.

Exactly what made him top choice for this assignment?

Maybe it was better if he didn't know, but there was a glimmer of something real between him and Isabel. He hadn't planned to tell her about his father and sister, to share intimate information. It'd flowed out of him naturally. No thought, no deception, no steering the conversation. One tiny connection sparked another and another, a flame in dry underbrush kindling unexpectedly on its own.

"Any updates from our contact on the inside?" Dutch asked.

A deep-cover FBI agent who'd infiltrated the organization learned about the plans for the auction set to happen at some unspecified time and got word to the Marshals. Though, this ticking time bomb wasn't the FBI's problem and they refused to get further involved, choosing instead to protect their agent's cover and pursue their own mission objectives.

"No." Draper shook his head. "As soon as I hear something, I'll pass it along."

Allison walked up to the doorway, her long black ponytail swaying behind her. "Did it work? Did Isabel agree to go out with you?"

Dutch folded his arms across his chest. "Not quite."

"Either you're in with her or not," Allison said. "Which is it?"

"I'm in, she just hasn't agreed to a date yet."

"What is that supposed to mean? Did you meet the objective?" Allison's eyebrows drew together, and she stepped deeper into the room. "She has to trust you. According to the profiler's report, it starts with you helping her in some life-threatening situation. Then there needs to be chemistry. We followed the recommendation by picking you. The only question is, are you the right guy for the job? Is she interested or not?"

Dutch drew in a deep breath. "She is, but cautious. If I push too hard, I'll lose her. She needed space, so I gave it."

"How can you be sure that she's interested and not blowing you off?" Allison asked.

He'd set out to do this assignment with cold detachment and unwavering objectivity, and after spending twenty minutes with Isabel, raw magnetism had punched a hole in his intentions.

That degree of attraction, which was scorching, wasn't one-sided. Of that, he was sure.

"Trust me—I've got her attention."

"Good." Allison's eyes were deadly serious, her composure so calm it was a little irksome. "You better keep it because there are families at risk. My family. I'm the one deputy marshal linked in the database to every witness who has gone into WITSEC as a result of testifying against the *Los Chacales* cartel."

"How is that possible?" Dutch asked.

"There have only been three and they were all women in fragile emotional states when the FBI brought them in. During the handover to us, they requested a female marshal to escort them to the safe houses and be on the protection detail until they testified. It was only me and Charlie Killinger in the San Diego office and her bedside manner left much to be desired."

Dutch had met Charlie out at Camp Beauregard. She ended up being his replacement on the Fugitive Apprehension Response Team. Kickass and fiery, Charlie wasn't the babysitting, hand-holding type.

"The only one I didn't protect every day was the last," Allison said. "Lori Carpenter. She was put in a safe house out in Big Bear for a year waiting for the trial to start. I've got a small kid and couldn't do something long-term like that, but I made the initial drive up and helped get her settled. My name is tied to all three women. Vargas is dangerous and vengeful. You mess this up and the deaths that follow will be on you."

Burdened with such an immense responsibility, Dutch compartmentalized his feelings. He never mistreated women, never used them, didn't even have one-night stands. His parents, the army, Delta Force, had taught him how to be a man with honor. If Isabel knew the truth about her uncle, then she was complicit, and Dutch need not feel an iota of guilt. If she were unaware, he'd do everything in his power to safeguard her heart in the process.

But this had to be done.

He pushed aside the doubt gnawing at his resolve to see this through. There was too much on the line not to give it his all.

# Chapter Four

Nightfall couldn't come fast enough. It was a new moon. The sky was pitch-black perfection, the ocean roiling darkness.

An ideal time to pay his doll a visit. To keep their one-of-a-kind connection alive. To stoke the passion between them.

Wearing dark clothes and ball cap pulled low, he strolled down the private beach off the north end of Malibu Road, cloaked in the night. Found his prime spot to tuck himself in among the boulders of the rocky outcrop, where he had a bird's eye view of her third-floor condo.

The corner one-bedroom in the small, exclusive building faced the water. There were no other balconies adjacent to hers, only above and below. Two-story houses on either side of the building sat lower than her place, giving her a false sense of security. Privacy. Large, expansive windows nearly surrounded the apartment, putting her on display in her glass cage.

*Isabel*, his doll. A thing of beauty and grace.

His lingering rage over her mugging and that man fondling her was a wild beast inside him, but the longer he stood there, watching her, the more the turmoil faded.

She was healthy and safe, with him now. Even if he was at a distance.

He could reach out and touch her whenever he liked and do as he pleased, caress her with care, or damage her a little. Dolls with flaws were the prettiest because they were unique.

Sometimes love had to hurt. A crazy-beautiful pain.

*Not so hard it made her black-and-blue.*

*Just enough to bring her back to you.*

He liked this game. It turned him on, whetted his appetite for her. One day soon he'd have another taste of her.

Isabel poured a glass of sparkling water and squeezed a wedge of lime in it. Six months ago, she stopped drinking wine. Probably her attempt to become her best self…for him, right along with getting fit. She'd started jogging.

So did he, even knew her favorite trails.

She took boxing once a week and Krav Maga on Tuesdays and Thursdays, always in the afternoons. He couldn't have them growing apart. To stay in sync with her, he signed up at the exact same places. Learned what she learned, but at an accelerated rate going twice as often as she did. He stayed two steps ahead.

Nothing like the element of surprise to fan the flames.

She strutted across the room in her skimpy nightgown, parading around, wanting to be seen, to be coveted. A lace chemise clung to her breasts, a generous 38F cup, and skimmed her thighs, showing off her curvy legs.

*Tease.* She knew that was his favorite one. Could she feel him watching now?

Of course she did. That's why she chose to wear it. For him. Their bond was special. Unbreakable.

She curled up on the sofa and turned on the TV with that stupid dog at her feet. Some reality show that she'd DVR'd was most likely on the screen.

Staring at her, he remembered the scent of her shampoo in her hair, the feel of her skin, the taste of her mouth.

*Isabel. I'll love you forever.*

The same way he'd loved Patricia.

Until the day she died.

# Chapter Five

Once Isabel had finished spilling her guts to her bestie, Brenda, about what had happened yesterday, she took a sip of her coconut-milk latte and set the cup on the front desk of the gallery.

"Oh. My. God." Brenda sat wide-eyed. "That's why we have the new electronic dead bolt on the door. Are you all right?" Her friend jumped up, blond curls bouncing around her shoulders as she enveloped Isabel in a tight hug.

The warm embrace was nice. A comfort she wished she didn't need.

"Yeah." Isabel pulled back. "I'm fine." Her face was still a little sore, but the slight bruise was easily concealed with makeup thanks to Dutch getting her an ice pack as soon as possible.

The whole incident had rattled her to the point that she'd imagined someone was watching her from the beach last night. That the crazy nameless one had been out there, hidden in the darkness, spying on her.

But she refused to close her windows and draw her blinds like she was living in a prison.

She had a waterfront condo in Malibu for goodness sakes. While she was in her home, she'd enjoy the temperate breezes and the relaxing sound of the waves rolling in.

The beach was private, and he stopped stalking her after the restraining order. The almost mugging yesterday had dredged old feelings to the surface, triggering delusions and nightmares. That's all. Nothing more, she told herself.

She'd barely slept and had brought McQueen up on the bed with her, but she'd gone for a jog this morning on her sore foot, even though she didn't have to.

No one was going to mess up her life and take away her sanity. She'd worked too hard to get to this mental place where she wasn't a trembling wreck.

One setback wasn't going to derail her.

"I'll cancel my Thursday yoga classes." Brenda sat down. "You're not locking up alone again."

"You're not canceling anything." She put her hand on her friend's. "We stick to our routine." The only way for things to feel normal was to pretend that they were until it became reality. "Nothing changes."

Brenda shook her head, familiar pity filling her eyes that made Isabel cringe inside. "At least take your uncle up on his offer to hire a bodyguard for you."

Her uncle Emilio would love nothing more than to hear that he was right and coddle her. "Absolutely not. I live in Malibu to get breathing room from him. It's like he didn't get the memo I'm a grown woman." The last thing she'd do was bolster his overprotective instincts.

Someone pounded on the back door. Isabel's hand flew to her chest as her gaze snapped to the rear of the gallery.

"It must be the delivery. The stuff we're renting for the party." Brenda stared at her.

Tomorrow night they were hosting their annual charity event at the gallery. Cocktails and canapés would be served as people mingled and purchased art. Fifty percent of the proceeds went to the local children's hospital. There'd be a huge turnout. It was their biggest event of the year.

"I forgot," Isabel said, her heart still racing.

"Are you sure you're okay?" Brenda stood and they walked toward the door in the back.

"Yes. Just a little jumpy." Isabel fluffed out her long hair to hide how her hands were shaking. "One good thing came out of what happened yesterday."

"The hunky hero who got your purse back?" Waggling her eyebrows, Brenda smiled.

Dutch had definitely been a welcome surprise, the best part of yesterday in fact. Isabel wondered if she'd see him again after rejecting not one but two offers to go out.

Brenda opened the door and waved the delivery guy in

who was carrying a tray of glasses. "Put it upstairs on the table we have set out."

The short guy nodded and walked past them.

"No, I'm not talking about the Good Samaritan," Isabel said as they stepped outside. "I made a bucket list."

"Really?" Brenda looked over the items they'd ordered in the van. "Let's hear it."

"Well, I only have five things on my list so far. I hope it doesn't sound pathetic. I want to fall in love. Get married. Have kids. Learn to surf. Have earth-shattering sex," she said, and Brenda chuckled. "And I want to see the northern lights, something magical and wondrous."

"That's six things." Brenda stepped away from the van and turned toward Isabel. Her eyes went wide as her mouth dropped open.

"Doesn't sound pathetic at all," a deep male voice said, and Isabel spun around to face Dutch. "I can help with at least two of those things on your list."

Isabel gulped, her heart fluttering and thighs tingling at the gorgeous sight of him.

Oh, goodness. How much of her list had he heard?

Well, if he thought it wasn't *pathetic*, then he'd heard everything. Including the part about sex. She couldn't have been more mortified if she'd been standing there naked.

"Hi," she said. Her cheeks were on fire.

"Hi." Dutch smiled, and the heated sensation in her face spread lower throughout her body.

"I didn't think I'd see you again."

"Hope that doesn't mean you're disappointed I swung by." Dutch flashed a sexy half grin. "When I invited you to lunch, you didn't say no. Only *good night*. I didn't take it as a definitive refusal."

"Hi, I'm Brenda." Her best friend shook his hand. "You're exactly as she described. Big and strong and...*mmm*."

Brenda acted like she wanted to eat him. "She raved about you all morning."

Isabel threw a warning look at Brenda. "I briefly mentioned how grateful I am that you'd been there."

"Nice to meet you." Dutch lowered his eyes like the comment embarrassed him and he shoved his hands in his pockets.

The young delivery guy zipped past them and grabbed more glasses.

"You need help with that?" Dutch asked.

"Sure, man. Thanks." The kid pointed out some racks and Dutch took them inside.

Once the guys were out of earshot, Brenda turned to her and clutched her arm. "He is so yummy. Why didn't you agree to lunch?"

"One-year moratorium on dating. Remember?"

With an eye roll, Brenda waved a dismissive hand. "You're always talking about how you want your life to be normal after what—"

Isabel lifted a cautionary finger.

"After what CNO did," Brenda finished, using the acronym for the crazy nameless one. "Every time you turn down a date or think about why you shouldn't get back out there, you're really thinking about *him* and giving CNO power. It's great that you got a dog, but you need a man. Someone hot and sweet to put a little sizzle in your life. Someone like that." Brenda pointed to Dutch, who was walking toward them through the gallery, chatting with the delivery guy. "His chakras are off the charts and when he was standing next to you your aura got brighter and turned fuchsia."

Before Isabel could ask what any of that meant, the men came back outside.

"Okay. The only thing left is the fridge." The kid pointed to the large glorified cooler that was a single-section unit with a glass door strapped to a wheeled hand truck.

"Use the elevator," Brenda said.

Isabel winced. "You can't. I forgot to tell you the repair guy had a personal emergency and canceled yesterday, but he'll be out tomorrow afternoon in time for the event."

"I can't come back tomorrow," the delivery guy said, rubbing the nape of his neck. "I'm going to be slammed with back-to-back drop-offs all day. Saturdays are always crazy."

Dutch patted the kid's shoulder. "You grab one end, I'll take the other, and we'll carry it up the stairs."

"No can do, buddy. I'm not covered for that kind of thing. If I slip and get hurt, I won't get worker's comp. I'm sorry. I'll have to leave it on the ground floor."

"We need to get the beverages in today, so nobody has a warm drink tomorrow," Brenda said. "Everyone will expect cold bubbly with the amount we hope people will spend. Maybe we have to set the bar up downstairs."

Isabel pressed a palm to her forehead. "The whole point of having it upstairs is to encourage everyone to see the paintings on the second floor."

"I can take it up for you," Dutch said.

Isabel turned to him. "How? You can't carry that up on your own."

He was strong and it was a single unit, but everyone had limits. The fridge had to be a good two hundred pounds.

"Do you have an extra strap in the van?" Dutch asked.

The kid nodded. "Yeah."

Dutch directed the delivery guy to wheel the fridge out of the van. Then he adjusted the two straps, removing them from the hand truck and retightening them around the cooling unit. He slipped his arms through the straps like someone would with a backpack and he had the delivery guy wrap the third one horizontally around the center of the fridge and Dutch's torso, fastening it tight.

Bending at the knees, Dutch shifted the weight of the unit around before he stood and leaned over with the fridge balanced on his back and headed inside.

Isabel, Brenda and the delivery guy followed. They stood at the stairwell, marveling at Dutch carrying the fridge upstairs as though it were a death-defying circus act.

"Whoa," the kid said low, amazement ringing in his voice.

Okay, Dutch was really strong. And smart.

"To hell with your moratorium. Are you seriously not going to give him a chance?" Brenda pointed at Dutch while staring at Isabel like she was crazy. "If you don't want him, can I have him?"

"Hell, I'd date him," the delivery guy chimed in.

Isabel sighed. "Maybe we can hang out. Baby steps. Get to know each other better without all the physical stuff."

Brenda threw her an unmistakable are-you-kidding-me look. "The physical stuff is the best part."

Isabel had jumped into bed with CNO and look where that had gotten her. "But it shouldn't be the best part. It should be the icing on a fantastic cake, the cherry on a sundae."

"I'd eat his cake with a spoon," Brenda said, staring at Dutch as he came back downstairs.

Isabel shook her head. Brenda could wrap men around her little finger like twine. Except for the yoga instructor she'd set her sights on. The limber yogi was proving to be the ultimate challenge.

Then there was Dutch. He hadn't given Brenda the once or twice-over most men did with her sunny curls and sparkling smile and swimsuit-model physique. All his attention had been focused on Isabel.

"Here you go." Dutch handed the straps to the delivery guy who gave him a two-finger salute and left.

"Thank you so much," Isabel said. "How can I repay you for everything?"

"The only payment I'd accept is the pleasure of your company over lunch."

"She says yes." Brenda shoved Isabel forward. "You two should leave right now."

"I can't," Isabel said, not enjoying the sudden onslaught of pressure. "There's too much to do before tomorrow." The charity event was highly publicized. Who's who of LA would be there, including the mayor. It had to go off without a hitch. Not to mention, she hated being put on the spot.

Hadn't Brenda been listening?

Chatting over coffee was a baby step. Not lunch.

Brenda's doe eyes shifted to her, a sad kind of pleading in their depths. "Please go," she mouthed.

Her best friend wasn't reckless, or impulsive, and tended to be more protective than her uncle Emilio at times. She also had great instincts.

The first time Brenda had met CNO she'd said, *His aura is so dark. He skeeves me out. Doesn't something about him give you the heebie-jeebies?*

*No.* He'd been the sort everyone wanted her to go out with. Wealthy, owner of several businesses, wore a suit and tie, held open doors for her, spoke three languages.

*He'll show you his true colors sooner or later and when he does, run like the wind and don't look back*, Brenda had said.

In hindsight, Isabel should've pulled the rip cord right then.

Her internal creep-radar might be broken, but Brenda's wasn't. Maybe one meal with Dutch would be okay, if he got Brenda's endorsement.

"I know you're busy, but you've got to eat," Dutch said. "As soon as we order, I'll explain to the waiter that we're in a rush and ask for the check, so you're not stuck with me for too long. What do you say?"

"She's starving and would love to," Brenda said to him, then turned and whispered in Isabel's ear. "Go, start living again."

The past six months, she hadn't been living. Only surviving.

Something about Dutch made her feel safe. Made her want

to toss her rule book into the trash and move forward, not worrying about the past or shadows or mistakes. To be her old self.

*Baby steps.* For now, she'd hang on to the rule book. "Okay. A quick, casual lunch between new friends?"

Disappointment flashed in his eyes, but he nodded. "Where to?"

"There's a grill. Ten-minute walk. They have a variety of fantastic burgers."

Dutch held the door open for her.

Isabel grabbed her purse and they headed out.

"I should've asked yesterday," he said as they strolled down the street. "Do you have a boyfriend?"

She flinched. "No. I don't."

"To be benched in the friend zone is a tough place to ever move out of."

"I'm sorry—it's just that I'm not dating right now. I haven't had the best luck in the men department."

"Ah, I see. You don't want to rush into anything?"

"Exactly," she said, brightly, relieved he understood. "I want to get to know a guy before I jump into something hot and heavy." No more sleeping with the enemy.

"I have to admit I have one technical concern."

Technical? He was a standard-issue guy. Of course there was a catch. "What's that?"

"It's the kiss of death for a guy to be labeled *friend*," he said as if the word stung his tongue. "Before you know it, you'll start looking at me as a big brother."

She swallowed a chuckle. The only way that'd happen was if she had a frontal lobotomy.

"It's all about the way we frame things in our heads," he said. "How about you think of me as a potential? A possibility. Just a prospect. And we take things as slowly as you'd like. I won't even kiss you unless you ask me to. Absolutely no pressure."

Stopping in front of the grill, she frowned at him, weighing whether he was serious or not. "Really?" What would it be like to have to *ask* this hot hunk to kiss her?

"You're gorgeous, Isabel, and I'm attracted to you on multiple levels, but I swear on my father's grave that I'm more interested in earning your trust, in getting to know you, than I am in sleeping with you." The way he spoke, holding her gaze, held no hint of deception. He meant the words and she believed him.

"You're attracted to me on multiple levels, huh?"

"I'm even having a hard time picking which feature of yours is my favorite."

Unease rippled through her, making her stiffen. She braced for the routine, where a guy looked her over from head to toe, cataloging her *features* like she was an object instead of a person.

"Your eyes," Dutch continued, "or..." He ran the pad of his finger from the bridge of her nose to the tip with the lightest, most intimate touch. "Your pert nose."

Oh, she was an idiot for assuming the worst. She wanted to crush the presumptions that had built over the years, but sometimes they flared to the surface with no warning. "If I put you on the spot and made you choose?"

"Then hands-down it'd have to be the freckles on your cheeks and nose. I love that you don't use heavy makeup and let those beauties shine through."

This man sure did know how to give a woman a compliment. She'd gone out with boob men, butt men, leg men and none were bashful about telling her which they found most attractive. But he was the only one to call a feature she'd hated growing up *beautiful*.

"Okay. Let's give the whole 'prospect' thing a try." Not dating, just entertaining the possibility. She liked it.

The smile that spread across his face was a ray of sunshine breaking through a cloud bank. Any lingering reservations she had dissolved.

For the first time in a long time, she was hopeful.

He opened the door to the restaurant and let her go inside ahead of him.

The grill was a large place that stayed busy from open to close. The hostess escorted them to a table near the front, handing them poster-sized menus. They were lucky to get a table without a wait. Sometimes eating at the bar was the only option for a quick bite.

She sat where she could see the entire bar and all the tables while Dutch faced the door.

A server came to them straightaway and took their order. What were the odds? Sometimes you had to flag one down. The universe seemed to be conspiring to get her through lunch as quickly as possible and Isabel wasn't sure that was what she truly wanted anymore.

"I'll have the salmon burger with garlic truffle fries," Isabel said, as Dutch looked over the menu. "And can I get the veggie burger wrapped in lettuce, no fries, to go." She glanced at Dutch. "It's for Brenda. She'd kill me if I didn't bring one back for her."

"That's considerate of you. I'm sure she'll appreciate it." He turned to the waitress. "The monster burger for me, medium well, with everything on it. Thanks. And one check."

"No, separate bills," Isabel said, then leaned over toward Dutch, dropping her voice. "This isn't a date. Remember?"

"If you could bring the one check as soon as you can, that'd be great." He gave the waitress a wheedling smile that was downright irresistible. "We're in a bit of a rush."

"No problem." The waitress flashed a pleasant grin and left, ignoring Isabel's request.

"Before you say anything, please let me explain." His tone was soft and unassuming.

She bobbed her head once for him to go ahead.

"I invited you to lunch and I was raised that the person extending the invitation pays. If not for Brenda's help, I'm not so sure you would've agreed to come with me to begin with. As far as I can tell, I owe you both."

Not wanting to make a thing out of it after she saw the logic of his rationale, she said, "Your accent. Where are you from?"

"New York and Chicago are both sort of home to me."

"What do you do?"

"I was in the military. Special Forces," he said, casually like it was no big deal. "I'm on terminal leave, using up the last of my vacation days. Before you ask, the answer is no, I have nothing specific lined up. And I'm okay with that."

She'd never gone out with someone on the verge of unemployment and once again he was easy-breezy about it. Leaning toward him again, she put her hand on the table between them. "Let me pick up the tab for lunch. You should conserve your resources. And you did save my purse."

He laughed and covered her hand with his large palm. Her skin danced beneath the warm weight of it, the solidity. "I don't know what kind of fellas you're used to, but that's not how I operate. Financially, I'm good, not destitute."

The down-to-earth air about him, devoid of pretenses, wasn't what she was used to. It was refreshing.

"I'm renting an apartment in Ocean Park."

Nice area. Close to her gallery. "Why did you pick California to call home?"

Moving his hand from hers, he sat back and held her gaze. "I've been stationed and deployed to some hellholes. I wanted sunshine. Perfect weather. The ocean. But continental US. What about you? Why do you own an art gallery? More specifically, how does one come to own one?"

The waitress brought them two ice waters and a basket of bread.

"I was an art history major. In college, I did internships at museums. I wanted to be a docent, giving tours and talking about my passion." She took a warm roll and slathered butter on a piece. "But my uncle told me to set my sights higher, to own a gallery instead, where I could control my own destiny. When I decided to buy one, he didn't want me to use my inheritance from my father and bought it for me."

"So, he owns the gallery?" Dutch asked.

"On paper yes, but it's mine. Other than using his accountants, I run it freely."

"Who's your uncle?"

"Dante Emilio Vargas." Her uncle was a bit of a celebrity on the West Coast, and she waited for the usual reaction of awe, but Dutch's eyes didn't so much as light up. For once, someone who didn't know him. "To me, he's just Uncle Emilio. Dante was my grandfather and my uncle has never appreciated the title *junior* and doesn't use it."

Dutch sipped his water. "I think I might've heard the name."

"He's a huge venture capitalist. What Elon Musk is to the car industry and space exploration, my uncle is to advancements in farming organically and education. Building a better world is so important to him." Her uncle was driven, shrewd and tough, but he had the biggest heart and would do anything for her.

"Are you some kind of socialite who comes from old money?"

Isabel laughed. "Oh gosh, no. I come from humble beginnings. When I was little my father and uncle started investing their money in technology and buying farms. I guess they got in at the right time. My uncle compares it to buying stock in Microsoft or Apple when those companies were just getting started. I don't know." She shrugged. "I guess they got lucky."

His brows knit as he seemed to study her closely in a way that made her self-conscious. "Does he live here?"

"Thank heavens, no. San Diego. He's such an important man he's surrounded by bodyguards. You'd think he was the president or something. If I lived down there, he'd insulate me with bodyguards, too." Trading one personal hell for another. "I need my freedom. To breathe." She was finally starting to get to a place where she could once again.

Maybe this lunch with Dutch was the first step in the right direction.

"What has your uncle thought of your previous paramours?"

Sighing, Isabel dropped her gaze to her lap. "I haven't introduced any to him. He'd never approve of someone he didn't pick and who didn't check every box on his list, which is different than mine."

He perked up at that with a bright smile and something in the conversation shifted from investigative to inquisitive. "What's on your list? What kind of guys are you into?"

*Someone like you.* Isabel blushed. "Excuse me a minute. I have to use the restroom."

She stood, grabbing her purse, and crossed the length of the restaurant down to the other side. All the tables were now taken and there were only a few open spots left at the bar. They'd arrived at the perfect time.

Inside the restroom, she checked her makeup, fluffed her hair, running her fingers through her brown curls, and washed her hands.

She threw away the paper towel and left the bathroom.

In the few short minutes that she'd been in there, every seat at the bar had been taken. Passing the row of customers parked on bar stools, she homed in on Dutch. Even from behind, he drew attention with his brawny build and the wink of tattoos she glimpsed through the crowd.

The food was already on the table, but it looked as if he'd waited for her. *Another good sign.* As she sat down, she spotted three to-go containers on the side of the table.

"It really picked up in here," he said. "I figured if you couldn't finish your meal, you'd want a to-go box. It might take the waitress a good ten minutes to grab one later."

"You're a planner. I like that." Isabel picked up a fry, took the first delicious, hot bite and glanced up toward the bar.

Her heart nearly stopped, the blood in her veins turning to slush as she locked gazes with *him*.

# Chapter Six

A thousand thoughts rushed through Isabel's head like a high-speed train derailing. She couldn't think. She couldn't move. Couldn't speak.

At the far end of the bar, *he* was seated in the very spot that she had passed on the way back from the restroom. He must've arrived while she was inside.

Well-groomed as always, wearing a tailored suit, he resembled a thirtysomething Hugh Jackman. Looking at him, no one would suspect what he really was. Isabel hadn't the first time they met. He'd lured her in with his good looks, smooth charm and sophistication, his ability to talk to anyone about anything. She'd been flattered when he'd asked her out.

He sat there in the restaurant, staring at her. Unblinking. His eyes rabid, excited. His body rigid. With his elbows propped on the bar, he brushed one index finger across the other and mouthed, "Shame on you."

Isabel choked on the French fry going down her throat. She coughed, patting her chest, struggling to breathe, to gain her bearings.

Why was he here?

But deep down she knew. He was here because of her.

"Are you all right?" Dutch asked, handing her a glass of water. "You look like you've seen a ghost."

More like a living, breathing nightmare.

Her nerves stretched tight as bowstrings as she tried to gauge how far away he sat. At least seventy-five feet in the large restaurant. The restraining order only stipulated fifty.

*He* was within legal bounds.

The last time he'd pulled a stunt like this, he had shown up at LACMA, Los Angeles County Museum of Art, when she'd been enjoying her time off with Brenda. For days she and Brenda had planned the excursion, texting back and forth about shopping on Rodeo Drive afterward and having a late lunch at the best Peruvian restaurant in town. Isabel had stood her ground and called the police.

And they had done absolutely nothing.

If the petitioner was aware the respondent was in the vicinity and wasn't violating the provisions of the restraining order, then it was the petitioner's responsibility to leave.

Not the other way around.

She had argued that it hadn't been a coincidence and the police had countered that LACMA was the largest art museum in the western United States with a new exhibit that'd just started. Could she prove that it wasn't a coincidence?

Of course not.

It didn't help the situation that *he* was well-known by the cops, well liked and respected.

Trepidation weighted every muscle in Isabel's body and her stomach clenched hard as a fist. "I have to go."

"What?" Dutch froze with the burger in his hand midair before taking a single bite. "What's wrong?"

Dropping her gaze, she said, "There's an urgent call I have to make. I need to leave."

"All right. Let's box up the food."

"No." Grabbing her purse, she stood. "I'm not hungry anymore. I lost my appetite."

"Isabel, what's happening right now?"

"I told you." Her gaze flickered up to the far end of the bar.

*He* was still staring at her. An ominous smile full of evil spread on his face. Like some demon sent from hell to torment her. That's what he wanted—to possess her, body, mind and soul.

A chill spilled down her entire body, and she had an almost uncontrollable urge to make the sign of the cross over her chest.

Dutch turned as if to see what she was looking at, and

that sicko glanced away almost immediately and called to a bartender.

Isabel could barely swallow, her throat growing dry as sandpaper. She spun on her heel and dashed out the door.

Heavy footsteps thudded after her. A warm, strong hand took her wrist, callused fingertips pressed against her skin, bringing her to a gentle stop on the sidewalk in front of the restaurant.

"I know something is wrong," Dutch said, facing her. "You just did a one-eighty on me for a reason. Please, tell me what it is."

Shame burned a hole in her heart. There was no clear way to explain—her lack of judgment and poor instincts, every twisted thing that man had done to her, the degrees of sickness she had tolerated, how she'd allowed him to steal her dignity. The ways he'd terrorized her after she'd ended the relationship.

How did she let any of it happen?

A sob rattled her chest.

If she told Dutch, once she finished spewing out the whole sordid story, he would no doubt see her as a victim.

It was bad enough her best friend looked at her with *poor you* in her eyes. She wasn't inviting another person to the pity party.

"I'm sorry. Today wasn't a good day for lunch. I have to go." Isabel turned and fled at a pace just short of running.

No wasting precious seconds glancing back over her shoulder. No waiting at the light to cross—she held out her hand to cars and dashed across traffic. No aching lungs or quivering thighs holding her back. No letting her three-inch heels slow her down. She'd scurry down the street on stilts if she had to.

Hot tears blurred her eyes, and she thumbed them away.

Shoving through the gallery door, she almost bumped into Brenda.

"Why are you back so soon?" her friend asked. "Did you have time to eat?"

She hurried up the stairs. "He was there."

Brenda stopped dead in her tracks and recoiled. "Not… *him*."

On the mad dash back to the gallery, the fear that had been bubbling inside Isabel had turned to boiling anger. Just when she thought she could pick up the pieces of her life and move on, that bastard came back. Taunting her. Admonishing her.

How dare he invade her life again. Who did he think he was?

"Yes. Chad Ellis." The sound of his name grated on Isabel's ears.

For months, she'd told herself that if she didn't say the name of that twisted man, refused to see his face in her mind's eye, started training, got stronger, that somehow it would take away his power.

But all it had done was make her hypersensitive to him. Left her weakened and unprepared for a face-to-face encounter.

That was a mistake she wasn't going to repeat.

Brenda's heels clacked up the stairs after her. "What are you going to do?"

"Stop pretending that he's going to disappear." Isabel sat behind her desk and picked up the phone. She dialed the One Stop Home Security Superstore that had installed the alarm system in her condo and where she'd also purchased the pepper spray.

"Hello, Douglas speaking. How can I help you?"

Good, it was the owner. "Hi, Doug, this is Isabel Vargas from—"

"I remember you. How is everything working out?"

"The last time we spoke about tools I could use for personal safety, other than a gun, you made a recommendation that I thought wasn't necessary, but I've reconsidered."

"Oh, you're talking about the *Pacifier*." A fourteen-inch

stun gun baton that delivered 10,000 volts. "Yeah, that'll make someone trying to attack you regret it. Guaranteed."

"Yes. That's it. I'd like to purchase five."

"Five? That's a lot. You sure you need that many?"

"You heard me correctly." Two for the gallery, one for her purse and two for her home. She'd never be caught without one. Ever. "Can you have them delivered to the gallery?"

"Sure can. They'll be there within the hour. Would you like me to use the credit card we have on file?"

"Yes. Thank you." She disconnected, raised a finger to Brenda, asking her to wait, and called her Krav Maga instructor at the self-defense school. "Hi, John. It's Isabel. I was wondering if you had room for me in your evening class tonight."

"Sure. No problem. Everything all right?"

"No. It isn't."

"I can have Abraham take the class later and we can work one-on-one, if you'd like."

She let out a deep breath, her muscles slowly beginning to loosen. "I'd appreciate that very much. Thank you." She hung up. Already the panic was receding, and she felt grounded.

"Did you tell Dutch?" Brenda asked.

"No," Isabel snapped. The answer to every problem wasn't a man.

"Why not?"

The only person she could depend on to always be there for her was herself. She'd relied on her father for everything from support, reassurance, comfort, to unconditional love. And one day, he was gone.

Killed in a drive-by shooting.

The pain, the hole his death left seemed never ending. The only way to get through it was to be the person her father had always wanted her to be.

Strong and capable and happy.

Two out of three wasn't bad, so that's what she'd focus on.

"I can take care of myself."

DUTCH SET THE to-go containers of food on the front desk of Kismet and wrote his cell phone number on the top of the carton. Something had spooked Isabel, but no sense in her or Brenda starving, especially since lunch was paid for.

Voices came from the office upstairs, but he didn't want to intrude. He'd followed Isabel back to the gallery, giving her plenty of space while making sure that she was okay. She'd almost gotten hit by a car crossing one street, but she seemed more concerned about whatever she'd been running from.

"Why do you have to be so stubborn?" Brenda asked, her voice heavy with concern. "You don't have to do this alone. I'm sure Dutch would help you, but you have to tell him what you're up against."

"I want him to see *me*," Isabel said, "not Chad Ellis's victim!" A hand slammed against a wooden surface and a chair scraped against the floor. "I have to help myself. Do you understand? I'm not going to accept my uncle's bodyguards who'd only spy on me and report every move I make back to him and I'm certainly not going to start leaning on a man I just met, expecting him to protect me from that maniac!"

Dutch stiffened as he eavesdropped on their conversation. *Maniac? Chad Ellis?*

The name hadn't been in Isabel's file.

"I like Dutch, okay! He's a solid prospect for once. I won't let Chad ruin that, too. He's taken enough away from me."

Dutch crept out of the gallery as quietly as he'd entered. His thoughts spun around Isabel's reaction in the restaurant and everything he'd overheard.

Not a lick of it added up with the information he'd been given, troubling him a little and angering him quite a lot.

Going around the back way, he went to the command center across the street, where he found Allison and Draper. Jake Prindle hadn't come back.

"How did it go?" Allison asked.

"Not well, but it had nothing to do with me." He looked at Draper. "Who is Chad Ellis?"

A stupefied expression crossed his boss's face. "Never heard the name."

"Cut the crap and stop playing me," Dutch said. "I can't do my job if I don't have all the information."

Draper put his hands on his hips. "You have the same file the FBI gave me."

"It's true," Allison said, as though she sensed Draper's word couldn't be trusted. "I saw it myself. The same behavioral analyst who recommended you put the file together on Isabel Vargas for us."

"I want a name," Dutch demanded.

"Sheila Rogers," Allison said. "Out of the LA office on Wilshire Boulevard."

Dutch turned for the door.

"Hold on, Haas. I can't have you stirring up trouble with the FBI."

"I'm going over there to get answers and there's nothing you can do to stop me."

"Fine." Draper yanked on his suit coat. "But I'm coming with you."

LESS THAN THIRTY minutes later, Dutch and Draper were seated in Special Agent Rogers's office that was the size of a broom closet. They were so close to her desk that Dutch's knees practically touched the hardwood.

"Thank you for seeing us on such short notice, Agent Rogers," Draper said. "We appreciate you taking the time from your busy schedule."

Agent Rogers responded with similar professional chitchat.

They didn't have time for pleasantries. The inconsistencies surrounding Isabel had been rolling around in Dutch's head like a pinball, ringing warning bells and raising red flags. He needed answers. To hell with the rest.

"The file we were given on Isabel Vargas was incomplete," Dutch said. "Why?"

Frowning, Draper threw him an irritated glance. "You have to excuse Deputy Marshal Haas. He can be overly direct."

Agent Rogers was a petite woman with long, straight dark hair framing her narrow face and elfin features. She looked between them, finally setting her gaze on Dutch. "Based on your mission objectives, the limited amount of time you had to prepare and your lack of undercover experience, I gave you the relevant information you needed to be successful."

Leaning forward, Dutch put his forearms on his thighs. "There's some maniac she's terrified of who's making her life hell."

"Chad Ellis," Agent Rogers said matter-of-factly. "She has a restraining order against him."

"What?" His elevated tone drew Draper's gaze and a reproving head shake. Dutch took a breath, trying to calm down. "I'd call that relevant."

"First, Ellis hasn't been in the picture for months."

"He showed up today in a restaurant where we went for lunch."

Agent Rogers straightened, a glimmer of concern passing over her face. "That's not good."

"You don't say. Isabel hightailed it out of there and I had no clue why. If I'd known, I could've confronted him. Warned him to stay away from her."

Agent Rogers folded her arms across her chest and studied him. "Did Isabel tell you about Ellis?"

Dutch sat back. "No. I overheard her talking about him afterward in her gallery."

Agent Rogers nodded slowly. "So, if you saw Ellis, a man you're not supposed to know, sitting in a place that he's not supposed to be, intimidating Isabel from afar, you would've done what? Went over, jerked him out of his chair by his shirt and threatened him?"

"Sounds about right," Draper said. "That's precisely what you did with Prindle when things didn't go the way you'd expected."

"And you would have blown your cover," Agent Rogers said in a soft, firm voice. "Believe it or not, I'm trying to help you. According to your profile, if you had known about Chad Ellis, your initial response to Isabel would've been overly protective and caused her to withdraw from you rather than endearing her."

"Speaking of my profile, why did you pick me?"

"*How* would be a better question," she said. "After discussing the situation with Marshal Draper, I did some research on Isabel Vargas with the help of our cyber unit. We issued a warrant and requisitioned her dating profile from a top-tier online matchmaking site and discovered she has a type. Not only physically." Agent Rogers gestured to Dutch. "But she's also attracted to men who are highly intelligent, but have a middle-class background, energetic, passionate, socially dominant and who exhibit appetitive-aggressive traits. Three out of the four she dated from the site also rode motorcycles and expressed an interest in extreme sports. In short, they were adrenaline junkies. Does this sound familiar?"

Dutch restrained the sigh building in his throat and refused to concede that she had just described him, although he wasn't certain about the appetitive-aggressive bit. "*How* me and not someone else?" He couldn't be the only guy in the USMS fitting that profile.

"The situation presented discriminating factors. No one from California could be used because of the data breach. We needed a single male, late twenties to early thirties, who wasn't on an active assignment, had been with the USMS less than three years and had a background we could tinker with, filling in your work history. The fact that you both lost your fathers in your early teens was a bonus. You were perfect. No one else came close to your numbers. Algorithms don't make mistakes."

That explained the easy, natural connection he formed with Isabel, but it also raised an important question. "This Ellis guy, are you saying he and I are alike?"

"Not quite. With Ellis, she deviated from her usual type. She met him at a function, not online. From what I can tell, Ellis exhibits psychopathic traits, which is quite common in the corporate world. Charming, arrogant, risk taker, no remorse, a master manipulator. Whereas you're honest, noble, and during your US Marshals assessment displayed a high degree of empathy. All strengths that could also be a weakness in this situation. The emotional handling required here is a delicate balance and having all the facts from her file would've hurt your ability to forge a bond with the asset."

*Asset again.* Dutch gritted his teeth. "I want to see the complete file."

"I have to advise against that. In this case, less is more where the asset is concerned. If you want to see more on her uncle, that's fine. But you need to trust that I've given you everything you need to succeed."

"I don't know you. I don't trust you. I need all the facts or I can't do my job effectively."

Agent Rogers turned to her computer and typed away on her keyboard. "I just emailed it to Marshal Draper and cc'd Deputy Chen-Boyd."

The hyphenated name wasn't a surprise to Dutch. Allison had never used Boyd around him, but some days she wore a wedding ring and some days she didn't, like someone with unresolved feelings going through a separation.

"But I must warn you," Agent Rogers said. "Give serious consideration to how you've interacted with the asset so far and what's elicited a positive response. Don't deviate from that. Above all, don't let details that you're not supposed to know slip."

Dutch stood and shook Agent Rogers's hand. "Duly noted."

# Chapter Seven

"Thank you for squeezing me in. I need this emergency session," Isabel said, grateful for John's help and happy that she kept extra workout gear in her trunk.

"No problem. We're here to help." John clasped her shoulder. Tall and built, he carried himself with the same confident awareness as Dutch. "What's up?"

"The guy I told you about popped up today out of the blue."

Concern tightened across his features. "Did he threaten you?"

This was where it sometimes got tricky with Chad. He hadn't violated the restraining order and he hadn't spoken to her. If she told anyone that he wagged his fingers at her as one might do a child, they'd blow her off. Tell her she was overreacting and to ignore the taunt.

But to dismiss the slightest action on Chad's part would be a mistake that could cost her life. Of that, she was certain.

"He intimidated me on purpose, but not in a way that I have a legal recourse." Not this time. Not yet. But she worried things might escalate. "And I froze when I saw him. The terror and panic came rushing back and I felt helpless."

"I understand." John tightened his hand on her in a reassuring way. "I want to be clear—it's not okay for someone to make you fear for your safety or cause you emotional distress. When you have the option to call the cops and not engage, take it. That's best."

"What if that's not an option?"

"Then you need to fight until you can get away from him and get help. I think we need to work on some extreme scenarios where you feel legitimately threatened. Get you to the point where you don't hesitate. Freezing, even for a few seconds, can mean the difference between living and dying."

She was in favor of living. "Sounds good."

"But it'll take time for practice to become habit and habit to become a reflex. It's not going to happen in one or two sessions."

If only she knew how much time she had until Chad finally snapped. "I can come in more often."

John nodded. "What's your parking situation like at the gallery and your house?"

She explained about the valet garage two blocks down and told him about the gated garage with security cameras at her condo.

"There's a luxury valet service I know of. They'll pick your car up for you in front of the art gallery, fuel it, wash it and deliver it right at your door. It's a little pricey, but you might want to consider it. Save yourself the two-block walk."

Jim, the valet at the garage, wouldn't be happy to see her go, but the premium service was exactly what she needed. "I think I'll try it."

"You can grab a card at the desk on your way out. Now, let's go work on your self-defense skills."

Her phone rang. She glanced at the caller ID. It was her uncle. "I need to take this, but I'll only be a minute." After John nodded and stepped away, giving her privacy, she answered. *"Hola, tío."*

*"Hola, mi hija."* Since her dad had died, her uncle started calling her his daughter.

His love for her was undeniable. She felt deeply for him, treasured their bond, appreciated his attempt to fill the void left by her dad. He was almost a second father to her. Almost.

"I won't be able to make it to your fund-raiser this year. *Lo siento,*" he said, apologizing in Spanish. "I know how much the event means to you."

"It's okay." She hid the disappointment in her voice. "I know you're a busy man."

"But I still want to see you." His deep voice and thick Mexican accent sounded so much like her father's sometimes it made her heart ache. "I have something to discuss. Next

Wednesday, I'll come up to LA and we'll have dinner. Clear your evening for me."

He didn't make requests. He made demands. Not just of her, but everyone around him. He'd been that way for as long as she could remember, and she'd learned it was easier to go along with him than refuse.

"Okay. What time?" she asked.

"Let's say seven. I'll send a car for you."

"Gracias, *tío. Te amo.*" *Thank you, uncle. I love you.* "See you soon."

"*Te amo.* Adios."

Isabel hung up with a fresh wave of tension rising inside her. She dismissed it, not wanting the tightness in her chest to be related to her uncle's call and whatever he wanted to discuss. Instead, she focused on not letting that psycho Chad catch her off guard again. "John, I'm ready."

CHAD PUSHED THROUGH the men's locker-room door into the hallway and stopped short at the sound of a melodic voice that made his pulse race. *Isabel.* He peeked around the corner, catching sight of her going into one of the empty workout rooms with John.

*What are you doing here in the evening? Not like you to deviate from your schedule.*

Had their encounter earlier stimulated her as it had him?

From the gleam in her eye at the restaurant and the way she ran out, she'd been aroused. Still was, and she'd come here to work it out physically since she couldn't have the type of release that he'd give her.

Fire sang in his blood even now. Growing hotter, burning brighter as he watched her.

Isabel's caramel-brown hair was pulled into a high ponytail, her luscious hips swaying as she walked. He saw how other men took notice of her, lusted after her with their eyes. She liked it and so did he. As long as no one else touched her.

John talked her through a movement, something basic and easy. She got into position and then John lunged at her. Without a second of hesitation, she responded the way he'd shown her.

*Are you thinking of me? Imagining us together, tussling, our limbs entangled, with me finally on top of you, holding you down?*

He smiled, sensing their connection getting stronger.

"Hey, Chad," Abraham said, coming out of the locker room.

Chad pivoted, facing him, and flashed a bright, easy grin.

Abraham glanced over Chad's shoulder at the room where Isabel and John were practicing, then looked back at him. "Ready for class?"

"Actually, I got an emergency call from the office. I need to go, but I'll be back tomorrow."

Part of him was tempted to stay, hoped she'd see him, giving her another spike of endorphins, making her skin flush only the way he could.

But that would spoil the foreplay.

He was eager to see what she'd do next and he had a few moves that she'd never anticipate.

"Before you look at the file, did Agent Rogers say why she withheld it?" Allison asked, sitting in front of the laptop in the makeshift command center.

Dutch set his motorcycle helmet on the table. "Something about not wanting me to treat Isabel in an overprotective manner because it'd push her away. And, uh, the more I knew, the easier it'd be to slip up."

"I'm going to make a coffee run. Anyone want anything?" Draper asked.

"Skinny cappuccino," Allison said. "Thanks, sir."

Dutch shook his head and Draper left.

"I've got to warn you," Allison said, her voice grim. "The redacted information made my skin crawl and it will definitely make your protective alpha instincts flare, so if you read it, don't go all caveman on the asset. Okay?"

Give him some credit. As an elite operator on the Fugitive Apprehension Response Team, restraint and patience were prerequisites. "Sure."

Allison got up and gestured for him to sit at the computer.

"Where should I start?" he asked.

"The restraining order." She clicked on the document and brought it up on the screen.

Dutch skimmed over it, trying to pinpoint the essential elements of information through the superfluity of legal jargon.

"You want to look at her allegations," Allison said, as if reading his mind. "She claims that over the course of their one-month relationship, Chad Ellis grew increasingly possessive, controlling and aggressive. She felt intimidated and scared and broke up with him."

"Any abuse?"

"Not physically, at least not while they were together. In her statement, Ellis comes across as charming and persuasive, like a cult leader. Isabel struck me as a bit inexperienced and too trusting."

"It's good she broke up with him before things got violent."

Allison grimaced. "But there's more. The night she ended it he tore up her apartment. After the breakup, the harassment started with him following her. She alleged that he called her at all hours, forcing her to change her cell number, but she still received calls at the gallery. Unfortunately, it was never proven. Ellis voluntarily handed over the records for his cell phone and all the landlines of businesses."

"It would've been easy enough for him to use a burner."

Allison nodded. "My thoughts exactly."

"What does the guy do for a living?" Dutch asked.

"Here's the creepy part," Allison said, bringing up other documents on the screen. "He owns a few car washes, several biohazard remediation cleaning businesses from Malibu to Laguna, and a couple of funeral homes with crematoriums."

Ice slid through Dutch's blood. "What is he, a serial killer in the making?"

"Maybe. With those resources at his disposal and his past behavior, he may have already killed someone and made the entire crime scene disappear. We may never know."

Dutch clenched his hand into a fist, thinking about how Ellis had shown up in the restaurant, intimidating and frightening Isabel to the point that she ran out. It made Dutch want to rip his head off.

"Isabel was never able to prove that he followed her or made the strange phone calls, but there was a witness who caught him accosting her. She was leaving the art gallery. Her car had been parked in a proprietor's spot around back, when he came up behind her, put his arm around her throat and allegedly told her that they'd always be together. The owner of the bookstore two doors down happened to be leaving around the same time. He testified that Ellis was shoving his hand up her skirt and Isabel stated that he tried to get her inside the car."

Dutch's fist tightened, the joints popping, his fingers beginning to ache.

Why would Agent Rogers recommend a mugging scenario with Isabel after what she went through?

Even though it had worked, the tactic was despicable, especially considering Isabel's history. Dutch hadn't known her long, but he had an overwhelming urge to shield her from violence and pain.

"Ellis claimed it was a misunderstanding," Allison said. "Isabel had called him earlier that day. She stated it was to demand that he stop sending her gifts, but he alleged she asked him to come to the gallery and that in the past Isabel liked him to be rough. Several police officers testified on Ellis's behalf, making him look like citizen of the year. He had a good lawyer who characterized Isabel as a scorned woman with a grudge, trying to defame Ellis. The judge issued a harassment restraining order for one year, where Ellis has to remain fifty feet away from her."

Dutch scowled, keeping a tight lid on the rage brewing inside him. "That's it. Only fifty?" He ran both his hands over his head.

Blood pounded behind his ears in a thunderous rush as his brain turned over the information, round and round, thinking of all the places where that freak could legally show up and still harass Isabel as he'd done earlier.

"It sucks. I know." Allison splayed her hands. "I'm sure the police testimonials were a factor, along with how careful Ellis had been. Thank heavens the bookstore owner came out when he did. I hate to think what could've happened to her if Ellis had gotten her into the car."

Biohazard remediation was another way of saying crime-scene cleanup. That would explain why Ellis had a good relationship with the police.

Allison pulled out the cell phone buzzing in her pocket. "It's my son—I've got to take it. My soon-to-be-former husband is already giving me enough hell over this short-term assignment. Like he doesn't get to jet off for his job whenever he wants. Damn double standards." She thumbed the accept button and strolled away. "Hey, munchkin." Her tone turned warm and cheerful. "How was school?"

Agent Rogers had had a legitimate concern. It was going to take every shred of Dutch's willpower to contain his protective impulses where Isabel was concerned. He wanted nothing more than to keep her safe from Ellis. Because he did care. Whether or not she was aware of her uncle's status as leader of a powerful and brutal cartel had nothing to do with this. In fact, it made him believe that she was completely unaware. Anyone familiar with the cartel and their vicious reputation could've had Chad Ellis disappear with one phone call to her uncle.

Isabel was innocent and suffering and needed help.

Dutch enlarged the picture of Chad Ellis. He wore an expensive suit and tie, clean-cut, with a practiced smile and Hollywood looks, but there was something cold and vacant about his eyes.

"So that's what a psychopath looks like," he muttered to himself.

Guys like Ellis didn't simply walk away on their own accord, or even when directed to by the law. Things would only build with him, getting worse until he struck out and physically hurt her. Did as much damage as possible.

Dutch had been right to push for the information. He had to know what Isabel was up against. The reason she'd been guarded, wary, fearful today.

Getting close to her without smothering Isabel in his red-hot need to protect her, to defend her against that violent creep wouldn't be a problem. His mother and sister had made him an expert in dealing with determined, independent women who could take care of themselves.

But he had to show Isabel that even the strong sometimes needed backup.

The next time Chad Ellis messed with Isabel, Dutch was going to see to it that he regretted it.

# Chapter Eight

The annual fund-raiser was winding down but had gone better than Isabel had hoped. The elevator had been fixed earlier that afternoon. Canapés were being served and chilled champagne flowed all evening. Her uncle Emilio had purchased a painting over the phone, showing his support as always even though he couldn't attend. They'd exceeded their mark, raising twenty thousand over their goal, and still had two paintings left.

The one thing that'd make the night better was seeing Dutch.

Isabel checked the door again, hoping he might show. Not that he had any reason to. She'd run out on him at lunch yesterday without a legitimate explanation, hadn't called him to say thank you for dropping off the food despite his laid-back way of giving her his number and she'd neglected to extend him a formal invite to the event.

He must think she was a total basket case. Why would he come tonight unless he was a glutton for punishment?

"It's haunting," the mayor said about the abstract expressionist painting, yanking her from her thoughts. "This artist has the depth and passion of Jackson Pollock. I'll take it."

"Fantastic." She plastered on a hollow smile. Pulling off her biggest event of the year with such a resounding success should've made her happy. But there was a gaping hole in her life. If only she knew how to fill it. "Thank you so much for your support."

The mayor shook her hand and they held the pose for a photo op in front of the painting. With any luck, the picture would make the front of the Art and Entertainment section of the Sunday newspaper.

Isabel directed the mayor's assistant to Brenda to complete the purchase.

*One painting left.*

The phone rang. Isabel made her way through the milling

crowd to the front desk and answered. "Kismet art gallery."
She pressed her opposite ear closed so she could hear over the
murmur of conversations in the background. "Isabel Vargas
speaking. How may I help you?"

Heavy breathing rasped through the phone. Isabel's stomach plummeted, her muscles tightening. Long breaths in and
out over the line in her ear, deep, slow grunting.

Her hand fluttered to her neck and she fiddled with the
string of pearls she wore.

"I hate your lipstick," an altered male voice groaned, and
the cold lump in her throat swelled to the size of a bowling
ball. "That shade of red makes you look like a harlot. But I
love the dress."

First, he'd shown up at the restaurant and now he was making harassing phone calls again. No matter how he disguised
his voice, she knew it was him. Chad Ellis.

"Sophisticated, yet, enticing. A second skin against your
body, showcasing your curves." He grunted, his breath growing heavier, deeper, viler. "You look beautiful tonight. Nice
touch with the pearls. Such a *tease*."

Bile burned up the back of Isabel's throat as she dropped
her hand from her neck and looked around out the front window. He wouldn't be easy to spot. That maniac was hiding
in the darkness, where no one else would be able to see him.

No witnesses.

"I bet you smell even better," he said, dragging out each
syllable in an eerie way that raised goose bumps on her skin,
but she swallowed the bitter taste filling her mouth. "Maybe
I'll come closer to take a whiff. I miss you. Can you feel my
eyes on you? Like a physical touch you crave. Watching you
makes me so hot—"

"Get a life, you sick pervert, and stay out of mine!" Isabel
slammed the phone down and caught the shocked glances of
those around her.

Embarrassment heated her face, her heart fluttering. "Sorry." She raised a trembling hand in apology. "Excuse me."

She was done. No more hanging up in silence. No more running away. No more living half a life because she thought there was something wrong with her. She wasn't the problem.

He was.

"Everything all right?"

Isabel turned around, freezing midspin. Dutch stood beside her, dressed in a slate-gray shirt buttoned almost all the way to the top and dark slacks. His face was tense, concern stamped across his features. The surprise was so pleasant and shocking she threw herself against his chest, hugging him.

An immediate spark of heat rushed over her skin at the contact, but she dismissed it as a histrionic reaction after the disturbing phone call from Chad. Still, Dutch's warmth and strength engulfing her took the chill away from her bones, nonetheless.

He held her, his arms banding tight around her in a comforting embrace.

"You came," she gasped.

Stroking her hair, he said, "All the work and worry you were putting into this event, how could I not come?"

She pulled back, regaining her composure, and looked up at him.

The relief in seeing his face and beaming smile was like a gift she'd prayed for but had given up hope on ever getting.

"When I walked in, you sounded upset on the phone. Who were you talking to?"

Isabel dropped her gaze to her peep-toed shoes. "No one worth discussing."

Brenda shimmied through the crowd and slid up next to her. "We just sold the last painting to that Hollywood producer."

"That's great," Isabel said, her voice flat and devoid of excitement.

"What's wrong?" Brenda asked.

"She just got an upsetting phone call from a *sick pervert*," Dutch said to Brenda while putting a comforting arm around Isabel.

Brenda's jaw unhinged and her eyes went wide. "The nerve of him."

"Him who?" Dutch asked.

"Chad Ellis," Brenda said. "Her ex."

"I don't want to talk about it." Isabel rolled her pearls through her fingers and remembered the disgusting things Chad had said to her. Was he still watching her? She lowered her hand, smoothing down the bottom of her Herve Leger crisscross bandage dress. "I think I need to get out of here. Would you mind if I cut out early?" she asked Brenda, hating to abandon her friend, but she needed to leave the gallery, needed air.

"Not at all. This soiree is almost over. I've already roped the gorgeous party planner into helping me close and we're going to have drinks after. Go somewhere with Dutch." Brenda shifted her gaze to him. "Do you promise to take her somewhere fun and make sure she gets home safely?"

"I can handle that."

"You don't have to," Isabel said. "Really. I can just go home."

"It'd be my pleasure to take you out," he said.

"There. It's settled." Brenda kissed her cheek. "You deserve a break. You did awesome tonight, working the room and convincing people to open their wallets. Get out of here."

"Are you up for dancing?" Dutch asked.

"Sure." It might be a good distraction. "My uncle owns a nightclub in downtown LA. We could get a VIP table and a bottle of whatever you want."

He shrugged, not looking the least bit impressed. "Sounds like a lot of unnecessary fancy stuff if you ask me. All I need is you and some good music. You game?"

She was so accustomed to using the perks of her lifestyle to ingratiate herself with other people that she didn't know how to respond when Dutch shot down her offer.

He frowned. "If going to your uncle's club makes you more comfortable, then we—"

"No. It's just surprising. Most people jump at the chance to have VIP treatment."

"I'm not most people."

No, he wasn't. He was a beautiful anomaly.

"I'm game," she said. "Just give me a minute."

After saying a few quick goodbyes, she grabbed her clutch from the bottom drawer of the desk. Since she hadn't realized the Pacifier required twelve hours to charge, all five were plugged in at home, juicing up. Rather than needing to lug a tote-size bag, she opted for something small and sparkly to match her shoes. It was only big enough to hold her driver's license, credit card, lipstick, pepper spray and EpiPen.

"Where are we going?" she asked.

"It's a surprise." Dutch took her hand in his, interlacing their fingers, and hauled her out of the gallery.

"Do I need to call for my car?"

"Nope."

Being led off into the unknown by a man she'd met two days ago should've felt reckless and risky, but it didn't. She didn't know Dutch well. His body was lethal, his face hard and rugged, but she was certain of two things. He was kind and considerate, and that made him exactly what she needed.

"Dutch, you're so right," she said, swallowing the words *almost perfect*, "that there must be something wrong with you. What is it? You don't have split-personality disorder or any other type of condition, do you?"

"I assure you, I'm as sane as you and Brenda."

Well, that wasn't saying much. Some days she was insane-asylum-batty, and Brenda was far from normal, in a wacky sort of way, but neither of them were psycho. Like Chad.

Something had been off about her ex, in his core makeup.

He had probably tortured animals as a child. She'd sensed it in his eyes, in his touch, without being able to pinpoint what it was until he'd let his maniac flag fly.

. Dutch was turning out to be everything she wanted in a guy, her wish list made into flesh and bone. If she were looking for a perfect partner.

"And you've never stalked anyone, have you?" she asked.

"Never. But in freshman year of high school, I had a crush on a cheerleader and went to every football game. Fortunately, she was a senior and when she graduated, my obsession ended."

She chuckled.

"You're safe with me, Isabel." He leaned in and put their joined hands over his heart. "I promise, no harm will come to you while you're with me." He spoke the words like a vow.

She always picked the wrong guy, but Dutch was different and had given her plenty of reasons through his actions to take a chance on him.

They walked four blocks down Santa Monica Boulevard and over to the Third Street Promenade—a posh outdoor shopping center with luxury boutiques, restaurants and lively events. Between Wilshire and Arizona Avenue was a festive public party with a diverse crowd. Salsa dancing on the promenade, from the young to the old, beginners and talented dancers displaying expert footwork and head rolls and dips she could only dream of doing.

It was unpretentious. A stark contrast to the vibe at any club. No one cared about how they were dressed or was concerned with appearances only. Everyone simply wanted to have a good time.

Isabel had no idea that this was going on a short five-minute walk from her gallery.

Dutch whisked her into his arms. "Disappointed?"

"Not at all," she said, her feet already moving to the music. Placing his hands in the right places, holding her in a firm yet gentle grip, he made it so damned easy with his *caliente* salsa moves. Their bodies pressed close, hips rolling in fluid sync.

She listened to the rhythm, surrendered to Dutch's lead and let go. He was a human live wire made of muscle.

*Dancing.* Who would've guessed it would feel so good?

Laughter, fun and romance were in the warm air as he held her closer, spinning away her worries to the energizing Latin beats.

Her blood heated. The provocative moves reminded her how sexual and carefree she used to be. Dutch's magnetism, the upbeat tempo, the sound of the trumpets in the music, the open-air environment, sparked life back in her veins and weaved a sort of magic around her.

She'd needed this. *Needed him.*

Dutch twirled her away from him. Smiling, she whirled with her arms extended. She did a two-count step, backing up to him, showing off a little.

Facing the large fountain topped with a dinosaur topiary, she spotted Chad watching her.

His jaw clenched hard. His eyes narrowed, his stare blistering. She could feel his fury like scalding lava on her skin.

If looks could kill, she would've been reduced to scorched earth.

Taking her wrist, Dutch spun her back into his arms. The unexpected touch made her catch her breath and sent her pulse hammering for good reasons. He smiled at her as if no one else in the world existed. Something in her chest lightened as fear evaporated.

God, she liked touching this delectable man, dancing with him, being near him. The way she felt safe with him. And nothing, absolutely nothing was going to spoil this moment.

Cupping his face in both her hands, Isabel rose on her toes and brought Dutch's mouth to hers. She didn't know if it was the adrenaline, her attraction to Dutch or her refusal to act as a victim that caused her to do it.

But he pulled her into the kiss, his lips hot and urgent, his tongue exploring deep.

And she didn't hold back. Nothing denied. Everything on public display for all to see.

Her body moved against his, sinuous and desperate for sweetness, for sanctuary.

Not that long ago, someone cruel had made her doubt herself and tried to convince her that love had to hurt.

But it didn't.

Dutch's hands were gentle and persuasive on her body. Each long, sensual stroke of his tongue stole her breath along with the ugly memories. Transcended her to the clouds, where she was floating. She moaned in his mouth and he held her tighter with those granite arms, flattening her against his rock-hard chest. They tasted one another again and again, sharing breath, fueling the mutual fire crackling between them.

In that moment, she was fearless and passionate, and had never felt more like her true self. A believer in happiness and romance. All from the most empowering kiss of her life with a man she was falling for. Against her self-imposed rules.

Dutch eased back and looked into her eyes. His hand came up to cradle her jaw. A smile spread across his face, brimming with heat that melted her. To heck with the rules.

"That's one hell of a way to ask a guy to kiss you."

She laughed, free and loud. The heartfelt sound emanating from deep inside her belly. Glancing over her shoulder, she looked at the fountain.

The demon was gone, banished back to hell.

*For now.*

DUTCH FOLLOWED ISABEL's directions as he drove her home in her Maserati. A fine piece of machinery that handled tight curves with smooth precision.

Her dog was curled up on the back seat, asleep. A soft smile rested on Isabel's face, filling him with a sense of joy the likes of which he'd never known. With her tension gone, she looked younger than twenty-eight, vulnerable, adorable. He hadn't thought making someone else happy could bring him such gratification.

No one deserved a fun evening more than her. The dancing had done the trick. She came out of her shell and had blossomed in front of him. As soon as he'd read about the Third Street Promenade free salsa dancing in a local magazine, he'd thought of Isabel.

Not as a manipulative ploy. She'd popped into his head and he'd imagined her dancing and letting loose. And she had.

But that kiss had been unexpected. Instead of his reaction being one of professional restraint, it had been visceral, instinctual, taking the chemistry kindling between them from sparks to a brush fire.

Remembering it had adrenaline pumping in his veins akin to standing on the edge of a cliff preparing to jump into the deep blue below. He *was* into extreme sports. Cliff diving. Rock climbing. BASE jumping. Snowboarding. You name it, he'd tried it, but none of it compared to kissing Isabel.

A hunger for more was growing inside him. More kisses and salsa and smiles, like the one on her face now.

Dancing had led to dinner at an Italian place with good vibes, where they'd split a Neapolitan-style pizza while he kept one eye on the door. Waiting, hoping that cretin Chad dared set a foot inside, but he hadn't shown his face.

Isabel had eaten with a hearty appetite that he appreciated and laughed with no shadows in her eyes. They had chatted about their childhoods and the importance of family and their respective difficulties making friends when they were younger. About the places they'd both traveled to for fun and deployments. His time in the Sandbox and the mountains of

Afghanistan. Even the gut-wrenching reality of what it had been like in spec ops.

He'd told her things he'd never shared with another soul, and she didn't diminish it with platitudes. She'd taken his hand in hers and showed her understanding through her eyes, through her touch.

Somewhere along the way he'd forgotten this was business and not pleasure, and the weight she carried seemed to lift from her shoulders, as well.

They'd only called it a night because she had to pick up her dog from day care before the place closed.

"Turn left here," she said. "That's my building." She pointed to a small modern complex with only six floors.

Dutch turned and she hit the remote, opening the gate to her garage. It was well lit and had plenty of security cameras, not leaving any blind spots.

Still, it was possible for someone on foot to slip in behind her car. Good thing she'd gotten the dog.

"Thanks for driving. I'll order an Uber for you," she said, as they had planned earlier, but he'd hoped to have a little more time with her.

They got out of the car and walked toward the door that led inside to the lobby. The well-trained dog stayed at her side without a leash.

"The app says it'll take twenty minutes." Her tone was disappointed, but he couldn't tell if it was because he wasn't staying longer or not leaving sooner.

"I can wait outside for it." The night had been the best date he'd had in a long time, but he didn't want to put any unnecessary pressure on her.

"No, please don't. I've got to take McQueen out one last time. Join us? The app will send an alert when the car gets here."

"Sure."

They strolled past the elevator and headed for the back deck.

"Since the gallery is closed tomorrow, if you don't have plans, I'd love to help you mark something off your bucket list."

"If you're talking about sex, I'm sure you're fantastic in bed, but—"

Dutch laughed. "I meant surfing. I'd love to teach you, but it's nice to know you have such confidence in my bedroom skills."

Cheeks turning berry red, she lowered her head and pursed her lips. "I'm sorry. I'd love to learn. Text me a time and a place and what I need to bring or wear."

He held the door open for her. Motion lights came on as they went outside. The dog ran past the swimming pool to a patch of fake grass on the far side of the large communal deck that had a locked gate.

"McQueen is such a kick-butt name," Dutch said, following Isabel to the railing, overlooking the beach. "I'm surprised you named him after the actor."

"Which actor?" She looked up at the stars.

"Steve McQueen. The king of cool. *The Thomas Crown Affair*, the original. *The Getaway*, once again the original. *The Magnificent Seven*."

Her gaze found his. "Let me guess. The original."

"Yes. And let's not forget *Bullitt*."

"Well, I named him after Alexander McQueen."

"Who?"

"The fashion designer."

After a beat of silence, they laughed in unison.

"Sounds like we'll have to have a movie marathon," she said. "I'll cook dinner and you'll…"

He brushed the hair from her face, caressing her cheek. Standing there, staring at her, he hid nothing, letting her see the cutting edge driving him, the genuine attraction drawing him closer to her. He was the kind of man who owned who he was and told the world to go take a flying leap if they didn't like it. But this was the best he could do, the most he could give in the moment. "Do the dishes and then rub your feet?"

She smiled, unguarded and bright. "You better stop, or I'll have to kiss you again."

"If that's your idea of a deterrent, you're going to have to work on that." He pulled her to him. But caught himself and lightened his grip, easing back.

"Do I still have to ask?" She tilted her head, wetting her lips.

"I want to respect your wishes and take this slowly." He had an important job to do and touching her was testing his willpower, but he had no intention of seducing her or using sex as a manipulation tactic. That was a line he wouldn't cross. "I want you to get to know me. To be comfortable around me. I want to understand what troubles you, keeps you up at night just like I know you want to see the northern lights." And he did, so damn badly. Not for his job, but for himself. "I get the sense this might scare you and I don't want to rush you."

"*You* don't scare me, Dutch. So stop talking and kiss me."

Lowering his lips to hers, he slipped an arm around her waist and gently touched her mouth, his tongue skating over hers. She leaned into the kiss, circling her arms around his neck. He threaded his fingers in her silky mass of loose curls cascading around her shoulders, breathing her in, molding her to him and savoring this.

He drank her in, the heady, delicate taste of her that was somehow wild and sweet at the same time. An enticing floral scent mixed with spice came from her hair and skin.

The soft heat of her, the way she smelled, how she tasted, the responding hunger in her touch, everything culminated in that moment of pure perfection.

No woman had felt better. So right.

Then her phone chimed, and he cursed the promptness of the Uber driver.

A PALL OF RED fell over the world as Chad seethed. Violent thoughts, gruesome cravings danced in his head the same way she had danced with that man.

*Isabel.*

He beat his fist against the boulder as he watched that man touching his woman. Kissing *his* precious doll, turning her into a wanton trollop.

*Isabel!*

The darkness around him on the beach seeped into his soul. His mouth tasted of ashes.

If that thug went up to her apartment, if she took him to her bed…

Chad squeezed his eyes shut, knowing what he'd have to do. Kill the interloper.

And cleanse Isabel of her sin.

On the deck, the two separated and Isabel pulled out her phone, then glanced at the screen. Her dog dashed out of the grass and ran around the pool, doing laps like it was racing around a track.

She snapped her fingers. The canine came to her and licked the man's hand. He bent down, rubbing its head. Even the damn dog liked him.

They traipsed back inside the building with her arm linked around his.

Chad's gaze slid to the third floor, to her apartment. He waited, growing still, the blood in his veins boiling, the leash slipping on the rage prowling inside him.

Finally, her lights came on and she entered her apartment. Alone. The inconvenient dog didn't count.

She'd come to her senses and sent that piece of garbage on his way for the night.

But she had put Chad in a difficult position. Now he had to save Isabel from herself before she violated the sanctity of their union.

He had no choice but to punish her.

*Because I love you, Isabel.*

Necessary preparations had been made. He'd anticipated this day might come, and he was ready to remind her who was in charge.

# Chapter Nine

The wind was mild, the sun bright, the waves cool and steady with a long swell period. Perfection conditions for Isabel's first lesson, Dutch thought to himself.

He was in the water waist deep. Next to him, Isabel was on his board, wearing a provocative one-piece with a zipper down the front and cutouts on her waist. Her killer curves had been apparent from the formfitting clothes she wore, but in a swimsuit, her figure was jaw-dropping.

For an hour or so, they'd practiced on the sand, going over training footwork, teaching her how to pop up on the board and read the waves. Then they'd spent another hour in the water. Sitting on a surfboard seemed easy, but as Isabel discovered, it wasn't. Simply something you had to learn, feel. Right along with falling over—a crucial part and inevitable for all, especially beginners—and paddling, a key to good surfing.

"Remember," Dutch said, "when you're riding on the board, bend your knees, not your back."

She pushed her wet hair back from her face, focused on the water. "Okay."

As a wave rolled in, Dutch positioned the board. "Go. Now."

Isabel paddled like the devil to catch the wave, got up into a solid crouch, then stood and balanced.

*Yes! She stood!*

Even better, she rode that wave all the way to the shore.

Dutch marveled at how well she was doing on her first day. She had the potential to be good at it.

He whooped and cheered and encouraged her to try it again. They did a few more sets and took a break on the beach.

Isabel went to shower off and Dutch ran a towel over himself. He opened the cooler, took out the food he'd packed and set it on a blanket. Surfing always worked up his appetite. He figured it'd do the same for her.

She returned wearing sunglasses and a white cover-up over

her bathing suit. Her skin was smooth and flawless. He loved her like this, carefree, no makeup besides a sheer lip gloss she'd applied. Not that she needed it with that natural rosy tint to her lips. She sat beside him, putting her tote bag down.

A breeze carried that divine scent of hers to him. Warm amber, floral and spice. "What perfume did you put on?"

"It's a perfume oil." She dug a delicate bottle out of the bag and showed it to him. "Marula Oil is the base, making it great for my hair and skin."

He leaned over and ran his nose up her neck, inhaling deeply. Vetiver struck him this time, the scent reminding him of Indonesia and wading through the tall, fragrant grass on an assignment. "I really love it on you."

"Then I'll have to stock up." As she was dropping the bottle back in her bag, the tote tipped over and a black baton rolled out.

Dutch picked it up, noting the wrist strap, rubberized armor coating and prongs on the end. "Stun baton?"

Turning her head away from him, she looked out at the water. "It's a deterrent."

"For whom? Chad Ellis?"

She went ramrod straight. "This has been such a lovely day." Reaching over, she took his hand in hers and looked at him. "I don't want to spoil it by talking about him. Please."

The vulnerability in her touch, her voice, tugged at his heart. Tied his gut into knots. He wanted to take away her pain, to mop up this problem of Ellis like a spill on the floor.

Isabel was an incredible woman, easy to fall for. Not at all the stuck-up princess he'd imagined her to be. If not for this assignment, their paths might never have crossed. He hated the circumstances and the necessary deception that had brought them together but spending time with her made him feel like the luckiest man on the planet.

Dutch put the baton back in her bag. "Okay." He rubbed her leg to reassure Isabel there was no need to discuss it, but his hand lingered longer than he'd intended. Her skin was so soft, supple as butter. "Hungry?" He started opening the containers of food he prepared.

"Starved." She flashed a bright smile. "You thought of everything."

AFTER CHAD PAID the parking fee, he pulled into a spot in the lot on the ridge above the beach. He double-checked that there were no CCTV cameras. Then he glanced down at the phone and read the text messages again.

Isabel: I'm excited, but nervous. Hope you're a good teacher, Dutch.

Dutch: You'll do great. Trust me, beautiful. Topanga Beach. 10 a.m.

Isabel: See you later.

ONE NIGHT SEVEN months ago, while Isabel had slept in his bed, Chad had taken her cell phone and the key fob to her car. He'd handed them off to his tech guy who did freelance work under the table. Two hours later, Chad had a clone of the RFID key fob and spyware had been downloaded on her phone. The malicious software gave Chad her GPS location, browser history, text messages, social media chats, emails and the ability to eavesdrop on her phone calls.

She'd been none the wiser. Still wasn't.

Despite the fact she'd changed her number, the mobile device itself and the SIM card were the same. Until she upgraded her cell, which wasn't going to be any time soon since he'd encouraged her to get the latest model shortly after they started dating, he was able to surveil her in ways even Olga couldn't. But the PI filled in the gaps.

If it hadn't been for Olga, it would've taken him days to find out about *Dutch*.

This was the first time Isabel had sent a message to another man.

Blood burned through his veins again, anger and adrenaline spurring him on.

Chad dialed Olga. She was somewhere down below on the beach. Like any good private investigator, she kept a variety of outfits in her car to blend in wherever she needed to and even had a bicycle in her trunk. "What are they doing?"

"Eating lunch."

"When they get ready to leave, I want you to film Isabel."

"I don't understand," Olga said.

"Record them saying goodbye and focus the video on Isabel getting into her car and driving off."

"Why?"

"Because I told you to," Chad snapped, letting his thinning patience resonate over the line. "No matter what happens, follow the man. Find out where he lives. Get me a full name."

"What's going to happen?"

Chad hung up, huffing his irritation. Olga was paid well not to ask questions and to do as she was instructed discreetly.

Before getting out of the car, he pressed down the fake mustache, ensuring it stayed in place, lowered the bill of his ball cap over his wig and slipped on gloves. He grabbed the robin's-egg-blue Tiffany box that he'd poked air holes in earlier, got out and walked quickly to Isabel's Maserati.

He hit the cloned key fob. Her lights flashed and the doors unlocked.

Grasping the handle, he opened the door and lowered to one knee. He slipped his little gift of *tough love* underneath the driver's seat, flicked off the lid—the faint sound of the box's inhabitants lifting his spirits enough for him to manage a smile—and slammed the door shut.

No fingerprints or any DNA traces of his left behind. His

brother Brett, a reliable alibi, would swear that Chad had been at his house the entire day, where his car was still parked in the driveway.

He climbed back into the Chevrolet that belonged to Brett's gardener, an undocumented worker who enjoyed living in this country and understood the cardinal Ellis principle.

*See no evil, speak no evil and no evil shall befall you.*

Or as their crass thief of a mother would've said if she were alive and hadn't died in prison—*snitches get stitches.*

He turned the key in the ignition and the old engine rumbled to life.

Turning onto the Pacific Coast Highway, his one regret was that he wouldn't be able to see Isabel receive the punishment she deserved firsthand.

The video would have to suffice.

BEING WITH DUTCH was like finding a haven during a storm. Isabel imagined spending time with him every day for the foreseeable future and her smile deepened. He was laid-back and thoughtful. Made things easier in a way no one else she knew ever had.

The spread of food he'd brought was simple. Peeled hard-boiled eggs, hummus, baguettes, Manchego and cheddar cheeses, grapes, figs, carrot sticks and prosciutto. Even two prepackaged slices of chocolate cake with buttercream frosting. The simple meal hit the spot.

"The only thing missing is a glass of chilled chardonnay," she said.

"I would've brought wine or champagne, but you said you don't drink."

"Not for a while." At his curious expression, she said, "I'm not an alcoholic, but I'm on medication that doesn't mix well with alcohol."

Pressing her lips together, she considered whether to go on without opening the door that led to the freak show of Chad

Ellis. Dutch had shared deeply personal things with her last night. About his call to serve in the army, losing battle brothers in dangerous military operations, how being in Delta Force took so much out of him that it'd scraped his soul bare and he needed a break.

She owed him the same transparency. In baby steps. "I'm on Ativan."

"I had a buddy who was on a cocktail of pills for his PTSD. Ativan was one of them. You don't have to tell me details, but I take it that you went through a rough breakup with Ellis."

"Yeah. You could say that." She was still going through it. Would it ever be over?

"I know you have Brenda, but with your uncle being down in San Diego, I'd like to be there for you."

Brenda was family. They'd been close since college, and she knew the ugly specifics of what Isabel had gone through. There were times she'd contemplated telling her uncle, since she shared everything else with him, but his support would've come with the strings of pity and bodyguards who'd spy on her. There had to be a happy medium.

Maybe Dutch was it. He was a good listener and didn't push.

"My uncle is coming up to have dinner with me on Wednesday," she said.

"Oh yeah. I'd love to meet him."

Lowering her shades down the bridge of her nose, she met his eyes. "Don't you think it's a little premature? We haven't even slept together. Why would you want to put yourself through such scrutiny?"

"You don't realize how special you are." He slung his arm around her, gripping her shoulder. "Maybe you should make all the men you date run that gauntlet. Trial by fire to see if they're worthy of your affection." His fingers moved along her arm, massaging, caressing. "Let me be the first. When I told you that I wanted to know you, I was serious. That includes meeting your uncle."

She enjoyed the possibility of endless tomorrows with Dutch and wasn't ready to lose him. "I don't think you understand what you're asking for. Once my uncle puts his stamp of disapproval on you…" That was it. There'd be no future.

Grasping her chin between his thumb and forefinger, he angled her face toward his. "I'm not a foregone conclusion, Isabel. *If* he doesn't approve of me, we cross that bridge when we come to it. But the way I see it, you're grown and financially independent. You date who you damn well please."

"He'll scare you off. He's very powerful, judgmental and can be a bit of a bully." A snobbish bully and that was putting it mildly.

"Do I seem like a man who's easily intimidated?"

No. He didn't.

"The only way I'll walk away from you is if you ask me to." Smoothing hair off her cheek, his fingers lingered, caressing her jaw, then gliding down her neck and back up again, sending tingles shooting through her. "I've gone up against my fair share of bullies. I can handle your uncle."

He drew closer, his hand tangling in her hair, bringing her mouth toward his. But he stopped short of giving her what she wanted, what she craved. Another taste of him.

So, she took it.

She kissed him and hummed her approval at the wet heat of his mouth as their breaths tangled. His eager tongue met hers, velvety stroke for stroke. Need drove urgency, bringing their bodies together into a hard squeeze of a hug that ended with him sucking on her tongue until her belly twisted with arousal.

"Isabel," he murmured against her lips, something raw and hungry in his voice.

She didn't want the kiss to end, didn't want to let him go. But she straightened, her thoughts bouncing back to the things he'd said. "Let me think about you meeting my uncle. Okay?"

He kissed the tip of her nose, trailed more across her cheeks. "Sure, beautiful."

Resting her head on his shoulder, she traced the lines of one of his tattoos. Inside the outline of an arrowhead were two black daggers crossed behind a skull with Latin inked beneath it, *De Oppresso Liber.*

*To free the oppressed.*

"I get how hard it was for you in Delta Force, losing your friends, having to kill people, the constant pressure, but you never told me why you stayed for twelve years."

He put his arm around her. "Just because it was tough doesn't mean it wasn't worth it. I believed in the mission, protecting our country, and the army gave me a family that had my back no matter what. That I could count on to pick me up if I fell, to hump me out if I got shot. Honestly, getting booted was harder than the grind of the high-ops tempo."

"Why?"

"Because I lost my battle brothers and my sense of purpose in one fell swoop. But I, uh... I know there's a new place for me out there, where I belong," he said, staring at the ocean, his voice somber.

She gave him a hard, quick kiss, wanting to erase his sadness.

"Promise me something," he said.

"Sure. What?"

"I hate the way we met, how the universe brought us together with you getting mugged, but I don't regret finding you, being with you." He cupped her jaw, brushing his thumb across her cheek. "This feels right. You and me. I want to keep doing this with you, see what's on the horizon for us, together. For as long as you want. Promise me you'll remember that."

She frowned, not understanding what possessed him to say that.

He must've read the concern in her face because he rubbed between her eyes with the pad of his thumb, smoothing away her worry lines. "Every relationship has highs and lows. When we hit a low point, I don't want to lose you. So, promise you'll remember."

"Okay. I promise."

Dutch kissed her nose. "Let's have dessert."

THEY FINISHED EATING, packed everything up and headed for the parking lot. Refusing to let her carry anything, except her tote bag, he managed the surfboard, blanket and cooler on his own.

After he got everything loaded into the bed of his truck, he walked her to her car.

"Hey," he said, and she stopped in front of her door and looked at him. Dutch wiped her lip and licked the chocolate frosting off his thumb. The gesture was intimate and assuming and she loved it. Dutch reached for her. "Come here," he said, roping his arms around her. He released a satisfied sigh as if he'd been aching to hold her. "When am I going to see you again?"

Sliding her hands up his bare chest, she appreciated that he was in magnificent shape, tip-top condition as one could get.

She was tempted to tell him *tonight*, but she was scared. Of how good his muscular body felt beneath her palms. Of how he stared at her with a mix of affection and attraction that made her knees a little weak. Of how the air, charged with desire, stimulated her skin, quickened her pulse. Of how his arousal pressed against her lower belly made her want to explore every inch of him.

"If you come by later, I think we might have sex," she admitted, her reservations lost in the enthralling deep brown depths of his potent stare.

"Would that be good or bad?"

"Both, I think." She chuckled. "It wouldn't be taking things slowly, but the more I'm around you, the more I feel my boundaries slipping away." Nerves fluttered in her belly and she chewed on her bottom lip.

"I don't want you to worry about stuff like that. Here's my promise to you. The possibility of sex is off the table until I meet your uncle."

Was he serious?

On her first date with Chad, he'd taken her to dinner at a Michelin-starred restaurant, they'd had dessert upstairs, drinks on the rooftop. Then he'd taken her home and swept her up in an aggressive tide of sexual energy, where she'd gone with the flow of it rather than drown.

Looking back on it, every time she'd slept with him had been more about survival than passion and she wanted to kick herself for being so easily manipulated. So weak.

One bad decision, one poor choice, and she was paying for it months later.

"Why?" she asked incredulously.

"Intimacy should be earned, and you should be treasured." He stroked her cheek and gave her a tender, slow kiss.

Dutch touched her the right way, with gentleness and respect, and said the perfect thing. Maybe he was too good to be true. This could quite possibly be the most brilliant use of reverse psychology.

Deny her sex to make her want it. But she still fell a little harder, faster, deeper for him.

"Well, that settles it, you're meeting my uncle on Wednesday," she said, and they both laughed. That was another remarkable thing about him. No guy had ever made her smile so much or laugh until her cheeks ached. "I want to see you later."

Spending time with him was the best kind of escape from her troubles.

"Then you will. I'll bring takeout. Thai or sushi?"

"Thai. Surprise me with your favorites." She hit the key fob, unlocking her door. "Spice isn't a problem."

"I'm not shocked you can handle the heat."

"How about seven?" She grabbed the door handle. "Is that enough time for you to miss me?"

He smiled and, cupping her face in his hands, kissed her. She lit up warm and bright as if she'd swallowed the sun.

"I don't need hours to miss you, beautiful. Before you make it out of the parking lot, I'll want you back in my arms."

"You're setting the bar pretty high for other men."

"Good. You should have high standards. Never settle for anything less than what you deserve."

She opened her door, slid in and tossed her bag in the passenger's seat. Turning the key in the ignition, she waved to him.

Dutch lifted his hand and stepped back while she put the car in Reverse.

After cranking the wheel, she threw the gear in Drive. Something buzzed past her head. She swatted it away.

A bee landed on her dash.

Isabel stiffened. Her gaze locked on the yellow jacket.

She was severely allergic to bee venom. A sting would send her into anaphylactic shock within minutes. How did it get in the car?

*Don't freak out.*

Rolling down the window, she prayed it would fly out as she drove slowly through the lot. Too bad she didn't have a magazine in her bag to help shoo it from the car. But the little insect stayed on the dash, unfazed by the breeze.

A second bee flew past her face, landing on the steering wheel. Dread slid down her throat and dropped in her belly hard and cold.

She pressed back against her seat, putting as much distance as possible between herself and the tiny flying killers, but the car cabin seemed to shrink around her.

A terrifying thought popped into her head. *Chad.* Did he put a couple of bees in her car?

Just as quickly, she dismissed the irrational idea. The

planning, the logistics it would've taken, not to mention, he would've had to have known that she'd be here.

That was beyond crazy.

Hitting the button to roll down the passenger window, she cursed the perfume oil she'd rubbed on her skin and hair. It'd only attract them. *Way to go to smell sexy.*

Another bee buzzed up between her legs. Then another and another and another, coming from the foot well underneath her.

*Dear Lord in heaven.*

Panic exploded across her nerves, her heart clutching. Bees swarmed near her head, hissed across her arms. The whirring drone filled her ears.

Isabel screamed, swatting at the yellow jackets. Impossible for her to duck and dodge, there was no place to run. She felt trapped in the car.

One buzzed up her leg. The creepy-crawly sensation inched past her calf, featherlight over her knee. *Oh, God.* Glancing down, she watched in horror as two bees disappeared under her cover-up and a third landed on her chest.

*No, no.* Fire nipped her. A pinprick of agony, a hot match to her skin.

When a bee stung, it released a chemical that attracted others. She jerked her legs reflexively, waving wildly to swat at the rest, and slammed down on the accelerator.

"Isabel!" Dutch called.

A telephone pole rushed forward to meet her. Isabel's heart flew up into her throat. The car smashed into wood, the crunch of metal ringing in her ears.

An airbag inflated, knocking her back.

Pain bloomed in her skull, punching behind her eyes. She coughed on dust particles saturating the air.

Dazed, she registered the familiar itch spreading over her skin, deep in her flesh. She'd been stung, more than once.

God, it hurt like hell. Pure agony.

She fumbled with her seat belt, groped for the door handle and fell out of the car onto the hard concrete. Kicking the frame, she pushed her legs free and crawled to get away from the bees.

Her body's autoimmune response was happening fast—skin itching so badly it burned, face swelling, her tongue growing thick and heavy, throat closing, lungs squeezing—too fast.

Dutch scooped her up into his arms. "Isabel?" His face was pinched in fear.

"Bees," she said, wheezing. "Allergic. Epi—Bag…"

He carried her several feet from the car, set her down and took off.

A woman stepped up beside her and lowered to her knees. She held up a cell phone over Isabel's face like she was recording.

Was she videotaping this?

"Are you all right?" The woman hit a button and the phone beeped. "Oh, my God! Your face. You're breaking out in hives all over." She lifted her cell and dialed 911. "We need an ambulance. Topanga Beach parking lot. Hurry."

Isabel's lips tingled, growing numb. It was getting harder to breathe, her airways shrinking to the size of straws. Tears leaked from her inflamed eyes.

Dark spots clouded her vision, distending, swallowing the sky.

Dutch's face came into view and then oblivion.

# Chapter Ten

Isabel's swelling had gone down somewhat. Her face was no longer so distorted that she was unrecognizable. But with the oxygen mask, puffy cheeks and swollen eyes, she looked fragile, wounded, not quite like herself.

The doctor estimated that six bees had stung her, on her feet, legs, arms and chest. Every spot was surrounded by inflamed skin and punctuated with an angry red mark.

According to the doctor, if she hadn't had an EpiPen in her bag, she would've died.

Dutch sat in a chair next to her bed, holding her hand. He'd never been so terrified in his life when she crashed her car and came crawling out, barely able to breathe, her face blown up worse than a prize fighter's.

His fear had nothing to do with his job, though it should've, considering how many people were counting on him. His only concern had been Isabel's well-being and safety.

There'd been so many bees in her car when he went to find her EpiPen. Not enough to constitute a hive, but more than two couldn't be discounted as a fluke or some bad stroke of luck.

"Hi," Isabel said, her voice faint and brittle, eyes finally open.

"Hey, beautiful. I was so worried about you."

"Liar."

Dutch was taken aback. "Honey, the only other time I've been more worried about someone was when a battle brother was bleeding out in my arms."

"Not that. I know I don't look beautiful right now."

He kissed the back of her hand. "The most beautiful part about you is on the inside. It's your heart. Your spirit. To me, you'll always be gorgeous." A tear slipped from her eye, and he brushed it away. "How are you feeling?"

"Like I went to war and lost."

He gave a rueful laugh. "I used your fingerprint to unlock

your phone and called Brenda. She's on the way. I hope you don't mind."

"She'll make a fuss."

"You need to be fussed over. Believe me. Do you want me to call your uncle, too?"

That would be one way to meet him. An unfortunate incident where Dutch had helped would ingratiate him, but it wasn't one he preferred. Dutch wouldn't be able to look at himself in the mirror if he played a card that low.

Whether or not her uncle was called had to be Isabel's decision.

"No." She shook her head. "He'll take over, hire a nurse. Maybe have me brought to San Diego by helicopter. I'd rather be at home."

"Whatever you want."

The door opened and Brenda rushed into the room. "I came as soon as I could." Her friend went to the opposite side of the bed and gasped. "Oh, sweetie. You look awful. How did this happen? You're usually so careful."

"I think…" Isabel touched her throat like it hurt to swallow. "I think Chad did this to me," she said, and Brenda recoiled. "I have no idea *how* he would've done it. Known where I was. Gotten into my car." Isabel's eyes found his. "It sounds crazy, far-fetched, I know, but please believe me. This was him."

Dutch ran through the possibility in his head and it didn't seem far-fetched at all. "Maybe he's having you followed. I mean, he had to know you were at the grill somehow when he showed up like that. Did he ever have access to your car keys?"

"Plenty of times."

"It's possible to clone a key fob. But I can't make sense of the bees. He would've had to have direct access to a hive and equipment to contain the bees without getting stung himself, which would mean this was planned. Well thought out. Not some impulsive act of jealousy."

"Do you think he was trying to kill you?" Brenda asked.

Isabel shook her head. "He knows I carry an EpiPen with me everywhere. I never leave the house without one."

Brenda took her other hand. "Then why would he do this?"

Chad went through all this trouble for what? To hurt her? To put so much fear in her that she never looked at another man?

"If he did this," Dutch said, "then that means he's dyed-in-the-wool nuts, Isabel. A bona fide psychopath."

"That's Chad Ellis," Brenda said. "You can't begin to imagine the depths of depravity in his dark soul."

But Dutch didn't have to imagine. He knew. He'd read the file.

"We need to have your car checked," Dutch said. "Dusted for prints."

"You won't find anything," Isabel said. "He's too careful."

That wasn't going to stop Dutch from trying. Everyone made mistakes. Sooner or later Chad would slip up and Dutch would be ready to dole out retribution.

Dr. Kiser came in and stopped at the foot of the bed. "You're looking better." She flashed a curt smile. "The meds are working."

"I'm tired," Isabel said, "and I hurt all over."

"That's natural, but you're out of danger. I'm going to send you home with a prescription for prednisone. It's a corticosteroid that will help with the inflammation and itching, and two days' worth of hydrocodone for the pain. Apply a topical analgesic to the spots where you were stung, calamine lotion or Benadryl gel. Get plenty of rest, drink lots of fluids and you'll be fine. Due to the severity of your reaction, I'd recommend immunotherapy. Otherwise, if you were to get stung by a bee again, your immune system could have a more severe response even faster. Do you have any questions?"

"Can I take off this mask?"

"Yes, of course." The doctor stepped around the bed and helped Isabel remove it. "I'll get your discharge paperwork started. It should take about an hour or so."

"Thank you," Isabel said before the doctor left.

"Let me run home and change." Dutch gestured to his T-shirt and swim trunks. "I'll come right back, take you home and stick around until you and McQueen are good for the night."

"I don't want to impose on you," Isabel said. "I'm sure you've got better things to do."

Dutch gave her hand a light squeeze. "You're not an imposition. I've been looking for an excuse to spend more time with you and now I've got it." He looked at Brenda. "Will you stay with her until I get back?"

He didn't want to risk leaving her alone on the off chance that Ellis decided to show up. It was highly unlikely he'd try anything with Brenda in the room as a witness.

"I'll be right here, glued to her side."

He kissed the back of Isabel's hand and stood. "I'll be back as soon as I can." He went to the door.

"He wants to take care of you *and* your dog," Brenda whispered, but he heard it.

Didn't occur to him that making sure McQueen was fed and walked was something special. It was necessary.

In the hall, he took out his cell phone. He called Allison, not having the tolerance to deal with Draper, and gave her the rundown on the way to his truck.

"It's good that Isabel is going to be okay and the dinner on Wednesday with her uncle is fortuitous. But do you really think that Ellis is responsible for the bees in her car?"

"I think it's possible. Underestimating him would be a mistake. We need to have her car searched and dusted for prints. And she needs a different RFID chip in a new key fob."

"That'll take a couple of days."

"Fine. She's got the time. I'll be with her to make sure Ellis doesn't hurt her again."

"Dutch, no matter what, you can't go after this guy like a vigilante. There's a process and we have to follow it."

"I hear you." But he wasn't making any promises.

His patience was threadbare where Ellis was concerned. If they found a shred of evidence connecting him to this bee-stinging incident, even circumstantial, Dutch was going to unleash holy hell on that man.

STROLLING HIS BROTHER'S YARD, eight acres in an exclusive gated enclave in Calabasas, Chad passed the beehive he'd had set up four months ago. The story for his sister-in-law had been that he wanted them to have fresh honey. Nothing tasted better and the kids loved the novelty of the idea although they never ventured to the far side of the property. As for Chad's brother, it didn't matter to Brett and no questions had been asked.

That was the type of courtesy between the Ellis brothers. The less one knew, the less one was complicit.

His cell phone rang. Chad checked the caller ID, hoping it was Isabel needing him after her ordeal. He longed to hear her voice, begging for his help.

*Olga.* His gut tightened.

With a sigh, he released his disappointment. "Yes," he said into the phone.

"I emailed you the video."

"Will I be entertained?"

Olga muttered a string of curses. That was out of character for her, Chad thought.

"I'm following the guy home," she said, her voice sharp and agitated. "If you want his address and full name, send my payment for the rest of the week now. Then I'm done, after what you did to her."

He didn't care for Olga's tone. Or the implication, no matter how spot-on.

"I didn't do anything. I've been at my brother's place all day." Other than the one hour he'd snuck out and used the gardener's car while Brett covered, telling his family they were in the office discussing business and not to be disturbed.

"Whatever," Olga snapped. "If you didn't do it personally, then you hired someone to do it. Either way, you're responsible. She almost died. I won't be an accessory to that. Understand?"

"But you already are, and you know it." Leaving the garden, he walked across the patio adjacent to the pool, where his niece and nephew were frolicking in the water. "That's why you're charging me such an exorbitant rate."

Some restraining orders stated "neither you nor your agent may" blah, blah, but not his. He was within his legal boundaries to hire a private investigator. But Olga knew this wasn't a situation where he was looking for proof that his girlfriend was cheating or gathering evidence regarding parenting or employability.

Olga spoon-fed his fixation on Isabel every day with updates and pictures and now a video. All the while in the loop that there was a restraining order against him. Chad hadn't even told Brett about the injunction, but he wanted a PI with loose morals who was willing to turn a blind eye for the right price.

The nerve of her to grow a conscience and get sanctimonious after pocketing his cash for the past six months.

"Send the money or I won't give you any more information about her new *boyfriend*," Olga said, deliberately taunting him. "For the record, Mr. Ellis. You disgust me."

The line went dead.

Clenching his jaw, Chad sat and reclined back in a chaise beside his brother, facing the pool. He accessed his banking app and wired the final payment to Olga.

Mindy, his sister-in-law, waltzed out of the house and handed him and Brett each a Tom Collins. Then she pranced away in her heels and bikini, flaunting her flawless figure that some cosmetic surgeon had given her.

Why couldn't Isabel be more like Mindy. Not the plastic body with implants. He liked Isabel all natural, preferred her a bit heavier before she'd started working out. Now she could wear anything she wanted. But Isabel needed to fall in line and meet expectations. Not give him a hard time. It'd only taken Brett two months to break in Mindy and within less than a year they were married and settled in wedded…contentment.

Bliss would be a bit of a stretch. Mindy either didn't know or simply didn't say anything about Brett's philandering and she'd learned to handle his temper, squirreling the children away in their rooms while she took her punishment if she dared violate one of Brett's rules.

They balanced everything, made it work for their family because they loved each other. For better or worse. Until death do them part.

That's all he wanted with Isabel. Why couldn't she see that?

He brought up the message Olga had sent him earlier and played the video.

Watching it, he sipped his drink. The low-class man with garish tattoos had his arms around Isabel, standing next to her car, as they spoke and kissed. Too bad there wasn't audio on their conversation.

It made little difference. From the lovey-dovey looks of them, Isabel deserved what she was about to get.

She climbed into her car, pulled out of the spot and rolled her window down. The angle and distance was lousy. He couldn't see the horror on her face, the panic in her eyes that she surely must've felt.

*Damn it.*

Then her car crashed into a telephone pole.

That was pleasantly unexpected. As Isabel was crawling from her Maserati, debilitated, face grotesquely swollen, Olga was on the move, drawing closer. The man left Isabel and ran toward her car. To fetch her EpiPen no doubt.

Honestly, Chad was a little shocked by the speed of her reaction to the bee venom. She'd been stung once when she was a child. After doing research, he'd learned that allergic reactions could be more severe in adults and in subsequent exposures.

On the screen, Olga lowered beside Isabel, the frame of the video zooming in on her face that had turned into a hideous mask. Not only was her face painfully swollen but her cheeks were drooping at the same time and her eyes were a glassy mix of agony and fear.

*Holy—* That was the money shot.

Chad chuckled at Isabel's monstrous image, the sound of her wheezing sending a thrill through him.

*You brought this on yourself, babe.*

Never should've gone out with that man. Chad bet lover boy would stay away from her until she was looking her best, which should take a day or two.

"Do I want to know what you're watching?" Brett asked.

"No."

"I should fire up the grill. Mindy has everything prepped and ready to go." He stood, grabbing his drink. "Burgers and chicken kabobs for the kids. Steaks and baked potatoes for us. I think Mindy is skipping lunch since I spoke to her about her weight. You're staying, right?"

The video ended and Chad muttered a curse under his breath over how short it'd been. "Steak sounds perfect."

"Hey, when are you and Isabel getting back together? Mindy misses her."

Of course she did. Isabel was the only friend Brett allowed Mindy to have at the house.

Starting the video over again from the beginning, Chad said, "I'm working on it."

# Chapter Eleven

*Lucky.* That was how Isabel felt. Dutch had taken care of her and McQueen for the past two days. First thing in the morning, he was there with her coconut-milk latte and take-out breakfast from a café, then he took her dog for a walk.

They'd watched the top five Steve McQueen movies along with her favorite films, snuggled together with no pressure for anything more than comfort and affection. He paid exquisite attention to her, giving his whole self and not asking for anything in return. Dinners had been delivered and after he took her dog for one final jaunt outside, he'd hold her, kiss her and leave.

Part of her didn't want her recovery to end.

She was back in her regular routine finally, but behind on everything. Work, jogging, Krav Maga lessons. Wednesday had rushed up on her and she was supposed to have dinner with her uncle in two hours and still hadn't told Dutch one way or the other if he was going, too.

Before her near-death allergic reaction, she'd been ready to invite Dutch, but now that he'd earned his place at the dinner table beside her, she could barely contain her excitement.

Isabel dialed her uncle as she grabbed her workout bag from the trunk of the loaner vehicle the car repair shop let her use and walked inside the Krav Maga school.

"Isabel, *mi hija*, I hope you're not calling to cancel."

"No. I wouldn't dream of it," she said, relieved her face no longer showed any sign of swelling. "It's just, I'd like to bring someone to dinner. A guy I'm seeing. I know how much you hate surprises."

"You haven't mentioned you're dating anyone."

"It's new, but he's special. I'd love for you to meet him."

"Not tonight," her uncle said. "I have business I want to discuss with you at dinner."

"How about we talk privately and then he joins us for dessert?"

"We'll discuss it when I see you later. The car will be at the gallery at seven."

Isabel groaned into the phone, wanting her uncle to hear every decibel of her frustration.

"Don't pout. It's unbecoming. I hate to disappoint you, truly, but I need some one-on-one time with you. That's it. *Te amo.*"

Isabel hung up without saying *I love you* back.

It was no wonder she'd gotten caught up with Chad and went along with his controlling behavior. She'd grown accustomed to similar treatment from her uncle, who was just as imperious. The same won't-take-no attitude. It was his way or consequences.

Thank heavens she'd met someone different like Dutch.

Isabel threw her phone in the gym bag and zipped it.

"You really pushed us today, John. Thanks," a male voice said, sending a hot rush of adrenaline shooting through her system.

Isabel looked up and stared at Chad. A class had just finished, and he was walking out with the instructor, John. The two of them were smiling and chatting. They were chummy.

What the hell?

A torrent of emotions flooded her.

Fear that he stood a few feet away, that she'd have to face him. That he'd never stop stalking her, terrorizing her.

Flustered. Out of all the self-defense schools between Malibu and Santa Monica he was at this one. But it couldn't be some bizarre coincidence. When it came to Chad, it never was. He was a planner, acted with deliberate, dark purpose. Controlled every facet of his life.

Isabel's heart hammered, her hands growing clammy. All she wanted was to crawl into a hole and disappear, but this was going too far. A violation she wouldn't tolerate.

Fury roared through her, burning through the stupefaction

that held her paralyzed. Only outrage remained. Outrage at his gall. At the narcissistic audacity it took for him to enroll at her school.

She stormed up to them, gave John a befuddled glance and glared at Chad. "What are you doing here?"

A ghost of a smile played across his lips for a second, maybe two. "For the sake of clarity, you came within fifty feet of me and initiated conversation," Chad said.

"What's going on?" John asked.

"This is *him*." Isabel pointed at Chad. "The one I told you about. He attacked me behind the gallery and popped up at the restaurant."

"Chad attacked you?" John asked with the skeptical tone she was used to hearing when it came to her ex.

"Yes!" Her voice drew attention from everyone in the hall.

"*Attacked* is a strong, ugly and untruthful word, Isabel. You called me that day. Remember?"

"I did, but—"

"You missed me, wanted to rekindle things and asked me to come to the gallery."

He was twisting the truth, spinning it into vicious lies. The same way he'd done in court, bolstering his position while tearing hers down.

Painful pressure welled in her chest, squeezing her heart. "That's not true." Her voice trembled.

To stop her hand from shaking she clenched her fingers around the strap of her gym bag.

Chad stood taller with a smug expression, his presence taking up the space, sucking up the oxygen. "You can't defame my character like this. It's not fair."

*Fair?* "I know it was you," Isabel said. Her pulse raced. Her breath was tight in her lungs. "The bees in my car. You wanted to hurt me. You wanted to scare me. You're a sick piece of work."

"What are you talking about?" Chad asked. "Bees?" His

features twisted in an expression of utter confusion that looked so real she half believed him. "Do you hear yourself? I think you need to talk to someone about your delusions. If this is another ploy to get attention, you should see a professional." He sounded calm, rational, looked like the sane one.

Anger bled from her as anxiety seeped through, sending her head spinning. "You put bees in my car, knowing I'm deathly allergic. Admit it!"

"Isabel, I love you." He took a step closer.

A terrible rush of energy flooded her system with no outlet, no conduit. It was like her body was in full-blown flight-or-fight mode, but she was frozen, stuck.

"Whether or not we're together, I only want what's best for you," Chad said, his voice so sympathetic he should've been struck by lightning. "Why would I put bees in your car? How? Unless you have proof, you can't go around tarnishing my reputation with such outlandish claims."

*Proof.* Dutch had asked a friend in the police department to have her car dusted for prints. Only hers and Dutch's were found, along with a jewelry box from Tiffany's that oddly enough had no prints on it at all.

"Stay away from me, do you hear me?" Everyone stared at Isabel like she was a raving crackpot.

Even John. But at least he moved up beside her in a physical show of support. "Chad, your membership is canceled, effective immediately."

"Hold on a minute." Chad raised his palms as though he were the victim. "You can't do that."

"I just did. We'll send you a refund in the mail. Abraham." John turned to the big, buff instructor. "Escort Mr. Ellis out and let everyone at the front desk know that he's no longer to be given access to the premises."

Abraham gestured for Chad to start walking.

"If you were stung by a bee, I'm glad you're all right," Chad said, his tone deceptively sweet—almost innocent. He had unbelievable gall. "You're looking good, Isabel. Call me if you ever need anything. I'm here for you."

"Stop talking to her." John stepped between them. "Leave. Now."

Abraham shepherded Chad to the front.

At the door, Chad glanced back at her, flashed a Hollywood smile—dazzling, polished, perfected—and brushed imaginary dust from his shoulder, radiating arrogance and superiority.

Her stomach roiled.

Chad pushed through the door, whistling as if he didn't have a care in the world, and got into his car.

Isabel deflated with relief that he was gone, but she was too far in the deep swell of a panic attack to stave it off. Digging in her bag, she grabbed her bottle of Ativan. She fumbled to remove the lid.

"I'm so sorry," John said, helping her to the water fountain.

She threw the pill in her mouth and washed it down with a swig of water. Shivering, she gripped the edge of the fountain and tried to breathe.

"I had no idea *that* was him," John said. "Chad has been so friendly, helpful in class. A great student. A fast learner. I can't believe I went bowling with him."

A sinking feeling slid down her throat like cold sludge, pooling in her belly. "How long has he been coming?"

"Well," John said, scratching his head. "He started around the same time as you. Maybe a week or two after."

She put away her meds. "Then we're at the same level, know the same moves."

John's gaze dropped. "No, Isabel. He's been coming twice as often as you. Four days a week. He's far more advanced. Just earned his orange belt."

Isabel was at the most basic level. White belt. She might be ready to test for yellow next month. But Chad had made it to orange?

Dread bubbled inside her. "What does he know that I don't?"

"A heck of a lot." John rattled off a mind-boggling list of moves, from choke holds, kicks and punches to body-defense postures. "He's getting really good at disarming an attacker."

"Get me ready," Isabel said. "Prepare me to defend against what he knows."

A grave look fell across John's face, and she wanted to vomit. "That'll take months, not days." He clasped her shoulder. "You don't want to engage in a physical confrontation with him. If you see him again, don't talk to him, don't go near him. Call 911."

THE LINES HAD blurred for Dutch. Over the past two days, he'd gone from marshal on a mission to legit boyfriend. *Damn.* What was he thinking?

But that was the problem. He hadn't been thinking or even trying to say the right thing. It was so easy with Isabel, talking to her, spending hours cuddled up in their little bubble while she recuperated, like they were two pieces of a puzzle fitting together. Caring about her was as natural as breathing. Every night when he left her condo something in his chest had ached and didn't subside until he saw her again.

He pushed through the door of the second-floor satellite hub.

"There's something I found out while you were off getting closer to the asset," Allison said as a greeting, cutting straight to it. "I dug deeper into Chad Ellis. Nothing concrete came up, but a woman did file a complaint with the police against him two years ago."

"Stalking and harassment?" Dutch asked.

"No. Virginia Campbell claimed that Ellis was behind the disappearance of her sister Patricia. Police investigated and couldn't find anything. Patricia had dated Ellis for a few months and broken up with him. Ellis dropped off the radar and Patricia started seeing someone new. Then she started getting strange phone calls and weird gifts in the mail. But when

Patricia disappeared, her new boyfriend was the top suspect. Not Ellis. She was never found. It's a cold case now."

The news only exacerbated Dutch's concerns. Ellis was slippery and careful. Methodical. The more Dutch thought about it, the more he believed the guy was behind Isabel's allergic reaction though they didn't have a shred of evidence to prove it. He hadn't pushed her to share the nightmare of what she'd been through in her relationship with Ellis. Survivors of trauma tended to keep their secrets, ashamed to share. No matter what happened with his assignment, Dutch wasn't going to abandon Isabel.

One way or another, something would have to be done about Ellis.

"We heard from the FBI," Draper said. "Their undercover agent passed along another message. The auction is going to happen this Sunday. The data is onsite at Vargas's compound, possibly in his biometric fingerprint safe."

"Can't they intercede?" Dutch asked, wanting to be done with this. To sit Isabel down and come clean. "Arrest Vargas for being in possession of classified data?"

Draper finished his coffee and crumpled the paper cup. "Since the information falls under the caveat of *Law Enforcement Sensitive* and not Top Secret, the most Vargas would get is two years since it'd be his first criminal offense. The FBI is putting together a RICO case. It could take down the entire organization and enable them to seize his assets. What they're going after is much bigger. This is as far as they'll go to help us."

Groaning his frustration, Dutch swallowed a curse.

"What's the status with dinner tonight and meeting her uncle?" Allison asked. "Are you in?"

"Dinner with Vargas is a no go."

Allison sighed, lowering her head in defeat.

"Damn it." Draper chucked his coffee cup in the trash. "Vargas comes to town for one night to have dinner with his niece and you can't manage to get yourself invited? Do you understand the mission objective?"

Dutch gritted his teeth at the rhetorical question and Draper's rude tone.

Allison looked up. "You just spent two cozy days at her apartment with her. I need to ask. Have you slept together?"

Rocking back on his heels, Dutch hadn't anticipated the question. "How is that relevant?"

"I'll take that as a no," Allison said. "And it's quite relevant. The deeper you get in with her, the easier it'll be to get access to her uncle."

"Chen is right," Draper said. "Women get emotionally invested once sex is involved. You've got to up the ante."

Allison narrowed her eyes at Draper. "That's a sexist stereotype. You know that, right?"

"But it's true," Draper said, doubling down.

"No, it isn't." Standing, Allison put her hands on her hips. "Women can have casual sex with no emotional investment. Trust me." Allison shifted her gaze to Dutch. "Isabel likes you. She's already invested, but you need to deepen the connection."

"Look." Dutch crossed his arms. "She wanted me to go to dinner, but her uncle didn't want me there."

"Then she didn't fight hard enough for you," Allison said.

Draper nodded in agreement. "Call her and have her press the issue."

"It doesn't feel right." Dutch shook his head. "She's on her way to meet her uncle now."

"Get her to tell you the name of the restaurant," Draper said. "Show up. Bring her flowers. Make it a grand gesture."

"You want me, the new guy, to pop up uninvited to dinner when she already has a stalker?" Yeah, that wasn't going to happen.

Allison raised a palm at Draper to back off. "We're desperate, here. Vargas knows where we live, the names of our kids, where they go to school. It's bad enough he has such sensitive information, but he's going to sell it to only God knows who. You've got to press a little harder. Please."

Turning his back to them, he scrubbed a hand over his face.

Maybe he could see Isabel after dinner and persuade her to arrange breakfast with him and her uncle before Vargas went back to San Diego. "Okay. I'll try."

Dutch took out his cell phone and sent her a text.

THE WAY TO find someone's weakness didn't always mean following a short, straight line. The trail to find Horatio "Dutch" Haas's was long and curved.

Prior military. Special Forces. La-di-da.

But Chad was getting closer. Or the new private investigator he'd hired to follow Haas instead of Isabel was. So far it didn't look like he was shagging Isabel, but with all the time Haas had been spending at her place, it would happen sooner rather than later.

Sitting in his car at the most recent address the PI had given him, Chad stared at Haas's motorcycle. The bike was parked in the rear of a supposedly vacant building that was conveniently located right across the street from Isabel's art gallery.

"What are you up to?" he asked under his breath.

Grinning, Chad couldn't wait to figure out the answer because it wasn't going to be anything good and might just be exactly what he needed to drive a wedge between Haas and Isabel.

# Chapter Twelve

Isabel's phone chimed at an incoming message. She slipped the cell out of her purse and swiped the screen to check it.

Dutch: Can I swing by after dinner? Go for a walk with you and McQueen.

She smiled and texted back.

Yes.

Uncle Emilio cleared his throat across the table from her, drawing her gaze. "Please, Isa. Shut that thing off while you're with me," he said, frowning.

Not only did her uncle find the use of personal devices during meals rude, but he was paranoid about some hacker eavesdropping through it to steal his corporate secrets. He was so cautious that when they met for dinners, it was always in private. Tonight, he'd arranged for the entire rooftop of a glamorous French bistro with spectacular views of the sky-line to be theirs. A bodyguard stood at either end—Rodrigo, who she'd known for years, and Max. She'd only encountered him a few times, but he'd risen in position quickly and flirted with her whenever her uncle wasn't within earshot. A third guard she didn't recognize, named Lucas, stood at the entrance to the stairs.

She powered down the phone and put it back in her purse. "Sorry."

"As I was saying, I'm planning to hold an exclusive silent auction at my compound for select pieces. I want you to organize everything and oversee the event from here. Handle the invitations, decor. Ensure the art is displayed properly with a floor plan and description of setup for Rodrigo. See to the menu with one of my vetted caterers, the music. Et cetera, et cetera."

"Don't you want me to come down and be there for the event?"

"No, that's not necessary. I don't want to intrude on your life. I know how you hate that."

Guilt poked at her. Her uncle had his faults. He was domineering and ran the family with a tight grip, but he only wanted her happiness. "I want to help you in any way. For how many people and when?" She took another bite of her smoked octopus with vadouvan and fennel citrus salad, humming her continued delight at the explosion of flavors on her tongue.

"An intimate gathering. Fifty guests. Sunday."

"You're joking. I can't organize an event that would be up to your standards in four days."

"I never joke, and I have the utmost confidence in your abilities. You could do this blindfolded, and I need someone I trust implicitly to see to things."

"Will your guests be able to attend on such short notice?"

"I have an exceptional item of great value that I'll be selling. One-of-a-kind. They'll clear their schedules for me. Have no fear. And you'll make the event happen for me. Yes?"

It wasn't really a question, even though he made it sound like one. "Yes."

Their waitress came out onto the rooftop and served the second course. *Loup de mer*, a Mediterranean sea bass, with white asparagus and couscous with squid ink paired with a glass of Sancerre. She tasted the wine, a sip to be polite and avoid an interrogation. The last time they had dinner, and she didn't drink, he'd accused her of being pregnant.

"So, what's the young man's name?" her uncle asked after the waitress left. "The one you want me to meet."

"Horatio Haas, but he goes by Dutch."

"Hmm. What does he do?"

Debating whether to tell him the truth, she tried the fish.

Buttery, silky, delicious. The wine complemented it perfectly with a hint of honeysuckle and flint. "He's between jobs right now."

A lie, once discovered, would only anger her uncle. She'd learned that the hard way as a teenager after her father died and she went through a rebellious phase. Better to be honest and mitigate the cons rather than incur his wrath.

Uncle Emilio shook his head. "I assume you pay for everything?"

"No. He hasn't let me pay for anything."

"Yet." He wagged a finger at her. "Give it time."

"*Tío*, he's the greatest guy. Truly. He makes me happy." She could envision a real future with Dutch. He had nothing to hide, was trustworthy, reliable. Unbelievably hot.

"What's so great about him?" Her uncle cocked his head to the side, waiting.

Mentally, she ran through the long list, deciding which thing would win over her uncle and sway him to give Dutch a chance. "I was stung by a bee the other day," she said, omitting the part about slimy Chad. "My allergic reaction was fast. It was bad—I'm not going to lie."

"*Dios mío*, Isa, why didn't you tell me?" He put his fork down. "I would've had you flown home to San Diego and ensured you were properly cared for while you recovered."

Where he would've smothered her to death with love. "That's precisely why I didn't want you to know. My home is here. In Malibu with my dog." With Brenda. With Dutch.

He tsked. "I would've brought the dog, too."

"My point is that Dutch kept a level head. Got my EpiPen and saved my life. He even took care of me for two days, walked McQueen, brought me food, breakfast in bed every morning."

He cleared his throat. "How generous of him."

"Not that it's any of your business, but I haven't slept with him." *Yet.* That would get his attention and should earn Dutch some brownie points.

Raising an eyebrow, her uncle shot her a dubious look that was also cautionary, warning her not to lie.

"Honestly," she said. "He's a good person, a gentleman, and wants to meet you. If you scare him off, I promise the next guy you meet will be on my wedding day."

Uncle Emilio laughed. "All right, my dear. I'll meet your new beau. On one condition." He raised a finger for emphasis.

"What's that?"

He smiled at her, the look tender and kind. "If I disapprove of this young man, you will stay away from him. Heed what I say as any daughter would."

Isabel sat back in her chair. "I'm entitled to date whomever I please. I respect your opinion, but I'll follow my own judgment." Or when it came to men, Brenda's. Her bestie had steered her toward Dutch and she'd never been happier with a match.

She wished her uncle was still dating Lori Carpenter. Although Lori had been young, about the same age as Isabel, when Uncle Emilio had been with her, his attitude toward everything had been more laissez-faire, less regulated. Lori had been the best distraction for him.

To this day, Isabel had no idea why they'd broken up a year ago.

He wiped his mouth with a napkin. "Would you show your father such disrespect? Talk to him like this, if he were the one sitting here?"

"Yes. Because I'm twenty-eight. I'm not a child." She thought of her cousin out in New York, Uncle Emilio's son, and her indignation ballooned. "Miguel is two years older than me and you'd never tell him whom he should and shouldn't marry, much less date."

"You think you are your own person, free to do as you please." His tone softened and sharpened at the same time, drawing her to lean in to catch his every word. "But you are part of a larger whole. This family." He slapped the table, and Isabel flinched at the sound, straightening in her seat. "Miguel wanted to become a hotshot corporate attorney, but instead he picked up the mantle I passed to him and will carry on the Vargas legacy. It's not what he wanted, but he's thriving. Because he understands the importance of family. Of being part of a whole. The same way my brother and I understood the need for sacrifice. I wouldn't tell Miguel who to date or not to sleep with because I don't care. But when he gets serious enough about someone to introduce her to me, or chooses a wife, I will have a say. He'll listen to me. He'll show respect. Just as you will now. Do you understand?"

Stunned to silence, Isabel nodded.

"I'm only looking out for your best interest," he said.

Chad's words rang in her ears. *I only want what's best for you.*

A lump formed in her throat at the similarity.

Her uncle took a deep breath, lightening his expression and his voice. "Your father would want me to. He was more than my brother. He was my mentor. My best friend. Losing him devastated me. When I buried him, I swore to raise you as he would've. I love you as my own. Don't dishonor his memory by disregarding what I say."

Always the expert at manipulating emotion to get what he wanted. Isabel wasn't surprised by her uncle's redirection. Expected it even. She'd spent fourteen years paying close attention, learning to do the very same thing herself when necessary.

She strategized while the third course was served. The waitress set down the plates in front of them and removed the stainless steel dome covers.

A delightful scent of lemon and herbs hit her.

"Veal medallions with brown butter and herbs de Provence," the waitress said.

Isabel reeled back. "None for me, thank you."

"What's wrong?" Her uncle cut into the meat and ate a piece. "Give it a try. It's delicious."

"I may wear leather and eat meat, but I draw the line at calves kept in small cages."

The waitress removed her plate and left.

Uncle Emilio chuckled. "If you object to eating baby animals, perhaps you should become a vegetarian. Do you think the broiler-sized chickens you buy are fully grown? Try eight weeks. Any idea the conditions they're kept in? Filthy and cramped." He took another bite. "Pigs are slaughtered at four months old. The same as calves for veal. Consider that the next time you're enjoying a piece of bacon."

Grimacing, Isabel tossed her napkin on the table. Maybe she *would* become a vegetarian.

Isabel had a choice. She could upset her uncle by confessing she'd lost her appetite or redirect the conversation to get what she wanted. "There's something I haven't told you. How I met Dutch. I was locking up the art gallery and someone mugged me."

His face went blank as he stiffened. "Oh, Isabel." He held out a hand to her.

Isabel placed her palm on her uncle's. "The guy grabbed my purse." She left out the part about the knife. "The Chanel bag that Daddy gave me." She tightened her fingers around his hand. "Dutch stopped him, brought him down like a superhero and got it back."

He lifted their joined hands and kissed her fingers. "You should've told me. This is why you need a bodyguard."

She cringed on the inside, not wanting her admission to backfire. "Dutch saved me twice. He treats me with respect. Dignity. Makes me feel like I should be treasured. No other man has ever done that."

"Not even the last one, who owns all those businesses."

Lowering her gaze, she swallowed past a flash of irritation. "No. Actually, that bigwig business owner turned out to be a real jerk."

"If a man ever disrespects you, puts his hands on you, I want you to tell me."

"Why? So you can sue him and punish me by shoving a bodyguard down my throat?"

He pursed his lips in obvious annoyance. "I would make the man rue the day he crossed the line with you, and yes, give you a bodyguard."

*No, thank you.* She didn't want help with strings attached. "Well, there's no need for you to worry about Dutch crossing the line. He's incredible. Though, you might not approve of him." He would never fit the image of what her uncle wanted for her. "But I do. I want him to meet you because I respect and love you. *Please*, don't ruin this for me. Okay?"

"I see this man is important to you. I'll meet him tonight."

A smile she couldn't contain broke on her face. "Really?"

Her uncle nodded. "I do what I can to make you happy. Tell him to come to my club at eleven-thirty as my guest."

"Thank you, *tío*." Lifting out of her chair, she leaned across the table and kissed his cheek. "I must warn you that he speaks his mind and can be blunt, but we'll be there."

"You misunderstand." He released her hand and picked up his wineglass. "I wish to meet him alone. Without you."

That was strange. "Why?"

He gave her a placating grin, ratcheting up Isabel's anxiety. "Because I said so." His tone brooked no argument.

# Chapter Thirteen

The call from Isabel canceling their plans had been unexpected, but worth it. Dutch was set to meet Vargas.

He pulled up to the valet in front of the Enigma nightclub in the heart of LA.

"Hey, man," one of the twentysomethings wearing an orange vest said, approaching him. "Insurance won't let us take it, but you can park right there." He pointed to a parking spot in the valet area.

Dutch gave the kid forty bucks, twenty for valet and another Jackson as a tip to make sure they looked after his bike as if it were their own. "Not a scratch on it."

The guy nodded enthusiastically. "Sure thing. No one will get close to it."

Dutch rode over and backed into the spot sandwiched between a Mercedes and a Tesla. He took off his helmet and raked a hand through his hair.

Isabel let him know about the club's dress code. But Dutch had deliberately dressed down, jeans and a V-neck tee. He got that Dante Emilio Vargas had an appreciation for the finer things in life and would judge a book by its cover, but there was no disguising that Dutch came from middle-class means. No hiding the way he carried himself, how he spoke, like a man born and bred on the streets.

Silk threads and putting on airs wouldn't win over Vargas anyway. Men such as her uncle respected two things. Power and strength.

At the core, neither had anything to do with money.

Besides, Dutch didn't know how to be anything other than himself, something that worked in his favor with Isabel. Other than the omission of why he'd stepped into her life—and granted, that was pretty big—he didn't have to pretend with her.

He strode past the long line to get in that wrapped around

the corner and went up to the bouncer at the door. "I'm Dutch Haas. Here to see Dante Vargas."

The burly dude dressed in all black checked him out from head to toe with a wary look, but Dutch knew the vibe he gave off and was used to the split-second assessment people made about him based on his appearance.

The bouncer lifted a tablet and swiped through a list of names. After a few seconds, he glanced up. "You can go on in." He opened a door that was set off to the side of the main entrance.

Loud, throbbing electronic music and colored strobe lights washed over Dutch as he stepped inside with his helmet tucked under his arm. On his left, the general public entering through the main door paid a cover charge and had to walk through a metal detector.

Weaving through the throng of gyrating bodies, he went to the bar. The line was long, but he waited, in no rush, not wanting to seem overly eager to Vargas and needing to be certain what was in his drink. He ordered, got his drink and tipped well. Then he made his way to the stairwell, leading to the VIP area.

Instead of a waitress serving as a gatekeeper to the exclusive section upstairs, there was a bodyguard. Dutch spotted the telltale bulge in his jacket. The man was armed.

"I'm Haas," Dutch said. "Here to see Mr. Vargas."

"Not with *that* you aren't." The bodyguard gestured to his helmet.

"Man, this is a Schuberth." The name was synonymous with top-of-the-line. Sure, his helmet was sleek and looked cool, but it was a piece of serious gear. The outer shell was made from three layers of patented fiber called S.T.R.O.N.G. and the interior padding had special hygienic material to prevent pathogens from building up while ensuring comfort, and it had a sophisticated ventilation system and noise dampening inserts for the quietest ride possible. "It's worth two grand.

Where I go, it goes. Besides, I'm here as a guest. Just ask Mr. Vargas if I can bring it with me?"

The guy touched his earpiece and spoke in Spanish, which Dutch understood, into the mic that extended to his mouth, even relaying the helmet brand.

Looking around as if bored, Dutch knew exactly what the response would be. Vargas, the kingpin of Southern California, wasn't going to be worried about his niece's date carrying a helmet. Not when he was surrounded by loyal, armed men.

"All right," the guard said. "The helmet is fine, but I've still got to pat you down."

Extending his arms and spreading his legs, Dutch assumed the position, letting the man do his job. First, the guard ran a wand over Dutch's body, scanning for listening devices. Even if he had one hidden on him, with the loud, pumping music, he'd have to be right next to Vargas for any equipment to clearly pick up both sides of the conversation.

Satisfied that he wasn't wired, the guard moved on to the pat down, going across his arms, over his torso, up and down his legs, getting a little too close to his groin.

"Watch it, buddy," Dutch said.

"Not my concern." Pursing his lips in a tight line, the guard unhooked the velvet rope and then hiked his thumb toward the steps, giving him the okay to go up.

Dutch ascended the industrial metal staircase only to be greeted by another guard at the top of the landing.

"The helmet," the second one with a manicured beard said. He had the build of a middleweight boxer, tall and lean, but wiry.

"This again?" Dutch asked. "I was given permission to take it with me."

"Well, I didn't give permission."

"Max!" Rodrigo called from the swanky seating area. According to the dossier, Rodrigo was Vargas's right-hand man and second in command. Beside him, Vargas sat like he ruled the world as young women in skimpy dresses danced around the VIP room. "Let him through."

"See. What did I tell you?" Dutch said.

Max narrowed his eyes and took a step forward, blocking him.

"You want to dance?" Dutch asked, referring to a tango with fists. He clutched the rim of his helmet so tight his knuckles strained.

"Maximiliano!" Rodrigo said again. "It's okay. He's Isabel's new admirer."

Clenching his jaw and his fists, Max hesitated before finally letting him through.

What was his problem? Did he have a crush on Isabel and wanted her for himself?

Dutch brushed past Max, deliberately making contact without being aggressive enough to start a fight. This was his element, his culture, and he knew exactly how to behave to survive. To thrive in it.

There was another set of stairs leading to a third floor, where there appeared to be only one room. An office?

He walked by two more armed guards and dancing women, up to the sofa.

Rodrigo rose. "Welcome." He ushered Dutch into the seating area and backed away as if to give them privacy.

Dutch nodded to him and strode closer to the man he came to see. "Mr. Vargas, it's a pleasure to meet you." He put his helmet and drink on the coffee table and held out his hand. "I'm—"

"Horatio Haas." Vargas shook his hand, and Dutch could tell the mob boss was assessing everything—Dutch's clothing, facial expression, exposed tattoos, the firmness of the handshake—and motioned for him to sit in the leather club chair on the other side of a round glass coffee table.

"Everyone calls me Dutch." He sat, not sure what he hated more, being called Horatio or having his back to the iron railing that overlooked the dance floor. At least he had a clear line of sight of the stairs and all the guards, and the other VIP tables were vacant and not a concern.

Dutch gave the appearance of relaxing in the plush chair while staying ready to spring into action, his senses dialed into the environment. All the women threw him easy smiles, from the ones lounging on the sofa to others dancing. They were beautiful. Blonde, brunette, redhead, curvaceous, slim, you name it and that type was there.

The women gyrating to the music and shaking their assets were a shiny lure, meant to bait him. To test him.

"Call me Emilio," Isabel's uncle said. "What are you drinking?"

Under normal circumstances, Dutch would've gotten a beer, but he had to set the right tone for the conversation. "Scotch. Macallan."

Surprise lit Vargas's cold, shrewd eyes. "I'm a Scotch man myself."

Dutch was aware.

To get her uncle's attention and keep it, Dutch had to defy expectations.

"Do you know why I asked to see you without my niece present?" Vargas asked.

How would the typical dude answer? Act as if he didn't know and perhaps, he wouldn't. Or soften the response to avoid coming across as brash.

Dutch decided to speak his mind. Unfiltered. "To size me up without the distraction of Isabel's interest in me, and if you deemed me unworthy, then try to scare me off." It wasn't a question. It was a statement. Dutch was certain that was the reason.

Vargas stilled, his gaze not faltering for a second from Dutch's. "Try? You don't think I'd do an adequate job of scaring you." His tone was teasing.

Her uncle wasn't what Dutch had imagined. Without a

doubt, he was vile filth, but the cultured packaging, the detached, refined demeanor, the imposing air about him was impressive. Now Dutch understood how Isabel could've failed to see through his charismatic thrall.

"I don't scare easily." Dutch took his first swig of the Scotch. Peaty, hot, not bad at all. He noticed Max speaking into his mic and covering his ear as if trying to listen.

Max pivoted and hustled to Rodrigo. "There's a problem with the *delivery*."

Delivery being drugs. Every business that Vargas owned or paid for, including Isabel's art gallery, was used to either deal drugs or launder money.

"I'll go handle it," Rodrigo said. "But I want you to come with me." He waved the other two guards over. "You come with us." He pointed to the taller, stocky one. "Stay here and keep an eye on things."

The trio hurried down the stairs while the stout guard went to the landing and stood as sentry in Max's place.

"My niece tells me that you're between jobs right now," Vargas said, crossing his legs.

"Actually, I'm on terminal leave from the army. So, if you're wondering whether I collect a paycheck, the answer is yes."

"For how much longer? A week? Two?"

"Three, sir."

"What are your plans when that runs out?"

"I've been working since I was sixteen and I've always had a steady stream of income. Plus, I've got a decent amount saved. But I won't need to dip into it. Once my background check is completed, I'll start a position at a private security company." Dutch finished his drink and noticed Vargas's glass was empty. "Why don't I get us another round?"

"I'll have Macallan as well, but since you're buying, make it the twenty-five-year-old."

Dutch got up, thankful for the reprieve and time to think.

He headed to the bar against the far wall in the area and ordered. "Macallan 25. Two."

The waitress poured a generous amount of liquor into the tumblers. "That'll be four hundred dollars."

Dutch coughed, choking on the price. The most he'd ever spent on booze was for a keg and that had cost a fourth of the amount. He couldn't whip out a credit card since there hadn't been time to make a fake one for him, so he slapped down the last of the petty cash he'd been given.

The bartender threw him a disgruntled look. The crappy tip was less than 10 percent.

"All you did was pour," he said.

She cocked a brow. "Without spitting in the glass first. I'll be sure to remember you next time."

Dutch picked up the rock glasses and walked back to the seating area, strategizing, his wits reined in tight.

Vargas shooed away a brunette who was in his lap and waved for Dutch to sit beside him.

Dutch handed him the drink as he lowered into the seat. They clinked glasses, and he took a sip. The smooth, silky heat slid down his throat.

That was what old and expensive tasted like.

"May I be frank with you?" Vargas asked.

"By all means. Cutting the crap will save us both time and energy. I'm nothing if not efficient."

Vargas chuckled. "I appreciate your directness. My niece warned me that you'd speak freely, and I see that she was right. What do you know of the Vargas name in this area?"

Dutch shrugged. "Your niece owns an art gallery and you're a big venture capitalist."

"Where are you from? I can't pinpoint your accent over the music."

"I was born in New York City. Spent some time out in Chicago—"

"I'm going to cut to the chase… *Dutch*. To put it simply,

we are royalty. My niece is a princess. Whereas you are a peasant. You *aren't* good enough for her and have nothing of consequence to offer."

Dutch sat up, setting his drink down. "What about companionship?"

"Isabel has a full life. She's active in the community and has plenty of friends."

"Not male friends who she feels safe around," Dutch said, and Vargas straightened, his brows drawing together. "She's leery of men."

"As well she should. Guys tend to think with the little head between their legs, only interested in what they can get from a beautiful woman like Isabel. A night or two of pleasure. A bit of fun."

Swallowing a groan, Dutch couldn't believe how arrogant the man was, making such premature judgments based on nothing but his appearance. Vargas was the worst kind, valuing money and influence over kindness and decency.

"If all I wanted from your niece was a night of pleasure, I could've had that and moved on. Instead, I've shown her the utmost respect, which is what she deserves," Dutch said, staying focused on Vargas as well as his surroundings. "I'm here tonight not because you wanted to meet me, but because I insisted on meeting you. Isabel is leery in the way a woman is when she's been hurt by a man. Physically."

Vargas uncrossed his legs and slammed his drink down on the table, spilling two-hundred-dollar scotch like it was well liquor. "What are you saying?"

From the corner of his eye, Dutch noticed the stocky guard distracted by a voluptuous woman in a glittering gold dress dancing beside him, flaunting her curves.

Then Dutch saw it. Someone trotting up the steps, hurried—cloaked in darkness. The person wore a funnel-neck hoodie. The thin material would appear stylish when pulled down, but raised, it'd obscure someone's profile.

Too late, the guard turned and drew his gun.

The person threw something—overhand for added power and velocity. The blade struck perfectly, lodged in the body-guard's right eye. Staggering back, the guard dropped his gun to bring his hands to the knife and fell to his knees.

Fast, so fast, the killer reached the top of the landing and raced toward the seating area while digging into a pocket. Drawing another knife, he held it by the blade. White. Synthetic. Maybe plastic or some polymer that a metal detector would miss.

The hit man threw the knife at Vargas.

## Chapter Fourteen

On pure instinct, Dutch grabbed Vargas and hauled him to the floor.

The sharp knife sliced into the back of the sofa where Vargas had been sitting, spraying feathers in the air.

"Stay down," Dutch said. Then he whirled on his knees and leaped up, tackling the killer to the floor.

Dutch grabbed his helmet from the table—the only improvised weapon within reach. He slammed the sturdy piece of gear into the man's face, throttling him over and over until he stopped moving.

From the corner of his eye, Dutch caught movement. Rodrigo and Max were racing up the stairs. Two more lieutenants were behind them.

What in the hell was happening?

"Don Emilio!" Max rushed to Vargas's side, got him up off the floor and ushered him toward the stairs.

Dutch followed them closely to the office off the landing on the third floor. Two guards brought up the rear, weapons drawn.

"Are you all right?" Max asked. "Were you injured?"

"I'm fine." Vargas waved him away. "Dutch saved my life. If it weren't for him, I'd be dead."

The realization chilled Dutch to the bone as all eyes in the room shifted to him. He'd saved the life of a cartel boss, a man the world would be better off without. A man whose death might've put the US Marshals in a better position if they already had the stolen hard drive.

Damn it.

"It was nothing," Dutch said. "Instinct kicked in. That's all."

"You have excellent instincts. And it wasn't nothing." Vargas straightened his shirt and smoothed down his jacket. "It had happened so fast. One minute, everything had been under control. The next… How could anyone have gotten that close to me? What was the problem with the delivery?"

"Miscommunication," Rodrigo said. "Some heated words were exchanged, but I handled it before it turned into something major."

"A distraction." Vargas wagged a finger. "To lure you away. To give someone an opportunity to get to me."

Rodrigo turned to the guards. "I want one of you posted at the door. The other, go make sure the mess downstairs gets cleaned up. Clean this up *pronto*."

The two men nodded and left, closing the door. Max turned his hard gaze to Dutch like he was an interloper instead of the guy who'd just saved his boss's life.

Vargas poured two glasses of Scotch from his personal en suite bar and handed one to Dutch. "Here."

Dutch took a sip of the amber liquid. It was just as full-bodied as the Macallan, but deeper, richer. Or maybe the adrenaline surge sharpened everything, including his taste buds. "Smooth."

"Isle of Jura. A thirty-year-old." Vargas poured more in Dutch's glass. "What did you do in the army?"

"I was Special Ops. Delta Force."

"Ah," Vargas said in a tone that implied he'd grossly underestimated Dutch. "That explains those finely honed instincts of yours." He sat behind the desk and gestured for Dutch to take the seat opposite him. "Why did you get out of the service?"

"I was kicked out."

Vargas raised his eyebrows in curiosity. "What did you do?"

"I killed a man." Dutch took another sip, not rushing to explain his cover story. Not giving any hint of shame. Not an iota of regret. "It was self-defense, but he outranked me and had a lot of powerful buddies. Fortunately, I had a stellar record and a few friends of my own. The army gave me the boot, but with a general instead of dishonorable discharge. To hell with them."

"Isa tells me that you stopped a man from mugging her. The thought of such an assault on my niece turns my stomach, makes me want to tear someone to pieces."

Dutch understood the sentiment far too well. "To be honest, sir, she saved herself. Kicked the guy's butt. All I did was pick up her purse, shoes and get a piece of glass out of her foot."

Vargas chuckled. "Sounds like her. The women in my family are headstrong, independent. Fiery. As my brother's only child, I have a responsibility to her. I love Isa as a daughter. When I say that the Vargas legacy is the same as the Five Families in New York or the Chicago syndicate, do you understand what I mean?"

It meant he was the top dog, the mobster who controlled this region.

Dutch straightened. "Yes."

"I'm going through a bit of a turf war at the moment," Vargas continued. He pulled something out of his suit-jacket pocket and tossed it onto the desk.

It was a playing card. Ace of spades.

"First they sent me the king of spades. Then that one. The death card. It's from the Guzman cartel and means they're coming for me. But I have something in the works to fix this problem." He leaned forward, putting his forearms on his desk. "Isabel doesn't know any of this. Her father wanted her sheltered from our affairs. She was sent to the very best all-girl boarding schools until she went to college. Scripps."

Once again, an all-girls school, just outside of LA.

"I wish to honor her father's desire to keep her in the dark," Vargas said. "But I worry about her up here by herself. She refuses to move back to San Diego and won't let me give her any bodyguards. I believe she thinks they'd spy on her for me."

"Would they?" Dutch asked.

Vargas waved his hands out. *"Por su puesto."* Of course. "I have the best of intentions." He sat back and crossed his legs. "I believe there is a place for you in the fold, where your skills could be of use to me. I would like to offer you a job."

"Doing what? I hope it's not spying on your niece because the answer would be no."

"You have integrity. I respect that." Vargas drained his glass. "I want you to protect Isabel. That's why I'm trusting you with this information. You need to understand what we're dealing with if you are to keep her safe."

"But Don Emilio," Max said. "You can't trust an outsider with her safety."

"Are you questioning my judgment?" Vargas said in Spanish.

Rodrigo stepped forward. "He would never. Neither would I, but we don't know him."

"Isabel knows him." This time Vargas spoke in English. "Likes him. Trusts him. She's rejected everyone else I've proposed, including you two." He cast them both a look that screamed *don't dare say another word.* Neither man spoke again as Vargas shifted his gaze back to Dutch. "It's no secret to my enemies that I love Isabel dearly. That could make her a target to some. I need to insulate her from danger. Immediately, with this attack tonight. I think you're the man to help me do that without frightening her. I doubt she'd have any objections to your presence and as you've stated, your loyalty is to her."

Dutch nodded, slowly, considering the surprising offer. "What does it pay?"

"Ten grand a month."

"Just to keep her safe?" Dutch whistled. "Heck, I'd do it for free." And he would.

"A man has to eat. Does he not?"

Dutch lowered his gaze and clucked his tongue. "Not all of us want to dine on white truffles and Strottarga Bianco."

"You know of the finer things," Vargas said.

What Dutch knew about them had come from reading an article after Googling *expensive indulgences of the stupid rich*.

"But you don't need it." Vargas studied him a minute. "I can see why Isabel is fond of you."

"I can't formally say yes to your offer until I know Isabel won't object to me working for you."

"And if she does?" Vargas asked.

"Then I'll still be there for her, to keep her safe as best I can."

"I will tell Isabel that I approve of you and I'll have a new helmet sent. A Schuberth, yes?"

"Yeah," he said, noticing that Vargas hadn't asked for his address.

"It was good to meet you, Dutch."

"Likewise, sir." He stood and shook Vargas's hand.

"Take my card," Vargas said, offering him one. "It has my private number in case you need to speak with me about my niece."

Dutch pocketed the card. On the way out, he met Max's glare and caught the suspicion in Rodrigo's eyes.

He closed the door and headed down the stairs, hoping that the USMS had taken the time to cement his cover story online and in hard records, making it ironclad, because Vargas was about to run a full-scope background check on him.

If one wasn't already underway.

THE CELL PHONE woke Isabel. After tossing and turning for hours, fretting over Dutch's meeting with her uncle, she'd finally managed to fall asleep.

She glanced at the caller ID, hoping it was Dutch with good news.

*Uncle Emilio.* And it was two in the morning.

*"Tío,"* she said, surprise brushing away the dredges of sleep. "Is everything all right?"

"Yes, my dear. I met Dutch. I wanted to let you know that I like him."

"You do?" The instant the words left her mouth she regretted sounding so shocked.

"I give my approval and won't interfere."

Isabel pressed her hand to her forehead. Was she dreaming? She must be delirious from lack of sleep. "That's wonderful."

What was the catch? Uncle Emilio wouldn't make it this easy unless there was one.

"But I have one condition," he said.

*Here it comes.* Isabel was half-tempted to hang up the phone. She was grown and independently wealthy thanks to the money her father had left her. She'd trade it all, the lavish lifestyle and the trappings that came with it, the eight figures sitting in her bank account, for a normal life, where she was safe and not subjected to the tight reins of her uncle. To live without anything hanging over her.

Sometimes freedom seemed more necessary than maintaining familial ties. But she loved her uncle Emilio and her cousin Miguel. They were the only family she had left. She had been raised to respect her elders, to seek their praise and validation. Also, dealing with the nightmare of Chad Ellis was quite enough. She didn't want to add her uncle to her list of problems.

"Why am I not surprised there are strings?" she asked.

"Watch your tone with me," he snapped in that stern way of his. "Dutch told me about his Special Forces background, something you neglected to mention. I offered him a job, but he was hesitant to take it."

"A job doing what?"

"Protecting you."

Isabel bolted upright in the bed unsure she'd heard him correctly. McQueen shifted on top of the covers near her feet.

"When he discusses the matter with you," he said, "I want you to take away his reservations."

"I don't understand."

"Do this and you get the relationship you want with a man I approve of and I'll know that you're safe. If I can ensure that you're protected and it happens to be by someone who makes you happy, then we both win. Yes?"

Her first instinct was to rail against the idea. It took extreme effort for her not to scream into the phone. She didn't want Dutch taking her uncle's money, beholden to do his bidding. The audacity to even propose such a thing to her boyfriend was unreal.

Churning it over in her head, she began to see the flip side. If she agreed, then she'd get to have Dutch around more often and keep her uncle off her back. She wanted both.

"Don't ask him to spy on me," she said. "It would muddy the waters between us."

"Your young man already told me in no uncertain terms that he would do no such thing."

Dutch stood up to her uncle.

She smiled, her cheeks heating, a dizzying sense of warmth seeping through her down to the bone. "I can't promise anything," she said. "He's his own man and will make his own decision, but I'll talk to him and let him know that I'm not opposed to the idea."

"Excellent. I'm running a background check on him, just a formality of course. I feel certain he will be able to handle any threat to you. Despite what you might believe, your happiness is important to me. Good night, *mi hija*. I love you."

"I love you, too." Isabel hung up, wondering what exactly had happened at the club for Dutch to have made such a profound impression on her uncle.

Going back to sleep was impossible. Part of her was ecstatic and eager to see Dutch, but there was a niggle of worry in the back of her mind that wouldn't let her rest.

The sun took its time cracking over the horizon. As she

sipped a cup of tea, watching daylight break through the sky, she got a text.

Dutch: We need to talk. Game for an early lunch?

Without hesitation, she messaged him back.

Let's make it dinner. My place. I'll cook.

She decided right then that her uncle's call last night was a good sign and not an omen that there was something wrong with Dutch.

Isabel went through her routine for the day, started the heavy lifting on planning her uncle's event, putting an emergency rush on the invitations, and had all but set aside her qualms until she updated Brenda.

"After one meeting, your uncle approved of Dutch instead of running him off with a shotgun?"

"I know, right?" Isabel went back to humming as she hung up the last new painting.

"What did Dutch have to do? Raid a corporation? Kill somebody?"

The melody died in Isabel's throat. What a bizarre response. "Why on earth would you say that?" she asked, turning to face her friend.

Brenda opened her mouth as if to speak, then pressed her lips together and walked to the front desk.

Isabel followed her. "Why would you think killing someone would impress my uncle?"

"It was a poor joke," Brenda said, avoiding eye contact while she shuffled paperwork around. "Sweetie, I know how much you love Uncle Emilio and because I love you, I'll never say anything bad about him."

"Bad like what?" The worst thing her uncle was guilty of

was eating veal. Which admittedly was bad, but Brenda didn't know about that.

Brenda huffed. "Nothing. I'm sorry." She met her eyes and smiled. "I have a surprise. I was going to wait until later, but drumroll." Brenda tapped imaginary drums in the air. "I told my hot yoga teacher how you were mugged and asked if he could start teaching a morning class or something and he offered to give me private lessons on Sundays. Just the two of us, where he can really help deepen my poses and give me a good stretch." She winked.

Isabel gasped with delight. "You've been trying to get him one-on-one for months."

"I know. He really made me work for it, too. I mean, you had to get robbed at knifepoint for Pete's sake." She walked back around the desk like she no longer needed it as a barrier. "I propose you skedaddle and go see your hottie early for *dinner*," she said, using air quotes with the last word.

Dinner and dessert with lots of icing and several cherries. Isabel's heart fluttered with anticipation, but guilt was quick on its heels. "I've already missed two days this week, leaving you to handle everything. I'd be a horrible friend if I skipped out early tonight, especially when I asked you not to change your schedule for me."

"Pish, posh. Make it up to me by sharing a few juicy tidbits." She waggled her eyebrows.

"Okay. You really are the best friend I could ask for."

Brenda nodded with a smug smile.

Isabel called for her car, wrapped up the rest of what she was doing, grabbed her purse from the office and went to the grocery store.

Inside, she headed straight for the fish department and waited in line for her turn.

A young man wearing Dickies work pants and a black shirt buttoned only at the top with a white tank top underneath, sneakers and a black-and-white bandana on his head came up to the front of the large case where the fish was displayed and looked around.

"How can I help you?" the fishmonger asked her after he was done with the last customer.

"I'm cooking seafood *fra diavolo* for two. Can you wrap up a mix of what's freshest?"

"I've got some nice lobster tails, scallops and these beauties." The fishmonger held up a handful of the plumpest shrimp she'd ever seen.

"Perfect."

"Want me to prep it for you, remove the shells and devein the shrimp?"

That was why this was her favorite grocery store. "Yes, that'd be lovely."

"Finish shopping, ma'am, and it'll be here on the counter for you."

"Thank you." Isabel strode off and grabbed linguini and a can of tomatoes. She turned to find the rest of the ingredients and spotted the same guy in a black shirt and Dickies strolling past her aisle.

He glanced at her for one heartbeat too long, but he kept going. A creeping tension sent a shiver up her spine when she realized he wasn't pushing a cart and didn't have a basket.

Her first impulse was to call Dutch, but she was in a well-lit public place and could handle herself. She didn't need anyone's help.

*Get a grip, Isabel. You of all people know better than to stereotype that guy. The whole world isn't out to get you. Only Chad.*

She mentally checked off what else she needed and hurried to get the items. As she picked out a couple of salad dressings Dutch might like, the guy with the bandana showed up again. He didn't look at her. Standing in front of the ketchup, he took a bottle from the shelf and turned it over, as if he was reading the ingredients.

"It's nothing," she said to herself, but she couldn't shake the feeling that something was off about the guy.

She went to the produce section. Looking over the herbs, she threw a bundle of parsley in her basket. The main dessert would hopefully be in the bedroom, but they'd cap off dinner with something light. Maybe a fruit salad.

Breezing past the stands, she tossed a ripe variety in her basket. She stopped in front of the cantaloupe, deciding if she wanted to dice one up or simply buy it chopped and pre-packaged.

Another customer waltzed up beside her, bumping her basket. A hand with tattoos inked on the back grabbed a cantaloupe. "Do you know how to pick a good melon?" he asked.

She glanced over at the man. The one who looked like a gangbanger and kept popping up in the same parts of the store. He had two teardrop tattoos below the corner of his eye.

"No. Sorry." Spinning on her heel, she walked away. Forget the melon.

"Hey. Your stuff is ready," he called to her.

She pivoted and looked back at him. "What did you say?"

"Your seafood." He hiked a thumb toward the fish department. "It's on the counter waiting for you."

All the spit dried in her mouth, but she managed to say, "Thank you."

It was odd, yes, but he was only being friendly, and she was being ridiculous, right? No need to be rude, as well.

She passed another man who didn't have a basket or a cart and because he was dressed in business attire, she didn't question *his* motives for being in the store.

Isabel grabbed the seafood bundle from the counter in the fish department, tossed it into her basket and went to a register. She loaded her stuff on the conveyor belt, itching to get out of the store. As she bent over to place the empty basket on the floor, she stilled.

At the bottom of the basket was a playing card. She picked it up and turned it over.

Queen of spades.

But it hadn't been in there earlier when she'd first taken a basket. She was certain.

She dropped the card in the basket and shoved it under the conveyor belt.

Isabel paid, opting for paper bags, and hurried to her car. Hitting the new key fob, the lights flashed on her Maserati, and the doors unlocked. She opened the trunk and set her bags inside. Before closing it, she unzipped her purse and grasped the handle of her fully charged Pacifier.

*Better safe than sorry.*

Trying to slow her breaths that started coming too quickly, she scanned her surroundings.

No sign of the man.

She slipped inside her car, locked the doors and started the engine. Putting on her seat belt, she noticed something on her windshield, trapped under her wipers.

The queen of spades.

Her whole body went cold, but every nerve pulsed with energy. Isabel looked around outside, twisting in her seat. There was no one near her car, but was anyone watching her? Waiting for a reaction to seeing the card? How did the same queen of spades get on her windshield without her noticing anyone?

She flipped on the wipers. The wind snatched the card, carrying it on a breeze across the parking lot.

A shadow moved up alongside her window. She almost jumped out of her skin, her heart throbbing in her throat.

An older woman got inside a sedan parked beside hers and pulled off.

Isabel took a deep breath, calming herself down. She threw her car in gear and drove to the doggie day care center, going well over the speed limit, not running red lights, but gunning it when any turned yellow.

Once McQueen was in the car she felt better, knowing she had immediate backup in case she needed it. He wouldn't let anyone get near her if he sensed danger. Too bad she couldn't take him with her everywhere.

On the way home, she checked her mirrors constantly, making sure she wasn't being followed. Not that she had any training in picking up a tail, but she'd notice if the same car stayed glued behind her.

Nothing unusual stuck out and by the time she pulled into her garage, her nerves had settled somewhat.

Entering her building, she waved hello to the concierge, who worked from eight to six at the front desk. "Good evening, Bill," she said with a shopping bag in either hand.

"Evening, Isabel. You got a package. I ran it upstairs for you, put it in front of your door."

"You're a saint," she said, wondering what it could be since she hadn't ordered anything. "Thank you."

"Need help with those groceries?"

"No, I've got it." She hit the button for the elevator. Normally she took the stairs, but tonight, she wanted to get inside her condo as soon as possible.

The chime dinged and the doors opened. She got in the lift with McQueen. The ride up was quick.

At her front door, McQueen ran up to the package and sniffed it. She put her key in the door and unlocked it. Inside, she shut off her alarm and set her groceries down, relieved to be home.

She put everything away, took out her phone and called Dutch. "Hi."

"Hey, beautiful." His deep, smoky voice brought another layer of comfort.

"Brenda is closing up tonight," she said, retrieving the package, with the phone sandwiched between her ear and shoulder. "I already swung by the grocery, where something weird happened."

"Weird how?"

She shrugged to herself. "I'm not really sure, but I'll tell you about it later." She locked the door and put the box on the counter. "I've had the busiest day, running around like crazy because my uncle wants me to organize an art auction for him down in San Diego."

"Really? When's the auction?"

"Sunday. Fifty guests. I can't believe it's such short notice. Talk about pressure." She sighed, hoping to pull everything together, not wanting to disappoint her uncle. "I'm set to cook dinner tonight, though. How quickly can you get here?"

The package was covered in brown shipping wrap and her name was typed on a label on the top, but there was no return address. Today was full of weird stuff. Was Mercury retrograde? A full moon or something?

"I just stepped out of the shower," he said, conjuring delicious images in her mind. "I'll throw on clothes and head over."

"I was thinking, why don't you bring your toothbrush and spend the night?" Smiling, she pulled at the taped-down flaps along the side and unwrapped it. "That's strange."

"What?"

"I got a package. It's a foam box."

"Foam?" Sternness spiked the word.

"Yes, an insulated cooler," she said, taking off the lid.

"Wait. Don't open it."

A rancid smell hit her as she peered inside. A strangled scream escaped her lips. The cell phone slipped from her hand, crashing to the floor. She gagged, her stomach convulsing.

McQueen started barking.

Sickened and terrified, she heard Dutch yelling to her from the phone on the floor. But her mind went blank. She squeezed her eyes shut, staggering back from the box in horrified revulsion, spun toward the sink and retched.

In her entire life, she'd never seen anything more gruesome.

# Chapter Fifteen

Twelve minutes. That's how long it had taken Dutch to reach Isabel and it had felt like a small eternity.

Staring at the obscene foulness in the box, a cold fist clenched his stomach.

*Dear God, Almighty.* Dutch had seen a lot of awful, sick things in his time in the army, but this still got to him.

Looking away from the mutilated pig's head, he put the lid on the box. He was outraged someone had sent that to her. The only reason he was able to muster a facade of calm was for Isabel's sake.

Dutch went to her in the living room. He sat on the coffee table in front of her, so close that his legs brushed the outside of hers, and he held her hands.

Her fingers were ice-cold and her face pale.

McQueen didn't know what to do. The dog vacillated between barking at the box on the counter and whining beside his owner.

Making sure Isabel was okay was Dutch's only concern after he'd called the police. His protective instincts had reached an all-time high. After grabbing the throw from the back of the sofa, he wrapped it around her shivering body.

She was in shock.

He put a mug of water with a chamomile tea bag in the microwave and poured her a small cup of pomegranate juice. "Here, drink this. It'll help." Once her blood sugar came up, she'd start to feel a little better.

She took the glass with both hands and sipped it. Her face twisted like she might be sick.

"Chug it, all at once." It was only four ounces and she needed to drink it.

A shudder rippled through her, making the glass shake in her hand, but then she did as he told her. After she swallowed, he noticed a slight lessening of tension in her muscles.

The microwave beeped. He took the glass from her, got the tea and shoved the warm mug in her hands.

"Why would Chad do this? Send me…that."

First the bees, almost killing Isabel, and now sending her such a disgusting thing. He was a sadistic monster.

Dutch clenched his fists, aching with the need to pound them into Chad's face.

"The stench." Fresh tears welled in her eyes. "I can still smell it. I need air. Please, I want to get out of here."

A loud rap at the door drew their gazes. "Police. We received a call."

Dutch got up, let the two officers in and showed them the contents of the box. They both gasped, their faces tightening with disgust as they reeled back.

"Damn," Officer Gibbs said.

Officer Lewis took out a pad and pen. "Ma'am, we're going to need to get your statement," she said, gently.

Dutch folded his arms, furious energy buzzing through him. "How long will it take?"

"It might take a while," Officer Lewis said. "We're also going to need you both to come down to the station to get your fingerprints to check them against what we find on the box."

"Can you take her statement at the station? The sooner we change the scenery, the better."

The female officer nodded. "Sure."

Dutch strode into the living room and hunkered down in front of Isabel. "After the police station, do you want to come back here? Or do you want to stay with me tonight?"

"With you," she said weakly.

He helped her up from the sofa and into the bedroom, where she packed a bag.

"Ma'am?" one of the officers called from the kitchen. "There's no postmark on the wrapping. It wasn't mailed. Did you see who dropped it off?"

"No." Isabel drifted through the room, stuffing some things

in an overnight bag. "Bill, the concierge downstairs might've. He brought the box up to my apartment."

"We'll need his statement and prints, too," Officer Lewis said.

Since Isabel was in no condition to get behind the wheel, Dutch drove her and McQueen in his truck. At the station, he stopped out front.

"Go inside with McQueen," Dutch said. "I'll be back as soon as I can."

She stiffened. "Where are you going?"

Taking her hand in his, he said, "I need to make this stop."

Her eyes widened with understanding and she shook her head. "Don't go. He's dangerous."

"Not as dangerous as I can be." Ellis had no idea who he was messing with and it was time he learned. "It's okay," he reassured her in a gentle tone. "I won't be gone long."

Worry didn't leave Isabel's eyes, but she nodded. "Be careful. He got his orange belt in Krav Maga," she said as if that made Chad a lethal weapon. "I don't want him to hurt you."

If anyone was going to get hurt, it'd be Chad. By the time Dutch was finished, Chad would wish he had a second degree black belt. "Don't set foot outside the station. Don't go anywhere without me."

She nodded again, opened the door and slipped out of the car. McQueen followed. Once she disappeared inside, Dutch sped off.

The wings of cold, black rage beat through him and thanks to the file from Agent Rogers, he knew exactly where to find Chad Ellis.

IN HIS BRENTWOOD OFFICE, Chad sat behind his desk, working at his computer. Business was doing better than ever at the funeral parlor as well as with biohazard remediation, thanks to the rise in crime. If he could send every murderer in the area a thank-you note, he would.

Shouting from the front of the building had him swiveling around in his chair to see what all the ruckus was about.

Horatio "Dutch" Haas was charging down the hallway, headed straight for Chad's office.

Chad hit the intercom button for his secretary. She was fifty-something, loyal as the day was long and had been with him from the beginning. Jill sat as a gatekeeper at a desk in front of his office.

"Don't try to stop him," Chad said. "Round up the boys— have them hurry on over. Then grab your phone and record everything. No audio."

"Okay," Jill said. Her gaze bounced up to Haas as she hung up and called the lounge, where his workers hung out between cleaning assignments.

At least five men were in the building, not that he needed or wanted them to intervene. He was stacking the deck of witnesses in his favor.

Dutch kicked open his office door, splintering the frame.

*What melodramatic machismo.* Chad suppressed an eye roll and stifled a chuckle. Playing the part of the victim meant he needed to appear frightened and intimidated on the video.

"How dare you," Chad said. "Who do you think you are barging in here like this?"

"You sick bastard!" Dutch stalked up to the desk, planted his palms on the surface and leaned over, bringing them eye level. "Did it make you feel like a big man to send a butchered pig's head to Isabel? You're a twisted monster."

"What?"

Rage boiled in Dutch's face as he swept everything off Chad's desk onto the floor. He stormed around, grabbed Chad by the lapels of his suit jacket, snatched him out of the chair and slammed him against the wall.

"Are you going to look me in the eye and deny sending it to Isabel?"

*Hell, yeah.* Not because he didn't do it, even though he hadn't, but deny, deny, deny was the second rule he lived by.

Rule number one—don't get caught.

Glancing over Dutch's shoulder, he saw Jill filming everything and the guys who worked for him gathering around the front of the office.

Chad raised his palms and pinched his features into those of a man terrified for his life. "I don't know what you're talking about. I didn't send her anything."

But he wished like hell he had. Damn, that was a good one. Why hadn't he thought of it?

"You're a lying sack of garbage." Dutch lifted his fist. "I ought to—"

"What?" Chad asked, maintaining his frightened expression for the camera and witnesses, but lowering his voice, taunting Haas. "Hit me? Go ahead. Beat me. Kick my teeth in. Make it hurt. Don't stop until you turn me into meatloaf. You know you want to."

Reason dawned in Dutch's eyes, breaking through the cloud of wrath. He looked over his shoulder at the crowd of employees and then back at Chad. Releasing him, Dutch stepped back.

Apparently, Dutch wasn't a mindless Neanderthal who'd be easily baited. Too bad.

Chad would love nothing more than to have this riffraff charged with assault and thrown in jail. Guess that meant Chad would have to work a little harder to push his buttons. "When Isabel and I came close to reconnecting a few months ago," he whispered, "behind her art gallery—"

"You mean when you attacked her?"

"She wanted me to be there. She wanted me to touch her."

"You're delusional." Dutch stared at him, his narrowed eyes darkening. His jaw flexed with barely contained anger. "If you go near her again," he said, dropping his voice to a whisper as well, "I'll kill you."

Isabel was his weakness. Chad's minx had gotten under

Dutch's skin, slinked her way into his heart. "Tell my Isabel she should keep better company. Or she might get stung by something worse than a bee."

Swift fury gleamed in Dutch's eyes as he cocked his fist back and launched it.

The first punch smashed into Chad's face, jarring his head. The second struck the wall when Chad ducked, his reflexes honed from training kicking in, and maneuvered to the side.

One blow was enough to do the trick. Blood poured from his nose. The pain made his head buzz. Covering his face, he hid his smile and swallowed laughter along with his own blood. He had six witnesses, a video and soon a medical report as evidence. "Kiss your freedom goodbye. I'm going to have you brought up on charges."

"Knock yourself out trying." Without a lick of worry in his expression, Dutch turned for the door.

Chad growled, "Maybe she needs to take a restraining order out on you since you've been watching her." He rattled off the address to the vacant building where Dutch's motorcycle had been parked.

Dutch froze. Then he pivoted. Fear, gut-wrenching fear was plastered on his face.

Chad was so thrilled he gave a mental cheer that would've rocked a stadium. He'd found the right thread. Now he needed to pull it until this thing between Dutch and Isabel unraveled.

"Stay away from her," Dutch warned while pointing a threatening finger, and then he charged out of the building.

Chad looked at Jill. "Call the police. Tell them I've just been assaulted."

# Chapter Sixteen

With a bag of ice on his bruised knuckles, Dutch sat on the sofa in the temporary one-bedroom apartment the USMS had loaned him. He stared at the new Schuberth that had been delivered, his mind spinning while Isabel was in the shower.

Everything had turned into a disaster.

An epic disaster of career-ending proportions.

Will Draper had had a conniption when Dutch was forced to call him and explain what happened at Chad Ellis's place of business. His boss had to intercede with the cops before a warrant was issued for Dutch's arrest.

Dutch had never heard such foul language from a superior, not even in the army. His ears were still burning. He was worried Draper was going to have a stroke on the phone.

The fact that Dutch was a deputy marshal had become a ticking time bomb bound to explode. The satellite hub had to be shut down. Draper and Allison would have to work out of the LA field office, putting Dutch's backup at a distance. Ellis was close to learning the truth and once he did, he wouldn't hesitate to rub it in Isabel's face.

Even worse, at the police station, the cops had found an ace of spades card underneath the pig's head. A warning to Vargas that the Guzman cartel was coming for Isabel. Chad hadn't sent that monstrosity after all and Dutch had gone off the rails over the one thing that sicko wasn't actually guilty of.

Dutch petted McQueen who was on the leather couch with his head in Dutch's lap.

He had to tell Isabel the truth. She needed to know that she was in danger, not only from Chad Ellis, but also the Guzman cartel because of her uncle Emilio.

Guilt coiled and tightened through him, leaving him queasy. He'd give anything to have a clean slate with Isabel, a fresh start, where she wouldn't hate him.

Going into this assignment he hadn't given any consideration to how he would exit.

Falling for her had been unforeseen, an impossibility he hadn't planned for. With Isabel, Dutch found everything he wanted, something he hadn't even realized had been missing in his life. The prospect of walking away from her, disappearing with no explanation, shredded him. He wouldn't be able to look in the mirror much less live with himself.

It all snowballed in his head into one gigantic problem with no easy solution.

Isabel opened the bedroom door and came out wearing a silky peach robe that complemented her olive complexion, her hair in a high, loose knot, the long line of her leg peeking out of the slit. The sight of her walking toward him, looking so fresh and clean, was a sucker punch to the gut. She was beautiful, full of sweetness, had such courage and absolute strength. It took hope for her to open her heart to him after everything she'd been through.

God, he didn't want to put her through more hell.

Dutch set his bag of ice on the end table and shooed McQueen off the sofa to make room for her. The dog jumped down and lay across his feet.

Isabel sat and leaned into him. Roping an arm around her, he brought her against his body. She rested her head on his shoulder, putting her palm on his chest.

She smelled good, that particular scent he now knew as hers enveloped him. Inhaling deeply, he breathed her in. *Vetiver.* They'd have fun together in Indonesia. He longed to show her the thousand islands off greater Jakarta one day. Swimming. Exploring the coves.

There were a million things he wanted to share with her.

Pipe dream or possibility?

Tightening his hold on her, he needed to believe there was a way for them.

"Are you hungry?" he asked. It was after nine and they

should've eaten hours ago. Not that he had much of an appetite. "I can whip something up."

"No, thanks. I don't want to eat." She tipped her head back, running her nose across his neck. "I don't need food right now. I need…"

"What is it, sweetheart?" He rubbed her arm, up and down, soothing, slow strokes.

"There's been so much ugliness. I need to forget the fear and horror for a little while." Angling her face up, she pressed her palm to his cheek and turned his mouth toward hers. Their lips a hairbreadth apart. "Help me forget, Dutch. I don't want to think. I just want to feel something good." She drew him closer.

Not holding back, he kissed her. Not a soft, flirty peck. No, this was greedy and reckless.

In a heartbeat it turned hotter, full of edgy desire. She lay back, pulling him on top of her. He felt every lush curve of her body as he slid against her. Loosening the tie on her robe, she let it fall open. He found her damp and bare, making him instantly hard.

Only Isabel had this way of luring him in and driving him wild like no one else.

He should pull back, pump the brakes, but she took his hand, guiding it to cup her breast. Velvety-soft skin. The touch sparked across his nerve endings, setting off something primal in him. He flicked his thumb over her nipple, and she moaned, arching beneath him, spreading her legs to better accommodate him between her thighs.

Need pulsed inside him, swelled, growing urgent.

"I want you." She unbuckled his belt, groped his straining erection through his jeans.

As she unzipped his pants, he stayed her hand.

"I can't." He wanted nothing more than to make love to her and show her how deeply he felt. That everything burning inside him for her was genuine, that when he was with her, he had a sense of peace, rightness he'd never had. But not like this, with lies between them.

"Are you married?" Her mouth went to his neck. She pressed a trail of sizzling kisses up his throat to his jaw, stoking his desire for her.

"No."

"Do you have children hidden away that you haven't told me about?"

He shook his head. "No."

"An STD?"

"God, no. Nothing like that."

Her hand dove down, where she palmed him through the denim. He wanted her so much that it hurt.

"Then I don't care." Her warm breath fanned his lips. "Whatever it is doesn't matter."

"You wanted to take things slowly. This is too fast," he said, not believing what was coming out of his mouth. Not once had he ever turned down sex and especially not with a gorgeous woman he yearned to have.

"I know we've only been together a week, but I feel closer to you than any other man I've ever been with. When we're together, I feel safe and happy. Special."

"You are special."

Everything between them fell into place right from the start, tumblers in a lock clicking into position. Her presence, her affection, her warmth, lessened the emptiness that gnawed at him.

She had a good heart and wasn't weak. This woman had grit. She was fierce and smart and trusting. An irresistible mix of qualities that were hard to find and it made him even hotter for her.

He'd never considered having a long-term girlfriend, or commitments outside the military and the USMS, but he wanted to give himself to Isabel, have a future with her.

"This may sound crazy," she said, raw vulnerability all over her face, "but I think I'm falling in love with you."

His heart ached because he was falling in love, too. For the first time in his life.

If he told her the truth about who he was, he'd jeopardize everything. But if he slept with her without her knowing, she'd never forgive him, and he'd lose her forever.

Dutch squeezed his eyes shut, the importance of the mission weighing on him heavy as wet sandbags, knowing what was at risk if he failed—the lives of fellow marshals, their spouses, their children.

There was no debate. He had no choice. Right or wrong, what he had to do next was clear.

"I TOLD YOU I love you," she said. And he hadn't said it back. Not that he owed her such a huge declaration.

Isabel drew in a shuddering breath, wondering if her admission was too much for him. Ill-timed? Too soon? Was she supposed to wait for him to say something so big first?

She'd had a handful of lovers, but none that she'd *loved*, and she wanted to share herself with someone who filled her heart.

Dutch opened his eyes, his gaze locked with hers, and she knew. Without him needing to say it, she saw it crystal clear, the same affection, the same passion, an absolute soul-deep connection glittering back at her.

She let out the breath she'd been holding. Her heart stuttered and swelled with relief. She brushed her mouth across his, but there was no answering pressure.

"Isabel," he said, and she put her hand to his chest, feeling the hard muscles bunch under his T-shirt, the hammering beat of his heart beneath. "I'm undercover."

"Huh?" That hadn't been what she'd expected to hear, and it made no sense. "What—what are you talking about?"

"I'm a US marshal. Undercover." His body flexed with tension. A dark sadness, pain, filled his eyes. "I was sent to get close to you. To recover something important that your uncle stole. To save lives." The words cut through her, leaving her raw, exposed.

She gathered her robe closed, covering herself as she pushed upright and tied the sash tight. Too stunned and confused to speak, she cradled her head in her hands. She tried breaking down what he'd said into tiny digestible pieces, but before she had a chance, he kept talking.

"Your uncle isn't who you think he is." Dutch sat up beside her. "He's not a legitimate businessman. He's the head of the *Los Chacales* cartel," he said, the name ringing bells in her head—big, clanging warning bells. "At least, he's in charge on the West Coast. His son, Miguel, handles things on the East Coast since your uncle put him in power."

A chill so cold that it burned raced over her skin.

Dutch put his hand on her thigh.

She flinched, jumping to her feet. "Don't touch me. Stay away from me."

"Your uncle Emilio peddles drugs and death," Dutch said, low and calm while a storm of emotion brewed inside her. "He's a man of violence with brutal tendencies. He's also a growing threat to national security."

"That's not true!" She stumbled back. "Why are you saying these horrible things?"

Dutch strode across the room to a briefcase. He entered a code, unlocking it, and pulled out a thick file. Sitting back on the sofa, he set it on the coffee table and opened it somewhere in the middle. "Do you know this woman?"

Isabel stepped closer and peered over at a picture of a young woman she recognized and stilled. Icy fingers closed around her heart and squeezed. "Yes. She's my uncle's ex-girlfriend."

"Your uncle uses every legitimate business that he owns, including your art gallery, to wash his money or sell drugs. Lori Carpenter," he said, pointing to the picture, "worked at a capital-management firm, where your uncle laundered hundreds of millions of dollars. After he started dating her, he put Lori in charge of his account. She saw all the dirty blood money coming in and ran to the FBI. He went to a lot of trouble to try to kill her. Silence her. But she survived, just barely. Turned state's evidence and testified."

A ringing started in her ears. She put her fingers to her temples.

*Seven days.* She'd only known Dutch seven days and as it turned out she didn't know him at all. The concrete number gave her something to focus on. A meter by which to gauge what he was saying. No reason to believe him. No reason to believe her own judgment that screamed what he'd said might be true. "Then why isn't my uncle in jail?"

"He's clever, insulated himself with layers of protection. The Justice Department couldn't go after him directly, so they went after the capital-investment company and shut down the major money-laundering arm of *Los Chacales*."

"I would've heard about it in the news, Lori testifying in such a big case."

"The DOJ tried to protect Lori's identity by keeping her name out of the press and had a closed-door trial. But in your uncle's attempt to kill Lori, the US Marshals building in San Diego was attacked. That was on the news."

It had been all over the television and in the paper for days. The USMS building under siege.

That had been Uncle Emilio?

"Your uncle came into possession of sensitive information that was stolen from the US Marshals Service. He has the personal data of every individual in WITSEC here in California, as well as that of our marshals and their dependents. Your uncle is planning to auction the hard drive with information this weekend to the highest criminal bidder."

Putting her hand to her mouth to muffle a gasp, Isabel turned away from him. The ringing in her head wouldn't stop. Like something was there, some horrible realization, only it was too terrible, and she couldn't wrap her head around it.

To do so would bring her whole world crashing down.

"I have to retrieve the hard drive before the auction," Dutch said. "It can't be sold."

The auction. The bizarre, short-notice auction.

*An exceptional item of great value. One-of-a kind. They'll clear their schedules.*

And she was organizing it.

Isabel was so furious she was sickened to her stomach. She was angry at Dutch. At her uncle. At every single person on the planet. But still she couldn't accept this because then everything in her life would be a fabrication of one shade or another.

"I can't believe I introduced you to him!" she said, storming around the living room. McQueen got up at Isabel's raised voice as if waiting for instructions. "Put myself on the line. For what? So you could create these lies? Drive a wedge between us? Why are you doing this?"

"When I met him at the club, there was an assassination attempt on him."

Isabel swiveled around, faced him, her arms falling to her sides, the breath knocked from her lungs.

"He's in a turf war with the Guzman cartel." Dutch stood and stepped closer to her.

McQueen moved between them, the dog's back to Isabel, his eyes locked on Dutch.

"But I saved his life," he said. "On pure instinct. Then he confided in me. Asked me to be your bodyguard because he's worried that you'll be in danger and he's right. The queen of spades, the ace of spades, those were from the Guzman cartel. It was a message for your uncle. They're going to try to kill you to hurt him. They sent him a similar message before the attack in the club."

Isabel reeled, her thoughts a jumbled mess. How could she have been so easily duped by every person in her life?

Was Brenda the only one she could trust?

Isabel staggered away to the window that overlooked the

building's parking lot. Half a mile in the distance was the ocean. Black and murky and endless. It mirrored the tumult of emotion raging inside her.

"Think about what I'm saying, Isabel. His lifestyle. The armed bodyguards." Dutch sighed, coming up slowly beside her. "The reason you were sent to boarding school was to create distance, to blind you from the truth."

She didn't want to acknowledge the legitimacy of his claims. She closed her eyes and pressed harder against her temples.

*Dutch is a US marshal undercover.*

"You lied to me!" The surge of pain eviscerated her. The stab of betrayal sliced deeper, past bone, down to marrow, hitting her soul. "Manipulated me."

"I'm sorry. I had to."

"I'm so stupid." She thought back to their conversations, the things they had in common, the ways that they'd clicked. "I thought this was real." But it had all been a web of lies. Layered fabrications to lure her in. To get to her uncle.

Dutch inched closer to her. "The fact that we didn't meet by accident was a lie, but everything else between us was real," he said, as if reading her mind.

It felt like another violation.

When he'd touched her, she'd never been so warm, so light, so happy. Like they were meant to be.

What rubbish!

Every fairy-tale book about the princess falling in love with some version of Prince Charming, or in her case a charming bad boy, and living happily-ever-after should be banned. Better yet, burned, so no little girls grew up with such nonsense poisoning their minds.

"Who are you?" she asked, facing him. "What's your real name?"

He looked at her, his eyes sad, his brow creased. She stared at him, studying him, trying to read his expression. But maybe she was a fool who knew nothing and had never had a thread of connection with him.

"My name *is* Horatio 'Dutch' Haas. They didn't have time to create an alias. I swear to God, you know me. About my father's heart attack, about my sister. How kids picked on me. My crush on that cheerleader. Finding the public salsa dancing to put a smile on your face. I've told you things, truths from my soul, that no one else in the world knows. Because I wanted you to *see* me. And the more you liked what you saw, the tattoos, my lack of finesse, my bluntness, my rough edges, the deeper I fell for you."

Tears prickled her eyes. The upsurge of belief in her was swiftly blunted by a daunting sense of betrayal.

"We came so close to making love, sweetheart. That would've been the easier thing to do. Sleep with you and maintain my cover. Instead I told you the truth."

Isabel slapped him hard. The sting in her palm and the flush in Dutch's cheek made the tears fall from her eyes. "Am I supposed to thank you for that?"

McQueen barked at Dutch. The dog stalked closer, teeth bared, growling.

Dutch raised his palms and softened his tone. "I told you all of this because I love you. You deserve the truth. I want to be with you. I can see a future for us, traveling, taking McQueen to the dog park, cuddled up on the sofa watching movies."

She'd wanted that too and so much more. She had been ridiculous enough to imagine what it'd be like to start a family with him. After he'd taken care of her and McQueen, she'd been certain he'd make a good father.

"You don't need to keep lying to me." Tears streamed down her face.

"Everything is on the line," Dutch said. "If we don't get that hard drive back, then good, hardworking, innocent people are going to die. But I risked it all for you. Because I couldn't live with the alternative." He grimaced, the wavy lines in his forehead deeper than before.

They stared at each other. The intensity of his eyes drew her in, made her want to believe him. But she'd been a naive fool lapping up the lies from those around her long enough.

How on earth could she trust him?

Her chest heaved as silence hung between them. He cupped her shoulders, bringing her against him into a hug and—

*Boom!*

An explosion shattered the quiet, rocking the night and driving them apart. Outside in the parking area, a fireball blazed, triggering every car alarm in the lot.

She leaned on the window, putting her hands to the glass in shock. A motorcycle had been blown to bits and the frame was on fire. The bike that was beside his truck.

Dutch's bike.

"Chad didn't send you the box, but I'm a hundred percent certain he's responsible for that." Dutch hitched his chin at the inferno outside. "I really hate that guy."

At least they were on the same page about something.

WATCHING THE FIRE rage in the parking lot, the aftermath of his homemade bomb, Chad stood in the darkness. A man who loved Isabel to the point that he'd do anything for her. Lie. Cheat. Commit arson. Murder.

And he would. He'd kill Horatio Haas given the chance.

How many women could say they had that?

Such devotion. Commitment. His passion could be overwhelming, sure, might even frighten her, but it was a singular love.

Why was Isabel so ungrateful?

If she didn't come to her senses and see the light, Chad would be forced to do the unthinkable.

He'd have to cleanse her.

Consume her soul so that they'd always be one and then lay her body to rest.

# Chapter Seventeen

After Dutch had taken her cell phone to keep her from making any rash calls, Isabel had locked herself in the bedroom with McQueen while he dealt with the police and fire department. She'd spent all night looking through the file he'd given her, every page, every line. Twice. Then a third time, letting it sink in.

One undeniable fact struck her like a lightning bolt. Uncle Emilio was the biggest drug kingpin on the West Coast.

And he was now embroiled in a turf war that endangered her life.

The truth was sobering. Painful.

Even her art gallery was a ruse. The FBI suspected he was using it to launder money.

How would Isabel know? He owned it and she used his accountant.

To think she'd bought into his story of him wanting to be a generous, loving uncle who didn't want her to touch her inheritance. So altruistic.

Dutch knocked on the door. "Are you ready to go? They're expecting us soon."

Fully dressed, Isabel rose from the bed, grabbed her handbag and the file. She opened the door, ready to go to the US Marshals office and unleash her indignation on his boss.

He stood with a badge and holstered gun hooked on his belt, offering her a cup of coffee in a travel mug. "I don't have coconut milk. I used a splash of half-and-half."

Two days with no real sleep, she would've slurped down a cup of hot sludge if it had caffeine in it. "No, thank you." Her pride refused to let her take his coffee.

"We can stop for food on the way, if you want."

She was starving. "I'm not hungry." She shoved the file at his chest, and he took it.

"Isabel." He scrubbed a hand over his face. "It'd be nice to know if you're going to help us before you meet my boss. I'd like to be prepared."

How could she not help? Her beloved uncle was the head of a notorious drug cartel and had been lying to Isabel her entire life and using her. The same way Dutch wanted to use her.

But if she could help save lives and undo a fraction of the wrong caused by Uncle Emilio, then she would. Obviously. It only outraged her more that he doubted her, so she was going to let him stew.

"It's a lot to think over," she said. "I have questions."

"What are they? I can answer them."

"For your boss. Not you. You're just following orders. It's not your fault you lied, manipulated and used me. It's your boss's, right?" She crossed her arms. "I want to look him in the eye and hear it from him. Let's go."

Without talking, they swung by doggie day care to drop off McQueen and went to the LA US Marshals Service building located downtown across from city hall. She wasn't sure what she'd been expecting, but not Dutch flashing a badge with ease, having her stun baton confiscated at the metal detectors, him signing her in like she was a visitor instead of a finagled informant.

In the elevator, she asked, "Are you trying to turn me into an informant? Is that the correct term?"

"*Asset* would be more accurate," he said in a low voice.

*Finagled asset. Lovely.*

The doors opened with a chime. Dutch stepped off first and led her to a conference room where a man and woman were seated side by side, dark suits, hands clasped on the table.

The fit, middle-aged man with an affable face and a dusting of gray around his temples greeted them. "Hello, Ms. Vargas. I'm US Marshal Will Draper. Call me Will. Please have a seat," he said, waiting until Isabel sat before taking a chair himself. "I'm in charge of the San Diego field office and this is one of my deputies, Allison Chen-Boyd."

"Just Chen," Allison said with a blank expression, giving off a no-nonsense vibe. She didn't look older than early thirties and wore her dark hair in a braid. In front of her was a tall stack of folders.

"Sorry. I forget." Will straightened his tie and folded his hands on the table, flashing a soft smile that said *let's be friends*. "Ms. Vargas, Deputy Haas has updated me on the current status of things. How can we put you at ease with assisting us?"

"You can start by explaining what gave you the right to invade my privacy and my life. I'm a law-abiding citizen and the only thing I'm guilty of is naivete. Stupidity for believing in those around me who I care about." She glared at Dutch and then refocused on the marshals across the table. "How could you send someone in to seduce me? What about common decency? Respect? Why didn't you bring me in, show me your file and simply ask me to help?"

"Forgive me, Ms. Vargas," Allison said, "but if you think that approach would work with ninety-nine percent of the assets that we recruit then you are naive."

Isabel recoiled from the harsh words and even harsher tone.

"Allison, back off," Dutch said.

"No, I'm not going to back off. If you had done your damn job and kept your mouth shut, we wouldn't be here right now."

"That's right." Isabel regained her composure. "He would've slept with me and I'd be none the wiser. I would've brought him to San Diego this weekend, he would've found a way to get back your precious database, and then what? He'd disappear?" She turned to Dutch. "Leave me behind? Like collateral damage."

"I wouldn't do that to you." He put his hand on hers and she yanked it away, clasping her hands in her lap. "Everything I said last night, I meant."

"The majority of assets have to be coerced," Will said, evenly. "Blackmailed. The FBI has more expertise in this area than we do and recommended this approach and selected Haas for the assignment."

"Why him?" Isabel asked.

"Something to do with his profile," Will said, "and an algorithm that selected him as a good match for you."

*Like a dating website profile?* She tamped down the discomfort and nerves rising in her. "I want to see the FBI agent who thought this was a good idea."

"I'm afraid that's not going to happen, Ms. Vargas," Will said. "If you want to feel better about Haas's involvement, then you should know, he objected to the approach we took from the get-go. He even confronted the FBI agent in question. He's demonstrated nothing but the utmost concern for you and your well-being during this difficult process."

"I'm sorry if we hurt your *precious* feelings with our methods." Allison stood, picking up one of the files in front of her, and opened it.

She started dropping pictures on the table in front of Isabel. Of dead bodies. Shot. Stabbed. One had been beheaded.

Isabel looked away, not needing the graphic images, and wrapped her arms around herself.

"That's what real collateral damage looks like, Ms. Vargas," Allison said. "Those are innocent people who got in your uncle's way."

"Stop it!" Dutch scooped up the pictures. "She's upset. But she'll help us. Isabel just needs time to cool off."

"You didn't seem so certain of her help on the phone." Allison dug through the stack of folders and pulled out a red file.

"Don't you dare show that to her," Dutch said. "It's going too far. She doesn't need to see it to help us."

Isabel swallowed past the tightening in her throat. What more could there be?

"During your heart-to-heart last night," Allison said, "you didn't tell her that her uncle is responsible for her father's death? That dear Uncle Emilio ordered the hit because there was an internal disagreement on how best to manage the cartel's operations?"

A shocking jolt ran through Isabel like a bucket of ice water had been dumped over her.

"Damn it!" Dutch said.

Allison slapped the red folder down on the table. "Open it."

Dutch sat and turned Isabel's chair toward him, taking her hands in his. "Sweetheart, now you know. There's no reason to open it. You don't need to see the pictures of your father. Of the informant who was going to testify, but your uncle got to him first. Please don't look at it."

After everything she'd already learned, *this* truth was the most gut-wrenching. Uncle Emilio's love for her, his attention, concern, generosity was bred from guilt for killing her father?

Isabel's heart sank. There was a heaviness in her chest, making it hard to catch her breath.

*This isn't real.* She must be trapped in a nightmare, unable to wake up. This was a movie, a sick novel. Not her life.

She looked at the red folder and shook her head, not wanting it to be true, but knowing deep down on some level that it was. She remembered the arguments and fights between her father and uncle.

Had she blocked it all out and simply gone along with the stories they'd told her?

"I asked to come here," Isabel said, growing numb inside, needing distance, "even though I'd already decided to help you because it's the right thing to do. This is what it has gotten me. The last truth I needed to know. Will you all please excuse me while I look at it?"

On her own, without any crutches.

"You don't have to and definitely not alone," Dutch said. "I'm here for you."

The sincerity gleaming in his brown eyes and radiating in his voice was heartbreaking.

"This is something I have to do," Isabel said. "Alone."

FOLLOWING DRAPER AND Allison into the hall, Dutch hated to leave Isabel. Her life had been torn apart and she needed comfort. Not isolation.

Draper walked away as if relieved things were settled, with no concern to the impact this was having on Isabel. Allison hung back at the end of the hall, waiting, like she knew Dutch had a bone to pick with her.

"What the hell was that in there?" Dutch asked her. "A good cop, bad cop routine? You're supposed to be the nice one."

"Did Draper ever tell you my specialty?"

Taken aback, Dutch paused for a beat, taking a breath. "No."

Allison clutched the folders to her chest. "Think of me as the closer. A witness gets nervous while waiting to testify, I put their minds at ease and bolster their confidence. An asset that we've reeled in needs the right push to seal the deal, they call me. I read the room, I read the person and do whatever is necessary."

His gaze dropped to the files in her arms. "What's in the other folders?"

"I was prepared for any angle I needed to exploit."

"You went too far. You didn't have to break her heart. She loves her uncle."

"That love was the last hurdle. If there was any doubt in your girlfriend's mind before she came here, I guarantee you there's none left now. And I'll sleep soundly tonight knowing that we've locked in our high-priority asset."

"She's a person, you know. With feelings."

"Tell that to my seven-year-old son who I'm trying to protect. You chose your fake girlfriend and her feelings over us, your fellow marshals and our families." She took a deep breath and sighed. "Getting the hard drive back is crucial. In the event you can't, destroy it." She took a small metal device that was the size of a hockey puck from her suit jacket pocket. "It's a degausser and will wipe the drive clean if it comes in contact with it for at least two minutes."

"You need to come up with an exit strategy for Isabel in case she decides to leave."

"An exit for you two together? Or separate?"

He lowered his gaze and rubbed his forehead. "I don't know yet."

"Once you figure it out, let me know. I'm heading back to San Diego today. But there's still a problem. Vargas has seen the files, which means every marshal in my office is in danger as long as he lives. I'm sure he has our personal information memorized. There's no telling how long it'll take the FBI to build their case. If you get a clear shot at Vargas, take it."

"Are you asking me to kill him?" In Delta Force, eliminating targets was a part of the job, but those days were behind him. He was no longer an assassin for Uncle Sam or anyone else.

"I'm asking you to secure sensitive information and to end this once and for all."

No TEARS SHED. No screams of outrage.

Isabel pulled herself together and closed the red folder on the pictures of her father's bullet-riddled body and the brutally killed informant who'd witnessed his murder and had intended to testify against Emilio.

Nothing in her life made sense.

"I'm sorry Allison was so horrible," Dutch said, coming back into the conference room. "Can I get you anything?"

"I'll help you retrieve the database, but he doesn't want me to come down for the auction."

"We'll brainstorm a reason for you to be there. A problem with one of the vendors maybe."

She stood and hiked her purse strap on her shoulder. "I want to leave."

"We should talk about what you learned."

Talk? She could barely stand. Her legs shook so badly, it'd take all her strength to walk to the car without falling over.

She glanced through the glass walls of the conference room at the marshals watching them. "Not here. Not now. Please, take me to the gallery."

Dutch nodded and got her out of the building as quickly as possible. Without pushing conversation, he sped to the I-10. He gave her silence, he gave her space, but it couldn't last forever.

"I don't think you should go to the art gallery," he said, exiting the freeway. "We should go back to the apartment, talk, sort through how you must be feeling."

"I have work to do. I need to finish organizing the auction for my…" The breath caught in her throat. "For Emilio. It's easier to do it from the office."

"We need to talk. I know this isn't easy for you."

"How will it work in San Diego? The ins and outs. What should I expect?"

"The database is on a hard drive in Emilio's safe. I need to find it."

"The safe is in his office. I know where, but it requires his fingerprint to access it."

He nodded. "We need to get the hard drive or erase it with a degausser."

"What's that?"

"It emits a high-intensity magnetic field that'll erase the data. We need to do it before the auction during a time when the guards will be distracted, then we get out."

"What happens to me? He'll know I helped you, that I was a part of it."

"You'll have a choice. I can make it look like you didn't know, leave you tied up, gagged."

For a second, when he'd said he wouldn't leave her behind, she'd believed him.

"Once the FBI is able to arrest him later," Dutch continued, "then we could be together if you wanted."

Her vision hazed. "Later when?"

"I don't know how much longer the FBI needs to build their case. It could be weeks, months. This isn't my first choice."

"Then what is?" she asked, looking at him.

The creases in his forehead were deeper, his eyes wider. "You leave with me. But that means walking away from everything. The gallery. Brenda. This lifestyle. The FBI will eventually seize all of your uncle's assets anyway."

"You're saying that no matter what, I'll lose the gallery?" The art gallery she'd poured her heart and soul into, built up from nothing and created a reputation that others envied. And lose her best friend.

She had the unsettling realization that her whole life was slipping through her fingers and she was powerless to stop it.

"Yes, you'll lose the gallery, and if they can tie the money your father left you to any RICO charges on your uncle, they'll freeze that, too," Dutch said. "We could go away together. I'll use my vacation days. We can take a long trip to give you time to decide if you still want to be with me."

She shook off the apprehension slithering through her. "And vice versa, I suppose."

"No, beautiful." He took her hand. "I love you. I want you. I've almost been fired twice in the last twenty-four hours because of it. For knocking the daylights out of Ellis and then for telling you the truth. Isabel, what we share is real. Realer than anything I've had before. Last night, I chose you over everything else because I don't want to lose you. We're just getting started."

It would've been the path of least resistance for Dutch to continue to lie, to sleep with her when she was throwing herself at him, but he hadn't. He'd turned down sex and chosen honesty.

Chosen her.

Dutch stopped in front of the gallery. "Don't you want to see what's possible for us as a couple? I do. We can find out, no matter how you want to play it in San Diego with your uncle. And if you decide that you want me to disappear, where you never see or hear from me again, it'll break my heart, but I'll respect your wishes. Just think about it. Okay?"

"You lied to me," she said, pulling her hand away. It was a hard thing to get over. Like climbing Mount Everest with no training, no gear, struggling through the change in altitude and lower oxygen pressure.

A wounded expression crossed his face. "Our chemistry is undeniable. My body reacts to yours, your touch, your kisses, hell, your voice. I love the way you taste, the way you smell. I think about you all the time. How to bring a smile to your face, to ease your troubles. And it's not just attraction. Think about those two days we spent together in your apartment. We mesh, sweetheart. You and I—it's kismet."

She looked out the window at the sign on her art gallery. *Kismet.*

There was no better word to describe how she felt about Dutch, destiny, fate, but a part of her couldn't help but wonder if he was playing her. Not that he had any reason to at this point.

Her uncle was the devil. Satan incarnate. He murdered her father. She was furious at Uncle Emilio. It didn't take a holier-than-thou angel to help.

"I don't know if I want to be with you," she said, the lie tasting bitter. God help her, she did want him and felt like the biggest fool for it. "I need to work for a few hours."

"Let me make sure it's safe for you to go in first."

He hopped out and ran inside. She watched him speak to Brenda for a minute, and he came back.

Dutch opened the door for her.

She climbed down from the truck. "I'll call you when I'm ready to leave."

"I'm going to park around back and order us some food to be delivered. You must be starved and I'm not leaving you," he said. Isabel opened her mouth to protest, but he went on, "It's too dangerous. I stay with you. Got it?"

"Fine," she said, too tired to argue. She turned and strode inside the gallery.

"How did it go last night?" Brenda asked, rising from her seat, bright-eyed and excited.

"Not as I expected."

"Oh, really?" Brenda frowned. "I was confident he'd be good in bed and I can tell that he's really into you. He seems like he'd be a generous lover. What went wrong?"

Isabel shook her head, not wanting to get into it. Not having the strength to say it all out loud. "The timing was off. We didn't make it to the bed. Then there was Chad. He blew up Dutch's motorcycle."

"What?" Brenda rushed around to her. "Chad is a total sicko. He scares me. I bet the cops won't be able to prove that it was him."

"Probably not." She set her purse down on the reception desk. "If you have any free time, I have a ton of stuff to do for my uncle's event in San Diego and could use your help."

"Sure, whatever you need."

A knock came at the back door.

"It's Dutch," Isabel said. "I'll let him in. He's going to hang around today."

"Aww. That's sweet."

If only her friend knew the ugly, bitter truth. Sweet had nothing to do with it.

Isabel went to the back door and put her hand on the handle. "Dutch?" No such thing as too careful.

"Yeah, it's me."

She opened the door for him. Stepping inside, he shoved his badge into his pocket, but kept his gun.

"How am I supposed to explain you're armed?" she asked.

"You've got a dangerous stalker who blew up my bike. That's explanation enough."

She turned to go to her office.

"Hey," he said, taking her wrist softly and a shiver ran through her at his touch.

Slowly he put her palm to his chest over his heart and cupped her face with his other hand, holding her gaze.

She tried to dismiss the way his gentle strength made her body thrum with electricity. The natural closeness that'd built between them, getting stronger each day. But how he made her feel was impossible to ignore. Impossible to deny.

"May I kiss you?" he asked, his voice deep and husky, stirring heat low in her belly.

The sexiest part wasn't that this gorgeous hunk of a man could have his pick of women and wanted her. It wasn't the tingles flooding her thighs or her chest tightening with anticipation. It wasn't even that he seemed unaware of the effect he had on her.

The sexiest, hottest part was that he knew she was vulnerable and emotionally fragile and rather than taking a kiss when he could've easily done so, he'd asked.

Because he'd never harm her.

Even in front of his boss and Allison, he stood up for her, sought to protect her, defend her.

So what if it made her a fool. "Yes."

He pressed his mouth to hers in the barest of touch. Brushed his lips across hers with such fierce tenderness in a whisper of a kiss that sent arousal humming through her body.

"If you can forgive me, if you come with me, I'll prove to you every day how much I care about you. Not just with words, but with my actions. I swear it."

A lump formed in her throat and she didn't know what to say. "I need to think about it."

He nodded and let her go.

Isabel smoothed down her skirt and walked back to the front. She felt his eyes on her and unlike creepy Chad, she liked the idea of Dutch watching her, wanting her.

"I ordered food for the three of us from the grill," he said. "I hope that's okay."

"Sounds great to me." Brenda put a vase of fresh-cut flowers on the desk. "Very thoughtful of you."

Deep burgundy long-stem roses called Black Pearl. Isabel hadn't noticed them when she came in. "You bought flowers to dress up the place?"

"No," Brenda said, arranging them. "They were delivered this morning without a card."

"Do you think they're from Chad?" Isabel asked Dutch, turning to face him, but his gaze had veered past her to something outside. She glanced over her shoulder.

A black van rolled by. The man from the grocery store with teardrop tattoos sat in the passenger's seat. He stuck the barrel of a machine gun out the window.

Isabel froze.

# Chapter Eighteen

Time stretched, slowing, moving at half speed as a black van inched down the street. A man stuck a Heckler & Koch MP5 out the window.

Dutch didn't have much time to think, to assess. They were all in serious trouble standing in front of the plate glass window with nothing to stop the rounds that were about to tear through them.

The man lifted the MP5 and let it rip, spraying the front of the gallery. Bullets shattered the plate glass, stitching in a fiery line toward them. Dutch grabbed Isabel, whirling her away from the incoming fire, as he dove to the floor.

Brenda was hit instantly and sent spinning and falling. The vase burst. Jagged shards of glass flew everywhere like tiny projectiles.

Shielding Isabel with his body, Dutch forced her to low crawl toward the back of the desk. He feared the men outside would stop the vehicle and come into the gallery to make sure they'd finished the job.

Rounds were still being sprayed on full automatic, punching into the walls, shredding paintings. He and Isabel skirted behind the desk, beating the deadly fusillade by a blink of an eye. Bullets pounded into the solid wood, thuds reverberating through his body.

"Keep your head down," Dutch said to Isabel and drew his weapon.

Flipping off his safety, he peered over the top of the desk and pulled the trigger, returning fire. Every shot he squeezed off was controlled and well aimed.

A hot slug slammed into the shooter, throwing him back into the vehicle.

The driver accelerated and the van hurtled forward with its tires squealing.

"Stay here." Dutch raced to the front, out onto the sidewalk, and watched the vehicle speed away. He scanned for any other threats.

No secondary shooters on foot. Only terrified passersby.

He ran back inside and checked on Brenda. She lay on her back, rolling left and right. A red blotch on her abdomen seeped wider, dripping blood on the hardwood. Another bullet got her in the shoulder just under her collarbone. She was alive, but not for much longer if she didn't get medical attention.

"Isabel, grab a towel, a piece of cloth, anything you can find."

Glass crunched as she scurried to her feet. Seconds later she came to him, carrying a silk scarf. She screamed, a blood-curdling cry that he'd never forget.

"Oh, God!" A choking sob left Isabel. "Brenda!"

Dutch snatched the scarf from her, tore it and pressed the pieces to Brenda's wounds. "Put your hands here," he said to Isabel. "Apply pressure. Don't worry about hurting her. We've got to slow the bleeding."

Isabel dropped to her knees with no care about the broken glass that bit into her skin and replaced his hands with her own. Dutch took out his cell phone and dialed 911.

Before he'd finished with the emergency dispatch operator, the sound of approaching sirens split the air. Someone else must've already called them. Help was on the way.

Brenda was still conscious, which was a good sign. Her blood wasn't a dark red like her liver had been punctured, but the bullet might've hit her stomach. It was a nasty wound.

The ambulance and police arrived at virtually the same time. EMTs rushed inside while the police cordoned off the area, driving onlookers back from the scene.

Dutch holstered his weapon and flashed his badge to the cops. After the EMTs loaded Brenda on a stretcher, he helped Isabel climb into the back of the ambulance to ride along.

"I'll give a statement and meet you at the hospital," Dutch

said. He'd call Draper and have him or Allison head over to keep Isabel safe until Dutch could get there.

Isabel swallowed hard and horror was stamped on her face. She brushed her hair back with a bloody hand, nodding that she'd heard him, but her glassy eyes were focused on her best friend.

"Brenda? Brenda!" Isabel took her hand, but her friend didn't answer.

Fear speared him as Brenda's head lolled to the side. She wasn't conscious.

"Why won't she wake up?" Isabel asked, her gaze bouncing from an EMT to Dutch.

His fear spread. If Brenda didn't make it, the loss would crush Isabel.

The EMT put an oxygen mask on Brenda. "We've got to get her to the hospital now." He closed the rear doors and the ambulance pulled away.

Life wasn't cutting Isabel any slack. It had been one horrible thing after another. No matter how strong a person was, everyone had a limit. A breaking point.

Dutch didn't think Isabel could take much more before she reached hers.

Even though she was justifiably ticked off at him, he hoped she'd let him be there for her to help her get through all this. She needed someone to lean on now more than ever.

He whipped out his phone and dialed Draper, updating him quickly so Isabel would be protected at the hospital.

"Sir," a police officer said, approaching him with two others, as Dutch hung up, "we're going to need to know exactly what happened here."

The cops didn't give Dutch a chance to catch his breath before they launched in with their questions.

"HORATIO HAAS IS definitely a US marshal," the new PI said to Chad. "First, they went to the US Marshals Service building earlier and now he's flashing a badge to every cop he speaks to about the shooting."

That explained why the police hadn't arrested him, giving Chad's attorney the runaround and flimsy excuses. But why would the Marshals be watching Isabel?

She wasn't into anything illegal and neither was her best friend, Brenda. But the Marshals had definitely been set up across the street from the gallery for a reason.

"Are you sure Isabel is okay?"

"Yes, she's fine. She got into the ambulance with the other woman."

*Good.* Chad didn't want anything to happen to his Isabel unless he determined that she deserved it. And even then, Chad would be the one to dispense punishment. Him and no one else.

"Find out why the Marshals are interested in Isabel."

"That means pulling my surveillance on Haas."

"Understood." On that front, the PI had served his purpose, and Chad could track Isabel from her phone. "This is more important."

"I still have a few contacts in the FBI. They might be able to find out something, but it'll cost you."

Tell Chad something new. He was used to paying to get what he wanted. "I need to know what the Marshals have on her. The cost doesn't concern me. I want answers ASAP."

ISABEL SAT IN the waiting room, wringing her hands, while Brenda was in surgery.

The two marshals she'd met earlier sat across from her, giving her breathing room. She didn't want to see or talk to either of them right now. If they hadn't insisted that their presence was necessary to ensure her safety, she would've thrown them out.

The nightmare kept getting worse, spiraling, growing bigger, darker, consuming every good thing in her life.

*Brenda.* What if her best friend died because of her?

Her bloody hands were shaking so badly she didn't know what to do with them.

Dutch shoved through the double doors, carrying the purse she'd forgotten. Her eyes fluttered shut on an overwhelming wave of relief. Then it morphed slowly with each step he took toward her, changing into an indescribable need to be held. By him.

She stood, dizzy, aching from head to toe, and reached for him. He pulled her into his arms. It was all too much being thrown at her, life forcing her to drink from a firehose of crap on full blast. She was drowning. She needed his comfort and was too weak to turn it down.

The other two marshals stood and headed for the door. "Dutch, give me a call when you get a chance," his boss said.

"Sure."

Once they left, Isabel let fresh tears fall.

"This is my fault," she said. "Brenda got shot because of me. Oh, God, she could die."

"No, sweetheart." Dutch stroked her hair, his voice calm and steady. "This is your uncle's fault. His and no one else's."

The realization hit her that if Dutch hadn't been there, if that stolen database hadn't brought him into her life—even by duplicitous means—she and Brenda would both be dead. Victims of her uncle's turf war.

Her knees gave out.

Dutch caught her and helped her sit in a chair. "Give me a minute." He got up to leave.

"Don't go." She clutched his arm, something in her chest unraveling like a pulled spool of thread. "I need you to stay."

He kissed her forehead. "One minute. Two tops. I'll just be in the hall, a few feet away, and be right back." Then he hustled out of the waiting room.

True to his word, he was back in two minutes, carrying a candy bar and a cup of coffee. He pushed both into her trembling hands. "You need to eat. We've got to get your blood sugar up and some caffeine in your system. It'll help."

She shook her head. The thought of eating repulsed her.

"You need your strength. For Brenda. Eat, honey."

She bit into chocolate and caramel, not tasting it, and washed it down with a few sips of coffee. One nibble after the other, she ate the candy bar and drank the black coffee.

Her nerves were still scraped raw, but her jitters faded, and her legs felt solid again.

For hours, they sat in the small room that had muted colors, waiting for an update on Brenda. Dutch's arms around her, enveloping her in his warm protectiveness, was the only thing holding her together.

Finally, a doctor came in, pulling off his green scrub cap. "Are you the relatives of Brenda Reaver?"

Isabel stood and Dutch was up on his feet beside her. "I'm her best friend, Isabel Vargas. Her parents live in Ohio, but I'm her emergency contact here in LA for everything. Is she going to live?"

"Your friend got lucky. One bullet broke her clavicle and the other just missed her stomach. She lost a lot of blood and we had to give her a transfusion, but she's going to pull through."

Isabel released the breath that had bunched in her lungs. "Thank God."

"You'll want to contact her parents and have them fly out. She's going to need help for the next few weeks while she recuperates."

Isabel had wanted to wait until Brenda was out of surgery to tell them their daughter would recover or...

"Okay. Can I see her now?" Isabel asked.

"The best thing you can do for her now is let her rest. Come by tomorrow."

Isabel nodded, not liking it, but understanding.

"Let's get you to the apartment so you can clean up," Dutch said. "You're covered in blood."

She didn't object when Dutch led her out of the hospital and guided her into the car.

While he ran into doggie day care to get McQueen, she called Brenda's parents. The machine at their house picked up, which wasn't surprising. For a couple in their sixties, they were active and social and were usually only home in the evenings, but Isabel didn't have their cell numbers. She left a brief message, focusing on the fact that Brenda was going to recover and that they should fly out.

Despite Dutch's assurances that this wasn't her fault, guilt plagued her.

The door opened and McQueen leapt in, tail wagging, excited to see her, but she couldn't even pet him. She was trapped in a miasma of fear and darkness. Dutch tossed a small bag of dog food into the back seat and she was grateful he'd thought of it. If not for him, poor McQueen would starve.

At the apartment building, Dutch parked away from the burned spot where his motorcycle had been torched. She drifted into the building, into the elevator, through the apartment, bedroom and found herself in the bathroom.

Kicking off her shoes, she started the shower. Her chest was tight, a crushing pressure building, coiling, winding deeper.

She stepped into the shower, fully clothed, sat under the spray and tucked her knees into her chest. Letting the hot water cascade over her, she prayed it might warm her. She was cold, so very cold, and trembling uncontrollably.

Everything she'd been through with Chad, everything she'd learned over the past twenty-four hours turned over in her mind. A sick feeling ballooned in her stomach. With a flash of panic, it dawned on her that life as she knew it was over.

The water slid from hot to lukewarm. She had lost track of time with no way to tell how long she'd been in there.

Dutch knocked on the door. It was still open. She'd never closed it. He peeked inside. The expression on his face was a heartbreaking mix of worry and affection. He came in, pulled off his boots and socks and climbed into the shower.

He lifted her from the tile floor, peeled off her top and skirt, leaving on her underwear. Then he washed her. Lathered her hair with shampoo, ran her bath sponge over her face, scrubbed the blood from her hands, checked for embedded glass in her legs. Holding her up under the spray, he rinsed the suds from her body.

No one had ever cared for her like this. Completely. Tenderly. Asking for nothing in return. There was no reason for him to go to such trouble unless he felt something real for her.

He turned off the water, grabbed a towel and wrapped it around her. Stepping out of the shower, he looked down at his sopping-wet clothes. A grimace crossed his face as he undressed like he wished there was a better alternative than tracking water through the apartment.

Keeping on his boxer-briefs, he lifted her into his arms and carried her to the bed. Dutch laid her down and threw the bedspread over her. He sat on the floor beside her, with his back against the nightstand, and stroked her hair, over and over, driving her mind to empty.

She was tired and aching and wanted to give in to the exhaustion that clawed at her. To surrender to Dutch's soothing caresses and close her eyes, to sleep. But she couldn't.

Pain churned, rubbing coarse as sandpaper against her insides.

Her heart wanted him, and her brain longed for an escape, but her body *needed* a release. "Dutch," she said, her voice hoarse and low, "make love to me. Help me forget every horrible thing that's happened for a little while."

He took her hand and kissed it. "I don't want you to regret this later."

"I'd only regret it if the way you say you feel about me is a lie."

"It's not. I swear. But your emotions are running high. This might be a bad idea."

"I'm an adult. I know what's best for me, what I need, what I want." Tugging his hand, she urged him up from the floor.

No resistance given, he slipped into the bed. "If you change your mind at any time and want me to stop, I will. No matter how difficult that might be. Just say the word."

This was why she trusted him in that moment, sought refuge and comfort in his arms. Even though he was strong and powerful, to the point of imposing in a scary way, and could be violent when necessary, she was safe with him, wasn't afraid of him.

There was no doubt in her mind that if she asked him to stop, he would. Every woman deserved that kind of sound assurance from the person they were with, but this was the first time she had it.

"I can just hold you if you want," he said, offering her another out, and it was another first.

She cupped the back of his head and brought his mouth to hers. In an instant, he covered her with his body, the contact lighting up her nerve endings.

Raising her hips to meet his, she telegraphed her urgency. He looked into her eyes, and she saw passion and heat and a similar plea for connection, for communion, that they were both powerless to deny.

Her whole body screamed for friction, for the need to have their bodies joined, for a release that could only be found in his arms.

He removed the little remaining physical barriers between them. There was heat and need in his gaze. He ran his hands over her body and moaned as if he'd been longing for this, too. Her nipples peaked and tightened beneath his tongue, and she was amazed by how quickly her body responded to him, growing soft and pliant and wet.

Moving his hand down to the welcoming spot between

her legs, he slid his fingers between her folds. He watched her face, reading her responses for what she liked and didn't. His thumb circled her tight bundle of nerves and she gasped with pleasure.

He kissed his way down her body, diving beneath the sheet, his face settling between her thighs, treating her yet again to another first.

The sensation of his tongue, his fingers and lips all converged, swelling, cresting. It was devastating in the best way possible as an orgasm tore through her. She clutched at his hair, wishing the strands were longer, the backs of her knees over his shoulders, her heels digging into his back, and screamed his name.

Once she settled, he crawled up and hugged her to him. Her breath slowly steadied, and she remembered her name.

Brushing the hair out of her face, he looked down at her. "Should we stop? Or should I grab a condom?"

An ache drilled deep into her heart. She'd never been with anyone so generous and kind. Who'd disregard their own needs for the sake of hers.

Never had she felt more connected to another. Cherished. This was what she wanted, someone who saw through the superficial and desired her despite her flaws. Someone who'd put her ahead of anything else.

If only she could get over the humiliation of being used, the betrayal that gutted her.

Hope welled inside her but didn't scare her. Quite the opposite. In a way, it was setting her free from her past and opening the door to possibilities she'd never dared entertain before.

She caressed his cheek and kissed him, hot and needy for more. For everything he had to give. At least for tonight. "Condom."

# Chapter Nineteen

Dutch awoke the next morning with Isabel in his arms, her head nuzzled between his neck and shoulder, her breath warm on his cheek, their legs tangled.

By nightfall last night, they'd both been famished. He'd whipped up spaghetti carbonara with the ingredients he had handy in the fridge. They'd eaten, made love again and went back to sleep.

Without a doubt, he knew in his heart he wanted to make her happy, give her everything she needed and asked of him and more. She deserved that and nothing less. It was staggering to realize how long he'd lived without ever knowing this feeling of rightness, completeness with another person. He never wanted to be without her again.

There were no presumptions on his part. She'd needed comfort and it didn't have to mean anything more to her. She was entitled to stay angry, but he hoped she'd agree to the trip he'd promised and then they could take it from there. No pressure. No stress. Give her time to sort through everything, and when she was ready, figure out her feelings for him. He'd be patient and wait, no matter how long it took.

First, he needed to keep her safe and get them both through the next couple of days unscathed.

Isabel roused, stretching. "I feel like I've been drugged. What time is it?"

He kissed her forehead. "Late. Almost ten."

"I can't believe I slept so long."

"You were exhausted and needed the rest. I crept out around dawn and took McQueen for a quick walk."

"Thank you." She rubbed his chest and sat up. "About last night. I needed to feel better, to lose myself for a little while, and you were there for me. I appreciate it. But I haven't made a decision about us and what I want to do."

"That's understandable. I don't want you to feel rushed, but you'll need to know by the time we take the hard drive."

She nodded. "I'm going to shower and dress. I want to go to the hospital and see Brenda."

"You need to call your uncle and give us a reason to go down today."

"My uncle's turf war has given us the best excuse. I'll need to finish the preparations on-site since I can't work from the office. Come to think of it, you should speak to him. If he knows about the attempted hit on my life, he'll welcome us with open arms."

"All right." He waited until she was in the shower and dug out the card that Vargas had given him at the club. Punching in the number on his cell, he considered whether to tell her uncle about Chad Ellis. The man was a threat but sharing that with Vargas had to be Isabel's choice, not Dutch's. The last thing she would want was for him to make decisions for her.

"Who is this?" her uncle answered.

"Dutch Haas. I'm not calling with good news."

"My niece hasn't pushed back on you being her bodyguard, has she?"

"No, it's not that. Unfortunately, she learned why she needs one. The Guzman cartel made a move on her. They sent her a pig's head with an ace of spades. Then they shot up her art gallery. Her best friend, Brenda Reaver, survived, but had to go through surgery."

"Damn it," Vargas growled over the line. "Is Isabel all right?"

"More or less. Physically she's fine, but she's quite shaken up. After what's happened, she wants to come to San Diego to take her mind off things and finish the preparations for your event."

"Yes, of course. Shall I send a helicopter for you?" Vargas asked.

"No, thanks. We'll drive." Dutch rubbed his forehead. "You said you were going to handle the Guzman problem."

"And I am. I'll move up the strike I have planned to tonight. Going after Isabel won't be tolerated. Retaliation must be swift and brutal and leave no doubt in the minds of my enemies what the consequences are."

No need to ask for the particulars to know that a lot of blood was going to be shed.

"There's something you need to understand," Vargas said. "Once Isabel is finished with the final preparations tomorrow, I want the two of you sequestered in the west wing of my villa. The individuals coming in for the auction aren't the sort I want Isabel consorting with. That's the reason I didn't want her here for the event."

"Okay. I'll come up with a reason for us to stay in the west wing." They needed to be out of the villa well before the auction, not locked inside. "We'll see you later." Dutch disconnected and looked at the clock.

The auction was set to take place tomorrow evening at eight. If they got on the road by three at the latest and didn't hit too much traffic, they'd have plenty of time to get the hard drive.

Dutch got ready as quickly as possible once Isabel was out of the bathroom. They boarded McQueen at the day care facility and swung by the hospital.

Brenda was sleeping when they arrived, perfectly natural according to the nurse and the best thing to help her recovery.

They sat quietly at Brenda's bedside. He held Isabel's hand, lending his strength, doing his best not to hurry her along.

Time ticked away, one hour slipping into the next. They were losing the day.

The USMS couldn't pull this off without her, but Dutch was painfully aware that few people in her life had put her first. There was no changing the fact that she was an asset the Marshals were exploiting, but he had to find a way to balance the constraints of the mission with Isabel's needs. He wouldn't let her become collateral damage.

Brenda stirred, her head moving from side to side. Her eyes fluttered open. She looked around, wildly, disoriented.

Isabel gently took her hand that bore the needle from the IV. "The doctor said you're going to be fine. I called your parents."

Brenda's gaze settled on Isabel. Her dry lips mouthed, *You okay?*

The woman had been shot twice, spent four hours in surgery fighting for her life and had slept nearly a day. Once she finally opened her eyes, her concern wasn't for herself. It was for Isabel.

Watching the two of them broke Dutch's heart.

Isabel nodded as a tear slipped from her eye. "I'm okay. Thanks to Dutch."

Brenda flashed a weak smile. Then her eyes closed, and she slipped back into unconsciousness.

A sob broke free from Isabel. She turned to Dutch and he brought her into his arms.

"I hate him," she said in a harsh whisper, her voice brittle. "I hate Emilio so much." She wept, her body trembling with what he guessed was a mix of sorrow and loathing.

Dutch shushed her, stroking her hair. The cold, hard truth of her words made something in his chest clench.

Would Isabel be able to face her uncle, hide what she'd learned, disguise her feelings? She wasn't an actress, a professional trained in deception.

Could she still be the asset they desperately needed? Or was she about to become their biggest liability?

THEY ARRIVED AT Vargas's place well after sundown, but there was no mistaking the villa was in fact a fortified compound crawling with guards.

Dutch had done his best to prep Isabel on the ride, guiding

her in how to behave around her uncle. He hoped it'd alleviate some of his worries, but he'd only reinforced his concerns.

She was too sad, too angry, too volatile—an emotional powder keg waiting for a spark.

The best thing to do was abort, but they were down to the wire. He had to roll the dice, have faith in Isabel and pray this worked out.

After the front gates opened, he drove his truck up the long path.

"I need to know why my uncle killed my father. How could he do such a thing? Over business? They were close. They loved each other. I don't understand."

"Money and power are strong motivators. They can make people do ugly, regrettable things."

Isabel trembled, rubbing her palms on her thighs. She looked fragile, on the cusp of breaking. "I'm not sure I can do this."

With all the new information thrown at her, he could only imagine how she felt.

"You can do this. You're going to be fine." She had to be, or he was as good as dead and there was no telling what Vargas would do to Isabel.

He drove around the elegant circular driveway with a large fountain in the middle.

Rodrigo stood at the bottom of the steps that led up to the main building and greeted them. He opened Isabel's door, and helped her from the vehicle.

Dutch cut the engine and came around the front of the truck.

"Keys," Rodrigo said to him. "I'll have it parked." He gestured off to the side where several black SUVs sat in front of a four-bay garage. "We'll have your things brought up to your rooms."

Dutch tossed him his keys.

"Rooms?" Isabel asked, emphasizing the *s*.

"Your uncle would prefer if you two didn't share a room. It's old-fashioned, I know, but he won't bend on it."

Rolling her eyes, she crossed her arms. "I can't wait to give him a piece of my mind."

Great. One more thing to poke the bear, Dutch thought.

"I've got to pat you down," Rodrigo said.

Nodding, Dutch extended his arms. Since he'd expected a pat down and to have his things searched, he'd given Isabel the degausser and the forensic lifting tape to get her uncle's fingerprint. She'd stashed both in her purse.

Once Rodrigo was satisfied, he said, "Your uncle is waiting in the courtyard to have dinner."

Isabel marched off, her heels clacking against the stone steps, spiking Dutch's trepidation.

He hurried after her. When he caught up, he took her arm, encouraging her to slow down. "Don't forget the objective. Dinner is perfect. He'll have something to drink and we can pull a print from the glass. Please, try to remain calm."

A guard opened the front door. They entered a palatial foyer, chandeliers glittering. He followed Isabel past a grand staircase. They crossed a room with a wall of windows thirty feet high that faced the ocean and went out through another door.

The courtyard was breathtaking, plucked straight from an Italian villa, and had a multimillion-dollar view of the ocean. Torches blazed and candlelight gleamed, bouncing off the silverware and crystal on the table.

*"Mi hija,"* Vargas said, standing with his arms outstretched to Isabel. "How are you?"

She went to her uncle, allowing him to kiss both her cheeks. "I'm fine." Her voice was cold and sharp, her face stern. She sat opposite him and draped her napkin across her lap.

"Mr. Vargas." Dutch shook his hand.

"Please, call me Emilio." He gestured for Dutch to sit to his right. "Your fortitude is remarkable, my dear. Dutch told me about the crazy, random drive-by shooting at your gallery. I'm sorry to hear your friend was injured. It's unfortunate such things happen in this day and age. How is Brenda doing?"

Isabel clenched her jaw. "She's going to recover, thankfully. Her parents will fly out as soon as they can."

"I'd like to pay for her medical bills as well as her parents' expenses. We have so much good fortune. It's the least I can do to help someone you're close to."

"Yes. It is the least you can do," Isabel said, her tone scolding.

Vargas narrowed his eyes, giving her a strange look.

"What's for dinner?" Dutch asked. "Isabel has low blood sugar and we're starving."

Isabel stared at her uncle, and Dutch could feel the animosity emanating from her.

A perplexed expression crossed Vargas's face, but he picked up a bell and rang it. The tinny sound grated on Dutch's nerves.

Seconds later, servants came outside in a single, orchestrated file and placed salads in front of them. Another poured chardonnay in their wineglasses.

"Let us toast." Vargas raised his glass and waited until they had all done likewise. "To you, Isabel. May you have a long, happy, healthy life, *mi hija*. And to you, Dutch, for protecting her when I could not. Thank you. I owe you a life debt. *Salud*."

They sipped the wine and set their glasses down.

Dutch dug into the salad, but Isabel pushed the food around on her plate with her fork.

Vargas stared at her, noticing her preoccupation, too. "What's wrong? I know yesterday was difficult for you, probably terrifying. But you seem off. Like you're angry with me for some reason."

Isabel glared at her uncle, saying nothing.

Tension mounted, growing so tangible it had taken on a pulsing beat in Dutch's head. *Tick. Tick.*

"It's nothing," she finally said, lowering her gaze.

"Don't lie to me." Her uncle's voice was warm and loving. "Whatever it is, tell me."

"You should try the salad," Dutch said. "Eating will help." Though he wasn't sure if anything would make this situation better.

"Dutch, please," Vargas said and then looked at Isabel. "There's obviously something troubling you. I want to know what it is."

She threw her fork down and it clattered onto the plate. "I can't do this. Pretend like everything is all right when it isn't."

*Tick. Tick.*

"Then don't pretend." Vargas cocked his head to the side. "What can't you do? Tell me what you mean."

"You're upset," Dutch said taking her hand, but she pulled it away into her lap. *Tick. Tick.* "It's being away from Brenda when you feel she needs you." His heart ached looking at Isabel, seeing the internal struggle evident on her face.

"Is that it?" Vargas asked. "Or is it something else? Talk to me. I love you. I'm here for you. No matter what it is, you can tell me." His tone was affectionate and coaxing, his eyes pleading.

"I'm talking about how you killed my father," Isabel said, reaching her breaking point.

Uncomfortable silence reigned for the longest moment. Dutch schooled his expression and tried to think of a way out of this situation, but nothing came to mind.

"Why would you say such a thing to me?" Vargas asked, his voice so pained, it'd make anyone who hadn't seen the evidence of a feud, the pictures of her father and a witness both gunned down, doubt the accusation.

"Don't try to change the subject." Isabel tossed her napkin on the table. "I know you did it. How could you? Your own brother?"

Dutch's ears rang, clear and sharp and loud as the bell had

earlier. Sitting at the table, he felt like he was watching a six-car pileup, helpless to stop it.

Vargas leaned back in his chair, picked up his wineglass and drank. Maybe he was stalling for time, but he appeared composed, as if he wasn't the least bit worried. "This subject is Pandora's box. If you insist on removing the lid, you'll never be able to put it back on. It'll change everything for you. I ask you, as someone who has loved you from the day you were born, to let this go."

"Why did you kill him?" Isabel pressed, ignoring the warning. "For power? For money?"

"Who told you this?" Vargas asked.

"You don't get to ask me questions. Not until you've answered mine."

"Isabel, I've only sought to protect you. Let me do so now. Drop this."

"Tell me. Why did you kill my father? I have a right to know."

"I didn't kill your father," Vargas said.

"Damn you to hell! May God strike you dead for lying to my face. I loved you, looked up to you, when all along…" Her voice trailed off as tears fell from her eyes.

Vargas sighed and clucked his tongue. "My brother and I reached an impasse, where only one of us could survive, yes, but I didn't kill your father. Because… I'm your father."

Silence. Complete and total silence.

Isabel blinked at Vargas. The shock in her eyes was palpable.

It was one of those surreal, precarious moments. Dutch was too stunned to move, afraid the tiniest action on his part could tip the scales in the wrong direction.

"Your mother and I had an affair. It's the reason my wife left me," Vargas said, the words flowing unpolished, tripping over one another in a rush. "It's not something I'm proud of. When she got pregnant, Luis suspected the baby wasn't his.

After you were born, the doctors found cancer in your mother. Metastatic. Stage four. She was gone so fast. The day we buried her, Luis sat me down, told me that you were the last piece of your mother that he had left. Then he recounted a story from the Bible. The judgment of Solomon." Vargas's eyes turned glassy and the heavy emotion in his voice was undeniable. "He told me that either you were his and all would be forgiven between us. Or he would cut you in two like the baby in the story and we could each keep half of you. He claimed you, and I let him, to protect you. It was the price for peace that he demanded I pay. But I'm your father."

"No." The clipped reply emanated disbelief. "This is just another lie," Isabel said, shaking her head. "You never answered my question. You'll never tell me the truth, will you?" She shoved her chair back and stood. "You're not even sorry that you killed him. Are you?"

"I have no regrets." Vargas got up and came around the table. "It's no lie." He wrapped her in a bear hug. "I'm your father."

She squeezed her eyes shut, lifting her hands away from him as if disgusted that they were touching. "Are you the leader of *Los Chacales*?"

He lowered his head but didn't let her go. "Yes. I never wanted you to find out. I wanted you to build a life free from the dangers of my world."

"Well, you failed. Horribly." She disentangled herself from him. "I almost died, and my best friend is in the hospital because of you."

His head snapped up. "How do you know any of this? Who told you? Who is trying to turn you against me?"

Reflexively, she glanced at Dutch. Vargas's gaze followed hers.

Dutch sat still as stone. His ears weren't only ringing now, they were burning. His entire face was on fire, but he kept his gaze soft, almost questioning.

"The playing cards. There was an incident in a grocery store I didn't tell you about." She stepped back. "A man from the Guzman cartel followed me in a grocery store. Put a queen of spades card in my basket. He spoke to me. You wouldn't believe the things he said. Do you have any idea what that was like for me? Did you really think I'd never find out?"

Vargas raked his hair back with his hands. "I've worked very hard to keep you in the dark about my affairs."

"And it almost cost me my life."

"You're safe," Vargas said. "I'm taking care of the Guzman cartel."

"What does that mean?" she asked.

"The head of their cartel and all their top lieutenants will be dead before sunrise. Their cartel is like a hydra—many new heads will sprout, and they'll be too busy fighting among themselves for power and control to worry about me."

"I can't do this with you right now." She pressed her fingers to her temples. "I'll finish organizing your event tomorrow. Then I'm leaving."

"I know you doubt me and question whether I'm your father but give me the chance to prove it."

Isabel backed up with tears welling in her eyes. "I need time away from you. To clear my head. To think." She turned and rushed off into the house.

Dutch slumped in his chair, his head pounding, and noticed Isabel had left her purse.

The tape was inside. A glass with Vargas's fingerprint gleamed in the candlelight.

Groaning, Vargas pressed his fists on the table. "Why didn't you warn me and tell me she knew all of that?"

"I didn't know that was going to happen," Dutch said, letting his natural shock over Isabel's admission come through. "She told me the man who left the queen of spades in her basket spoke to her, but she didn't tell me what he said. Then everything at the gallery happened."

"I've spent three decades protecting her from the truth. Damn it!" Vargas swept his hands across the table, knocking his dishes to the floor. His glass shattered. He paced back and forth in front of the table, then caught himself and regained his composure. "Go to the kitchen. They'll give you a plate to take to your room. Get some rest. The sun will rise on a new day."

And it would be their last chance to get the hard drive. If they let emotion stop them from succeeding again, a lot of innocent people were going to die.

Dutch stood. "Let's hope tomorrow is better."

"One more thing. Respect my wishes. Stay away from Isabel's room tonight."

Isabel needed him. She needed comfort, a compassionate ear to listen, now more than ever, but under the tenuous circumstances as they were, what choice did he have? "Yes, sir."

# *Chapter Twenty*

Isabel awoke with a start, jackknifing upright in bed. She squinted against the sunlight streaming in through the windows.

The dream stayed with her, vivid, in high definition. She remembered being six or seven, Emilio buying her toys, playing with her in the yard, him making her giggle, holding her tight and singing her songs, but only when her father wasn't at the house.

She closed her eyes and heard Emilio's voice as if he was beside her. *Our little secret, mi hija. Don't tell I came to visit. Te amo.*

The fights between her father and Emilio came back to her, as well.

*Isabel is my daughter,* her father had said. *Don't ever forget that unless you want a war.*

A shudder slipped down her spine.

When she was fourteen, her boarding school in Palo Alto had held a father-daughter dance. Her dad was stuck in Mexico on important business. She'd thrown the worst fit over it, and had said ugly, bratty things to him. Emilio came, not wanting her to be disappointed. But at the end of the dance, her dad had shown up as a surprise. There'd been such tension radiating between them, but her father hadn't spoken to Emilio that night, not a single word exchanged. Like the calm before a Cat 5 hurricane.

Two weeks later, her father, Luis, was dead.

They hadn't fought over the cartel. They'd fought over her.

The pain that came from the memories was almost too much to bear, like someone had slammed a dagger in her heart and twisted.

Emilio wasn't lying. She was a product of infidelity, the cause of violence and revenge. Some truths were too terrible and should never be brought out into the light.

*Pandora's box.* He'd warned her and now she wished she never knew.

Releasing a hiss, she brought her knees up to her chest and leaned against the headboard. She wanted to leave the villa that very instant, but she had to stay and see this through. For Dutch. For the marshals who were in danger. And maybe for her own sake, too.

As she got ready for the day, she set aside her personal issues and steeled herself for what had to be done.

She went downstairs, wondering if Emilio would show his face at breakfast.

Pushing through the door that led to the courtyard, she stepped outside and had her answer.

Of course he was there. He was playing host to them and he hadn't the decency to feel any shame. Emilio sat proud as a peacock, talking to Dutch, speaking in his animated way, waving his hands.

Isabel held her head high and strode to the table. "Good morning." She kept her tone light and neutral, hiding the enormous burden weighing on her.

Dutch stood, kissed her cheek and handed her the purse she'd forgotten last night. The way she'd rushed from dinner had been clumsy and reckless. She wouldn't blame him if he was furious with her, but when she glanced at him all she saw was compassion in his eyes.

"I'm pleased you joined us, my dear," Emilio said and took a sip of his fresh-squeezed orange juice.

"I'm not here for your pleasure. I have to eat." She sat and poured herself a cup of coffee.

"Ah, so you're still cross with me." His voice was mild and amused, and it made her want to scream. "I was hoping that tomorrow we could spend the day together. Go shopping, take a walk on the beach."

As if buying her new clothes and jewelry and taking an oceanside stroll would make everything better. "Prepare for disappointment," she said. "As soon as I'm done arranging your event, Dutch and I are leaving."

That wiped the smug look from Emilio's face. "I under-stand you're angry and want to punish me, but not like this. We're family. I love you, Isabel. You must find a way to em-brace what you've learned. Or move beyond it. But I won't let you shut me out."

Emotions raged inside her. Isabel sucked in air, filling her lungs until she couldn't take in more. She shut her eyes and gritted her teeth, struggling for some semblance of control. *Keep it together. You have to do this.* "I won't be getting over it today or anytime soon."

Rodrigo entered the courtyard, came up to Emilio and whispered in his ear.

"Where do I know that name?" Emilio asked in response.

Again, Rodrigo whispered.

This time, Emilio's gaze flew up to Isabel and then whipped to Dutch. "Excuse me. I have a phone call I must take." He stood and walked into the house with Rodrigo following him.

"I'm sorry for losing it last night," Isabel said, mortified over how distracted and distraught she'd been. A complete wreck almost ruining everything.

"Don't worry about it." Dutch unzipped her purse and fished out the special tape.

God, she needed to quit getting sidetracked.

Working quickly, he ripped off a piece of tape, carefully took Emilio's glass by the top, and pressed the adhesive to where his thumb had been minutes ago.

Dutch peeled off the tape and held the small strip up to the light. There was a clear, solid print.

They got it.

Dutch lowered his hand seconds before the door to the house opened.

Emilio waltzed out with Rodrigo and Max. And two more guards.

She clenched her napkin in her lap. "Is everything all right?"

"I received a call from your ex-boyfriend, the business

owner," Emilio said. "Chad Ellis. He's concerned about you and had some very interesting things to say."

Why would Chad call her uncle... Emilio? How did he even know she was there? "You shouldn't listen to anything he says. Chad hasn't gotten over the breakup. He's having difficulty letting go. I'm sure he's just trying to stir up trouble." To make her life miserable.

"That may be," Emilio said. "But I think Dutch can help me get to the bottom of it. Dutch, would you come with me?"

It might've sounded like a question, but it was an order.

"Can this wait?" Isabel asked, tension surging through her. "I need Dutch's help with the final preparations."

"No, it can't wait." Emilio delivered the statement like the crack of a whip. "Max will stay at your side and assist you with anything you need."

Her stomach plummeted to her toes. The plan was to show Dutch the office and let him take it from there. She wasn't a marshal or a spy or remotely capable of handling this.

Dutch flashed a cool smile. "It's okay, Isabel." He got up and leaned over toward her. As he kissed her cheek, he slipped the strip of tape with the fingerprint into her hand. Then in her ear, he said, "The degausser needs to be in contact for two minutes. Leave me behind."

Her breath hitched. *No, no, no.*

She couldn't do this without him, and she certainly wasn't leaving him.

Isabel went to grab his arm and keep him there with her, but he stood, moving out of reach.

Dutch looked at Emilio. "There must be a misunderstanding. I'm sure we can clear it up."

"I hope so."

The two guards seized Dutch by his arms.

Her pulse skyrocketed. She didn't understand what was happening, but she knew it wasn't good. Dutch was in trouble.

"This is ridiculous. Where are you taking him?" she demanded.

"It's okay," Dutch said. "Don't worry about me. Focus on why you're here."

The auction. The hard drive.

She swallowed hard, hating the sensation of being trapped in an impossible situation.

Emilio spun on his heel and stalked back to the house with Rodrigo beside him, and the other guards hauled Dutch along.

What could Chad have said to upset Emilio?

The prospects had her growing lightheaded. With someone as deranged as Chad, there was no telling.

"What's going on?" she asked Max and sipped her coffee, trying to appear casual instead of freaked out.

He clasped his hands behind his back. With his sunglasses on, she couldn't read his eyes. "Nothing to concern you. Your uncle wants you to worry about the auction."

Part of her wanted to follow them and do everything in her power to help Dutch. But she had to think strategically, not based off emotion. This was the opportunity they'd been waiting for. One where her uncle and the main guards would be focused on something away from the office.

If she had any hope of pulling this off, it'd have to be now, while they were distracted, but the one thing they hadn't accounted for was Max.

"Once you're done eating," Max said, "I'll help you in any way you require. The great room is being set up now per your instructions."

To hell with breakfast.

"I've lost my appetite." She grabbed her purse and discreetly slipped the piece of tape with the fingerprint on it into an inner compartment of her bag. "Let's go take a look at the progress."

EMILIO LED DUTCH downstairs to an empty alcove in the wine cellar. Thanks to the stone walls, it was dank and ten degrees cooler than the rest of the house.

With a flick of his hand, Emilio gestured to his guards.

Someone hit Dutch across the back of the head. The world blurred and he fell off his feet. They slapped handcuffs on Dutch and lifted him from the ground, catching the chain on a hook suspended from the ceiling.

They must've used this space for interrogation before. It made sense. There were no windows and the stone walls would act as natural soundproofing.

"Chad Ellis tells me that you're a US marshal," Vargas said. "Care to explain?"

Dutch's head pounded. "Ellis is a psychopath. He's obsessed with Isabel. He can't be trusted."

Rodrigo punched Dutch and pain flared in his jaw. The taste of salty copper hit his tongue.

Vargas held up his cell phone. On the screen was a picture of Dutch, flashing his badge to the cops. "I asked Mr. Ellis to email those to me. He was more than happy to oblige."

Good old Chad. "Bet he was." Dutch spit blood from his mouth onto the stone floor.

"He even offered to drop off glossy five-by-sevens personally, but I said that wasn't necessary."

Did he follow them down here? Dutch hadn't been looking for a tail. So stupid of him. He'd been too preoccupied with Isabel, trying to help her contain her emotions, and prepare for how things might go. He hadn't considered the possibility. "Is Ellis in San Diego?"

"I'm the one asking the questions. Why are you here?"

"Ellis is dangerous." Dutch had underestimated him and look at where that had gotten him.

Vargas gave a curt nod. Rodrigo hit Dutch in the gut and a sharp pang shot through him.

"Why are you here?" Vargas asked. "Is it to stop the auction?"

"I'm here because you hired me to protect Isabel and invited me."

"Does Isabel know what you are?" Vargas asked.

Dutch shook his head. "No. She doesn't."

"Are you the one who told her the truth about me?"

"It was the Guzman cartel," Dutch said, determined to stick with the lie.

Another fist connected with his jaw.

"Anyone worth asking in the Guzman cartel is dead," Vargas said. "But I can't take your word for it. Not until I've broken you. When I do, you'll tell me everything I want to know."

The other two guards replaced Rodrigo and took turns punching Dutch in the sides, making his ribs and lungs ache.

"You don't have to," Dutch said, coughing. "Go to extremes. I'm a straight shooter."

"Not yet, but you will be. Even if it takes hours. Days. Eventually, everyone breaks."

Vargas had a point. Everyone's body did break, literally, but the spirit was a different beast, different rules.

A blow to his kidneys sent stabbing pain in a fiery arc across his back.

"You marshals have been a vexing thorn in my side, protecting my enemies and traitors." Vargas circled him. "Helping them testify against me, trying to dismantle my business. But the people coming here tonight to buy that hard drive will gladly root you out for me. *And* they'll pay me in the process. A firestorm from hell is about to rain down on every single marshal, not only in the San Diego office, but the entire state, and there's nothing you can do to stop it."

"Smart to get others to do your dirty work. Keep your hands clean. But I still don't know what you're talking about." Dutch had to stall long enough for Isabel to complete the mission, prevent the sale and get away.

During the car ride down here, he'd talked her through a worst-case scenario. If she got off the compound and made it to the rendezvous point four miles away off Del Mar Heights

Road, where Allison and Draper were waiting, it'd be worth every bruise, broken bone and scar.

As for Dutch, he'd trained for this in the army. Delta Force had fortified him, had ingrained one thing in him above all else. SERE—survival, evasion, resistance, escape.

# *Chapter Twenty-One*

In the great room, Isabel told the staff where to place the remainder of the furniture and discussed lighting and music and ways to drive bids higher. For two hours, she gave directions on autopilot because as it turned out, Emilio was right. She could do this blindfolded, but all she thought about was Dutch, what was happening to him, and how to get clear from Max and up to Emilio's office.

Ten polished mahogany tables were set up, displaying sculptures, paintings and pieces of antiquity such as a spectacular fossilized gem of opalescent ammonite and a sought-after Roman coin, an ides-of-March denarius minted to celebrate the assassination of Julius Caesar. The items would catch the attention of any serious collector, but there was no reason for her uncle to sell them unless he was facing bankruptcy, which he wasn't.

The tenth table didn't have any art, only a laptop.

That was for the hard drive and to show off its contents. It had to be.

"It's always nice when I get to spend time with you," Max said, glued to her side.

Moving away from him around a table, she pulled on a polite smile. "That's sweet. You know, the caterer should be here any minute. Could you check the kitchen and see if they're prepared?"

They were using a vendor to supply the food and drinks, but only Emilio's personal staff was permitted on the premises during the auction. *For security reasons.*

Max's eyes flashed up to hers as a grin spread across his face. "I'm sure they're ready. Your uncle has such high standards."

*Uncle.* She had no idea how to think of Emilio. The very idea of him stirred conflicting emotions, dredged up uncomfortable memories that she had blocked out. But when she thought of him alone with Dutch, doing only God knows what to him, there was only impotent rage coupled with a pervasive sense of dread.

She couldn't lose Dutch. The connection between them had been sparked by his job, by Emilio's crimes, but their bond was real. Truer than anything she'd ever experienced.

"Because of those high standards, I need you to double-check," she said, pleasantly, but firmly. "We can't have anything go wrong this evening. The event is too important."

His grin fell as he studied her a long moment. "As you wish." He bowed, with great formality—for some reason he did things with flourish around her—and headed to the kitchen.

As soon as he disappeared out of sight, Isabel grabbed her purse and hurried for the staircase. Max would only be gone for a minute, two at the most, and she needed every precious second.

She took off her heels to move quietly and faster. Holding her shoes in one hand, she padded up the steps and ran down the hall to Emilio's office.

Grabbing the knob, she prayed the door wasn't locked.

The knob turned. She ducked inside.

She caught her breath, letting the slightest bit of relief seep through. Her gaze darted around, finding the painting that concealed the safe. Many times, she'd been in here with Emilio while he wrapped up work on his computer and they'd had a drink together and chatted. It was in this room that he'd steered her toward running an art gallery and away from taking a low-paying job at a museum.

Mentally kicking herself for letting him use her, she hurried to the original Renoir she'd purchased on his behalf at Sotheby's. She dropped her shoes, unlatched the right-side mounting on the painting and swung it out as one would a door.

The wall safe was sixteen by twenty, had a smooth matte-black finish, a biometric scanner and a handle. She pulled out the strip of tape, turned it the right way so his print was in the correct position and pressed it to the scanner.

A white beam of light ran across the thumbprint, once, twice, three times. Her chest squeezed, her pulse throbbing. *Come on, work.* Tension wormed in her veins.

The lock disengaged and the safe door popped open. On the bottom shelf were various documents and two envelopes. One addressed to her and the other to Miguel.

She took the one that had *For Isabel* scrawled across the front. The envelope wasn't sealed. Quickly, she opened it and took out two sheets of paper.

One was a paternity test dated twenty-four years ago, stating that with 98.9 percent certainty Emilio was her father. Seeing it in black and white was like taking a blow to the chest.

The other sheet was a handwritten letter.

*To My Beloved Isabel.*

*If you're reading this, then I am dead.*

A wellspring of emotion bubbled up inside, but Isabel closed the letter and stuffed it into her purse. Now wasn't the time. All that mattered was the hard drive and saving Dutch. Not her deep-seated issues with her uncle who was in fact her father.

On the top shelf was an internal hard drive that'd been pulled from a laptop. There were three thumb drives beside it. Those could've been copies or contained completely unrelated data.

Not willing to take any chances, she snatched all four devices. She shoved them into the zippered compartment inside her purse and pushed the button on the degausser, activating it.

Isabel hurriedly closed the safe door, locking it, and put the painting back into place. She grabbed her shoes, whirled around to get the hell out of there and gasped.

Max stood in the doorway, watching her. "What are you doing?"

"Looking for Emilio." Her heart fluttered like a caged bird's wings. "I need to speak to him about Dutch."

His gaze swung to the painting, down to the shoes in her hand and back up to her face. "What were you doing in the safe? Better still, how did you get into the safe?" He closed the door and walked toward her.

"I wasn't in the safe." She slid her hand in her bag and felt around for the Pacifier.

"I'm not sure what your uncle would do if he knew you were sneaking around in his office, rifling through his safe. But I don't think you'd like to find out."

She gripped the base of the stun baton and positioned her finger over the switch to flick it on if necessary. "I just want to find Dutch and I want to go. Please."

He came closer, so light-footed that he didn't make a sound. His hard gaze pinned her in place.

Waiting for him to be within reach, she steadied her breath, calmed her thoughts down to one. Freedom.

Freedom from the villa, from Emilio, from the Vargas name, from its cursed legacy.

Max stepped up to her. Flipping the switch on the baton, she jammed it up toward him.

But he caught her by the wrist, not going for the baton itself as a typical attacker would naturally. There was a special *grab-guard* stun strip carrying an electric current that would shock anyone attempting to take it. Unfortunately, Max wasn't typical.

"You don't want to do that," he said in a low, flat voice.

Bright electric current pulsated and crackled from the tip of the Pacifier.

"Shut it off and put it back in your purse," he said, and she did as he demanded. "Dutch is in the cellar. You should hurry."

She scrunched her face in confusion. "Why are you telling me this?"

"If you can convince your uncle to let him go, I'll have his truck ready out front for you and ensure the gate is open."

Was this a trick? Was he going to double-cross her and use this to get in tighter with Emilio? "Why are you helping me?"

He shepherded her to the door. "Because you're a good person and you need it."

A thousand questions rushed through her head. "What about the other guards? Won't you get in trouble?"

"Heads will roll, but not mine. I'm Teflon. Nothing sticks to me." He put his hand on the knob. "Your uncle loves you, Isabel. More than you know. He'd do anything for you, which gives you the power. If you want to get Dutch out alive, use that love like a weapon."

What did he mean? How was she supposed to do that?

Max cracked the door open, peered out and then ushered her into the hall and down the stairs. He gave her a nod, like they were on the same team, and they went in separate directions.

She hustled to the basement door and flew down the steps barefoot, not wanting to alert Emilio of her presence too soon.

Once she reached the stone floor, the sound of flesh beating against flesh echoed in the corridor, making her quicken her pace. Fear for Dutch flooded her.

She followed the sounds and hesitated before going around the bend. Gathering her strength, Isabel put on her shoes and took a deep breath. She rounded the corner and stopped short at the sight of Dutch. Hanging from a hook, bloody and bruised.

"Isabel," Emilio said, his face growing pale. "You shouldn't be down here. I don't want you to see this."

He rushed to her, taking her by the arm and dragging her around the corner.

"Don't touch me." She yanked free of him. "Why are you beating him?"

"He's a US marshal. Spying on me through you. Did you know?"

"Of course not."

He eyed her as if trying to gauge her credibility. The doubt in his eyes was clear. "Go back upstairs. Let me handle this and tomorrow—"

"I'm not going anywhere without him."

"I'm afraid I can't let him go, my dear."

As she straightened, their gazes locked. She wanted to curse at him. To slap him. To scream at him for every awful thing he'd ever done. But there was only one way to get through to him and that was by using her wits. She drew on her anger, her hatred, her pain and even her love for Emilio, and she knew what to do.

"If he's a marshal like you claim," she said, "then obviously they know he's here. Right? If he disappears, that's only going to cause trouble for you. Let him go and at most, one of your minions gets charged with assault, but I'll tell Dutch not to pursue it."

He considered what she'd said. "After the auction, I'll release him. All right?"

Once the auction started, Emilio would find his safe empty. It wouldn't take him long to connect the dots to her. After he discovered that she'd erased the drive, he might not hesitate to kill Dutch out of sheer anger. "I'm not waiting. If you don't uncuff him right now and let us leave, I'll never give you what you want most."

He narrowed his eyes at her. "And what's that?"

"For me to call you Father." She let that hang in the air. The impact on him was immediate and splashed all over his face, but she had to dig deeper. "I remember your secret visits when I was little, how you played with me, always found ways to make me smile, how you used to tell me that you'd give me the world if you could."

"I thought you'd forgotten." His voice was forlorn. "I tried to be there for you as much as I could."

He had. She saw that now and clashing emotions ripped through her.

Isabel put her hand on his chest over his heart, hoping

he still had one. "I don't want you to give me the world. I'm asking for Dutch. You owe him a life debt and I love him." It was fast and she despised what had brought her and Dutch together, but in her heart, it made sense. Felt right. Good. She wanted to explore the possibilities with him and if she didn't, it would be her biggest regret. "Let us leave, now, or I'll never speak to you again. You'll be as good as dead to me. On my mother's grave, I swear it."

His face and posture softened. Emotion clouded his eyes as his shoulders slumped forward. "You are my pride and joy. The one true light in my life. We'll get through this, Isa."

The sounds of a scuffle came from around the corner. Isabel and Emilio rushed down the corridor and around the bend to the alcove.

Still hanging from the hook, Dutch had managed to knock one of the bodyguards out. He swung his legs up, wrapped them around Rodrigo's neck, and using him as leverage, Dutch hoisted himself off the hook. Then he rotated, bringing Rodrigo crashing down onto the stone pavers.

Spinning up from the floor, Dutch pulled Rodrigo's gun at the same time the last standing guard drew his weapon.

Both men pointed the guns at each other in a standoff.

"Please," Isabel said, clutching Emilio's arm, not wanting Dutch to get shot. Though he seemed to have the situation under control.

"Lower your weapons," Emilio said, stepping between them. First the guard complied, and then Dutch. "You're free to leave."

Dutch gave her a questioning glance. She nodded, beckoning to him so they could get out of there. He wasted no time going to her side.

She wrapped her arms around him, needing to hold him for a moment. After a hard, quick hug, she looked at Emilio. "Thank you. Father."

Emilio nodded and they turned to leave, but then he said,

"Dutch, I know the Marshals can't get a warrant in time to stop the auction. But if you interfere, in any way, there will be the harshest of consequences. I will show no mercy."

The threat had been issued in no uncertain terms, chilling Isabel's blood. "Let's go."

Emilio would keep his word, but for now, they needed to get out of there. They'd have to deal with the rest later.

She grabbed Dutch's hand and fled out of the cellar. He was close behind her going up the stairs and again at her side once they cleared the front door.

There were no guards in sight to question them and Dutch's truck was parked out front running as Max had promised.

"Good work," Dutch said, gesturing to the truck.

"I had help. From Max."

They hopped into the truck, Dutch shifted into Drive and hit the gas. They sped down the path toward the open gates and out onto the road. "Either he's got a crush on you or he's the FBI agent who's been deep undercover in the organization for a while."

"FBI?" Isabel glanced back through the windshield. No one followed. The road was clear.

She sucked in a deep breath, forcing air into her lungs. Her hands were trembling. She felt wrung out and nauseated.

"Thank you for coming to get me, even though I told you not to."

"I couldn't leave you behind." She put her hand on his leg. "I was afraid I'd lose you."

"You're not going to lose me. I'll be with you for as long as you want." He covered her hand with his. "Did you get it?"

She nodded. "Three thumb drives, as well. I took them all and used the degausser. They're in my purse."

"You're amazing."

"I feel like a wreck. Like I want to cry and sleep and rage and hold you all at the same time."

"Oh, honey."

"Not that I should complain. You're the one who's been beaten to a pulp." He had a split lip, and bruises on his face that would turn purple by tomorrow.

"I don't look that bad. Just a little banged up. They didn't break anything."

How could he take this in stride? He was the amazing one.

"We're almost there," he said, referring to the rendezvous point with the other two marshals. "Draper will take you to the hotel and get you settled. Relax in a bath, order some food, maybe take a nap while I go to the office."

"We're not going to be in a safe house?"

"Technically, you're not in witness protection and I have to get off the grid since I used my real name. The steps they're taking to keep us safe are a little unorthodox."

"How long will you be?"

"It might take a few hours to finalize our exit plan."

"What about McQueen? Brenda? I have to see her."

"Call the day care and give permission for a US marshal to pick up McQueen. As for Brenda, it's too dangerous for you now to go back to LA to see her. Your uncle, I mean dad, is going to know you helped me. He'll expect you to be there."

Isabel wrapped her arms around herself and shuddered at the thought of Emilio's consequences. A part of her was glad that his auction was going to be a disaster with him surrounded by a bunch of disappointed criminals. But she'd assumed she'd get to hug her best friend again and say goodbye. Not just disappear without a word.

They pulled up alongside a sedan.

Will and Allison got out, and Dutch lowered the window.

Allison passed Dutch his service weapon. "Don't leave us in suspense."

Isabel handed her the drives, the tape and degausser.

"Good job, you two." Allison glanced at Dutch. "The other thing?" she asked, cryptically.

He shook his head.

Allison muttered a string of profanity and lowered her head. "Vargas might not be able to sell the hard drive, but I bet he pored over every bit of information on the marshals in our office. We're going to need protection for our families."

Will nodded. "I'll square it away."

"Isabel had help from someone inside. Do you have any idea who the undercover FBI agent is?" Dutch asked.

"The FBI keeps their identities close hold," Will said. "All we know is his code name. Teflon."

*Max is FBI?* He'd moved up fast in the ranks. Emilio and Rodrigo trusted him implicitly.

"Sir, would you mind taking Isabel to the hotel," Dutch asked, "while Allison and I finish the rest? And it might be good if you stayed with her until I get back. No guards followed us here, but I'd feel better if she had protection while I'm gone."

"No problem," Will said. "We appreciate what you've done for the US Marshals Service, Ms. Vargas."

"What's it going to be?" Allison asked. "Double the work hashing out separate plans for each of you? Or will you two lay low for a while together?"

Isabel looked at Dutch, without a doubt in her heart, and said, "Together."

## Chapter Twenty-Two

The hotel was on the waterfront of the San Diego Bay and the US Marshals Service had booked them a large suite with a separate living room, which gave Isabel her privacy and a generous amount of space to unwind in the bedroom, even though Will was there for protection.

Isabel dropped down on the comfy bed, wanting to sink into it, close her eyes and fall asleep. Maybe by the time she woke, Dutch would be there, and they could make love again. She'd missed sleeping with him last night. They needed time away together without the current stressors.

She took out her cell. Five percent battery life remaining. She'd left her charger back at the villa in her overnight bag.

Going through her phone, she found the number to the hospital in LA that she'd saved and dialed it.

"Hello," the female voice was familiar, but not Brenda. Someone older.

"Mrs. Reaver, is that you?"

"Yes, may I ask who's calling?"

"It's me, Isabel."

"Oh, sweetie, Brenda's been asking for you," Mrs. Reaver said.

"She's awake?" Isabel almost cried tears of joy.

"Yes. She's been lucid since we got here this morning. They just took her to run some tests, but she'll be back any minute. She can't wait to see you. Are you coming by soon?"

Her stomach clenched with regret. "No, I can't stop by. I'm in San Diego. Can you take down the number to my hotel? My phone is about to die."

"Sure."

Isabel rattled off the number, along with which room she was in and the fake name they were registered under. "When she gets back, if she's up to it, have her call me."

"She'll be up to it. She's dying to talk to you. It shouldn't be long."

"Okay. Thank you, Mrs. Reaver."

Isabel hung up. Her phone was at one percent and as good as dead. She climbed onto the bed and turned on the television, afraid to shower or fall asleep and miss Brenda's call.

She turned to a show about decorating houses for background noise more than anything else. One program ran into the next while her thoughts whirled, spinning around the last two days, coming back to Emilio and what she'd learned.

Glancing at her purse, she picked up her bag and put it in her lap. She thought of the letter and wondered if she was strong enough to read it. Curiosity won.

She read the letter, slowly, shocked by every line that brought tears to her eyes. Emilio had poured his heart and soul and pain out onto the page. He had written poetic lines about the depths of his love for her. Apologized for everything. Took responsibility for her mother's last days being difficult, for Luis's anger, for ripping the family apart with his selfishness, for her confusing childhood, for his brother's death. In the end, he begged her forgiveness.

He'd confessed to murder in the letter, sort of.

Could it be used as evidence to put him away? Would she use it against him?

He was flawed, corrupt and was guilty of monstrous things. But he was her father and regretted everything, despite what she had thought. Emilio was suffering, too, and he loved her deeply.

With her heart bleeding, she folded the letter, put it back in her bag and zipped her purse closed.

There was a loud knock at the main door of the suite.

"Hey," Will called from the living room. "You could've let me know you ordered room service. I'm hungry, too."

But she hadn't ordered any room service. She still didn't

have an appetite and after reading that letter, it would be hours before she'd eat.

It was probably the wrong room.

There was a thud and then nothing besides the sounds of the two televisions.

She shut off her TV. "Will? Is everything all right?"

Something was wrong.

Under the door, she saw a shadow move up to the bedroom. "Will?"

The door burst open. A man loomed, wearing a hotel jacket and holding a gun with a suppressor pointed at her.

A chilling, mind-numbing fear speared her. The man with scraggly hair, a mustache and glasses seemed vaguely familiar, but she couldn't place him.

"Hello, Isabel," he said.

*That voice.* Chad!

Her skin prickled, her jaw coming unhinged as she pressed back against the headboard.

"If you scream, I'll kill the US marshal and anyone else who comes running to help you, and when I leave here, I'll pay Brenda a visit in the hospital. Nod if you understand."

Isabel's breath snagged in her chest, but she nodded.

As Chad walked up to her, getting closer, she noticed he wore gloves and the suppressor was homemade—two PVC pipes, one inside the other, with some sort of end cap, attached to the barrel of the gun with a...*hose clamp*?

He pressed the gun to her temple. "Get up. Put on your shoes." His voice was deadly calm.

Trembling, she did as he told her, holding on tight to her purse.

"Come on. Walk." He nudged her forward.

"Are you going to hurt me?"

"Not unless you make me."

She stepped out of the bedroom and he pushed up against the back side of her, pressing the gun against her kidneys.

"When did you get a gun?" she asked, feeling cold down to her bones.

He hadn't owned a firearm before.

"When I found out Dutch used to be in Special Forces. I have a bullet with his name on it. I'd expected to find him in here with you. Not that one."

Isabel looked down at Will. Flat on his stomach, knocked out, but alive.

"Behave. If you don't and draw attention, I'll be forced to hurt others." Chad opened the door, keeping her close to him, and they walked down the empty hallway toward the stairwell.

Fear raced through her bloodstream. "How did you find me?"

"I suppose I can tell you since it doesn't matter anymore."

Why? God, why didn't it matter anymore? Was he going to kill her?

No, he wouldn't.

Chad wanted to be with her in a sick, abusive relationship that mirrored Brett and Mindy's, where she played the doting partner, tending to his every need, subjected to his every whim. He didn't want her dead.

"I found you through your phone," he whispered in her ear, his voice dark and pure evil. "I've been tracking you," he said, "listening to your calls, reading your emails and texts. I knew you were at this hotel, but not what room until you told Brenda's mom."

Isabel's heart nose-dived. How could she be so stupid? How could he be so twisted? So insane?

They entered the stairwell. Cupping her shoulder with his free hand, he steered her up the stairs. Not down, out of the hotel and into a car.

"Where are you taking me?" She clutched her purse against her belly and used the noise of their footfalls to cover the sound of the zipper as she inched it ever so slowly, in the slightest degrees, trying to get the opening wide enough for her hand without him noticing.

"It's a surprise."

She swallowed the scream churning in her belly, rising in her throat, and reminded herself there were cameras everywhere. Someone in security would see this, find it odd, report it.

They reached the landing one floor up and he opened the door.

In the hallway, there was a family leaving their room. Two kids were fighting, a girl and a boy, maybe eight and ten respectively. The boy hit his sister and their father snatched him up by the collar and reprimanded him as the mother closed the door. The girl smiled and stuck her tongue out at her brother behind her parents' backs.

A similar incident from her past flashed in her mind with her and Miguel. Emilio had been furious that Miguel had hurt her one day and when he'd been punished, she'd remembered feeling special, untouchable.

*I have a brother.*

"Keep quiet unless you want kids to die," Chad whispered to her.

The family seemed a million miles away as they walked to the elevator, not noticing them at all.

Chad stopped her in front of the first door on their left. Took out a key card and inserted it. The green light flashed, the door unlocked, and he shoved her inside.

Something creaked under her feet. She looked down. There was a thick layer of plastic covering the carpet. Industrial strength.

She stepped deeper into the room. Plastic covered the surfaces in the bathroom. More plastic had been placed over the rest of the carpet, the dresser, nightstands and the bed.

A large suitcase sat near the window.

Dear God. He intended to kill her.

*Don't panic.*

Too late. Her mind was being sucked down a dark vortex, chased by pure terror.

"There's security footage of us together. You can't," Isabel said, her brain reeling. It was all she could do not to beg, plead, offer to do anything he wanted, if he wouldn't go through with this.

He chuffed a smug laugh behind her back. "The security guards here make fifteen dollars an hour. I just paid two of them fifteen thousand each to ensure technical difficulties of the security cameras. Nothing is recording."

She spun around. Chad had put on a plastic coat and had the gun aimed at her head.

"I'm sorry…about everything," she said, lowering her eyes, recalling the time when she'd come out of the bathroom and overhead Mindy speaking in private to Brett. "Let me make it up to you."

The gun lowered to his side, and she looked up at him. Chad stepped closer with his brow furrowed. "If you're sorry, prove it."

"Take off your clothes," she said, digging her fingers in the leather of her purse, rubbing the outline of the stun baton. "Make love to me."

Chad backed up to the edge of the plastic near the dresser. The opening of her bag wasn't wide enough yet to get the baton out and his gaze was pinned to her, watching her every breath. He pulled the plastic down and placed the gun inside the bottom drawer. Then he replaced the thick covering.

Even if she got away from him, he'd overpower her before she'd get the gun.

Keeping the plastic coat on, he reached underneath it and removed something hidden behind his back. Steel glinted in the dim light from the drawn curtains. He tossed a large hunting knife with at least a nine-inch serrated blade on the floor in the corner of the room near the suitcase.

She'd be crazy to go after it and that was probably exactly what he was counting on.

Chad slipped the strap of her purse down her arm and tossed the bag onto the bed by the pillow. Her chest rose and fell with tight, anxious breaths.

Isabel kicked off her shoes, realizing at some point that she'd need to run, sat on the bed, scooting up, and lay back as close to her purse as she could get.

Chad pushed her down against the mattress, the eerie sound of the plastic creaking underneath her. Grasping her jaw, he kissed her aggressively, almost violently.

Worse, she had to sell him on her performance as she kissed him back. Her stomach roiled. With her right hand, she stroked his hair and her fingers found the strange strands of the wig. She groped for her purse with her left hand, gently, quietly, trying not to disturb the plastic and draw his attention to what she was doing.

Chad undid his belt and unzipped his pants, the distinct sounds slicing through her ears, echoing in her soul. He lowered his full weight on her, pinning her to the bed.

Hot bile welled in her throat. The backs of her eyes stung with tears, but she surrendered herself to the kiss. To survive, she had to.

Her fingers snagged soft leather. She reeled it closer, drawing the zipper open more.

Chad's hands wandered, up her skirt, cupping her butt, groping her breast. She shuddered in revulsion.

*God, please get me out of this.* Tears leaked from her eyes.

She dug her hand in her bag and rummaged for the baton.

"I missed this, Isabel. Missed us." His eyes burned with his obsession. "I just want it to go back to the way it was."

She cringed. The fear he'd cultivated in her over the past several months bloomed, like nightshade in the darkness. Invasive vines, strangling, poisoning, blocking out the sunlight and smothering every good thing.

*Don't give up! Don't let him win!*

Her fingers grasped the baton. She pulled it from her purse and swung with all her might.

*Crack!*

The shaft of the baton struck hard against the side of Chad's head, knocking him off her. Isabel kicked him, hard, with both feet, propelling him to the floor.

She launched herself up from the bed, holding the Pacifier and leaving her purse. She ran to the door, grabbed the knob and pulled.

It didn't budge. The door was stuck. For a split second she thought of Dutch.

She tried the door again. Still nothing. She looked around, frantic to get out.

There was a doorstop wedged under the door.

Plastic squeaked as Chad righted himself. Isabel bent down and wiggled the rubber stopper. Desperation sizzled in her blood. She wrenched it from under the door.

As she stood, Chad charged toward her.

*No!*

She yanked the door handle.

The safety latch at the top caught and the door wouldn't open.

Chad was almost on her.

Her heart was hammering so fast that she could barely breathe. She flicked the switch on the stun baton, heard the crackle of electricity and lunged at him. Chad snatched the grab guard and an electric current flooded his body. His muscles spasmed and his eyes rolled up into the back of his head. She jammed the prods into his neck. He lost his balance, crumpling to the floor. Then she held on for a couple of seconds longer to be sure he was down.

Isabel flipped the safety latch off and threw open the door. She pressed across the threshold to the stairwell. Ran back downstairs one flight barefoot. But the stun baton slipped from her hand over the railing. It clattered along the descent several flights below.

Damn it.

She bolted onto her floor and dashed to her room. "Will?" Isabel pounded on the door. "Will!"

Was he still unconscious?

Adrenaline propelling her, she hurried for the elevator. She glanced over her shoulder, looking for Chad. The stun baton wouldn't immobilize him for long.

She slapped the button, summoning a car.

The *L* was illuminated. It was in the lobby and she was on the sixth floor. She hit it again and again, knowing it wouldn't make the elevator arrive any faster, but what choice did she have?

Number two lit up. Then three.

At the far end of the hall, the door opened to the stairwell.

Even though she already knew it was him, she pivoted to see Chad.

Isabel slapped the button repeatedly. The car was at the fourth floor.

Growling like a wild animal, Chad bulldozed down the hall with the hunting knife raised in his hand, his face taut with blind rage. The fury pumping through him was terrifying.

If he reached her, got his hands on her, he'd kill her.

*Dear God, help me!* He was almost to her.

Panic exploded in her chest. She hit the button again, cursing and screaming.

A chime sounded, and the elevator doors opened. Isabel stumbled inside and landed against a wall of solid muscle.

"Isabel!" Dutch's face was ashen and bruised as he held her closer. He glanced up, drew his weapon and put her behind him. "Stop! Or I'll shoot," he warned.

But Chad kept charging, yelling obscenities, shouting hateful, violent things.

A shot rang out. The force of the bullet stopped Chad and

made him stumble. Blood poured down his body from the chest wound.

Was it over? Would he just die already and let this nightmare end?

Chad lumbered forward a few quick steps, raising the knife again.

As if reading her mind, Dutch stepped out of the elevator, and fired once more. The second bullet to the head flung Chad backward to the floor.

He lay in the hall, still, his eyes open and unmoving.

The demon was dead.

Dutch turned, wrapping her in his arms.

She fell against him, collapsing in the safety of his heat and strength. It was all she could do not to break down. Relief cascaded through her as she clung to him. "Oh, Dutch."

A few guests opened their doors and peeked out. Others left their rooms, gathering in the hallway.

"Are you okay?" His arms tightened around her.

"I will be." Now that he was there.

"God, I'm sorry it took me so long."

She buried her face in his chest, took in his scent, relieved, comforted. Safe. "You were right on time."

# Epilogue

*Magical.* Sitting beside Dutch in front of their campfire, Isabel stared up at the majestic aurora borealis. Green ribbons of light tinged pink danced high in the sky. Pure, vibrant waves of energy. It was wondrous.

The US Marshals Service had flown them on a military plane to Eielson Air Force Base near Fairbanks, Alaska. Arrangements had been made for them to embark on the last camping tour of the season to Chena Hot Springs to catch the northern lights.

Conditions had to be optimal for them to see it. The night as dark as possible, little to no cloud cover and there had to be enough solar activity. Those elements had converged perfectly, gifting them with this.

Sort of like her relationship with Dutch. It boggled her mind to think of all the factors that had to sync up at the right time, in the right way, to bring them together.

Dutch being picked for the assignment. Her needing someone like him to walk into her life. Chad spinning out of control. The auction that never happened because they'd stopped it.

*Kismet.*

Emilio must be livid, plotting his revenge. She'd considered showing Dutch the letter her father had written her, had contemplated using it against him, but she couldn't and had burned it.

There was no denying her father was a monster, capable of unspeakable things. But he loved her, and she loved him. In a weird way, if it weren't for him, she never would have met Dutch, the man who might end up being the love of her life.

Even more remarkable, roughing it in the Alaskan wilderness, without the danger and adrenaline and creature comforts, they were truly happy together.

"This is incredible." She rested her head on his shoulder, snuggling against him in the frigid night air, thankful for everything. From being with Dutch to her toasty goose-down puffer coat.

He wrapped his arm around her and kissed her head. "More hot chocolate, beautiful?"

"No, I'm good." She brought her denim-covered legs up to her chest, basking in this moment. The serenity. The safety. The splendor. "Thank you, for getting Allison to make this trip happen."

"She just wanted us off the grid. The farther away from civilization the better. She didn't care where."

"You know what I mean."

"I know. I love you," he said, tightening his arm around her. "Once it's safe, we'll visit Brenda. I promise."

Who knew how long it would take before she'd be able to see her friend again?

Max was working hard to build a case against Emilio. He was smart, cunning. If anyone in the FBI could do it, it was him. *Teflon.*

"I love you, too," she said.

McQueen's collar jingled as he got up and came out of their tent. With his ears up, he stood on alert, staring at the woods. Then he started barking.

Dutch fished his gun out of his backpack, stood and aimed in the direction that McQueen was looking.

"Stand down, Haas," said a man coming out of the tree line, wearing a parka and backpack. "It's me, Captain Williams."

He was their liaison from the air base.

"What are you doing out here?" Dutch asked.

"It took me two days to find this campsite." Captain Williams approached, looking winded. "You guys really picked a remote location. I couldn't even get here with a vehicle."

"What's up?" Dutch asked.

"We got a call for you two on base from Deputy Marshal Allison Chen-Boyd. Her son's been kidnapped, and she needs to speak with you."

"Oh, God." Isabel jumped to her feet.

"Do you have a satphone we can use?" Dutch asked.

"You can't," Captain Williams said. "We might even have to trek back to base. The aurora borealis occurs during solar storms. The massive bursts of charged particles create satellite disturbances and mess with our satphones."

Isabel swallowed around the cold lump in her throat. "Does she know who took her son?"

"She said that you guys would know," Captain Williams said.

"This is my fault," Isabel said. "He took Allison's son because of what I did."

Dutch grasped her shoulders. "No, sweetheart. He's mad at the Marshals. Not you."

"He gave me a letter. Confessed to murdering his brother. I should've told you, but I burned it."

"What?" Dutch sucked in a breath. "Did he explicitly state that he pulled the trigger? Did he write the words, *I killed him? I ordered a hit?* Or was he vague and left some loophole?"

The exact wording had been vague, implied things that led her to draw conclusions.

"He wrote that it was his fault the family was torn apart and he was sorry. That he was responsible for Luis's anger, for his death. I know what he meant, but the verbiage wasn't explicit." Thinking back on it, he hadn't even admitted to having an affair on paper.

But she couldn't shake the sense of guilt. Maybe if she'd stayed behind in San Diego, she could've prevented this.

"He never would have left an incriminating letter anywhere that could send him to prison," Dutch said. "Besides, he has the best lawyers that money can buy at his disposal. They would've had it thrown out of court because we didn't get it with a warrant. This is not on you."

"We have to help her get her son back," Isabel said, panic bubbling in her stomach.

He nodded with a worried look.

"What is it? What aren't you telling me?"

"It took Captain Williams two days to find us. Kidnapping cases where there's ransom or demands are usually resolved within forty-eight to seventy-two hours. One way or the other."

One way was rescuing the hostage. The other?

Her heart sank. She couldn't bear to think about it.

If her father took that child, then she needed to speak to him, bargain, negotiate. She'd do whatever he wanted as long as Allison got her son back.

"I think this is out of our hands," Dutch said. "Beyond our control." He brought her into a hug. "It's going to be okay. You'll see. They kidnapped the wrong kid."

"What do you mean?"

"Allison would move heaven and earth for her son and her husband works on the FBI's Hostage Rescue Team. They're trained by Delta Force. If anyone can get him back, it's HRT."

It was a small comfort but did nothing to erase her sense of guilt or helplessness.

Dutch pulled back and met her gaze. "We did the right thing stopping the auction."

"And no good deed goes unpunished."

He shook his head. "That narrative isn't true. Good will prevail. And love might not conquer all, but it's pretty freaking powerful."

Staring into his eyes, Isabel felt the impact of those words, deep in her heart, and hope welled. They'd stopped the auction and had beaten Chad. Against the odds, they'd won together.

He put his forehead to hers, their noses touching. In his arms, she chose to believe in that different narrative. One of goodness and love, where it would all work out.

\* \* \* \* \*

# COLTON
# CHRISTMAS
# CONSPIRACY

## LISA CHILDS

With great appreciation for all our wonderful
romance readers!

# Chapter One

*No. No. No.*

It wasn't possible. But the little mark was there on the calendar on her desk, the mark that meant she should have started her period a couple of days ago. Sure, she was only a couple of days late, but Elise Willis was never late.

She could not be pregnant. Well, she could be… after that amazing night a month ago. But she *shouldn't* be—because that night had been a horrible mistake. A mistake that never should have happened and that could never happen again.

So why had he called?

Her fingers trembled as Elise reached for the note her assistant had left on her desk next to her calendar. Scrawled across the page from Carmen's memo pad, the note read: *Neil Colton wants you to meet him at Crest View Center.*

Crest View Center was an old warehouse that Elise and the city council had approved for renovations several months ago. But construction had been halted when dead bodies had been discovered in the walls of the basement a few months ago. It was a crime scene now, and the bodies that had been found there might not have been the only people who'd died because of the place. The health department was investigating that Colton Construction site as well as other sites Neil's father's company had renovated. And all Colton Construction operations had been suspended until the health department finished their investigation.

Was that why Neil wanted her to meet him there? Did he think that she, as the mayor of Braxville, Kansas, could somehow help his family?

A chuckle slipped out at the irony of a mayor helping Fitz Colton, Neil's hardheaded father. He'd hated her predecessor, former employer and mentor, and he probably did not think too highly of her, either. But that might have had less to do with her job than her former marriage…to his son.

Neil…

Her pulse quickened at the thought of seeing her ex-husband again. Dare she meet with him?

Hell, all she had to do to see Neil was close her eyes. Every time she did, he appeared with his bright blue eyes, dark brown hair and that faint scruff of reddish-brown beard clinging to his chiseled, stubborn jaw. He was too damn good-looking.

Always had been, from the first moment she'd noticed him across a law school lecture hall. When he'd caught her staring at him, she had quickly turned away from him. But it had been too late—despite her determination to stay focused on her education and on establishing her career.

"Mayor Willis," her assistant called, drawing Elise's attention to the open doorway to her office where Carmen stood, her purse dangling from her shoulder. She was a little older than Elise, with a few silver strands winding through the dark curls that brushed her shoulders. Her eyes were dark, too, and warm like her personality. "Is it all right if I leave now?"

Elise nodded. "Of course. You stayed later than you needed to."

"The phones don't stop ringing," Carmen said with a weary-sounding sigh.

"I know…"

Braxville was in crisis right now and not just because of the dead bodies that had been uncovered at Crest View Center. Those old murders were less of a concern than more people getting sick. Too many residents, most of them current or former Colton Construction workers, had cancer. A couple had even died.

Years ago, Colton Construction had renovated another old warehouse into what was now Ruby Row shopping center. If the mall truly was contaminated, like the state health department inspector—who was also Elise's ex-sister-in-law—was concerned that it was, then she would have no choice but to shut it down during the busiest shopping season of the year, Christmas.

But the results of Bridgette's tests weren't back yet. Every time the phone rang Elise worried that it was her calling to confirm contamination.

"Are you all right?" Carmen asked with concern.

Elise nodded. Maybe all the stress was the reason why she'd missed her period. Maybe it had nothing to do with what had happened last month...between her and her ex-husband. She held up the message her assistant had taken. "Did Neil say anything else when he called?"

"He didn't call," Carmen said. "Someone from his office did."

Someone from his office...

Who?

Elise knew most of them since that office had once been hers, too. She preferred this one, though, with its coffered ceiling and dark-paneled walls, mostly because she had it all to herself. But it was late, and she needed to leave. Should she go meet Neil, though?

"So no reason for the meeting was given?" Elise asked.

Carmen shook her head. "And I didn't feel right asking since he's your..." Color flushed her face as her words trailed off.

"Ex-husband," Elise finished for her. That had been his decision, not hers. He was the one who'd given up on them—on her. So if she didn't show up to this meeting he'd proposed, he would probably give up again.

But because they'd once been partners, in more than marriage, they'd vowed to try to remain friends. She glanced into the purse she'd dropped next to her chair. The leather bag gaped open, revealing the box she'd bought at the pharmacy that morning—the pregnancy test.

If only they'd remained *just* friends…

She needed to take that test. She needed to know.

"Are you sure you're all right?" Carmen asked again.

Elise forced a smile and nodded. "Yes, I'm fine. Please, go home to your family."

In addition to her three kids and husband, Carmen's in-laws also lived with her, which might have been why she didn't really seem to mind working late. At least she had help at home, though.

Unlike Elise's mother, who'd raised her alone. Was that how Elise would raise her child, if she was pregnant? She grabbed up her purse from beside her desk and slid the strap over her shoulder. She needed to talk to Neil and not just to find out why the hell he wanted her to meet him at a crime scene. Given the way they tended to communicate, though, the place might wind up being a crime scene once again.

"So Crest View Center, the warehouse, isn't a crime scene anymore?" Neil asked his older sister for confirmation.

"No, Yvette and the rest of the techs thoroughly processed the site for evidence months ago," Jordana said, her voice emanating from the speaker of his cell phone.

The glow from it illuminated the dark interior of his SUV. He'd shut off the lights some time ago while he waited in the parking lot for Elise to arrive.

"So I'll be able to get inside?" he asked.

"Yeah, if you have a key to it," Jordana said. "Did Dad give you one? Why the hell would you want to go there anyway? You know Bridgette took samples from it to test for contamination?"

"Yeah, I know," he said. "She doesn't have the results back, though." Unless she'd contacted Elise before anyone else in the family.

But if the place was contaminated, why would Elise have wanted to meet him there?

"So why are you going there?" Jordana asked. Then she gasped aloud, and it echoed inside his vehicle. "You're not representing Markus Dexter, are you?"

"Has he been arrested?" Neil asked, hoping like hell that he had been.

"No," she said. "But has he been in contact with you? Did he try to hire you?"

"I damn well think he would know better than to try to hire me after he shot my brother," Neil said. Not to mention how he'd betrayed his business partner, Neil's father, as well.

"If he hasn't hired you, why are you so interested in the crime scene?" Jordana asked with suspicion, like he was a suspect the Braxville detective was interviewing.

A criminal lawyer, he was often present at those interviews. Being the interviewee had him smiling with amusement. "I'm not interested in it." In fact, he was kind of loath to find out anything else about his father's business and his business partner. "I'm meeting someone here." And before she could ask again, he assured her, "It's not Dexter."

"Then who?" she asked.

"The mayor," he replied.

Her sigh rattled the cell now. "Of course."

"What does that mean?" he asked.

She sighed again. "Just that the two of you have some strange divorce."

He couldn't deny that they did, not after what had happened between them last month. "We're friends."

"With friends like that, who needs enemies?"

"Just because we got divorced doesn't make Elise my enemy," he assured his overprotective sister. Despite only being a year older than he and the other triplets, Jordana acted like she had to take care of all of them. Maybe because of her military background...

"Dad might not agree with you," Jordana warned him.

His father always struggled with mayors, but it didn't help that Elise was determined to carry on her predecessor's legacy of limiting urban sprawl. But that wasn't the only thing adversely affecting his father's construction business right now. There were also the open investigations by the police department and the health department.

That was why he hadn't taken on any new clients lately; he was going to wait to see what happened with his family. And with Elise.

He sighed. "I'm sure you're busy, Jordana, so I'll let you go now."

She was stammering something in protest when he clicked off the cell. But he didn't want to hear whatever his older sister had to say about his ex-wife any more than he ever wanted to hear what his father had to say about Elise and her politics. His family didn't understand Elise like he did.

He chuckled at his own joke. Hell, he didn't understand her, either. Never had. Probably never would.

He stared through his windshield at the dark building. Why the hell did Elise want to meet him here? So there would not be a repeat of what had happened the last time they'd met?

That was a damn shame.

His body tensed just remembering what had happened that night—how a friendly hug good-night had turned into a hot embrace.

A brush of his mouth across her soft lips…

He groaned—like he had that night—as desire overwhelmed him. Hell, he didn't care where she wanted to meet—just that she wanted to meet again. He needed to see her…see her beautiful face, her green eyes sparkling with amusement and intelligence as she challenged him, as she always challenged him.

That was probably why she'd left the message for him to meet her here—to challenge him about something to do with his family. He was aware that one of his sisters—his fellow triplet Bridgette—had talked to her about the health department's concerns regarding all Colton Construction projects, including the mall. But he and Elise had agreed, during their last meeting, to not talk about his family or city business…which was probably how they'd wound up making love instead. They'd had nothing left to argue about.

Yet they weren't ever able to completely agree on anything.

His mouth slid into a grin, though, as he remembered the lobbying for position, her pushing him onto his back so she could straddle him…her long golden hair falling in a curtain around them both as she leaned down, brushing her breasts over his chest as she pressed her mouth to his.

He groaned again, and his body throbbed with need—need for her. He wanted her so damn badly. Always had.

Probably always would. Damn it.

But Elise didn't want him. At least not for more than that one, passionate night last month.

So why had she called him here tonight? Was it possible that she'd finally changed her mind about them? That she wanted what he wanted now.

No. Elise did not change her mind once she'd made it up. She had undoubtedly called this meeting about his family.

If she wanted to talk about the possible health hazards of the Colton Construction projects, why not call Bridgette? Or his father?

He groaned again, but it had nothing to do with desire now, just dread. Elise and his father had never gotten along. It was clear that she suspected Fitz Colton was more involved with what had happened in this building, with what his business partner had done, than he was willing to admit.

And Neil was afraid she might be right. That was why they'd banned the topic of the Coltons during their last monthly dinner. But apparently she thought that ban had expired.

Lights illuminated the warehouse as another car pulled into the lot. He recognized the two-door compact as Elise's little vehicle, and he wished again that she would drive something bigger, safer.

But if he suggested as much, again, she would accuse him of being controlling or overprotective. If only they could agree not to argue every time they'd met, like they'd agreed last month.

If only they could do *that* every time they got together...

He had no such expectations for this meeting, though—not when she'd called it here. She must have been in a hurry to get it started, because she pushed open the driver's door and stepped into the parking lot. Because of the tinted windows, she must not have noticed him sitting inside his SUV, since she headed straight toward the building.

He sucked in a breath over her walk. At five-six, she wasn't tall, but her legs were long enough that she moved quickly and easily, her hips rolling beneath her tightly cinched trench coat. He wanted to imagine that she wore nothing beneath the coat, that that was the reason for asking him to meet her. But why here? Of all places?

He had only one way of finding out—to actually

ask her. So he pushed open the door to his SUV and stepped out. A sudden chill rushed over him. Maybe it was the cold night air. Maybe it was something else...

He glanced around the lot. Was somebody out there? Because he had the sudden, unsettling sensation that someone was watching him.

HE WATCHED THEM from the shadows at the far corner of the parking lot. He watched first the woman as she walked into the building, into the trap he'd set for them. Then, finally, the man got out of his vehicle. But Neil Colton hesitated a long moment.

And his head turned from side to side as he looked around the lot, as if he somehow sensed his presence. He held his breath, not daring to move even his lungs in case he was discovered.

His plan could not fall apart now, not when he was just getting started with it. He'd waited too long and had planned too well. And he'd chosen to start with the couple because they would be the easiest to eliminate.

They were lawyers. Book-smart. Not street-smart. But the man was more cautious than he'd thought he would be. But then he was a Colton.

The Colton family had reason to be cautious since bodies had already been discovered in this building.

Finally the man stopped looking around and headed toward the warehouse, too.

He wrapped his hand around the detonator he held. How long should he wait before he pressed the button? How long before he ended their miserable lives?

## Chapter Two

A chill chased down Elise's spine as she walked farther inside the abandoned warehouse. The door was unlocked, and she'd noticed Neil's SUV parked in the lot. She'd purposely parked a distance away from it because she remembered what had happened the last time she'd parked next to him. What had happened when they'd left the restaurant and walked back to their vehicles.

The hug that had turned into more...

The kiss.

The passion between them had drawn her to him, her body demanding the pleasure and the release she knew he could give her. And damn, after dealing with everything that had happened in Braxville over the past few months, she had desperately needed that release, that mindless pleasure.

But she should have known that there were always consequences for her actions. What would be the consequence for coming here?

Would it end as that night last month had ended? In his bed? Her pulse quickened at the thought, but it wasn't racing just with excitement but also with fear. She couldn't get used to going home with him—to the home they'd designed and had his father's company build for them after they'd settled in Braxville.

She was not going to go home with him. That wouldn't be a consequence of this meeting. But getting hurt might be.

She stumbled over something in the dark. The only light in the warehouse came from her phone. Where was Neil?

"Hello?" she called out, her voice echoing off the brick walls and concrete floor. "Hello?"

Was it safe to even be here?

Neil's triplet, Bridgette, had insisted that construction not start again on the warehouse until her investigation was complete. What kind of contaminants might be in this place?

Elise ran a hand protectively over her stomach. Could coming here cause problems with her potential pregnancy? Was it safe healthwise?

She needed to get the hell out of here, but she hadn't realized how far she'd walked into the warehouse until she heard the far-off creak of a door opening. If that sound had come from the outside door, she'd walked quite a distance into the building without even realizing it. But then she'd been lost in thought, in memories...

She pushed those from her mind now as she turned toward the noise she heard and the faint light moving toward her. A big shadow loomed behind it, and her pulse leaped again with fear and excitement.

"Neil?"

It had to be Neil; he was the one who'd asked her to meet him here. Then her excitement waned until just the fear gripped her.

"Neil? Is that you?"

"Elise?" he called back to her. "Damn, it's dark in here." He must have been using his cell phone as light, too, because only a small beam moved toward her with that shadow behind it. "Why did you want to meet here?"

"Me?" She tensed with indignation and uneasiness. "You were the one who wanted to meet here."

Even during their divorce, she and Neil had never played any games with each other. They'd civilly handled separating their personal and professional lives. So why would he be playing games with her now? Or wasn't he the one who was playing?

THAT STRANGE SENSATION that Neil had had earlier overwhelmed him now. He'd suspected then that something wasn't right about this meeting, at this location. It hadn't made sense then and made less now.

"What?" he asked. "I didn't ask you to meet me here. You asked me."

She shook her head, whipping her long hair around her shoulders. "I did not. You said to meet here."

"When?" he asked. "I didn't call you. You were the one who called—"

"I did not!" she interjected. "You had someone from the office call and leave a message—"

"Who?" he asked. "Who called? You know everybody." She had helped him hire everyone, and all the staff—albeit small—had stayed with him. She was the only one who'd left the practice.

"I didn't answer the phone. Carmen did."

"So this person didn't call your cell? They called the main switchboard for City Hall?"

"You know who this person is," she persisted. "You had them make the call for you."

He shook his head now. "No. I didn't. I also received a message my assistant took…from someone from the mayor's office." He cursed. "I should have known."

"What?" she asked, her eyes wide in the dim light.

"That you would have called me directly if you wanted to see me." But he'd thought that she might have been embarrassed, after what had happened the last time they saw each other.

But he should have known better. Elise didn't get embarrassed. She was strong, independent and, most of all, direct.

She cursed now. "And you would have done the same if you'd really wanted to see me. I should have known."

But she must have initially drawn the same wrong conclusion he had—that their night together last month had made him uncomfortable. He wasn't uncomfortable, though, except for the frustration gripping his body. He needed another release like she'd given him that night—one so intense it had shaken him to his core.

"So what's the deal?" she asked. "Why would someone leave those messages for us?"

He shrugged. "Maybe they're playing matchmaker? Trying to get us back together."

She chuckled, emitting that throaty sound that had always driven him wild with desire. "Nobody we know actually wants us back together," she said.

"Your mother," he said, a smile curving his lips as he thought of her.

"Yes, but she's too busy with her college classes to play matchmaker." Her voice was soft with pride and happiness that her mother was finally getting the education she'd been denied when she'd been forced to raise her daughter alone. "And she's too far away, back in Michigan, to be meddling in our lives."

Her mother was not a meddler. She also knew her daughter too well to try.

Elise continued, "And your family certainly isn't going to play matchmaker for us."

"My mother loves you," he insisted. "And my siblings—"

She chuckled again. "Your mother, yes, but not your siblings. I don't know if they liked me before the divorce, but now they certainly don't."

He sighed. "I don't even know if they like me half the time, so don't worry about it."

"I don't," she said, but her brow furrowed, and she glanced around the warehouse. "I am worried that someone tricked us into showing up here, though."

"Me, too." He glanced around, but he couldn't see anyone else in the place. And he didn't feel like he had outside, where he'd sensed someone had been watching him.

"Let's get out of here," Elise said with a sudden shudder.

When she headed toward the door they'd entered, Neil caught her arm and pulled her back. "Not that way."

"But the door is that way," she said.

"Was it unlocked?" he asked. It had looked like she'd walked right in.

She nodded.

"I don't like this…"

"Me, neither," she agreed. "So let's get the hell out of here."

"There's got to be another way out of here," he said. "One that doesn't open onto the parking lot."

"What are you worried about?"

"Dexter is still on the loose," Neil said. "This feels like a setup, and I thought I felt someone outside, watching the warehouse."

She sucked in a shaky-sounding breath. "Okay…"

He raised his phone and waved it around the space until the faint light reflected off a sign on the other side of the building: EXIT.

"This way," he said, and he tugged her through the warehouse toward the sign. At the door, he pushed against the steel, but it didn't budge. And another curse slipped through his lips.

"Push it down," she said.

But before he could figure out what she meant, she shoved him aside and slammed her hands against the handle, which was a bar stretching across the steel. The bar popped and the door opened.

A cold breeze blowing across the field behind the warehouse wafted inside the brick building, stirring dust and another strange smell. It could have been anything—since some of the construction materials might have been substandard, or so his sister Bridgette suspected. But this building had been abandoned before it could be renovated like the mall and some other structures in town.

The smell that tickled his nose didn't come from building materials, though. It reminded him of the times his father had convinced Neil to go hunting with him—of gunpowder!

A sudden urgency came over Neil, and he grabbed Elise's arm again, pulling her along with him as he ran through the door and away from the building.

"What the hell…" Elise murmured in protest, gasping for breath as they waded into thick, dead weeds in the small field behind the building. "You know I don't exer—"

She stopped talking as the ground shook and shuddered beneath them. Then the building exploded, bits of glass and debris propelling toward them. The force of the blast knocked them to the ground. Then flames reached out, too, like tendrils trying to pull them back—into the fire.

But then everything started going dark for Neil as he struggled for consciousness. He had to make sure that Elise was all right—had to make sure that whoever had been watching them didn't realize they'd gone out the back way. That they'd escaped the blast.

But had they?

His ears buzzed from the explosion as dizziness overwhelmed him. He was only able to murmur, "Elise…" And hope that she was all right, before consciousness slipped away from him.

"DEXTER MIGHT BE BACK!" Reese Carpenter said, his deep voice rattling Jordana's phone.

She smiled apologetically at her date—and the love of her life, Clint Broderick—and mouthed the words, "I'm sorry."

She really needed to stop answering her cell, though. Clint, determined to stop obsessing over business, always shut his off now when they were together. She would have done the same…if not for her job. A detective needed to be available, especially when there was a suspected killer on the loose.

"Dexter? Where was he seen?" she asked.

Clint tensed and sat up straighter in the chair across the candlelit table from her. The flame of the candle illuminated a flicker of concern in his blue eyes. He worried about her, but he also trusted that she could take care of herself.

Damn. She was lucky she'd found him—that they'd found each other. If only they had more time together.

His business was in Chicago, but he came back to Braxville every weekend to stay with her. If only she wasn't so damn busy.

"Nobody reported actually seeing him but dispatch just got a call about an explosion at the warehouse where the bodies were found. He must be trying to destroy evidence." Reese chuckled. "Idiot. It's too late for that. Yvette wouldn't have missed anything."

"Neil!" Jordana exclaimed as she jumped up from the table. Other diners whirled around to stare at her in alarm. She was aware she'd attracted some attention since she walked in but wasn't sure if it was because they knew she was a detective or because they knew she was a Colton.

Clint jumped up, as well, and tossed some bills next to his untouched plate of food. She would have told him to stay, to finish eating, if she wasn't so damn worried that something had happened to her brother.

"What about Neil?" Reese asked.

Her heart pounded fast and hard with fear. "He was meeting the mayor at the warehouse."

"Why?"

"I don't know," she said. She headed toward the door with Clint sticking close beside her. "But send an ambulance out to Crest View, too."

"Jordana…" Reese began.

More dread gripped her. The explosion must have been big, so big that her partner doubted anyone could have survived it. But they had to have.

She couldn't have lost her brother. And despite their divorce, Elise was still family, too. They had to be okay. They had to be…

# Chapter Three

Was he in shock? Or was he seriously wounded?

Elise closed her eyes as she remembered those first moments after the blast when she'd rolled to her side to see if Neil was all right.

His eyes had been closed, his body shockingly still for a man who was usually always in motion. Neil paced his office. He paced a courtroom. He even moved in his sleep. But now...

He was so still.

So lifeless.

She forced her eyes open to assess him, to see if his life was truly gone.

"Neil!" she shouted at him over the roar of the flames, over the ringing in her ears and the pounding of her heart.

And he blinked open his eyes to stare at her with first confusion, then concern. "Are you all right?" he asked, his first question about her. But he was that way, always fiercely protective and defensive of everyone else.

She flopped onto her back in the scratchy weeds and considered…

She could move. She hadn't lost consciousness. But what about the baby? Was the baby all right?

If there even was a baby.

There was.

She knew it—even without being able to feel anything. She knew she was pregnant, that she was carrying the child Neil had always wanted. If she hadn't lost it from the explosion propelling them to the ground.

"What the hell happened?" she mused aloud.

"We were set up," Neil said, his voice gruff.

Wondering at his paranoia, she turned back to him. Surely the explosion had just been an accident. "Are *you* all right?" she asked. The glow from the burning building illuminated his handsome face. His hair was mussed and matted with bits of debris and weeds. But she couldn't see any obvious injuries.

He levered himself up to his knees and nodded. "I'm fine. But we need to get the hell out of here."

"How?" she asked.

Had their vehicles survived the blast? They'd been parked fairly close to the building. If he hadn't dragged her along with him to the exit and out to this field…

But she could feel more than dirt beneath her. The weeds had grown up through the crumbling asphalt of an old parking lot. Using the asphalt as leverage, she pushed her hands against it and sat up. Then she stared at the building. Flames rose through gaping holes in the roof. At the realization that they could have been inside, buried under debris, burned, she shuddered.

"You saved my life," she murmured in awe. "How did you know this was going to happen?"

He stared at the devastation, too. "I didn't know this was going to happen," he said. "But those messages luring us here were obviously a setup for something."

"Certainly not for matchmaking," she murmured with another tremor of fear.

"And I felt somebody outside watching us," he added. "Probably waiting for this…" He gestured toward the building with a hand that shook.

"Do you think it was Markus Dexter?" she asked. His dad's business partner was the prime suspect in the murders of the people whose bodies had been discovered in that very warehouse. So it must have been him.

Neil just continued to stare at the fire.

The most important thing she wanted to know, though, was "Why us?"

He shook his head. "I don't know. I just know we need to get out of here in case he's still around."

Sirens wailed and lights flashed on the road behind the field, which was really an abandoned parking lot, as fire trucks and police cruisers approached.

"If Dexter was still here, he'll leave now," she told Neil.

But she needed assurances herself. She slid her hand over her stomach.

And Neil's hand followed hers, covering it. "Are you hurt? Did something hit you?"

Fear. She was so damn scared. She hadn't even been sure that she wanted a baby...until now. She wanted *this* baby.

Neil didn't wait for her reply. He closed his arms around her and lifted her up as he staggered to his feet. She didn't know if it was because she wasn't all that light or if he had been hurt.

"I can walk," she told him.

"You don't like exercise," he reminded her, his lips curving into a slight grin.

God, she...

Was so relieved that he was all right. Wasn't he?

He stumbled again, but maybe he'd just gotten caught up in the dead weeds pulling at his legs and at their clothes, as he walked through the abandoned rear parking lot and headed toward the front of the building. Before he rounded the corner, people emerged from the shadows into the glow of the fire.

Paramedics rushed toward them. "Are you all right?" a male EMT echoed the question Neil had asked of Elise.

"I—I don't know," she stammered, fear gripping her even tighter than Neil held her in his arms.

The man shone a small light in her eyes. "Did you hit your head? Lose consciousness?"

She squinted against the light, tears springing to her eyes. "No. But he might have," she said, gesturing toward Neil.

The light turned toward his face.

"I'm fine," Neil insisted.

"You must not have been inside the building, then," the female EMT remarked as she stared at the burning structure.

Neil shook his head. "No."

"So neither of you need treatment?" the male EMT asked.

"I—I might…" Elise continued to stammer over the words that she needed to say, just in case…she was carrying Neil's child.

But she hadn't wanted to tell him until she knew for certain and had had a chance to process for herself. And when she told him, she hadn't wanted it to be like this. The explosion had taken that choice away from her, though, and had potentially put her unborn child at risk. She had to know for sure that the baby was all right.

She drew in a deep breath and finished, "I might be pregnant."

Neil tensed and sucked in a breath, as well. Then, still clutching her closely in his arms, he strode toward the front of the burning building, where the ambulance was parked among police vehicles—all with lights flashing. He lifted her through the open back doors of the ambulance and laid her on the gurney sitting inside it.

Would he drop her and leave? Was he angry? She stared at his face, but he was stoic. Then he settled onto a bench seat on one side of the ambulance, as if to make it clear that he wasn't going anywhere.

The male paramedic jumped into the back of the

ambulance while the female one climbed into the driver's seat. She turned back and asked, "Nobody else was hurt in the explosion?"

Maybe she thought someone else might need help more than Elise did. She slid her hand over her stomach again, already protective of the child she might be carrying. "There was nobody else inside the building," she said. "Nobody that we saw as we ran out of it anyway."

There could have been someone else, though.

"If someone was inside the building, they probably didn't survive," the male paramedic remarked as he slid an oxygen sensor onto the tip of one of her fingers before wrapping a blood pressure cuff around her arm. "Let's head to the hospital."

*Yes.* Now finally Elise would have the confirmation she needed—that she was pregnant, and if she was, that the baby was all right.

He or she had to be all right.

Was Neil? He was so quiet. Maybe he had been hurt during the explosion. She'd thought he'd lost consciousness for a moment, like the paramedic had suspected. So had he hit his head on the asphalt?

Fumbling with the oxygen sensor on her finger, she clasped the paramedic's arm and murmured, "Please make sure he gets checked out, too. We were knocked down from the blast."

The paramedic glanced at Neil and nodded. "He could also be in shock."

But maybe Neil wasn't quiet because he was hurt

or in shock. Maybe it was because of what she'd just had to admit to the paramedic. That she could be carrying his child…

NEIL WAS IN SHOCK. So much so that he didn't move when the doors opened onto the ambulance bay at the ER. The paramedics whisked Elise out on the stretcher and disappeared with her down a hallway before he realized they were taking her away from him.

Dazed, he lurched to his feet and jumped down from the ambulance. Weakness had overtaken his leg muscles since he'd been sitting for a while, causing him to dodder as he walked toward the entrance to the ER.

"Sir," a nurse exclaimed, rushing to him. "Are you all right?"

He shook his head.

No.

Not now…

"Let me get a wheelchair for you," she said. "Or a stretcher."

He shook his head again. "No, I have to find my…" Wife. The word nearly slipped off his tongue. But she wasn't his wife anymore. What was she?

*Pregnant? She might be pregnant.*

Was that possible? She was always so vigilant about taking her birth control—so much so that she'd assured him last month that it was fine that he didn't have a condom. She wasn't seeing anyone else anyway.

So if she was pregnant…

The baby was his. His and Elise's.

That was once all he'd wanted, so he should have been overjoyed. But instead, he was just shocked. And scared…

What if something had happened to the baby? What if she actually wasn't pregnant? What if she was but didn't want the baby any more than she had when they'd divorced three years ago?

She hadn't been pregnant then. She'd refused to get pregnant…until she was ready. Neil had suspected that she would never be ready, and he hadn't wanted to fight about it anymore, or worse yet, turn into the painfully civil, cohabiting strangers his parents were. So he had filed for divorce.

Elise hadn't fought him on that like she usually fought him on everything. Apparently, the divorce was one of the few things on which they'd agreed.

"Sir," the nurse spoke to him again with an urgency in her voice, as if she'd called out to him a few times. She had a wheelchair now and tried to ease him into it.

But he shook his head again. "I don't need treatment."

He needed answers.

He needed to make sure that Elise and his…baby… were all right. "The paramedics just brought back a woman. I have to find where they've taken her, see how she's doing."

"I'll check on her for you while you're being seen," the nurse offered. "You were at the explosion?"

He nodded. "With her. We were already out of the

building when it exploded, though." But had they gotten far enough from it before the big blast? Had anything hit Elise? How hard had she been knocked to the ground? He'd hit it so hard that the air had momentarily left his lungs, and he hadn't been able to draw in another breath. That was probably why consciousness had slipped away from him for a minute, because he hadn't been able to breathe.

"You should still be checked out," the nurse insisted, and she shoved a little harder on his shoulder, trying to push him into the wheelchair.

The weakness had left his legs now, and he had no problem walking. But he didn't get far before another woman joined the nurse.

She wore scrubs, as well, with a name tag on the pocket that he didn't need to read. He knew her better than any other woman in the world.

Her blue eyes glistening with tears of concern, she pulled him into a tight embrace. "Neil!" his mother exclaimed, and her slender frame trembled. "Are you all right?"

"Yes," he insisted as he pulled away from her. "I'm fine."

"Really?" She scrutinized his face, furrows forming in her forehead. She wore her dark auburn hair up in some type of messy bun. Her fingers trembled as she ran them lightly over his face, knocking dirt and briars from his short beard. "What happened?"

"We got knocked down—by the explosion," he admitted.

Then she knocked him down, gently shoving him

into the wheelchair the other nurse had failed to get him to use. His mother didn't give him a choice. "You are getting checked out," she insisted.

"I'm—"

"A lawyer," she interjected. "Not a medical professional. We're going to let someone else evaluate your health."

She propelled him down the hall and through double doors that opened automatically onto a big room. A nurses' station sat to the left, while the rest of the area was cordoned off with walls that didn't reach entirely to the tall ceiling. Each of those walled-off cubes had a curtain that was either pulled open or shut.

Elise had to be in here, too. The paramedics must have rolled her back into one of the walled-off spaces. He glanced around, but he couldn't see behind the closed curtains.

"Where's Elise?" he asked his mother. "I need to find her."

"Elise was with you?" Lilly asked with concern. "Is she all right?"

"That's what I need to know," he said. "But where is she? Please, Mom, find out what's going on with her."

His mother's voice, which had been all warm concern, changed to chilly professionalism. "I can't tell you her medical condition."

He jumped up from the wheelchair and whirled toward her. "Why the hell can't you?"

"Privacy laws—"

"She's my wife."

"She *was* your wife," his mother corrected him. "She isn't anymore. She has every right to her privacy."

"But…"

"But what?" his mother prodded.

"She might be carrying my child," he admitted.

His mother's mouth dropped open as she drew in a sharp breath. Then a smile curved her lips. "That's…"

"Surprising," he finished for her.

She shook her head. "No, not really, not with how close you two have remained even since the divorce."

"So find out where she is and how she is," he persisted. "I need to know that there's nothing wrong with her or the baby." *And that there is a baby…*

Elise had told the paramedic that she wasn't certain she was pregnant. But she was never late, either. He knew that from when they'd lived together.

His mother's hands closed around his shoulders as she moved him toward one of those partitioned-off areas with an open curtain. She pushed him onto the stretcher and said, "Sit down and get checked out."

The other nurse must have summoned a doctor, because one joined them now, firing questions at him that he ignored. Fortunately, they hadn't closed his curtain, so he could peer around the open area. Maybe he had to pull open every other curtain to find Elise. She was all he could focus on right now.

As if his mother had read his mind, she said, "You're going to stay here and get examined, and when Elise has been released, she can update you on her condition…if she chooses to."

"But if something's happened, she might need me," he said, but the words sounded hollow even as he uttered them. Elise had never needed him; in fact, she'd done much better without him in her life.

She'd gone from being his partner in a fledging law firm to running the whole damn town. Had she been the target of the bomb? It had to have been a bomb that had caused the explosion. Someone must have rigged up one in the abandoned warehouse and lured them there.

"She could still be in danger," he said, panic pressing on his madly pounding heart as the thought finally occurred to him. Maybe he had struck his head when the blast pushed him to the ground. Maybe that was why he hadn't considered that the bomber could have followed the ambulance away from the burning warehouse.

"We have good security," his mother said with pride in the hospital at which she spent so much time. He could understand that she would prefer being here to spending time at home with his father. There had always been so much tension in their house, but it had to be even worse now, because of the ongoing investigation.

"The security might be good, but I don't trust anyone," Neil said. Not with the life of Elise and their unborn child. "I can't…"

"Being a criminal lawyer has made you cynical," she admonished him.

"Being a criminal lawyer has made me a realist," he corrected her. He knew there were really bad people in the world. She had to know that, too, as a nurse.

But his mother always insisted on finding the good in everyone. Maybe that was why she'd stayed with his father so long, even though they clearly weren't happy.

"The police are also on their way to question you about what happened," his mother said. "You do trust your sister, right?"

He groaned. "Jordana called you," he said. That was why their mother had rushed to the ER area, when usually she was involved only in training and administration now.

"She knew you were going to the warehouse," Mom said. "And when she learned about the explosion, she got worried."

"She's not the only one," he bitterly remarked. He was worried, too, so damn worried about Elise.

THE FLASHING LIGHTS and blaring sirens on the ambulance had drawn him to follow as it sped away from the burning warehouse. Somebody was hurt.

Not dead…

They were supposed to be dead. They couldn't have survived the explosion. Unless…

Had they been inside?

He'd watched them enter the building—falling into the trap he'd set for them—but had they exited some other way? Had they escaped before he'd detonated the bomb? If they had, they would not be so damn freakishly lucky the next time.

And there would be a next time.

He wasn't going to stop until they were dead.

# Chapter Four

"You're sure?" Elise asked, anxiety fluttering through her stomach. Or was that fluttering she felt due to some other reason? No. It was too soon for her to feel the baby move. It might have been the ultrasound wand they'd had to insert inside her, though. The young female resident had informed Elise that at approximately four weeks, she wasn't far enough along for them to see anything with a traditional ultrasound.

"Your blood work confirms you're pregnant," the resident said as she read the results the nurse had brought to her.

"But is the baby all right?" Elise needed to know.

"You're not bleeding, and you've said you have no pain?"

She shook her head. "No. No pain," she confirmed. Just fear…

The doctor moved that wand inside her and something appeared on the machine's monitor. Elise stared at it, but she couldn't see anything. Tears stung her eyes. She hadn't realized how much she'd wanted to be pregnant. "There's nothing there. Are you sure…?"

The doctor pointed at the screen. "This…this is the gestational sac."

"What is that?"

"It's where the fetus is developing," she said. "It's intact. Your pregnancy is definitely still viable."

"The explosion didn't hurt…him or her?"

"It's way too soon to tell the gender," the doctor said as she pulled out the wand. The image remained on the screen, though.

"I'm not worried about the gender," Elise said. She didn't really care. "I just want to make sure the baby's all right."

"You're in the early stages of development, so you don't need to worry about injuries to the fetus. You have no injuries, so I see no risk of a miscarriage from what happened tonight."

Elise expelled a shaky sigh of relief. "Thank you."

"I had nothing to do with it," the doctor replied. "I'm just the messenger."

It was Neil who had saved her life, his and their baby's. She owed him her gratitude. She owed him the truth. "How is the man who came into the ER with me?" she asked.

But he hadn't actually come in with her. When the paramedics had whisked her out of the ambulance, Neil must have remained inside it. He hadn't followed her. Was he really all right? He'd been knocked down even harder than she had. And when she'd first called to him, he hadn't immediately responded. Had he lost consciousness briefly? Did he have a concussion?

"Man?" the doctor asked.

"She's talking about my son," she heard a voice say as the curtain slid aside.

Elise closed her eyes for a moment, but when she opened them, Lilly Colton was there in the small ER space with them. Not that Elise disliked the woman...

Lilly was actually Elise's favorite Colton. But she couldn't deal with her now, not when she was reeling from everything else. And Neil deserved to know before his mother did, that he was going to be a father.

Lilly's blue eyes, so like her son's, were focused on the monitor and that strange bubble that had remained on the screen even after the doctor removed the wand. Unlike Elise, who had no idea what she was looking at, Lilly, as a nurse, must have recognized the image. A soft sigh slipped out of the older woman's lips.

The young doctor lowered her voice and stepped closer to Lilly. "Should you be in here, since you know her?"

"No," Lilly admitted. "I stopped Neil from barging in and then I..."

"It's okay," Elise said, even though she wasn't entirely sure about that herself.

The doctor looked at Elise for a moment, as if assessing the situation. "If you're sure..."

"I am," Elise said.

And Lilly released another little sigh. "I'll help her get dressed," she told the doctor, "while you write up your release orders."

The doctor hesitated yet.

"She is being released?" Lilly asked with concern.

"Of course," Elise answered for her. "You told me that I'm fine."

The doctor nodded and finally stepped out of the small area, pulling the curtain closed behind her as if she suspected she and her former mother-in-law needed privacy.

"She's right," Lilly said as she stepped closer to the gurney. "I probably shouldn't be in here, but she's a resident who comes from a big city, so she doesn't realize that most of the staff here winds up having to treat people we know. Even though we do, we abide by the privacy laws, and we don't share what we learn." Lilly covered Elise's hand with hers and gently squeezed. "This is your business. No one else's."

"I wish…" Elise murmured ruefully, but she hadn't conceived this baby via artificial insemination.

"Even the mayor is entitled to privacy," Lilly assured her.

Elise groaned. She hadn't considered yet that being an unwed mother could impact her career, at least in a town as conservative as Braxville. Fortunately she had a few years to go on her term before needing to worry about a reelection campaign. "I wasn't worried about voters, at least not all of them. Just one…"

But had Neil voted for her?

If he had, he'd probably been the only Colton, with the probable exception of her ex-mother-in-law. Lilly had always been very sweet and affectionate and welcoming to her. The other Coltons had been, too, until the divorce and until she'd gone to work for her predecessor.

"If you're talking about Neil…"

"I know," Elise said. "You're his mother, and your loyalty will always be to him."

"My loyalty is to all my family," Lilly said. "And you will always be family."

"So is this baby," Elise confessed as she moved her hand, still clasped in Lilly's, to her stomach. "This is Neil's baby."

Lilly smiled, but there was no surprise on her face. She'd already known. Neil must have sent her back to check on Elise or maybe just on his unborn child. A baby was all he'd really wanted from her, not the complete partnership he'd promised, or he would have given her the time she'd wanted before starting a family.

"I already informed him about the privacy laws that preclude him from learning your medical condition. I won't tell him anything," Lilly promised.

"I will," Elise assured her.

"Take your time," Lilly advised. "Make your decisions based on your needs, nobody else's. You have to do what's going to make you happy. Life's too short to live with regrets."

Surprise widened Elise's eyes. "I didn't expect you to say that to me."

"Because I'm Neil's mother?"

Elise nodded.

Lilly released her hand and stepped back from the gurney, and she murmured wistfully, "I'm also a woman."

A woman who obviously had made some decisions

in her past based on needs other than her own—decisions she apparently regretted now.

Elise held out her hand for Lilly, wanting to offer comfort to her, but the older woman was already reaching for the curtain. Maybe someone had called out to her, because she rushed away without another word, leaving Elise reeling from what she'd said or rather what she'd left unsaid.

Lilly had just offered Elise more support than even her own mother would have in this situation. Her mother would urge her to tell Neil, to let him be involved in his child's life. Although, that was because Elise's own father had abandoned them, and Aubrey Willis knew how hard being a single mother was.

Elise knew, too, because of all her mother had sacrificed for her. She didn't want to make those kinds of sacrifices; that was why she hadn't been in a rush to start a family, like Neil had been.

He deserved to know, though, that he was finally going to get his wish. He was going to be a father.

*They must be in shock...*

Neither Neil nor Elise had spoken since walking through the door of the room that the head nurse—aka Mom—had provided for the police interview. While the head nurse had refused to comment on their medical conditions, Mom had revealed that they were being released. So they hadn't been seriously hurt in the explosion.

Once she'd learned that, Jordana had assured Clint that he could leave the hospital. Reese, her partner, would drop her home when they took a break in their investigation for the night.

"Are you both really all right?" she asked again. Those had been her first words when each had walked into the room just seconds ago. In reply, all she'd received were head nods. Well, actually just a head nod from Elise. Neil had been too busy studying his ex-wife's face to do even that.

This time he did. But that was all he did. He remained silent, just like Elise—which was so totally out of character for the lawyers who rarely stopped talking or arguing. Concern gripped Jordana. Were they really all right?

"We need you to answer our questions," Reese said, irritation making his voice gruff. "We need to know what the hell happened tonight."

Neil shrugged. "I don't know."

And Jordana wondered if he was talking about the explosion or something else—something that had him staring so intensely at Elise that her own heart ached over the look of longing on her brother's face.

Like her brother, she focused on her ex-sister-in-law. "Why did you ask Neil to meet you at the warehouse?" she asked.

Elise shook her head now. "I didn't."

Jordana's brow furrowed and she turned to her brother. "You told me that—"

"I got a message that was supposed to be from her," he said. "But it wasn't."

"And I got the same from him," Elise said, "asking me to meet me there."

"A setup," Reese said.

"The explosion wasn't an accident, then," Jordana said. Neither was Neil and Elise being there at the exact time of the blast.

"Did you see anyone?" Reese asked.

They both shook their heads this time.

"No sign of Markus Dexter?" he asked.

"No," Neil said. "What about you? Do you have any idea where he is?"

Jordana shook her head. "No. Ever since we served a search warrant on his house, there's been a unit sitting on it, watching it to see if either he or his wife returns. The evidence is still being processed from the search. But so far there have been no clues to lead us to where he's gone."

"He must not have gone far," Reese remarked.

"You think he was behind the explosion?" Elise asked. "But why would he try to hurt me and Neil?"

Reese shrugged now. "You're not the only Colton he tried killing recently."

Jordana flinched with a twinge of pain and fear over how the family could have lost Ty when Dexter had shot him. He was pretty much fully recovered, though—albeit more from love than medicine, probably. Like her, her brother had recently found love, too.

She could only hope that her relationship fared better than Neil and Elise's had.

"I'm not a Colton," Elise said. "So it doesn't make sense for him to try to kill me."

"Maybe he blames you for the bodies being discovered—because of your plans for the city," Jordana suggested.

"I guess he wouldn't be the only one to have problems with my politics," Elise admitted.

A smile tugged at Jordana's lips. Her father had made it clear what he thought of Elise's plans to continue her predecessor's policy of limiting urban sprawl. Not damn much...

"We really don't know anything to help with your investigation," Neil said, and now irritation was making his voice gravelly. "It's late. If we think of anything else, we'll let you know."

"We need those messages that lured you both to the warehouse," Reese said.

"My assistant received a call from who she thought was someone in Neil's office," Elise said.

"Same here," Neil added.

"Then we'll need to talk to your assistants," Reese said.

"In the morning," Jordana told her partner. She wanted to get back to her house and to Clint. He'd come down early for a long weekend. Unfortunately, she still had to work tomorrow, since it was Friday.

"We don't have anything else to tell you, so we're going to leave now," Neil informed them. Without waiting for the interview to officially end, he clasped Elise's arm and escorted her toward the door.

A strange look of dread and resignation crossed Elise's beautiful face. She obviously didn't want to leave with Neil. Of course, most women didn't want to hang out with their ex-husbands, but Elise wasn't most women. She and Neil were that rare couple who'd managed to maintain a friendship even after their divorce.

So what was going on with them?

"What the hell?" Reese asked after the door closed. "Why'd you let them walk out of here?"

Jordana sighed. "I know them." And how damn stubborn they both were. "They're not going to answer any more questions tonight."

Reese shook his head, mussing up his already mussed-up, overly long hair. "It's crazy. If someone tried to kill me, I'd be the one asking the questions. I'd be so damn mad...unless..."

"Unless what?" Jordana asked.

"I know they were married before, so was this some kind of murder-suicide thing? One of them trying to take out the other?"

Jordana gasped with shock, then laughed. Like her, Reese had been a detective too long—so long that he'd grown cynical. "That's crazy."

"He's your brother, so of course you'd have trouble suspecting him."

"And you suspect everyone of everything," she admonished him. "I know them both, and they're not murderous or suicidal. They've been divorced a few years, with no animosity between them."

"I'm not so sure about that," Reese said. "I could feel the tension in this room. Something's going on with them."

Jordana couldn't laugh off that suspicion. She'd suspected the same damn thing.

"They're keeping something from us," Reese said.

She nodded in agreement. "But it might not have anything to do with what happened tonight."

And everything to do with the two of them.

"Whatever it is, we need to know," he said. "And they need to know that their lives are at risk."

Jordana sucked in a breath of fear for her brother. Her partner, however cynical, was right. Neil was in danger and maybe not just from whoever had caused the explosion.

"WE'RE IN SERIOUS TROUBLE," Neil told Elise, his stomach knotting at the thought of how bad the threat was. They could have been killed earlier. And if they had…

He nearly choked on the emotion rushing over him. "We need to get out of here."

What if whoever had set them up had followed the ambulance to the hospital? Neil suspected he might have, because once they stepped out the doors of the hospital, that sensation rushed over him again—of someone watching him.

It could have been Jordana and her partner, though. Detective Carpenter obviously hadn't wanted to end the interview when Neil had. But the detectives weren't who either he or Elise needed to talk to at the moment.

They needed to talk to each other. He had so damn many questions for her. One more important than any other.

"How are we getting out of here?" Elise asked.

"Our vehicles are back at the warehouse and might be burned up."

He held up a key fob. "My mother loaned me hers."

Elise expelled a ragged sigh. "Good. Then you can drop me home."

"I'm taking you home," Neil said. To the house they'd designed together. The one they had intended to share for the rest of their lives. The one Neil had wanted to fill with children…

He clicked the fob, and the lights flashed on his mom's vehicle. Hastening his step, he made it to the passenger's door before her and pulled it open. But she didn't slide onto the seat. Instead, she just stood and stared at him.

"I want to go to my place," she said.

"The security is better at mine," he said. His brother, Tyler, being a security expert, Neil had the best alarm system on the market. That wasn't the only reason he wanted Elise to come home with him, though. "And we need to talk…"

"We can do that here," she said.

That strange sensation—of being watched—continued to chill his flesh, though, and he shook his head. "Not here."

She sighed. "What's to talk about, Neil? You know I'm pregnant."

A sharp pain jabbed his heart. "You are?"

She nodded. "Yes, I am. And as I told your sister, I'm fine. I am also exhausted, so talking about anything else can wait until tomorrow."

"This can't," he insisted.

"What?"

"My proposal," he said.

She sighed again, clearly getting frustrated with him. "What do you propose, Neil?"

"That you marry me."

# Chapter Five

"Did you hit your head?" Elise asked. Again. She'd asked that the moment Neil had proposed to her in the hospital parking lot.

He'd claimed he was fine. But suspecting that he had a concussion, she'd agreed to go back to the house with him and also because she had the same uneasy feeling he had, that they were being watched.

Maybe someone had been watching. Or maybe they were just being overly cautious after what had nearly happened to them. They'd nearly been killed.

Would have been if not for Neil's quick thinking. She owed him for saving her life, but becoming his wife wasn't the correct way to repay him. They'd tried that already. He'd been the one to end it—to end their marriage.

But that was because…

She pressed her hand against her stomach. It was still flat, or as flat as it ever was, since she never had the time or the inclination to work out. He had either proposed because she was pregnant or because he was concussed. Maybe both.

He hadn't forgotten the code to the security system at the front door, though. He punched in the number—the date he'd originally proposed to her—and the red light flashed to green on the console. Closing the door, he glanced around the darkened foyer as if looking for someone hiding in the shadows.

"You said it's the best security system," she reminded him. And she doubted anyone could have guessed the passcode. Nobody else knew how soon he'd proposed after their first meeting in that law school lecture hall.

He poked his head in the door off the foyer, to the den, before heading cautiously past the stairwell toward the open area at the back of the house, which combined the kitchen and great room. As he walked, he flipped on all the lights.

"I'm sure nobody got inside," she assured him as she peered around the space. "Not even a decorator..."

"Decorator?" he echoed the word, finally seeming to emerge from the coma he'd been in since the explosion, or at least since she'd told the paramedic she might be pregnant. "The house looks the same as it did when you lived here."

They had decorated it together, just as they'd designed it. They'd picked out every cabinet, every paint color. That was why she hadn't wanted it in the divorce, but she hadn't been surprised that he had. Obviously he hadn't been as sentimental as she was, or he wouldn't have filed for divorce in the first place.

"You haven't decorated for Christmas yet," she

said, clarifying her remark, as she pointed toward the empty space in front of the tall windows where they'd put the tree in the past.

"It's barely December," he said.

Braxville had put up the twinkling lights and wreaths in the town square even before Thanksgiving. She'd thought the tradition a bit premature, but after she became mayor, she didn't dare discontinue it. To do so would cost her votes in the next election. Would being a single mother also cost her votes?

Not that she would ever consider accepting Neil's proposal, even if he was serious.

But he couldn't be serious.

"See, I remember what month it is," he said. "I don't have a concussion. What about you?"

Maybe she had hit her head; it would explain why she'd come back here again, especially after what had happened the last time she'd come home with him.

She moved her hand over her stomach and sighed. "I told you I was fine," she said. He could have found out for himself if he'd really wanted to know. She hadn't removed him as her next of kin or durable medical power of attorney. She had no one else in Braxville.

Her mother lived in Detroit, Michigan, where Elise had been born and raised. She might have returned there after law school if she hadn't met and fallen so hard for Neil that she'd moved to his hometown.

"What you said earlier…" His hand covered hers on her stomach. "You really are…?" His voice trailed off as if he couldn't utter the word, as if he didn't dare believe it was possible.

"Pregnant?" She nodded.

"That's why you need to marry me," he said.

She snorted. "You might not have hit your head, but you've lost your damn mind. I am not marrying you."

"But you're pregnant."

"And this isn't 1920," she said. "I can be a single mom." Not that doing so was something she had ever planned.

In fact, that would have been the last damn thing she ever planned on being, after watching her mom struggle so much to raise Elise on her own.

"But you don't want to be a single mom," he said.

*Damn it.*

He knew her too well. Sometimes.

Other times it was as if he'd never known her at all.

"I'm not going to marry you," she said. Not because of the baby.

Now, if he loved her—just her—she might have been tempted to accept. But he'd never really loved just her, or he wouldn't have divorced her in the first place.

Tears stung her eyes, but she blinked them back. Damn hormones. She never cried. Not even when she'd received those divorce papers.

Neil must have noticed her struggle with emotion because he reached out, cupping her cheek in his palm. "Are you really okay?"

She nodded. "Yes, the blood work confirmed the

pregnancy. And although it's too soon to see much of anything, the doctor also confirmed that I didn't miscarry. That everything looks fine."

"Are *you* fine?" he asked.

No. Not now...

Not with him staring at her so intently, touching her so gently.

"WHAT'S WRONG?" HE ASKED.

Neil's stomach clenched, knots forming as he gazed at the tears shimmering in Elise's green eyes. She never cried. Not even when he'd told her that he couldn't stay married to her. If she had, he might have known that she cared, that she loved him as much as he loved her. But she'd given him no indication that it mattered to her whether they were married or not.

She was giving him a clear indication now that she had no intention of accepting his proposal, though, of ever being his wife again. So obviously she preferred their divorce over their marriage.

She blinked, her lashes fluttering over those green-green eyes. "What do you think is wrong?"

He didn't want to believe that she was upset about being pregnant, that she regretted that night they'd spent together a month ago.

Fortunately, she answered her own question. "We could have been killed tonight," she said, her voice cracking with emotion. "If you hadn't gotten us out of there when you did."

"I should have realized right away that it was a setup," he admonished himself. "I should have gotten us out of there sooner." Hell, he never should have let her walk into the warehouse.

Not only was it a crime scene but it could potentially pose health risks if Bridgette was right, if the buildings Colton Construction had renovated were somehow contaminated.

"Are you sure you're okay?" he asked again. "That the doctors thoroughly checked you out?"

"I'm fine," she assured him. "I'm just tired and overwhelmed."

It was late. And they'd been through so much that evening. Now was not the time to press her to accept his proposal, if he could even come up with an argument that could convince her. He moved his hand from her face, and then he swung her up in his arms.

She clutched at his shoulders. "What are you doing?" she asked.

"Bringing you to bed," he said as he carried her through the great room to the double doors on the other side of it. He'd left them ajar that morning, so he was able to push easily through them to the master bedroom. The bed was unmade, the sheets rumpled from his restless sleep the night before. Next to the four-poster bed, he released her, letting her soft, curvy body slide down his.

"I should sleep in one of the guest bedrooms," she said. But she made no move toward the doors.

She might need to be with him as much as he needed to be with her. He could have lost her tonight. Could have lost *them*…without ever knowing that they'd conceived a child together. The child he'd wanted so badly.

Emotion rushed over him now. "Please," he implored her. "Marry me again, Elise."

"Why?" she asked.

Because he never should have divorced her in the first place. He'd been such a fool. So stubborn...

He realized that now. Hell, he'd realized that then. But as well as stubborn, he was proud—like his father. Too proud to admit to all the mistakes he'd made.

"Last month you told me that you weren't seeing anyone else," he reminded her. "So this baby is mine. I want him or her to have my name."

"What's wrong with my name?" she asked. "Isn't Willis as good as Colton?"

"Right now, being a Willis is probably better," he assured her.

Nobody in Braxville was happy with his father right now. While Fitz Colton might not have known about his partner allegedly being a killer, why hadn't he done something about so many of his workers getting seriously sick? A couple had even died.

"And I'm fine if the baby has your name, too. But I want..."

Her.

She pressed her finger over his lips. "Shh...it's late, Neil, and I don't want to fight."

Neither did he. Unfortunately they did it entirely too often. Sometimes fighting with her—matching wits with her stimulating mind—was exhilarating. Other times—when she was as stubborn as he was and refused to concede defeat—fighting with her exhausted him.

And she had already admitted to being tired. He wasn't going to push her tonight, not when he could see how determined she was. She wasn't going to give him a win and let him put her ring back on her finger. Not tonight.

"Let's just go to bed," he suggested, and he flicked his tongue across the finger she held over his lips.

She shivered and murmured, "Neil…"

"We're alive, Elise," he reminded her. Despite someone's effort to end their lives. "Let's celebrate that tonight." And that they were having a child—whether they had decided to have it together or apart.

He pushed that horrible thought from his mind, though. He would come up with a better argument. He would eventually convince her to marry him again. He couldn't live without her. If something had happened to her tonight…

He shuddered and closed his arms around her. She stood for a moment in the circle of them, her body tense. Then she slid her arms around his waist and clutched him tightly. Like the hug at her car a month ago, passion ignited over the closeness of their bodies.

Hers so curvy and soft. His so hard he ached with tension, with need…for her. After nearly losing her tonight, he had to be close to her again—part of her again.

She must have felt the same desire, because she moved her arms from his waist to his neck and pulled his head down to hers. She kissed him passionately, hungrily. Like she had the night they'd conceived their baby. Remembering that, remembering what they'd been through, he pulled back. "Are you sure it's safe to do this?"

She chuckled. "I'm already pregnant."

"That's what I mean," he said. "We're not going to hurt the baby?"

She shook her head, but she studied his face for a moment…like she was looking for something. She had to see how much he wanted her, how much he always wanted her. And in case she didn't see it, he showed her.

He leaned down and kissed her back with all the passion he felt for her. And as he kissed her, he pushed her coat from her shoulders. He needed nothing between his skin and hers. She must have felt the same, because she dealt with his buttons and zippers with as much impatience as he showed in tackling hers… until they stood naked before each other.

No. They weren't entirely naked. There were always thin walls between them, holding them apart. He knew it. Some of those walls were his, his way of avoiding getting hurt. Were hers the same?

Was that why she'd turned down his proposal? She didn't trust him again.

With her heart…

She trusted him with her body. So he made sure to give her pleasure. Gently tugging her onto the rumpled bed, he made love to her with his hands and his mouth before she pulled him down on top of her. She guided him inside, joining their bodies.

He moved slowly…until she began to move beneath him. She knew just what to do, how to move, where to touch him, kiss him…so that he lost control and found his release, his mind-blowing release.

Despite the pleasure they'd given each other, though, his body was still tense, his mind unable to shut off the flow of all his concerns. All he could do was hold her tightly against him and try to keep her safe through the night…but he worried that someone was out there, waiting to try for them again.

HIS CELL PHONE vibrated across the surface of his nightstand, and a groan slipped out of Ty Colton's mouth. He ran his hand over his head, mussing his dark brown hair. It was getting too long, starting to curl too much.

"What?" a soft voice murmured as Ashley shifted against his side. Her silky dark hair fell over his arm as she snuggled closer to him.

Love warmed his heart, making it swell in his chest. Ashley Hart was such an incredible woman. A socialite. A philanthropist. A freaking genius. Not to mention drop-dead gorgeous.

It made total sense that he'd fallen for her after he'd been hired to protect her. But that she'd fallen for him, too…

How had he gotten so lucky?

The phone continued to vibrate, drawing his attention back to it and another groan from his throat.

"Nobody ever calls at this hour with good news…" Not that he was entirely sure what time it was. They'd been eating dinner and she'd looked so damn beautiful that he'd wanted her instead. Tempted to ignore the call and focus on Ashley, Ty groaned again into the cell phone as he swiped his hand across the screen.

"Are you okay?" his sister asked, Jordana's voice gruff with concern.

"Yeah," he said.

"But you're groaning," she said. "Is your gunshot wound bothering you?"

"The only thing bothering me is someone interrupting my sleep," he said. "What's going on?"

"You need to come home."

"I am home." Never more so than now, since Ashley had moved in with him.

"You're in Wichita," she said. "You need to be here in Braxville."

He sighed. "I'm a security expert, Jord. I'm safe here. And I doubt Markus Dexter will try to get to me again."

"He might have tried getting to Neil tonight."

He cursed and jolted upright in bed. "Has Neil been shot? Is he okay?"

Ashley sat up next to him, her big brown eyes even wider with concern.

"He was nearly blown up," his sister said, her voice shaking with emotion. "But he got out of the building in time. The bomb was set at the warehouse where the bodies were discovered."

He sucked in a breath.

"Is Neil okay?" Ashley asked.

He nodded but repeated the question to Jordana.

"Yes, he's fine. But he shouldn't have been there."

"What the hell was he doing there?" Ty asked. "He has nothing to do with the investigation, nothing to do with Colton Construction. Unless…" A horrible thought occurred to him, but he shook it off. Neil was a criminal lawyer, but he was too loyal to his family to ever represent the man who'd tried to kill Tyler.

"Unless what?" Jordana asked.

"Nothing. What was he doing there?"

"He thought Elise wanted to meet him there."

Ty cursed again. "Of course." And for some reason, despite divorcing her, his brother could not stay away from his ex-wife.

"She thought the same," Jordana continued. "It was a setup."

"It would make more sense that the mayor would be the target," Ty said. "Maybe Dexter blames her campaign against urban sprawl for those bodies being discovered."

"So you think Dexter killed those people?"

"Don't you?" Ty asked. "One of them was probably his mistress, since he's been rumored to have many. And the other body was the private investigator trying to find her after she was murdered. How can you not think Dexter killed them?"

"I'm waiting for conclusive evidence," the detective maintained.

Ty snorted. "Yeah, right. Has any been found?"

"His house was searched—"

"Bet his wife loved that," Ty remarked.

"She'd already left town."

"Alone?"

"Don't think she wants anything to do with her husband or the scandal, but we have a unit watching the house in case anyone comes back. Nobody has come back yet."

"That you've seen," Ty said. "But who else besides Dexter would want to blow up that warehouse?"

"Since they were lured there with those messages, Neil and Elise might have been the targets more than Crest View Center. That's why you need to come home. You need to help me keep Neil safe."

"Of course," Ty agreed.

He could protect his brother from whomever had set that bomb, but who would protect Neil from his ex-wife? Ty had a feeling that Neil's life wasn't the only thing in danger; his heart was, too.

# Chapter Six

*What the hell did I just do?*

Her body answered that question. Limp with sexual satisfaction, Elise nearly melted into the tangled sheets. Maybe it was the hormones that had had her reacting so passionately to Neil's kiss. Or maybe it had been their close brush with death that had heightened all her senses.

But what had been her excuse a month ago when she'd gotten pregnant? At least that couldn't happen again. She was already as pregnant as she was going to get.

She pressed her hand over her stomach but felt nothing until Neil's hand slid over hers. Then her skin tingled, and her pulse leaped. Even after what they'd just done, how much pleasure he'd just given her, she wanted him again.

Damn hormones.

"Are you really all right?" he asked.

"Me?" she asked. "Or the baby?" That was whom he was really concerned about, the only reason he wanted to marry her.

"Both of you," he said. "I could have lost you tonight."

"Last night," she murmured, as she glanced at the clock beside the bed. She corrected him about the time but not about the fact that he didn't have her, that he hadn't had her since he'd divorced her.

Even that night…

It had been a lapse, a slipup. It had been passion, not love. He couldn't have ended their marriage if he'd really loved her.

"You need to rest," he said. "Especially now."

Now that she carried his child. In the past she'd worried about losing herself to him. That was why she hadn't fought the divorce. She'd known then that he hadn't been with her for her but for the life they could build together: the life he'd wanted, the law practice, the kids…his family.

She gasped as she felt now like she'd felt then, like she was drowning under all the expectations, of all the responsibilities of being a Colton.

"What is it?" he asked. "Are you all right? Did you feel the baby move?"

"No. Although the doctor assured me everything was normal, I couldn't even see anything on the ultrasound, so I doubt I'll feel anything for a while."

"Oh…" he murmured with clear disappointment. Then he clutched her hand in his, entwining their fingers. "I want to be there when you have the next ultrasound. I want to be there when you first feel the baby move. I want to be there for you during this pregnancy, Elise. Please marry me again."

She closed her eyes against the tears rushing to them. "Neil…"

"You don't have to do this alone, like your mother did," he persisted.

She cursed. How could he know her so well in some regards and so little in others? He knew how she'd felt about the struggle her mother had had raising Elise on her own, but he didn't fully grasp how that had affected her.

"I will be there for you," he vowed, "if you'll let me."

No. He would be there for the baby and that baby was the only reason he would be with her. She wanted more. She deserved more.

"I am not my mother," she said through gritted teeth. "I will be fine."

"You don't know that," he said. "Not after what happened."

Making love with him or the explosion?

A ragged sigh slipped through her lips. "What the hell did happen?" she wondered and not just to her common sense but in the warehouse. "It doesn't make sense."

None of it made sense. Making love with him and someone trying to kill them. The explosion could have been an accident, another side effect of some of the faulty construction that had gone on in Braxville. But why had someone lured them both there?

"We'll figure it all out in the morning," he said. "You need to rest now."

With all the thoughts and fears swirling through

her head, she wasn't sure she would be able to sleep. But she intended to pretend that she was…just until he fell asleep. Then she would be able to leave without an argument. Without another proposal.

Without any temptation to accept that proposal and stay with him forever.

No. She needed to get the hell out of there before she did anything else crazy, like falling in love with him all over again. But even as she resolved to stay awake, her lids began to droop over eyes gritty from exhaustion and maybe debris from the explosion.

It had to have been accident. Somebody couldn't really be trying to kill them. Could he?

SHE WAS GONE. Neil knew it before he even opened his eyes—because he was cold, his skin chilled by the loss of her warmth, her presence.

Damn.

He shouldn't have fallen asleep again, shouldn't have risked her leaving without him. Not when she was in so much danger.

Something creaked and the security system alarm sounded. Maybe she wasn't gone yet or maybe someone had broken into the house.

He jerked fully awake and jumped out of the bed. The minute his feet hit the floor, he ran for the front door where the alarm control panel was. But the high-pitched siren cut out, as someone pushed the buttons for the security code.

"Elise…"

He'd caught her trying to sneak out, just as he'd

suspected she might. He shouldn't have fallen asleep, but she must have, as well, because the sun was high and bright, casting a glow through the front door that shimmered in her golden hair.

She sighed, and her shoulders slumped as if defeated over being caught. "I don't want to fight," she said before she looked away from the panel to focus on his face.

Dark circles rimmed her green eyes, making it clear she hadn't slept, or at least not enough that she was rested.

"I don't want to fight, either," he said. "I just want to make sure you're safe."

"I'm fine," she said. "And I need to get to work."

"You don't have a car," he reminded her. "And I need to get my mother's car back to her."

She sighed. "I'll call a cab. I need to go home first and change before going into the office anyway."

His skin chilled, reminding him that he hadn't bothered to dress when he'd run out of his bedroom at the sound of his alarm. At least, sometime during the night, he must have pulled his boxers back on, though. He wasn't as physically cold as he was emotionally—at the thought of her running around town without protection.

"Before I return my mother's car," he said, "I'll take you to your condo and then to the office."

She grimaced. "You don't need to do that. I'm not helpless."

"No, you're not," he agreed. "But you are in danger."

She shook her head. "I don't think so."

"That building blew up—"

"It could have been an accident," she said. "More faulty construction."

"And it was just a coincidence that it blew up after fake messages lured us both there?" he asked, shaking his head now. "You don't really believe that any more than I do."

She narrowed her eyes and glared at him. "It doesn't matter what happened or why. It and you are not going to stop me from doing my job."

"I don't want to stop you," he assured her. He knew how much her job meant to her. "I just want to make sure you're safe when you're working."

She sighed again, but this time it sounded as if it was with resignation. "Okay, but you might want to get dressed first."

Suspicious of her sudden agreement, he narrowed his eyes and studied her beautiful face. Was she going to run out of the house the minute he went back to the bedroom to dress? He wouldn't put it past her.

"Elise, I know you're anxious to get to work, but I hope you're taking this threat seriously. You could have been killed."

Her hand pressed against her flat stomach. And he knew she wasn't thinking just of herself anymore. "I'll wait for you," she promised. "You can even shower if you want…"

He wanted her—in the shower with him—water sluicing over her naked skin. "You need to shower, too," he said as he stepped closer to her so their bodies just brushed. She had on too damn many clothes now, her jacket over her black slacks and heavy sweater. He wanted—*needed*—her naked again. "Want to join me?"

Her pupils dilated, swallowing the green irises, but she shook her head even as her lips curved into a slight smile. "You need to get to work, too."

She was right. He needed to get to work—not at his office, though. He wasn't currently representing anyone. He needed to get to work finding out who had left those messages for them—who had tried to kill them.

And he had to make sure that person didn't get the chance to try again.

YVETTE COLTON STARED at the blackened shell of the warehouse from which she'd collected evidence months ago. If she'd missed anything then, it was probably gone now. Had that been the purpose of this explosion?

Or had it been an accident?

The sun had risen over what remained of the warehouse while she waited in the parking lot for the fire department to deem it safe enough for her to enter the structure. Their arson inspector hadn't had to wait like she had, though.

He walked out now, and as he ducked under the yellow tape, she rushed up to meet him. He was an older man, older probably even than her father and Uncle Shep, because his hair was completely gray and his face was lined with age.

"So?" she asked. "What do you think?"

"You don't need to go in," he said, and he held up a bag. "I got what you're looking for."

"What is it?" she asked, trying to visually examine the contents through the plastic, since he still held tightly to the bag.

"Incendiary device," he said.

"So it wasn't an accident."

"Nope. Looks like the type that had to be detonated. You might find that out here," he said as he glanced around the lot. "I was told there was nobody inside the building when it exploded, so no casualties, fortunately. But if nobody was inside, whose vehicles are these?"

Like the warehouse, the little hybrid coupe was a blackened shell of what it had formerly been. The plate, though, was intact enough that a detective had made out the raised letters and numbers in the metal and run them through the department of motor vehicles.

"That's the mayor's," she said.

"And that one?" He pointed toward the SUV parked farther from the building. It had a fine sheen of soot on it and some debris, but it wasn't burned up like the hybrid.

If it had been closer, though…

If he had been closer…

Yvette's heart did a little flip in her chest as fear and panic rushed over her again. She knew he was okay; Jordana had assured her of that. But it could have been so much worse. "My brother's."

"The security guy?" the inspector asked.

"Not Tyler. Neil, the lawyer," she replied.

He chuckled. "Not surprised someone might have tried to kill a lawyer."

She was. Even though people often made derogatory remarks about lawyers, especially those who practiced criminal law like Neil, she hadn't thought anyone would actually act on that prejudice. And she couldn't believe that now.

Was Markus Dexter involved, like he'd been with Ty's shooting? Was her father's friend and business partner going to go after all of them?

She found it hard to imagine that he'd risk coming back to town now—with an outstanding warrant for his arrest.

No. More than likely this attempt had been personal.

Had Neil ticked someone off? Someone other than Elise?

Her cell vibrated inside her pocket, startling her. She quickly pulled it out and glanced at the screen. "It's Neil calling me now," she said.

"Tell him to be careful," the arson investigator advised. "He and the mayor got damn lucky this time. They might not be that lucky the next time."

The next...

If someone had meant to kill Neil or Elise, they probably wouldn't give up after one failed attempt.

# Chapter Seven

Someone had tried to kill them.

Elise had known that the second the warehouse had exploded, but she hadn't wanted to admit it, even to herself. Because then she would have had to accept that Neil was right to be so overprotective of her.

He'd insisted on driving her back to her condo and waiting while she showered and changed. When she was getting ready, she'd heard the rumble of his voice as he spoke to someone on his cell. She'd thought he might have been checking in with his office, but when she joined him in the living room, he'd told her to pack a suitcase.

"Why?" she asked, glancing around her condo. Had something happened while she was in the bathroom?

"You need to stay with me," he said. "My house is safer than this place."

She didn't have the high-tech alarm system he did, but with curious and concerned neighbors close, she'd always felt safe in the complex. "You're overreacting," she told him.

But he shook his head. "The arson investigator confirmed that was a bomb in the warehouse, one that someone detonated thinking we were still inside."

"You called the arson investigator?" she asked.

He shook his head. "No, my sister."

"Jordana knows more than she did last night, then," Elise mused.

"Yvette," he said, identifying his youngest sister, the CSI. "She's processing evidence from the crime scene and was with the arson investigator when I called. So there is no doubt that someone tried to kill us last night."

Her knees trembled a bit, but she locked her legs, refusing to give in to the fear that crashed over her. She would not let what happened weaken her.

"What else did your sister say?" she asked.

Hopefully, Yvette had found evidence that would help identify the bomber.

"You're going to need a new car," Neil said.

Tempted to curse, she chuckled instead. With her life being threatened, the car was the very least of her concerns at the moment, so she quipped, "Now you know what to get me for Christmas."

"You know what I want to get you," he said as he reached out for her hand. "A diamond ring."

"Neil…" She pulled her hand free of his, but her skin tingled yet from even that brief contact.

"Come on, Elise, look at this place." He gestured at the close confines of her townhome-style condo. "You can't raise a baby here."

"I can if I want," she said. "They don't take up much room." In the beginning...

"I have more than enough room," he said. "We built that house for our future family."

"You did," she said. "I thought we were building it for us." But she hadn't been enough to make him happy. He'd wanted more.

"We did build it for us," he said. "Move back in with me. Marry me."

That curse slipped out now. "Neil, you have to stop. This isn't an argument you're going to win. And I don't have time for you to keep trying." She glanced at the thin gold watch on her wrist. Her mother had saved and saved to be able to buy it for her for her college graduation. "I need to get to the office before word gets out about what happened last night."

"That you were nearly killed." He shuddered, and his blue eyes gleamed with emotion. "Elise..."

She felt the same way. No matter what had happened between them, no matter that she wouldn't accept his proposal, she couldn't imagine a world without him in it. "I know."

"So will you pack a bag?" he asked. "Will you come home with me tonight?"

"I want to talk to Jordana and that other detective first," she said. "I want to know how the investigation is going. Maybe they've found Markus Dexter."

"I'm not so sure it was Markus Dexter who tried to kill us," Neil said.

"Who else would it be?" she wondered.

He shrugged. "I don't know."

"It has to be him," she persisted. "Obviously he has access to explosives since he was in the construction business with your father."

"But it makes no sense for him to come after us." He ran a hand over his head, mussing his thick brown hair. "We'll figure it out. But until we do, you need to be safe, so you'll stay with me."

"I have to get to work," she said as she jerked open her door and stepped outside.

He must have finally realized he wasn't going to win this argument, either, because he followed her out and locked the door behind them. Then he clicked the fob for his mother's vehicle and opened the passenger's door for her.

"What about your SUV?" she asked. "Did it survive the explosion?"

A slight grin curved his lips. "I parked far enough away from the building that it's fine."

She glared at him because she suspected he was teasing her for her penchant of finding the closest parking spot in order to avoid a long walk to whatever business she was patronizing. Parking close was convenient in case she had a lot to carry out to her car.

It hadn't been convenient in this case, though. She hated car shopping, but at least she was alive to do it. And Neil was alive, too.

He chuckled as he closed her door. Then he walked around to the driver's side and slid behind the wheel. "You might be safer with your vehicle out of commission."

"Are you calling me a bad driver?" she asked,

anger beginning to bubble up. Didn't he think she could do anything right or at least on her own? His overprotectiveness had been another issue in their marriage, his wanting to take care of her.

In the beginning she'd thought it was sweet that he hadn't let her be alone with any of their clients who'd been accused of abusive behavior. Eventually it had worn on her that he hadn't treated her as an equal. She'd just wanted him to trust her to take care of herself.

"No," he said. "I meant that whoever is after us won't be able to put a bomb in your car." He hesitated for a moment before turning the key in the ignition, as if worried that someone had put a bomb on this one.

But this was his mother's vehicle, not his.

"I still need to have a car," she said.

"Maybe you should wait until we find out who lured us to the warehouse."

"Has to be Dexter," she said.

"Why?" he asked. "Because you prefer to think that he's the only criminal in Braxville?"

"I know better than that," she said. From the years she'd been his partner in their criminal law practice, as well as from her time in the mayor's office. While Braxville had far less crime than where she'd grown up in Detroit, it wasn't entirely safe—as last night had proved.

City Hall wasn't far from her condo, so they pulled up in front of the building in just minutes. They weren't the only ones arriving at the scene; news vehicles had lined up along the curb. Neil was lucky to find a spot at one of the meters, and she wasn't even concerned it was just a two-hour meter. She didn't want him staying to babysit her.

And she definitely didn't want the reporters seeing them arrive together. She groaned. "Word must have gotten out about last night." She'd hoped it wouldn't have, at least not until a suspect had been apprehended.

"Want me to drive you around to a rear entrance so you can avoid them?" he asked.

She shook her head. "No. I better deal with this right away."

"Are you going to address your pregnancy, too?" he asked.

"Why?" she asked. "I'm still in the first trimester. There's a chance…"

He gasped. "That you could lose the baby? But I thought everything was okay?"

She found herself reaching across the console to grasp his hand, to reassure him. "That's what the doctor said, but things can happen at any time, just like us nearly getting blown up last night."

"That's why you need to stay with me," he persisted. "Why you need to marry me…"

She groaned. "I'm not going to discuss this pregnancy with the reporters or with you anymore until you stop spontaneously proposing to me."

Before he could continue arguing with her, she pushed open the car door and stepped onto the sidewalk. She'd only made it a short distance from the vehicle before a reporter spotted her. Then they all swarmed like shoppers over Black Friday specials.

An unfamiliar sensation rushed over her, making her pulse quicken with anxiety. She had never minded talking to reporters before. But maybe it was because of what had happened last night, and the uncertainty whether it would happen again, that made her uneasy.

Someone had tried to kill her and Neil. And now, knowing he or she hadn't succeeded, that person was bound to try again.

NEIL COULDN'T LEAVE Elise unprotected, so he jumped out of his mother's car, fed some coins into the meter and joined the reporters on the sidewalk. Anger tightened his stomach muscles as he listened to them bombard Elise with questions without giving her a second to answer any of them.

"Mayor, was there an attempt on your life?"

"Do you know who's responsible?"

"Were you seriously injured?"

"Were you alone at the time of the attack?"

"Will you be able to continue your duties as mayor?"

He was just lifting his fingers to his lips when a whistle rent the air and silenced the reporters. He chuckled at Elise's tactic to gain their attention, one that an old law professor of theirs had used to silence an unruly class or to end an argument between him and Elise.

"Apparently, you've all learned that I was at the

scene of the Crest View Center warehouse explosion last night," she began.

The reporters started speaking again, not giving her a chance to continue. But before Neil could step in, she let out another ear-piercing whistle.

"Last chance," she warned them. "I'm going to make a short statement before I get back to work. My statement will answer all the questions you need to have answered."

A grin tugged at Neil's lips. She was so damn tough and independent. So independent that she didn't need him. She never had.

He had been a fool to try to scare her about being a single parent like her mother. Nothing scared Elise. And he would make certain that even if they didn't get married again, she would not be raising their child all on her own like Aubrey Willis had raised Elise.

"The cause of the explosion last night is under investigation, and out of respect for the Braxville Police Department, I will not comment on their open case," she said. "I will assure you all that I was not hurt, and I will not only be able to continue in my duties as mayor, but I will also be more focused on making sure that Braxville is safe for all our citizens."

The reporters began to speak again, but Elise turned away from them and headed up the steps to City Hall. She wore a long black coat, belted around her slim waist, over a sweater dress and tall black boots. She was so damn sexy.

He would have pushed through the reporters to follow her, but he suspected she would be irritated if the media realized they'd arrived together and that he was chasing after her. So he raised the collar of his jacket, tucked his head down and circled around to the back of the building. As he did, he glanced around to see if anyone had followed him or if anyone watched him like he and Elise had been last night.

Someone had waited until they'd gone inside the building before detonating the bomb, intending to kill them. Why?

It didn't make sense for Markus Dexter to come after them. They had nothing to do with the investigation into those murders.

But if not old Dex, who?

Who wanted them dead?

Anxious that he'd lost sight of Elise, Neil rushed to the back door. The security guard assigned to that entrance knew him, knew that he frequently visited the mayor, so he was allowed inside with only a cursory pat-down.

How safe was Elise here? Who else might be allowed up to see her without being thoroughly checked for weapons?

Maybe because of that cursory pat-down, Neil met Elise at the elevator bank. She'd gone through security in the main lobby and had probably had to answer questions from those guards about last night.

She sighed when she saw him. "I thought you left."

"Hoped," he surmised as the elevator doors opened.

She nodded as she stepped inside the car. "You

need to stop being so overprotective. I'm in the build-ing. It's secure. Nobody's going to get to me."

"I got to you," he said as he joined her inside the elevator.

She glared at him. "Because the guard at the back door knows you."

"He might know whoever set that bomb, too," Neil pointed out.

She sucked in a breath. "You really think it's some-one who knows us?"

"Why else would someone lure us both to that warehouse?" he asked, hoping she might have some idea, because he didn't. But he would, once he gave his total attention to what had happened and not to what was going to happen.

He was going to be a father.

That news had hit him harder than the blast had knocked him to the ground. But in order to make sure he became a father, that his baby and the baby's mother lived, he needed to figure out who was be-hind that attack.

The elevator pinged as it arrived on the floor with her office. Her assistant jumped up the minute she saw Elise and rushed toward her. "Are you all right?" she asked. "When I saw the news this morning about the explosion and I knew you were meeting…" Her voice trailed off as she turned toward him, then her dark eyes narrowed with suspicion.

"I'm all right," Elise assured her. "And so is Neil."

"Why did you tell her to meet you there?" Carmen

fired the question at him, but not as amiably as the reporters had questioned Elise.

"I didn't," he said. "You talked to the person who did. Was it a man or woman?"

Carmen pursed her lips as if searching her memory. Then she shrugged. "I don't know. It could have been a man or a woman with a raspy voice. She or he claimed to be leaving the message on your orders, though."

Neil shook his head. "Not mine. Nor did Elise leave the message that asked me to meet her at the warehouse."

Carmen gasped. "What the hell is going on?"

He shrugged but promised, "I'm going to find out."

"No, you're not. We're going to leave the investigation to the police." Elise turned to him as she said that, her green eyes narrowed like her aide's. "And you can leave me alone. I'm safe here." Without another word to either him or her assistant, she headed toward her office. But when she pushed open her door, she gasped.

Fear stabbed Neil's heart. Had a bomb been set up in her office? He rushed to her, edging around her in the doorway to confront whatever had shocked her. Someone sat in the chair behind her desk.

"What the hell," he murmured.

She edged him out of the way now as she pushed past him and walked to her desk. "Good morning, Jeremy, I see you've made yourself comfortable in my office. Unfortunately, the reports of my demise were greatly exaggerated."

The guy jumped up so quickly that her chair knocked against the wall behind her desk. "Elise! Oh, thank God you're all right."

"No, thank Neil," she said.

Neil chuckled as the man, whose face had blanched white with shock, glanced at him. Well, he turned as white as he could with his artificial tan, which set off his blond hair and too-polished good looks.

"Uh, hi, Neil," Jeremy stammered. Usually the guy was a smooth talker, too smooth, but then he was a politician.

"Yeah, I'm alive, too," Neil informed him. "Hope you're not too disappointed."

"You were with her at the warehouse?" Jeremy asked. "The reports said her vehicle had been identified as the one destroyed at the scene."

"Mine survived," Neil said, "as did the two of us, which much have really upset whoever tried to kill us."

Jeremy gasped. "I—I can't imagine that was intentional," he said. "Elise is the most beloved mayor we've ever had."

Neil had always suspected Jeremy Lyons, her deputy mayor, was in love with her. But now he wondered…

At forty, Jeremy was ten years older than he and Elise were, and from his previous positions on the city council, he had more experience than she did. Was it Elise the man wanted, or was it her job? And what lengths would he go to in order to get what he wanted?

Murder?

ATTEMPTED MURDER...

The attempted murder of the mayor. That was what the reporters claimed had happened the night before, when the warehouse exploded.

He knew better.

It wasn't murder.

It was justice.

And he was damn well going to get it.

Of course, it might be harder now. They would be expecting another attack. But maybe that was good. The bomb would have been quick, would have spared them the fear and misery they deserved to feel.

He wanted them to feel all the pain he'd felt.

So he moved his hands to the keyboard of the computer, and as he typed, the words appeared on the monitor in front of him.

He'll get what's coming to him.

# *Chapter Eight*

She'd gotten rid of Neil—after many assurances that she wouldn't leave the building or let into her office anyone that security hadn't thoroughly vetted. Before Neil had agreed to leave, he'd called down to security to make sure that Jeremy had come through the metal detectors at the front entrance of City Hall.

She was well aware that her ex-husband was not a fan of her deputy mayor, and vice versa. But to consider Jeremy capable of murder?

She couldn't, but...

He had been very quick to take her office. Carmen hadn't even realized that he'd been in it. So he must have arrived before her assistant had, but to do what? Check Elise's schedule as he'd claimed, so that if necessary, he would be able to fulfill her obligations?

How had he known that she might not be able to fulfill those obligations on her own? News reports about the explosion, and her possible presence at the site, hadn't leaked until the morning. So what had compelled him to come in so much earlier than he usually did?

How had he known something had happened to her? Or nearly happened…

She shivered as a chill rushed over her at how close they had come to dying. If Neil hadn't reacted as quickly as he had, they would both be dead. No. She pressed her hand over her stomach. They would all three be dead.

But why? Why would someone want to kill her and Neil at the same time?

If Jeremy wanted her job, he would only need to take out her, not her ex-husband, too. Unless he'd wanted it to look like something else. Like a murder-suicide so the case would be closed without much of an investigation. Maybe that was why the messages summoning them to the meeting had been made to look like they were from each other.

"Elise?"

Startled, she jumped in her chair, knocking it against the wall behind her like Jeremy had when she'd startled him earlier. The deputy mayor stood in the doorway, his handsome face tense with concern. For her? Or for himself?

"Are you all right?" he asked.

"Yes, I just didn't realize you were standing there," she said.

"I knocked," he claimed.

But it was a lie. She would have heard a knock. If he was lying about that, what else might he lie about?

"Do you need something?" she asked.

"No, just checking to see if you need anything," he replied solicitously. He'd been trying to ingratiate himself with her since she'd caught him in her office. He'd brought her coffee and doughnuts and asked her several times how he could help her. She didn't like all the groveling and fawning.

Maybe that was why she'd fallen for Neil. He wouldn't know how to do either. Although she'd once wished he did, after he'd served her divorce papers.

She'd wanted him to come to her and beg her forgiveness for making such a horrible mistake. But he hadn't.

And that had proved to her that the divorce wasn't a mistake. Marrying him again would be, though.

"Do you?" Jeremy asked. "Need anything?"

"A car," she quipped.

"I know a dealer," Jeremy said. "If you know what make and model you'd like, I could have him bring one to the office along with the paperwork."

"That would be helpful," she admitted. She really hated car shopping, but what she hated even more was relying on someone else to drive her where she wanted to go. Like Neil.

Before leaving her at the office earlier, he'd vowed he would return at the end of the day to take her home. He undoubtedly meant to his home.

She couldn't keep going back there, back to him.

"What kind of vehicle?" Jeremy asked. "Two-door, four-door?"

Less than a year from now, she would need a four-door—one with a back seat easily accessible for buckling in an infant carrier.

"Something safe," she replied. For herself and for her unborn child.

"I'll check the safety reports for you," Jeremy offered.

Those reports would tell him how well a vehicle would perform in a crash. But what about an explosion?

She needed to make sure that she wasn't at risk of one of those happening again. She needed to find out who the hell had lured her and Neil to that warehouse.

While she'd told Neil to leave the investigation to the police, she wasn't any more likely to do that than he was. She just wasn't sure where to start her inquiries.

With Jeremy?

Could he really want her office—her job—so badly that he would kill to take it?

He'll get what's coming to him.

THE WORDS WERE eerily familiar to Neil. He'd heard them before. But then, as a criminal lawyer, it would have been more surprising if he hadn't.

District attorneys said that. Victims said that. Police officers and detectives.

But who had said it this time? Who had sent him the strange email message? And was he the only one who'd received it?

He could have called Elise to ask her, but he'd wanted to see her again. Had needed to see her again...

To make sure she was all right, that she and the baby were safe.

Maybe she was—because security hadn't allowed him through the back door again. He'd had to use the front entrance with the metal detector. But a gun or a knife weren't the only weapons a man could use to get rid of someone—as that bomb had proved the night before.

A man could use his hands, too. And if someone hurt Elise, Neil might use his to dole out what that person had coming to him: justice.

Her assistant wasn't at her desk; maybe Carmen had already left for the day. It was after five. Neil wasn't sure how he'd stayed away so long, except that he'd been busy with calls to Jordana and Yvette— trying to determine if the police had any leads yet. And when the email had come through, he'd turned that over to Braxville PD as a possible lead—which had led to another interview with his detective sister and her partner.

But he had nothing more to tell them than he'd had the night before. No idea who might want him or Elise dead.

Or was it just him?

Was he the *he* who would get what was coming to him?

If only Elise was what was coming to him…

He wanted her to come to him, to stay with him, to marry him again. But he'd already pushed her too much about that, which he saw the moment she glanced up from her desk and noticed him standing in her doorway. She uttered a weary-sounding sigh and shook her head.

"What?" he asked.

"I'm not leaving with you," she said. "I have too much work to do."

He suspected that wasn't the only reason she didn't want to leave with him, though. "You're going to need a ride home," he said.

She shook her head again. "No. I replaced my car already," she said.

"You hate car shopping."

"Jeremy helped."

"I'm sure he did," Neil said. Was the man trying to replace Elise or him?

With Elise being as beautiful, sexy and damn smart as she was, the deputy mayor probably wanted to be with her—like Neil wanted to be with her. But being with Neil might have been what put her in danger the night before.

The email hadn't said that *she* would get what was coming to her.

"Is that all you're going to say?" she asked, obviously expecting him to say more. Given their history of disagreements, he couldn't blame her.

"No."

She squared her shoulders as if bracing herself for a fight. His stomach muscles, which were already tense with anxiety, tightened more with regret. He didn't mean to argue with her…all the time. Maybe it had just been inbred with him, as a triplet, to fight for what he wanted—the time, the attention, the love.

But love wasn't something a person could take; it had to be given. Freely.

So he swallowed down another proposal before it could escape his lips. And he asked her a different question instead. "Did you get any strange emails today?"

"Emails?" she asked, furrows forming on her forehead. "What kind of emails?"

He'd printed off his—more than one copy, since the police had one that they were going to try to track back to the server from which it had been sent. He pulled the paper from his pocket, unfolded it and slid it across her desk.

The furrows deepened as she read it. "He'll get what's coming to him." She studied it for a moment before raising her head to stare at him. "Who's *he*? You?"

He shrugged. "I don't know. You didn't get one like it?"

She shook her head. "Not unless it went to my junk mail…" She moved her fingers from the note to her keyboard. After striking some keys and moving her mouse, she peered at the computer monitor and shook her head. "I don't see anything like this."

He breathed a sigh of relief. He must have been the target the night before. Not her.

"I'm sorry," he said. "That bomb must have been meant for me."

"I got the phone message yesterday," she pointed out. "I was lured to that warehouse, too."

He flinched with regret. "You must have gotten drawn into my mess for some reason…"

"What reason?" she asked.

He shrugged. "I don't know."

"You don't even know the *he* in that email refers to you," she pointed out. "It could be about Markus Dexter or your father."

"My father?"

"People are starting to blame him for the illnesses Colton Construction employees are suffering from," she said. "A couple of his former employees even died."

Neil refused to believe that his father could be responsible for those deaths any more than he had been responsible for the dead bodies found within the walls of the warehouse. He shook his head. "If those illnesses have anything to do with Colton Construction, Dex was responsible—not my father."

Elise stared at him for a long moment, her green eyes soft with sympathy or pity. "You really believe that something happened at Colton Construction without your father knowing about it?"

"He didn't know about those bodies in the warehouse," Neil insisted. "There's no way he had anything to do with those murders. So Dex was doing things without my father's knowledge. If there is any contamination at those job sites, it's because of Dex—not my father."

Elise didn't look as convinced of her ex-father-in-law's innocence. But just as she and Neil butted heads, she also butted heads with his father. Like her predecessor, she was opposed to Braxville becoming too urban, too commercial. She'd promised her voters that she would keep it the quaint town it had always been. That was why developers like Neil's father were forced to renovate old buildings instead of building new ones.

"Have you talked to your father about what happened last night?" she asked. "Hell, have you talked to him about anything that's happened?"

That knot of dread in his stomach tightened even more, and he admitted, "Not yet."

"Don't you think it's time that you do?" she asked. "Especially if he's the one who's put you in danger?"

"He isn't responsible for what happened last night," Neil insisted.

Because his father had always been working while Neil was growing up, he had never been that close to him, but he had no doubt that the man loved his family, loved all his children, and would never consciously put them in harm's way. Neil hoped the same was true of the Colton Construction employees. But if someone blamed Fitz for the men who'd gotten sick and died, maybe they'd figured they would hurt him most by taking away his loved ones.

"I'm not saying he set the bomb," Elise said almost begrudgingly. "But he might know or suspect who did. You need to talk to him."

Even though he knew she was right, Neil groaned with reluctance.

She chuckled then urged, "Talk to him."

Neil owed it to her—if he was the one who'd put

her in danger. But just because she hadn't received that email, she wasn't necessarily out of danger now. "I will," he assured her. "As long as you promise me that you'll be careful."

"Of course," she said, and she pressed her hand over her flat stomach as if to shield their unborn child.

Neil wanted to protect them both. In case his father had any information about what had happened at the warehouse or about who might have sent the email, he had to talk to him. He wasn't sure if he wanted his father to have any answers, though, or if he hoped he was as clueless as Neil was.

He reached for the email printout on Elise's desk, reading those words again. He'll get what's coming to him.

In this context, what the hell did it mean?

Did someone want revenge against Neil? Or against his father?

Before he could pull his hand away from her desk, Elise slid her fingers over his. "You be careful, too," she advised him.

But it was already too late for that warning. Neil was already in too deep—with her. He already wanted too much. And he was undoubtedly going to get his heart broken all over again.

FRUSTRATION GNAWED AT Fitz Colton. He had been in limbo too long, waiting on the health department's report regarding his company. Waiting on his partner being found...

Where the hell had Dex gone?

And what had he done before he left?

He must have murdered those people whose bodies had been found in the warehouse. Had he tried killing Tyler, as well?

And now...

He left his truck parked on the circular drive in front of the house and rushed inside, slamming the door behind himself as he stepped inside. "Lilly!" His voice echoed off the two-story foyer.

She'd worked late yesterday, so she should have been home already. But then she seemed to prefer working to being with him. He felt her slipping away from him just as he felt everything else slipping away— his business, his reputation, his family...

She didn't answer him, but a metallic clang emanated from the vicinity of the kitchen. He found her standing at the sink, staring out the window as she almost absentmindedly scrubbed a pot. The lake, with a light dusting of snow across its partially frozen surface, was beautiful, nearly as beautiful as she was.

But her beauty only intensified his frustration. She wasn't just slipping away from him now. She had slipped away long ago. He'd been gone so much, working so hard to support their family, that he hadn't even noticed until it was too late, until she was too far gone.

"Why didn't you tell me?" he asked.

He hadn't yelled, but she jumped as if he had. "What? Tell you what?" she asked, her voice shaky.

"About Neil, that he was nearly blown up last night," he said. "What did you think I was talking about?"

She shrugged her slender shoulders, then squared them before turning around to face him. "I don't know."

"Why didn't you tell me what happened? I heard he was taken to the hospital last night. Were you there when he was brought in?"

She nodded, and a piece of auburn hair slipped loose from the knot on the back of her head to slide down her cheek. He would have brushed it away for her…years ago. But now, if he tried to touch her, she would push his hand away, push him away. "Yes, I was there," she admitted. "But there are privacy laws—"

"He's my son," he said. "I had a right to know that he was hurt."

"He wasn't hurt," she said. "He's fine."

"What the hell happened?"

"You tell me," she said. "I think you know more than you've told us, Fitz. You're keeping secrets."

"Am I the only one, Lilly?" he asked. But he wasn't sure he wanted to know her secret any more than he wanted everyone to know his. But he knew it was only a matter of time before it all came out.

Hell, he needed to come clean to his family. They deserved the truth.

"I told you that there are privacy laws," she said.

He furrowed his brow and stared at her, failing to comprehend what she was trying to tell him. "I still should have learned about what happened to my boy from my wife, his mother, instead of hearing it in town."

At the coffee shop. He shouldn't keep going to La Dolce Vita, not with how the owner felt about him. Hell, the whole town was starting to feel that way now, but he was too damn proud to hide in shame. Megan Chase, the owner, had taken great delight in telling him about the explosion at the warehouse and, that rumor had it, his son had been inside.

"You were asleep when I came home last night," Lilly said.

He doubted she'd even checked, since he slept in a separate bedroom down the hall from the master suite, which was hers. "You could have woken me up," he suggested. But she hadn't done that in years.

"It's not my place," she murmured.

"You're my wife, his mother. Of course it's your place," Fitz said, frustration nearly consuming him now. What the hell had happened to them?

And was it all his fault?

"It was my place," a deep voice murmured.

Fitz glanced to the doorway, where Neil stood. He wore a suit, like he had come from his office or court. His beard was a little scruffy, though, and his hair a little disheveled, but that was normal for him.

But Fitz had to be sure. "You're okay?"

Neil nodded. But he didn't look certain. He looked unsettled. What did he know?

"We have to talk, Dad," he said.

Fitz had wanted to see his son—to make sure that he was all right. But he didn't want to talk to him…not yet. He wasn't ready to confess all to any-one—least of all someone who might have nearly been killed because of the mistakes that his father had made. Like Dex had gone after Ty, had someone else gone after Neil to get back at *him*?

# Chapter Nine

If she hadn't planned on working late, Elise would have had the dealer park her new vehicle on the street in front of City Hall. But because she'd known she would surpass the two-hour time limit on the meters, she'd had it delivered to the parking garage down the street, on the other side of the park.

So she had to walk past the park while she was wearing high-heeled boots and a dress. She had the coat on, too, but it wasn't thick enough to ward off the cold. The wind blew through the park, whipping snow flurries around her face and legs. What the hell had she been thinking to dress like this in winter?

Had she dressed up because she'd guessed reporters might be waiting for her? Or because of Neil?

She'd wanted to look good for him. When would he stop affecting her? When would she stop caring about him?

Never.

She'd accepted that a while ago, that she would always love him, but despite how much she loved him, she couldn't marry him again. Not even for the baby.

At least, not just for the baby.

Which was the only reason he wanted to marry her. To protect the child.

From what?

Had last night really had nothing to do with her? But then why had a message lured her to that warehouse, as well?

She hadn't received the email he had today, though, but maybe it had had nothing to do with what had happened last night.

*He'll get what's coming to him.*

She shivered, and not just from the cold wind. She'd heard that phrase before, just like Neil must have, during her years as a criminal lawyer in their partnership. Prosecutors said it, police officers, victims.

Was the *he* Neil?

What could he have done that made someone want to kill him, though? Even as hurt, as shattered, as she'd been during their divorce, she had never wished him harm.

No. Whatever was going on, it had nothing to do with Neil personally. It had to be about his family.

Or maybe about her...

That chill rushed over her again, making goose bumps rise on her skin beneath her dress and her coat. Her heels clicked against the sidewalk as she hastened her step. A sound echoed that click, a heavier, scraping sound as someone followed her. She peered over her shoulder, but she couldn't see much in the faint glow of the twinkling lights wrapped around the street poles. The lamps had been dimmed so that the decorations sparkled more. But now there were too many shadows from the tall trees in the park for Elise to see if someone stood there, watching her.

She was paranoid. Maybe it was just someone else heading to the parking garage for his vehicle. But why had the sound stopped when she turned back?

Why hadn't the person continued walking? There were no shops in this section of street between City Hall and the parking garage, no business into which someone could have gone. Just the park.

So whoever had been behind her was there, lurking in the shadows, not wanting her to see him. Yet…

Not until it was too late?

She reached into the bag slung over her arm, feeling around inside until she found something cold and metallic. She pulled out the small canister of pepper spray. But she should have already had it in her hand; she should have been being careful like she'd promised Neil she would be.

But since she hadn't received the email note that he had, she'd thought she was safe. Maybe that was what the person had intended by not sending her the email. So she would let down her guard. So that she would be alone for the next attack, so that Neil wouldn't be able to save her as he had the last time…

HE COULD HAVE sent that email to the woman, too. But since she was the mayor now, she probably had a more secure network and other people who screened her correspondence. She might never have seen it, and he'd wanted to be more direct in his threat to her.

He'd already determined that it was good that they'd survived the attempt last night. Dying in the explosion would have been too quick and maybe even a painless way for them to go. They wouldn't have suffered like he'd been suffering for so long.

Going out that way would have been better for them but not for him. No. Now he had time to scare them, to make them rue all the mistakes they'd made.

It was going to be better this way. This way they would learn exactly why they were going to die. And he would be able to make sure that there was no chance of either of them surviving.

Was Elise right…about everything?

Did the attack have everything to do with his father?

Neil should have manned up and had this talk with him long ago. But he hadn't wanted to hear what his father might admit to him. He hadn't wanted to know if the man he'd always idolized had done things for which people might want revenge.

Following his father down the hall to his den, Neil couldn't help but notice how much slower the man moved, how his once-broad shoulders stooped as if carrying a heavy burden. Neil had passed him a little bit in height a while ago, but Fitz seemed even shorter now, as if he were somehow shrinking in size or maybe importance.

With all the problems Colton Construction was

facing, Fitz Colton was not the revered and all-powerful man he'd once been in Braxville.

Fitz stepped inside his office, waited for Neil to cross the threshold and then closed the door behind them.

"Mom can't hear this?" Neil asked.

His father shrugged. "I don't know. What do you want to talk about?"

Neil snorted. "Somebody tried to blow me up last night. What do you think I want to talk about?"

"With me?" Fitz asked, his eyes narrowed behind the wire-framed glasses he pushed up his nose. "I didn't even know about it until someone mentioned it in town today."

Neil flinched. "Sorry about that. I thought—"

"Your mother would tell me?" Fitz asked, arching a brown eyebrow, strewn with gray hairs, toward his high forehead. Like his height, his light brown hair had slipped away more and more until he had little left.

"I should have called," Neil said, "but things were crazy after it happened."

He'd found out that he was going to be a father, too. Since his mother hadn't told Fitz about his ER visit last night, she undoubtedly hadn't shared that news, either. He hadn't come here to talk about that, though. Not yet.

Not until he got Elise to accept his proposal. He didn't want his father to think he was shirking his responsibilities again. At least he was pretty sure that was what Fitz had thought when Neil had chosen law school over the family business. His father had never voiced his disapproval, though, but he'd never voiced his approval, either.

"I heard you were with the mayor when the building blew up," Fitz said, his gruff voice emphasizing *mayor* like it was a dirty word.

Neil sighed. "You mean Elise?"

"What were you doing with her?" Fitz asked. "You know she's pretty much shut down my whole company."

"*She* didn't do that. First the police did, and then the health department," Neil reminded him. "But it's your business partner who caused all these problems with your company. Do you know where he is?"

Fitz's face flushed crimson, his eyes widening with shock behind those small lenses. "What the hell do you think? That I'm protecting him?"

"I don't know what to think, Dad," Neil admitted. And he hated having these doubts about his own father. But with all the long hours he'd worked and the events he'd missed because of it, Fitz had proved that Colton Construction meant more to him than his family. There was no way that he could have been completely unaware of everything that had been going on in the company he'd built.

"Wow," Fitz said as he dropped heavily into the chair behind his desk. "Do you actually think I could have had something to do with that explosion last night? That I could have harmed you and Elise?"

Neil shook his head. "No, of course not. But I think your partner might have."

"Why?" Fitz asked.

"The man tried to kill Ty," Neil reminded him.

And his father flinched. "But he thought Tyler was onto him."

"That justifies what he did?" Neil asked, appalled.

Fitz sighed. "No, hell no. But it must have been his motive for shooting at Tyler. What motive would he have for going after you or after Elise?"

"Maybe, like you, he blames the mayor's stand against urban sprawl for everything, for those bodies being discovered."

Fitz glared at him. "The only thing I blame Elise for is not having her own ideas but for blindly carrying on those of her predecessor."

Neil shook his head. "You don't know Elise." She was tough and independent and would never blindly carry on anyone else's ideas. Fitz had never bothered getting to know his former daughter-in-law, though, just as he had never really cared to know his own children.

He hadn't been the one who'd sat with them after school, asking about their days. That had been Mom. She'd always been there for them.

"You didn't give me much of a chance," Fitz said, "before you divorced her."

Neil flinched now. If only he'd given her the time she'd wanted.

But he hadn't wanted them to wind up like his parents, cohabitants in a house but nothing more. How had they had so many children with so little emotion between them? Elise had suggested once that maybe their lack of intimacy was the result of having so many children, that they'd gotten stressed out and drifted apart.

Even divorced, he and Elise were closer than his parents were. But Neil wanted more now. He wanted to be her husband again.

"The divorce was a mistake," he admitted to his dad. An ultimatum he should have known better to ever issue to Elise.

Fitz arched a brow. "Really?"

Neil nodded.

"One you intend to fix?"

"If she'll let me," he said. "But at the moment, we just want to find out who the hell lured us to that warehouse last night to blow us up."

"You were lured?" Fitz asked.

"Yeah, someone left messages claiming the other asked to meet there," Neil shared. "But we didn't."

"So this person is after both of you," Fitz said with surprise. "Not just the mayor?"

"Of course you would think she's the target," Neil murmured.

"Her politics have pissed people off," Fitz said. Furrows formed on his high forehead. "But I doubt that anyone's mad enough to want her dead."

Neil shoved his fingers through his hair, frustrated enough to pull it out. "Then what the hell could this be about?"

"Why are you asking me?" His father's gruff voice had gone even gruffer with his question. "I'm not a detective like your sister. And I certainly had no idea what the hell happened last night, let alone know why."

Neil tilted his head and studied his father's flushed face. "Really? There's no one who might want revenge against you?"

His face turned redder as he blustered. "For what? What do you think I've done?"

That was his father—always going on the defensive instead of admitting any fault. "Your employees' illnesses—"

"Have nothing to do with you and the mayor," he said. Then added, almost as an afterthought, "Or with me."

"But what if somebody thought you hurt somebody they cared about, and wanted to harm someone you cared about—"

"You're talking nonsense," Fitz interjected. "All of it. What happened to you and the mayor has nothing to do with me or Colton Construction."

Neil wondered if his father truly believed what he was spouting, though. "It happened at a Colton Construction site. The one where those bodies were found. Dex—"

"*Was* my business partner," Fitz said. "So I know one criminal. How many have you and Elise come into contact with in your practice? You certainly know more criminals than I ever will."

*He'll get what's coming to him.*

Neil had already concluded he'd heard that phrase before, probably many times, during the course of his career in criminal law. But he hadn't always been alone in the practice. Elise had been his partner before she'd become the deputy mayor.

And whoever had left those messages for them the night before had lured both of them to the warehouse before detonating the bomb.

Someone wanted them both dead. Someone from their shared past...

He cursed.

"What?" Fitz asked.

"You're right," Neil said. "This has to have something to do with the practice."

Which meant that Elise was not safe. In fact, far from it.

He pulled his cell phone from the inside pocket of his jacket.

"Who are you calling?" Fitz asked. "Your sister?"

Jordana might have already figured out what Neil just had. He shook his head. "I need to call Elise." He'd already brought up her contact information, but his call went directly to her voice mail. He cursed again.

He needed to find her. To make sure she was all right. He jerked open the door and rushed out into the hall. His father must have managed to move faster now, because he caught him in the foyer, his hand on Neil's arm holding him back from opening the front door.

"Let the police handle this," Fitz urged him.

"I have to make sure Elise is all right," he said. Because he had that damn feeling again.

That feeling he'd had just minutes before the

bomb had exploded. The feeling that compelled him to run…but this time he wasn't going to run away from danger. He would run toward it.

Because he suspected that Elise was in danger.

## Chapter Ten

Elise held her breath as she stepped inside the dimly lit parking garage. The click of her heels echoed off the concrete floor and walls, louder than her breath would have been had she released it.

She was intent now on listening for the sound of footsteps other than hers. Had that person followed her into the garage?

She clasped the canister of pepper spray more tightly in her hand, which had gotten clammy with sweat despite the cold. She should have been wearing gloves, but she hadn't been thinking of the weather that morning when she'd gotten ready, or she wouldn't have worn the dress and high heels.

Snow swirled even in the garage, through the space between the low walls and low ceilings. Like all new construction, the building was less than two stories high, with plenty of open space. Fortunately, the snow wasn't accumulating enough for her heels to slip, so she hastened her step, nearly trotting as she headed toward the spot where her new vehicle had been parked. She slid her hand, the one not holding the pepper spray, into her pocket and pulled out the key fob. When she clicked it, lights flashed on directly in her face. Blinded, she squinted and looked away, and as she did, a blur of movement caught her attention. Someone jumped out at her.

She spun, the can of pepper spray raised to defend herself. She pressed on the button, but she hadn't taken the safety clip off the top, so nothing came out.

The man held up his hands over his handsome face, though, almost as if he'd been pepper-sprayed before and knew what had nearly happened to him. "It's just me," Jeremy exclaimed. "It's just me."

"What the hell were you doing following me like that?" Elise demanded to know, her heart pounding madly with fear. She wasn't relieved that she knew him, not after the way he'd stalked her down the street.

"I wanted to see your reaction when you saw your new vehicle for the first time," he said, reminding her of a child wanting to surprise his mother with a bouquet of some weeds he'd picked on his way home from school.

Of course, the SUV wasn't a bunch of weeds, though, and Elise had written the check for it. Still, Jeremy had helped her purchase it and had arranged the delivery.

She released a shaky sigh, finally succumbing to relief. Yet she felt compelled to remind him, "I was nearly blown up last night. You didn't consider how that might have made me a little jumpy?"

He gasped and pressed a hand over his heart. "I'm

sorry. I wasn't thinking…" He shook his head, but not a single golden strand moved out of place. "But surely what happened last night had to be about Colton or that crazy family of his? It couldn't have had anything to do with you."

She would've liked to think that, too, but she wasn't so sure. Someone had made certain to lure her to join Neil at that warehouse. She shrugged. "I don't know. And because of that, I need to be careful."

And to take the safety cap off the damn can of pepper spray. She wouldn't make that mistake again. She couldn't afford to. She'd been lucky that Jeremy had been the one following her.

Or was she?

He had the most to gain if something happened to her. And he'd been quick to fill her chair before it had even gotten cold this morning. Maybe sending that email to Neil, and the message luring him to the warehouse, had been to make it seem as if he was either the target or the perpetrator.

"That's another reason I followed you," Jeremy said. "To make sure you're safe."

She narrowed her eyes. "But you just said you didn't think I was in danger."

"Not the target," he said. "But because of your association with the Coltons, you could be in danger. Somebody might be trying to get back at them by hurting you, too. I wanted to make sure you got safely to your new car. I would hate for anything to happen to you, Elise."

She nearly snorted in derision. He'd been sucking up like this all day. She hated it.

"I can follow you home, too, and make sure you get safely there," he offered.

She shook her head. "I'll be fine."

"You are going home, right?" he prodded.

Where did he think she was going? To Neil's?

Temptation pulled at her to head in that direction, to head to what had once felt like home to her—the house they'd built together, just as they'd built their law practice.

*He'll get what's coming to him.*

That phrase in the email sent to Neil sounded so damn familiar. But she'd probably heard it several times while she'd been a criminal lawyer.

Was that what last night had been about? About something that had happened during the years they'd run the practice together? Was that why someone had gone after both of them?

Where she was going wasn't any of her deputy mayor's business, and she was tempted to tell him that. But he had helped her replace her vehicle, so she replied civilly instead. "Yes, I am going home."

"Do you want to stop for dinner somewhere first?" he asked. "You must be hungry."

She should have been; she usually was. But while she hadn't gotten true morning sickness with her pregnancy, she felt slightly nauseated all day instead, just enough to curb her appetite.

Maybe that was less a physical side effect of her pregnancy and more an emotional one. She was tough and independent, but she'd never wanted to be a single mother like her mom. She wasn't going to accept Neil's proposal, either, not when the baby was the only reason he was proposing. "I'm too tired to be hungry," she admitted. "I didn't get much sleep last night."

"Of course—because of the explosion."

The explosion hadn't been the reason; Neil had. When was she going to be able to resist her attraction to him? Maybe when she was too big to see her feet.

"Yes," she replied. "So I'm going straight to bed." Alone. Not that Jeremy was inviting himself to join her. Despite how solicitous he was with her, he had never crossed the line into open flirting. She had no idea if he had a crush on her, or if he was just sucking up to the boss.

The person she didn't want in her bed tonight was Neil—because she wanted him more than she wanted sleep. But she needed to get some rest—for herself and for the baby that was developing inside her.

"Thank you, Jeremy, for helping me get this vehicle," she said. "I'll see you in the morning."

Before he could say anything else, she quickly climbed into the new SUV and closed the door behind herself. She drew in a deep breath of relief while also inhaling the scent of new leather. Maybe car shopping wasn't so bad after all.

If she hadn't been so tired, she might have taken the new vehicle for a spin around town to take in all the Christmas decorations. But she drove directly to her condo. As she headed down the street toward her unit, she automatically lifted her hand toward her visor. The garage door opener was in her other vehicle, though, and had undoubtedly burnt up with it. But between the dealer, Jeremy and her condo association, the new SUV had been programmed with the information from the opener so that the garage door began to lift as she approached.

She smiled with appreciation—until she noticed that the service door between the garage and the house stood open. She hadn't left it that way.

Someone else must have left it open. When they'd gone inside or when they'd left?

She stopped the SUV on the condo's short driveway while she pondered what to do. Chances were that the person had already left, though. And she had the pepper spray and knew to remove the safety cap now. So she turned off the SUV and stepped out onto the driveway. The smart thing to do was call the police, though. So she pulled out her cell instead of the pepper spray and hit the emergency call button.

While waiting for the operator to pick up, she moved closer to the condo, listening for any sounds from inside. But she hadn't noticed the sounds right around her—of someone approaching.

Strong arms suddenly closed around her as someone grabbed her. A scream burned the back of her throat, but before she could release it, a hand covered her mouth.

And just then the operator picked up, her voice emanating from the cell phone. "What's your emergency?"

"WHY THE HELL are we responding to a B&E?" Reese grumbled from the passenger seat as Jordana turned on the lights and sirens.

She only spared him a glance, her total focus on the road. She had to get there before anything happened, like another bomb being set to explode.

"You should have recognized the address," Jordana admonished him. "It's the mayor's."

Reese cursed. "You think someone's trying to make another attempt on her life?"

"I don't believe it's a coincidence that her condo's getting broken into a day after the explosion. Do you?" she asked, well aware of her partner's cynicism.

There was no way Reese Carpenter believed in coincidences or fate or maybe anything at all. She had once been like that herself until she'd met Clint and fallen so deeply in love.

Reese cursed again. "No, it's not a coincidence."

"So she must have been the target," Jordana mused, and some of the tightness in her chest eased somewhat. Hopefully, Neil was not in any real danger, then.

And maybe this was all about the mayor. Not him…

She'd nearly lost one of her brothers the month before, when Ty was shot. She did not want to lose Neil. But if he knew that his ex-wife was in danger…

Jordana doubted she would be able to keep him away from the mayor's condo, especially if Elise was anywhere near it. The dispatcher hadn't known who'd called to report the break-in. It could have been Elise.

Hell, it could have been Neil who'd called, or who had broken into the place.

Even after divorcing Elise, he never seemed to stay away from her. But if she was the one in danger, he might get killed, too, if he got too close to his ex.

NEIL BREATHED A sigh of relief that stirred Elise's hair. He was so damn glad that she was all right. But then he turned her in his arms. "What were you thinking?"

"What the hell were you thinking to grab me like that?" she asked.

"I was stopping you from going inside," he said, "when I noticed that the door was open between the garage and your utility room."

"I noticed that, too, so I damn well was not going inside," she assured him.

"Good. Get in your SUV and drive away from here," he instructed her. But knowing that she rarely listened to him, he guided her toward her new vehicle and the driver's door she'd left open.

"You want me to leave?" she asked.

He nodded. "At least until the police arrive and secure your place."

"Okay…" But she stopped before climbing behind the steering wheel and turned back to him. "What are you going to do?"

"I'm going inside," he replied.

Elise's hands went to his chest, but instead of embracing him, she pushed him back. "What the hell are you thinking?"

"I'm thinking I might be able to catch the damn

person before he gets away." Unless he spent too much time out here arguing with her. But when he turned toward the garage, Elise grabbed his arm.

"You can't go in there."

"I can't let him get away," Neil said as he pulled free of her. "Get in your SUV and lock the door!"

"Neil!"

"I'm sure he's already gone," Neil assured her. But as he got closer to that open door, noises emanated from within the condo. A heavy thud as something struck the wood floor.

Careful to be quiet, he eased through the opening and stepped inside the back hall. The doors to the closet on one side of it stood open, as if someone had been looking for something. Coats had been knocked from their hangers. He turned the other way and walked down the hall to the kitchen, where he found cupboard doors and drawers open.

Someone had ransacked the place. And must still be ransacking it…

Another thud echoed from just beyond the kitchen.

He moved toward the noise, but as he did, a shadow rushed toward him, shoving him so hard down the hall that he was knocked all the way back into the open closet. Losing his balance, he fell into the pile of coats.

The shadow passed by him, out the open door, to where he'd left Elise alone on the driveway.

What the hell had he been thinking?

He shouted her name in warning. But it was too late. The person had to have reached her already and maybe hurt her or worse.

## Chapter Eleven

He came barreling toward her, such intensity on his face that Elise had no idea what he might do to her. She knew what she wanted to do: launch herself at him and lash out at him for what he'd put her through.

Fury gripped Elise so fiercely that she trembled with it, her body shaking. "You could have been killed," she admonished Neil.

"I'm fine," he said. "What about you?" His hands shook a little as he reached for her, helping her out of the SUV.

When he'd gone inside the house, she'd thought about following him, about trying to protect him. But he wasn't the only one she needed to worry about protecting.

She pressed a hand over her stomach. Fearing for the baby as well as for Neil, she'd hopped into her new vehicle and clicked the locks. Guilt had gripped her, though. Guilt that she wasn't backing up Neil inside the condo, but she'd known the police were due to arrive soon. Sirens had been wailing in the distance, just loud enough that if the intruder was inside the condo yet, he would have heard them.

She wasn't sure if the intruder had heard them or if he'd heard Neil instead. But he'd erupted from the house just seconds ago. Luckily, he'd run past the SUV without noticing her. He'd probably been in a hurry to escape the police cars that arrived, with flashing lights and ear-splitting sirens, just seconds after his departure.

She flinched over the noise and the glare of the lights but nodded. "I'm fine."

Her heart and pulse raced yet with the fear she'd felt for Neil's safety. She'd been so scared for him, and when the other man had run out first, she'd worried that the police were going to be too late. That something had already happened to Neil—something horrible.

Fortunately Neil had been just seconds behind the intruder, moving with such speed that he seemed to be unharmed. She had thrown open the door of her SUV to stop him from pursuing the guy, though.

"Did you recognize him?" Neil asked. "Do you know who he is?"

She shook her head. "No. Did you?"

"I didn't get a look at his face," Neil said, his voice gruff with disappointment.

"Me, neither."

The man, tall and muscular, had been wearing a hoodie pulled tight around his face. All she'd seen was the side of that hood, not any of his profile, as he'd rushed past her. But he was big, bigger than Neil.

When Neil had helped her out of the SUV, her entire body was shaking with fear, and she'd grabbed his arms to steady herself. Now she clutched his forearms, which tensed beneath his jacket. She was tempted to pull Neil even closer. To hold him tight with relief that he was all right.

But she was still so damn mad that he'd put himself in danger. She was not the only one, as Detective Colton ran up to join them.

"What the hell are you two doing here?" Jordana demanded to know.

"I live here," Elise reminded her ex-sister-in-law. "I don't know why your brother is here." She hadn't had time to ask him why he'd showed up when he had. She'd been too worried about that open door. "And I sure don't know why the hell he's trying to play superhero."

The only thing she knew for certain was that if he kept it up, he was unlikely to live to see their child born. If whoever was after them didn't kill him, she probably would, for risking his damn life.

When Jordana whirled toward him, Neil held up his hands to ward her off like he should have warded off the intruder. But there hadn't been time…

No time for him to catch the guy or catch himself from tumbling into the closet. Despite the cold night breeze blowing around the driveway, heat coursed through Neil—the heat of anger and frustration.

If only he'd been faster. If only he could have

stopped the man. Then this would all be over; they would be safe.

He wasn't safe now, not from the angry women glaring at him.

"You're a lawyer," Jordana said, as if he had to be reminded. "Not a police officer. Once you two realized the place had been broken into, you should have left until the police could get here to secure the scene."

"Instead he went inside," Elise informed his sister. "He tried to catch him."

Jordana gasped and whirled toward him. "That was so damn stupid, Neil. And dangerous."

He shrugged off her concern. "I'm fine." Only his ego—and maybe his ass—had gotten bruised. Which made him wonder.

"I'm not even sure it was the person who set up the bomb," he said. "It could have just been a burglar."

"We'll have Elise check to see what's missing," Jordana said. But when Elise started toward the open door to her condo, she caught her arm. "After we clear the place."

"Clear the place?" Elise asked, her voice cracking with fear. "You think there could have been a couple of them inside the condo?" She reached out and smacked Neil's shoulder. "And you went in there unarmed and outnumbered! You could have been killed."

"I'm fine," he repeated.

But why hadn't the intruder taken the opportunity to kill Neil when he'd had the chance? Or Elise, as well? She'd just been sitting in the SUV in the driveway. The man had probably heard the sirens, though, and had worried that he was about to get caught if he didn't leave in a hurry. And he had left in a real hurry.

"Even if there was just one guy, he could have had a gun," Elise said. "You're lucky you didn't get shot."

"Or worse," Jordana added. "He could have been setting another bomb in there. That's why you two need to clear out of here."

Neil sucked in a breath of shock. He'd been so intent on catching the guy that he hadn't realized what the man actually might have been doing inside Elise's condo.

Setting another explosive device.

That was why he hadn't bothered to stop and kill Neil. It was why he'd been in such a damn hurry to get the hell out of there, too.

Even now he could be out there, somewhere beyond the police cars, waiting to detonate it.

Jordana must have considered the same thing because she waved toward Elise's SUV. "Unless you want to lose this one, too, I suggest you get in and get the hell out of here until the bomb squad clears your place."

Elise gasped and nodded. For once she was speechless.

So was Neil.

He hadn't considered that just being in the proximity could have put her in danger, too. He should have made her leave the area, and he never should have gone inside alone.

"I'm sorry," he murmured, to both women.

Sorry that he hadn't been thinking.

He had just been so intent on ending this so that they were no longer in danger. But they weren't just in danger. They were waiting for this person to strike out at them again and not knowing when it might happen.

Was it now?

*DAMN IT!*

Once he'd broken inside her condo through the side door of the garage, he had allowed himself to get distracted with thoughts of how unfair it all was. How she had so much while some other people had so little.

Not even life.

And he'd let his rage over the injustice of it all consume him.

Instead of putting his plan into motion, he'd smashed her stuff, taking his anger out on inanimate objects instead of the people who deserved it.

Who'd earned it.

And their reward for what they'd done was going to be death.

He stared through the windshield of the vehicle he'd stolen in another city, from a retirement center so that the owner might not even realize it was gone for a while. He'd parked it on the street outside the complex, and he sat inside it, in the dark, watching. Waiting.

Lights flashed as more official vehicles rolled into the complex. He chuckled as he saw the special response vehicles. What the hell did they think he'd done?

There hadn't been time for that.

No. His plan tonight had been to just send them a message. And maybe he had.

But now he wanted more. He wanted this over. *Them* over…

He couldn't get to them here, though, not with all the police officers swarming around. So he would wait until they left.

And he would follow.

The next time he came this close to his prey, he would take them out for good.

# *Chapter Twelve*

Worried about the danger to her neighbors, Elise had refused to leave the condo complex. She'd gone only as far as the entrance, where everyone stood after being evacuated.

"I'm sorry," she murmured to her neighbors, like Neil had murmured to her and his sister earlier.

She hadn't accepted his apology. She was still too angry with him. But most of her neighbors accepted hers. "Not your fault, Mayor," one of the older men assured her. "Can't help that some crazy is going after you." He cast a suspicious glance Neil's way.

He was some crazy—or at least he'd acted crazy when he'd charged into the condo unarmed and unprepared. She sighed and shook her head, amazed and grateful that he had not been injured. She was still angry that he'd taken such a chance with his life.

She slid her hand over her belly, thinking of the life growing inside her—the one that Neil had helped create. He'd wanted so badly to become a father, and he could have missed the opportunity entirely if something had happened to him.

Still could miss it if he kept taking foolish chances like that…

She'd been tempted, too, though. She wanted this over, and the real crazy person who was determined to kill them caught, as much as Neil wanted him caught. But before she'd let herself walk inside the condo, she'd reminded herself that she wasn't putting just herself in danger. She was endangering the baby, too.

"Bomb squad is leaving," Neil remarked beneath his breath, as he pointed toward the black panel van passing the entrance to turn onto the street.

Elise expelled a shaky breath of relief. There must not have been a bomb, then. She hadn't put her neighbors in danger. This time.

Until this person was caught, however, she could unwittingly cause them harm.

"You can all return to your homes," Detective Carpenter told the crowd gathered around the entrance. "Everything is fine. We've thoroughly searched the entire area and determined there is no threat."

The intruder was gone, and he'd left nothing dangerous behind him. Elise couldn't summon any relief, though. She knew he'd be back.

"We can leave now," Neil said. "We know your neighbors are okay."

Maybe he knew her better than she thought he did—since he knew her neighbors' safety had been her primary concern. "I'm not leaving," she said.

"You can't stay," Neil argued. "If you do, he'll come back."

She doubted that he would return tonight—with all the police officers on the scene. But he would come back…sometime.

"You can't leave," Detective Carpenter interrupted them. "Not until you give your statements."

"I already spoke to my sister," Neil said.

Reese shook his head. "I don't think she heard much of what you told her. She was too damn mad. In fact, she hasn't cooled off a whole hell of a lot yet." He sent Neil a pitying glance. "Maybe you should leave."

"I'm staying," Elise said. The thought of someone inside her home, touching her things…

She shivered.

"Then let's get you inside, Mayor," Detective Carpenter said. "It's freezing out here."

She'd been so angry she hadn't noticed the cold. But she gratefully followed him back to her condo.

Neil, of course, was right behind her. But when she started across her threshold, he caught her arm. "You may not want to see this," he warned her.

"What happened?" she asked. "I thought there was no bomb."

"Still looks like one went off inside," Reese remarked. "The guy was sure angry about something."

"I can relate," Elise murmured as she stepped inside her condo. From the mess, it looked more like a tornado had swept through her home than an intruder. Everything had been upended, with pictures torn from the walls, drawers emptied onto the floor.

She gasped as she noticed the contents of one of

those drawers. Broken glass surrounded the cracked frame of her and Neil's wedding portrait.

Instead of being upset, as she was, Neil grinned when he saw it. He picked it up from the floor and stared at their smiling faces. "You kept it…"

"In a drawer," she pointed out. "I'd pretty much forgotten it was there."

Except for all the times she pulled it out and stared at it, at how happy they'd been that day…and wondered what had happened, how it had all gone so wrong.

That was why she couldn't accept his proposal— not when she knew how devastated she would be if they failed again. They'd started out last time with so much love and hope and promise.

JORDANA HAD NOTICED the shattered wedding portrait when the bomb squad had first cleared her to enter the condo. She couldn't understand why her brother would grin at the broken picture.

She and Clint weren't even married yet, but she could already imagine that she would be as shattered as that portrait if they ever divorced. But they would never do that. They loved each other too much.

She'd once thought that Neil and Elise had loved each other, too. The way they were looking at each other now, though, wasn't too different than how they'd looked at each other in that portrait. Maybe the love was still there. But there was also pain and disillusionment, which reminded her of her parents.

She cleared her throat, drawing their attention

to her. "Have you had a chance to look through the condo and determine if anything's missing?" she asked Elise.

Elise shook her head.

"It's late," Neil said. "She doesn't have time to do an inventory. I'm going to take her home with me."

"I'm not a stray dog," Elise said, her voice sharp with indignation.

"It would take you all night to do an inventory of this mess," Neil pointed out. "And you need your sleep, especially now."

If not for the dark circles beneath Elise's pretty green eyes, Jordana would have asked why he'd said that, but the mayor looked so tired it was easy to understand why she needed sleep. She probably hadn't gotten much rest after the explosion the night before.

And now this.

"Did either of you get a good look at the intruder?" Jordana asked. She hadn't had time to question them earlier—given how angry she'd been with them for putting themselves in danger and with the potential hazard of another bomb being planted in the condo.

Elise described a big man with a hood pulled tight covering most of his head and face, and Neil nodded in agreement but added nothing more.

Jordana sighed with frustration. It was pretty damn hard to put out an APB for someone matching that description. If she did, almost half of Braxville would be pulled in for questioning.

"You have no idea who might be coming after the two of you?" she asked.

They both tensed, as if they were holding something back. Or had come to some kind of realization they were hesitant to admit.

"What?" she asked when neither answered her. "Who?"

Elise gave her an almost pitying glance. "Maybe it has something to do with your father—"

"We're already looking at Markus Dexter for it," Reese interjected.

"I meant someone else—someone who might have gotten sick or worse while working for your father."

"We don't know that Colton Construction is really responsible for anybody getting sick," Neil said, coming to their father's defense. But then that was what he did—he defended criminals.

Jordana didn't want to believe that their father could be one, though. It wasn't possible. But what if someone else believed that? "Why go after you two, though, to get back at Dad? Why not all of us?"

"Maybe we're just the first two," Elise suggested.

Neil shook his head. "It doesn't make sense. If somebody really wanted to hurt my dad, why hurt you?"

Elise flinched. "True. Something happening to me would make him happy."

Neil shook his head again. "No."

"I did have another thought," Elise admitted.

And Neil finished that thought for her as if he'd read her mind, "That it could be someone from when we were in practice together?"

Elise nodded.

"Of course," Reese said, "you guys represented criminals, so maybe one of them didn't like the deal you got him."

*He'll get what's coming to him.*

That was the email Neil had received earlier that day. "Or maybe someone thinks you got a criminal too good a deal."

"But why wait until now to come after us?" Elise asked. "We've not been partners for a few years now."

In business or in their personal lives.

Jordana shrugged. "I don't know. But *we'll* look into it. Not you two. We're the detectives. You need to stay out of this."

Neil held up his hands. "I just want to take Elise home."

"This is my home," Elise said, but as she looked around the ransacked condo, her shoulders slumped with defeat.

"My home," Neil said. "I have the top-of-the-line security system. You have just that doorbell camera."

Which hadn't helped when the intruder had come through the garage.

"Just to be sure that your system is really top-notch, we'll check out the house before you go there," Jordana recommended. "We'll make sure it's clear for you."

Neil must have been tired, too, because he didn't fight her on this, either, while the lawyer in him usually argued so much that it seemed like he had come out of their mother's womb arguing. That was why she didn't tell him about the other thing she'd done.

She didn't want him protesting or claiming that she was getting overprotective. After what had happened tonight—what could have happened—she wasn't being protective enough.

Neil was so damn stubborn and independent that he would get himself killed if he wasn't careful. Tonight he'd proved he wasn't being wary enough, so Jordana would be cautious for him.

Neil's eyes narrowed as he studied her face. Clearly he suspected that she was up to something. But once again he didn't argue. Maybe he'd realized that she was only concerned about his safety.

He turned his attention to Elise then, urging her to pack up a suitcase so they could leave. And the look on his face...

It was so like his lovesick expression in that wedding portrait that Jordana wasn't just worried about his physical safety now. She was concerned he might get his heart broken all over again.

NEIL FOLLOWED ELISE'S new SUV away from the condo toward his place. But he was tense with apprehension that she might suddenly turn off and head to a hotel instead of his house. The fact that she'd agreed to come home with him either meant that she was scared or just too exhausted to protest.

Either reason had his heart aching with regret. He'd fallen for Elise because of her fierce independence, because of her conviction to her opinions. Unfortunately, those were also the things that infuriated him the most about her. But he still didn't want her to lose them—to lose herself—like she'd once admitted she feared would happen when she moved to his hometown and became a Colton.

But Neil didn't want to lose her, either. That could have happened tonight if she had gone inside her condo before he got there, or if the intruder had harmed her when he ran out of her place. Or another explosive had been put in the condo.

His stomach lurched with dread over the danger she was in, over the danger they were both in.

Had a bomb been planted at his house?

Braxville PD vehicles filled the driveway. They were checking it out, as Jordana had insisted. He didn't mind his big sister's protectiveness, not in this case, not when she was also protecting her unborn niece or nephew, albeit unknowingly, as well as him and Elise.

Elise parked alongside the curb outside the home she had once willingly left just as she'd left him. Of course, he'd asked for the divorce, but he would have taken it all back…if she'd opposed it. But she, who fought over everything, hadn't fought for them.

She stepped out of the SUV and pulled open the passenger door of his to say, "Where are we going to go until they clear the house?"

"Have you eaten?" he asked.

She shook her head.

"Elise, you need to eat." She should be eating for two now, resting for two. Everything she did affected their baby as well as herself.

The fear, the danger, the exhaustion.

She grimaced.

And his heart thudded with alarm. "What's wrong? Are you all right?"

She sighed. "You know how much I usually love food, but I've been queasy the past few weeks."

"Morning sickness?"

"All-day-long sickness," she said. Her stomach grumbled, and her grimace turned to a smile. "But I should probably eat something."

"Me, too," he said. He'd been so consumed with finding out who was after them that he probably hadn't eaten, either. He couldn't remember grabbing much more than a snack earlier. As he turned off his street to head back toward town, he noticed headlight beams in his rearview as another vehicle followed them.

Jordana was checking out his house, but what about everywhere else? She couldn't keep them safe—not from someone following them.

It was up to Neil now. He had to keep his family from harm.

## Chapter Thirteen

For someone who kept proposing to her, Neil sure wasn't paying Elise much attention. Instead of talking to her, he stared silently out the restaurant window. Hungrier than she'd realized, she had been preoccupied with shoveling the diner special of meatloaf and mashed potatoes into her face, so she hadn't noticed his silence until now.

He hadn't even touched his plate, which tempted her to reach across to steal his burger. Instead, she settled for just a fry. Then another...

As she swiped one through the ketchup he'd squirted onto the plate, she remarked, "What's got your attention outside?"

He glanced at her then—just briefly—before gazing back out the window.

She turned to peer out, as well, but saw only her own reflection and his in the darkened glass. "What is it?" she asked.

Was someone out there?

"Uh, just all the decorations," he said. "They're really pretty this year."

"They're the exact same ones we had last year." Twinkle lights and lit-up wreaths wrapped around every light pole. But they were pretty.

She glanced at Neil's phone that he'd left sitting on the tabletop next to his formerly untouched plate. She grabbed another fry and remarked, "Since your sister hasn't called with the all clear, we should get a tree before we head back, and decorate it."

Neil whirled away from the window and toward her now, his blue eyes wide with surprise and delight. "You want to get a tree with me?"

She chuckled. "Well, it might be a good trial run. Make sure we can keep that alive before we have a kid." She trailed off as her joke fell flat to her own ears. With someone trying to kill them, keeping their child and each other alive wasn't going to be easy. "Who do you think it is?" she asked. "Who's after us?"

He shook his head. "I don't know."

"Maybe we should skip the tree and head back to your office and go through our old case files," she suggested.

"Jordana said to leave the investigation to her," he reminded her, and his attention returned to the window.

She narrowed her eyes and studied his face. "And since when do you leave anything to anyone else?"

"You should talk," he shot back at her.

She chuckled. "I know. That's one of the too many things we have in common that make us incompatible."

He flinched. "We are not incompatible."

"If we weren't, we would still be married," she pointed out.

A twinkle brightened his blue eyes, and he said, "We could be if you would say yes."

Her heart leaped—at that twinkle—and at the temptation to say yes. But she couldn't summon the trust to make the leap—not in herself and her judgment, and not in him. Not after he had ended their marriage so easily.

She shook her head. "Don't…" Her appetite gone, or at least finally sated, she pushed her empty plate away. "I'm tired. I think I should just check into a hotel."

"No, Elise," he said as he shoved his plate aside, too. "I won't pressure you anymore."

"It's not just that," she said. "I really am tired, and it's taking them too long to clear the house." Which meant that they'd probably found something they'd had to clear. Another explosive?

He glanced at his phone. "She texted a while ago. It's clear. We can go home."

She shook her head now. "No, you can never go home again."

She had to remind herself of that more than him. The house they'd built together wasn't her home. Not anymore.

And it never would be again…

NEIL WANTED TO take Elise home more than anything. But he didn't want to take along whoever was following them. And he was certain that someone was.

He hadn't been staring out that window at decorations. He'd been watching the car parked a little way down the street, and the dark shadow behind the wheel, to see if the person would step out. Why just sit there?

Unless he'd been staring at Neil and Elise through that restaurant window, waiting for them to leave.

Neil probably should have texted Jordana back and let her know that someone could be following them. But what if he was wrong? Then he would be upsetting Elise for no reason. And in her current condition, he didn't want to keep upsetting her, especially after what had happened earlier at her condo. She'd been furious with him and devastated over the damage to her things. All this fear, stress and anxiety could not be good for their baby.

"Let's get that tree," he suggested as they stepped out of the diner.

She tilted her head up toward him, tempting him to lower his head, to brush his mouth across hers. He wanted to kiss her so badly. But she narrowed her eyes and studied his face. "What's up with you?"

"It was your idea," he reminded her. He also wanted to walk a little closer to that vehicle, to see if the person was still sitting behind the wheel. The Christmas tree stand was in a small parking lot just a couple of storefronts from the diner. When Elise started toward it, his stomach tightened. He didn't want her any closer to whoever might have followed them, but he also didn't want her out of his sight, out of his reach. He caught her hand in his.

Startled to find her skin so cold, he remarked, "You're not wearing gloves."

"You're not, either," she pointed out.

They'd both been so preoccupied that morning that he understood how the gloves had been forgotten. He was still preoccupied with her safety. One of her boots slipped on the sidewalk, and she stumbled into him. He caught her, holding her upright. He'd been concerned about the man in the parked car; now he was worried about her. He glanced toward that vehicle and noticed the shadow was gone. Nobody sat behind the steering wheel of what was actually a station wagon–type SUV.

Where the hell had the driver gone?

Neil swiveled his neck, looking behind them— in front of them—and to the side. He hadn't noticed anyone getting out of the vehicle.

"You lost him?" Elise asked, her voice pitched to a low whisper.

"Who?" Neil asked, feigning confusion.

"Whoever you were watching from the diner window."

Of course she'd noticed. Elise rarely missed anything, except how much he loved her. But he wondered if she had ever really trusted his love or him. And thanks to the stubbornness that was so much a part of both of them, she probably never would.

"I thought someone might have been following us," he murmured. "I could just be paranoid."

"Probably," she agreed. "But call Jordana anyway."

"For paranoia?"

"You don't believe it's just that," she said.

He sighed and shrugged. "I don't know what to believe." But he wanted to find out. Where could the person have gone from that vehicle?

He peered around him, looking more for hiding places than at the trees on the Christmas tree lot. Elise's attention left him for a moment as she walked around a few of the cut trees. She stopped near a giant fir tree, gestured at it and murmured, "That would look beautiful in the great room."

He loved the look on her face, the awe. It was the same as it had been the first time they'd gone Christmas tree shopping. She and her mother had never had a real tree. The apartments where they'd lived hadn't allowed them nor had the space for one like this. They'd only had room for a small artificial tree. So when they'd designed the house, Neil had made certain that there was room for the biggest tree he could fit inside the house. For her…

And for the little girl she'd once been, the one who'd longed for more than her single mother had been able to provide.

"That's an awesome tree," he agreed. "But it's not going to fit on the roof of my SUV."

"We deliver," the attendant said.

Neil paid the man before giving him his address for delivery tomorrow. But he pitched his voice low as he did, not wanting anyone to overhear the details. But if that vehicle had followed him from his street, then the driver already knew where he lived.

The house was clear and safe, though. Jordana had assured him of that. He needed to bring Elise home.

But that sensation…that creepy sensation of being watched…

It had the skin crawling on his back as a chill raced down his spine. Whoever it was must have been behind them, staring holes into him. That was where the driver had gone; he'd gotten out to follow them on foot.

Neil led Elise quickly across the street to his SUV, keeping his arm around her until he opened the passenger's door for her. Then he helped her onto the seat.

She caught his arm before he could pull away and close the door. "What are you going to do?"

While she didn't know how much he loved her, maybe she knew him a little better than he'd thought she did. A smile tugged at his lips. "What makes you think I'm going to do anything?"

"Because I know how damn stubborn you are," she said.

"I'm just going to walk around a little bit, see where the driver of that car I was watching might have gone."

She shook her head, tousling her golden-blond hair around her shoulders. One tendril brushed against his cheek. Her hair was so soft, so silky. He wanted to lose his fingers in it while he kissed her lips. "It's too dangerous," she protested.

"Not if it's just someone shopping in one of the stores around here," he pointed out.

"Do you know what the person looks like?"

"I'll know when they return to their vehicle."

"Watch it from here," she said.

He shook his head. "I can't see it."

But the driver could see them if he was inside the vehicle; he could see when they pulled out and then follow them. But if the person intended to follow them, then he had to return to his vehicle. Now. Before Neil drove off.

"It'll just take a second," Neil assured her. "And I'll be right back."

"Neil!"

He covered her mouth with his, kissing her quickly but hotly before pulling back to close her door. He clicked the fob to lock the SUV, but that didn't mean she couldn't unlock and step out of it.

He only hoped she waited long enough that he had time to draw the attention of whoever was following them and lead him away from her.

HE HAD TO end this. He had to end *them*. Soon.

When they'd left the condo in separate vehicles, he hadn't known which one to follow, but at least they'd headed the same direction, to the same place. The lawyer's house. But there had been police vehicles parked there, too. Thinking they'd had too much protection, he'd almost left. But just before he'd pulled away, he'd noticed the mayor get into the lawyer's vehicle. And they'd driven off again—with him following.

This was going to be his best chance to take them

both out. But he had to be patient. He couldn't act rashly or let his rage control him, as he had earlier, at the mayor's condo.

What he'd done to her place—to her things—had to have sent her the message, though. That she didn't deserve the things she had, the life she was living...

Not after the mistake she'd made. It was past time she paid for it, for the justice she'd cost him. He'd had to wait so damn long.

And now he was able to act, to release all that rage.

His fury had earlier gotten out of hand, at her condo.

He could have been caught. And that wouldn't do. He was doling out justice; he wasn't going to have it dealt to him.

## Chapter Fourteen

He could not have gone far, not if he was following them.

Not even if he was just someone from Neil's neighborhood who had decided to head downtown at the same damn time they had.

He wouldn't have parked far from whatever business he intended to patronize, especially if he was like Elise, who had an aversion to walking too far or too fast. So the driver of the car, which Neil was pretty damn certain had followed them, had to be close.

Close to him and close to Elise. Neil shivered at the thought. She hadn't put herself in danger back at the condo, though—not like he had. So she would stay in the locked vehicle.

At least that was what he was counting on.

He hadn't counted on it taking so long for whoever belonged to that vehicle to come back, though. But maybe the person had noticed him loitering near it and knew that Neil was waiting for him to return.

A shadow fell across the sidewalk a short distance away, where a narrow alley separated a couple of shops. If he ducked in there, the person wouldn't see that Neil was still watching his vehicle. He glanced around, making certain no one appeared to be looking at him, before he eased backward into that space between the buildings. He wasn't sure it was actually an alley, though; it didn't seem wide enough for even a small car to traverse. It was also so dimly lit that he didn't notice anyone else standing in the shadows.

Until strong arms wrapped around him, pulling him farther from the street. He'd walked right into the trap of whoever was following him.

"Son of a bitch!" he yelled as he began to struggle.

He had to fight—for himself, for Elise and for their unborn baby. And it was a fight he couldn't lose—for all their sakes.

Ty GRUNTED WITH pain as Neil's elbow struck close to his healing wound. "Damn it! Stop! And you better watch what you call me—since we share the same mother."

Neil jerked free of his hold and whirled around on him. "What the hell are you doing grabbing me in a dark alley?"

"What the hell are you doing walking into dark alleys when someone's trying to kill you?"

"I didn't realize it might be you," Neil sarcastically replied.

"If it was me trying to kill you, you would already be dead," Ty warned him. "Jordana was right to call me. You need protection all right—protection from yourself."

Neil cursed. "I don't need my older siblings acting like I'm a stupid little kid anymore."

"Then don't be stupid," Ty replied.

Neil cursed again.

Ty chuckled, but he wasn't amused. From what Jordana had told him about the explosion, their brother was in serious danger. "Do you really want to be Dex's next victim?"

Like Ty very nearly had been, when the son of a bitch had shot him. A twinge of pain passed through his old wound again. He was healing, but not as quickly as he wanted. He had to be a hundred percent, especially now...because he wanted to keep his brother safe.

"I don't think I'm in any danger of that," Neil replied.

Ty snorted. "You just nearly got blown up and you don't think you're in any danger? You must have hit your head—hard—in the blast!"

"I don't think I'm in any danger from Dex," Neil said. "He has no reason to come after me and Elise."

"He didn't really have a reason to come after me, either," Ty said. "He just thought he did. Maybe, for some reason, he thinks he has a reason to take out the two of you, too."

Neil shook his head. "No, Elise and I are both pretty certain this is related to one of our cases when we were in partners in the law firm."

Ty groaned.

"What?"

"You guys handled a lot of cases…" Which meant a lot of potential suspects.

"Yes, we did," Neil said.

"So it might take a while to figure out who the hell is coming after you," he said.

"Jordana tells me to stay out of it, but she has you helping her?" Neil asked, his voice gruff with indignation.

Ty could have teased him about his resentment, because teasing was one of an older brother's responsibilities, but taking care of his younger siblings was also one of them. "Jordana has a partner. She hasn't asked me to play detective like you're trying to do. She asked me to watch out for you and make sure the person trying to kill you doesn't succeed before she has a chance to figure out who it is."

All wounded pride, Neil tensed. Maybe that was part of a younger brother's role—to get all defensive. "I can take care of myself. I can also figure out who's trying to kill me and Elise."

Ty snorted in derision. "That's why it was so damn easy for me to grab you."

"Seriously, if I hadn't noticed you following me, I wouldn't have stepped into this alley to wait for you to go back to your car," Neil said. "So it's your fault for blowing your security detail."

"I didn't blow it," Ty said.

"Then how did I see you?" Neil challenged him. "Jordana shouldn't have called you. You must be still recuperating from your gunshot wound."

"I'm fine. Fully recovered," Ty said, and it wasn't

a complete lie. He was pretty much recovered. "And you didn't see me. I'm driving a truck. Not a car."

Neil shook his head. "It might be a small SUV, but I wouldn't call it a truck."

"No, it's a truck," Ty maintained, his brow furrowing as he pondered his brother's confusion. "Are you that unaware of vehicle makes and models?" Wouldn't a lawyer have to have some knowledge of them to defend alleged hit-and-run and under-the-influence drivers?

"I know the difference between a truck and a car," Neil assured him. "Some people call their SUVs trucks."

"Not me," Ty said. "What the hell did you see following you?"

"A station wagon–type vehicle. Some kind of crossover SUV thing."

Ty's blood chilled. How the hell had he missed that vehicle? Maybe Neil was right; maybe he wasn't fully recovered yet from his gunshot wound.

"That's the driver I'm waiting for to return to his vehicle, so I can see if it's just a coincidence he headed to town when we did," Neil explained. "But you grabbed me, so I probably missed him."

"I hope you did," Ty replied. Because then that meant it had just been a coincidence.

If the person was still here—somewhere—then there was a chance that he was the one after Neil and his ex-wife.

"Where's Elise?" he asked.

"She's in my locked SUV. She's safe," Neil said, as if trying to reassure himself.

"And she would stay there?" Ty asked—because he knew his former sister-in-law. She was as independent and stubborn as Neil was, which was probably why they hadn't been able to make their marriage work.

Neil tensed, probably with fear, because he knew Elise far better than Ty did. So why the hell would he have left her in the SUV in the first place? He had to know that she wasn't going to stay there.

WHY HADN'T HE returned yet? He'd promised he was only going to take a quick look around and then come back to his vehicle, back to her.

Elise had been waiting a few years for that to happen, though, for him to come and beg for her forgiveness, to beg her to give them another chance. Sure, he'd recently been proposing, but that was only because of the baby. She'd wanted him to come back for her—for *them*—not out of some archaic sense of obligation. But because he loved her and that she was enough for him.

Now she just wanted him back in the damn SUV—safe—with her.

"Neil…" she murmured.

It had been too long. She needed to do something. She reached inside her purse for her cell. She needed to call his sister, to tell Jordana that he'd done it again—he'd put himself in danger.

But was he in danger?

She hadn't heard any gunshots or the blasts of any explosions.

Maybe he'd found the person who'd followed them off his street, and he was having a friendly conversation with a neighbor. The neighbor was sure to have been curious about all the cop cars in Neil's driveway.

With a weary sigh, she pushed open the passenger's door and stepped onto the sidewalk. A dull ache throbbed in her feet. Not only were the heels too high, but the boots had gotten too tight. Maybe swollen feet were another side effect of pregnancy, like the all-day nausea. Or maybe the swelling was an effect of all the fries she'd eaten off Neil's plate.

How far had Neil gone? He hadn't told her which vehicle he'd thought had followed them. And she hadn't noticed it at all. Not that she'd been looking for one; she wasn't used to someone trying to kill her.

And she didn't intend to get used to it. She intended to find out who was trying to kill them.

Not by trying to confront or trap them like Neil, but by going through old records from their former partnership. Despite what he'd said in the diner, she knew he had no intention of leaving the investigation to his sister. Hell, he couldn't even legally let Jordana go through their case files—not without violating lawyer-client confidentiality.

"Neil?" she called out as she glanced up and down the sidewalk. Other people walked along, some with shopping bags dangling from their gloved hands, some with dog leashes as they walked their pets. But she didn't catch a glimpse of Neil's lean body, of his dark hair, of his neatly trimmed beard.

Where was he? Which way had he even gone?

The guy at the Christmas tree lot could have seen him. From the big tip Neil had given him, the guy would remember him for certain. Since the lot was across the street, she stepped off the sidewalk between two vehicles parked at the curb.

While she waited for a break in the slow-moving traffic, a strange sensation rushed over her, like she could feel someone watching her.

Neil?

Was he close?

He had to be. A protective as he'd been of her—probably because of her pregnancy as much as their would-be killer—he wouldn't have gone that far away from her. He probably wouldn't have gotten talking to someone and forgotten all about her, either.

Had something happened to him?

Maybe she just needed to call Jordana. Better that she had the detective come over a false alarm than wait too long to get help for Neil.

First she would talk to the Christmas tree seller, though. Hopefully the young man had seen Neil and knew what had happened to him.

Finally the traffic cleared. As she headed across the four lanes toward the lot, lights flashed on and one of the vehicles at the curb pulled into the street.

Then an engine revved and those lights bore down on her as the vehicle headed directly toward her. With it gaining speed after shifting into Drive, she had only moments to react, to run…

And Elise was not a runner—especially not in those damn high-heel boots. But if she didn't move, she was going to get struck.

Hard.

# Chapter Fifteen

Worried about Elise, Neil had hurried out of the alley to make sure that she was safe and still locked inside his SUV. But before he could get to his vehicle, he had to pass the one he'd been watching when he'd stepped into the alley.

It was still there, and now there was someone behind the wheel, clad in a hoodie pulled tight around his face, just like the intruder had been. Of course, many people owned dark hoodies, so it might not have been the same person. But Neil damn well intended to find out.

The driver must have noticed him approaching, because the lights suddenly flashed on and the engine revved to life. In that flash of light, Neil noticed the woman starting across the street.

Elise.

The headlamps illuminated her face, which was white with fear. She saw the vehicle headed toward her. Neil started running, but he doubted he would reach her in time. The vehicle was too close.

And Elise, who hated to run, did not. As the vehicle bore down on her, she dove back toward the sidewalk she'd stepped off and onto the hood of one of the vehicles parked against the curb.

The brakes on the SUV squealed as the driver swerved back to the right and into the side of the vehicle whose hood Elise was sprawled on. Her body limp as a ragdoll, she tumbled off the hood and onto the sidewalk, and the SUV sped away.

Despite the horror gripping him, Neil moved. Running to where she lay on the sidewalk, he dropped to his knees next to her. Her long hair was tangled across her face, so he couldn't see it—couldn't see if her eyes were open—if she was unconscious or...

He couldn't even consider that—that she might be *gone*. Not Elise.

She had to be all right. He reached out, his hand shaking, to brush the tendrils of gold hair off her face.

A strong hand gripped his shoulder as Ty leaned down. "Is she all right? Elise?"

Her eyes opened then, and she stared up at them both. But her expression was blank, as if she was just too stunned—or too injured—to speak.

"Call 911!" Neil shouted at his brother, surprised that he could speak for the fear clogging his throat.

"Are you hurt?" Ty asked her again.

"Call!" Neil shouted. "And then go after that damn vehicle! Catch him!"

"You don't think it was an accident?" Ty asked. But at least he had his cell out.

"That was the vehicle that followed us, that was

the intruder from her condo earlier this evening." He was sure of it now, after the man had tried to kill her.

Had he been successful?

Her eyes were open, but she still hadn't spoken. And her stare was so vacant.

"Elise?" he called to her, his voice cracking with the emotion overwhelming him. He wasn't used to her not speaking to him. As angry as they'd gotten at each other during their marriage and partnership, they had never given each other the silent treatment.

Maybe they should have.

At least, he should have. Because when he got upset and hurt, he said things he didn't mean —like he wanted a divorce. He hadn't really wanted to end their marriage. He hadn't ever wanted that. But he hadn't wanted to wind up like his parents either, just sharing a house and nothing else.

"Elise?"

His hand shaking, he cupped her cheek. Her skin was so cold. He wanted to lift her up from the concrete sidewalk, but he didn't dare move her—in case something was broken, or she had internal injuries. Or a serious head wound.

He moved his hand from her cheek to the back of her head. Her hair was cold, too, and silky and dry. She wasn't bleeding. But that only meant that she didn't have an open wound.

He glanced up to look for his brother. But Ty must have left to pursue the vehicle like he'd told him to.

Had he called 911 like he'd asked?

He couldn't hear any sirens, nothing but the mur-

murs of the people who stood nearby, watching them
with curiosity and concern. "Did anyone call 911?"
he asked.

A few of them nodded.

And a breath eased out between his lips. So even if
Ty hadn't called, help was still on the way. But would
it get here soon enough?

Elise still hadn't spoken. Still hadn't moved.

Tears of fear and frustration stung his eyes. If only
he hadn't left her alone.

If only he'd made certain she was safe.

"I'm so sorry," he murmured.

He had failed her. He had failed *them*.

Again.

SHE WAS AFRAID to move. Afraid to speak.

Afraid that she'd done something to hurt the baby.

That was probably why Neil was so upset. She
could hear the fear and concern in his voice. But when
he leaned back and his handsome face was no longer just a shadow to her, she saw everything else: the
guilt, the pain.

His blue eyes were dark with it, his handsome face
contorted into a grimace of it. He was in far more
pain than she was.

Hell, she wasn't hurting at all. She was just
stunned. So stunned that it had happened, that she
had managed to jump through the air like she had.
But her instincts had warned her that if she continued to cross the road, the SUV would have pursued
her. By jumping back toward the sidewalk, instead,

toward the protection of the other parked cars, she'd had a chance.

For herself...

For her baby...

That was why she was lying so still on the concrete. She was waiting for the pain. For the loss.

Wasn't she supposed to be in pain? Bleeding?

But she felt nothing except concern for Neil. So finally she moved, reaching up to cover his hand that cupped her face. "I'm okay," she assured him.

He leaned closer. "Oh my God, you scared the hell out of me! I thought you..." His deep voice cracked with emotion. "You weren't talking or moving."

"I just had to catch my breath," she murmured, but she still wasn't able to draw in a deep one, not with how awkwardly she was lying on the sidewalk. "Although, I'm sure my not talking scared the crap out of you." She managed a chuckle.

And so did he. "It did. You've never not spoken to me."

And there had been times that she shouldn't have, because maybe he would have listened more to her silence than he had the things she'd told him, like she just needed time before starting a family.

"I'm sure you enjoyed my not talking," she said. "But I'm fine now." She reached out with her other hand and grasped his shoulder, so she could pull herself up.

But he pushed her back gently. "Don't move," he told her. "You might be hurt worse than you realize."

She'd lain there motionless partly to wait for the

shock to wear off, so that she could assess whether or not she had any injuries. She might be sore tomorrow, but at the moment she was just cold. And lying on the sidewalk wasn't warming her up any.

"I'm fine," she insisted. "Nothing hurts."

"You might be fine," he said. "But what about the baby?"

And suddenly something hurt—as pain stabbed her heart. Of course. The baby was all he cared about.

But because she was concerned, too, she lay back on the sidewalk and jerked her hands away from him. Her eyes stung with emotion, and she quickly closed them to hold in the threatening tears. She'd already cried too many of them over Neil Colton.

"Elise?" The concern was back in his voice, but now she knew it wasn't for her.

She just shook her head.

He might have said something else, but sirens from the arriving emergency vehicles drowned him out. Not that it mattered.

She doubted that he was ever going to say what she wanted to hear. That he loved her.

She knew that if she lost this baby, then she'd lost Neil, too. He wasn't going to want to marry her. Hell, he probably wasn't even going to want to see her again.

She kept her eyes closed so she couldn't see him. And so she couldn't shed the tears that threatened to overwhelm her.

HE GLANCED INTO the rearview mirror, watching for lights. Neil Colton hadn't been alone when he'd run out of wherever the hell he'd been hiding. While the lawyer had stayed behind, the other man had jumped into a truck.

He'd noticed the vehicle earlier on Colton's street. It had followed them, too. Was it following him now?

And who the hell was it? Had Colton hired security? He wouldn't put it past the spoiled rich kid.

Neil Colton had everything given to him from his daddy who ran the construction company. He probably didn't even have to work. But he had chosen to—and what a damn profession he'd chosen.

He worked at helping criminals get away with their crimes. And the mayor had worked right alongside him when she first came to Braxville. But she'd been too damn ambitious to stay in private practice.

Hell, she wasn't even a local and now she was running the place.

Until he'd run her down. She had to be dead. Or hurt very damn badly.

Either way, they were both suffering—she and Colton. But their suffering would never compare to his.

## Chapter Sixteen

What the hell had happened?

One minute Elise was touching him, almost comforting *him*, and the next she'd pulled away from him…physically and emotionally.

Was she worried about the baby? Was that the reason?

Neil had never been as relieved to hear sirens as he'd been when the ambulance had arrived. But when he started to climb inside the back with her, she'd held up a hand in protest.

"Stay here," she said. "File the report. You saw more than I did."

He should have. He should have made note of the license plate, but all he'd focused on was Elise, flying through the air and then tumbling off onto the concrete. His gut clenched with the horror he'd felt watching that, watching her while being so damn helpless to protect her.

Maybe that was why she'd withdrawn. Maybe she was angry with him. And he couldn't blame her. He was so damn mad at himself.

"I want to go with you," he said.

"Meet me at the hospital," she said. "You need your vehicle anyway."

It was clear that Elise didn't want him riding in the ambulance with her.

She even urged the EMT to close the doors and drive away. Was she worried about the baby? Was she scared that she was losing it?

Desperate to make sure that she and the baby were all right, he headed toward his SUV, but he hadn't made it more than a few steps before a hand on his arm jerked him to a stop. He whirled toward Detective Carpenter.

"We need your statement," Reese said.

Neil shook his head. "Not now."

Not when he could be losing Elise all over again. Because if she lost the baby, he had no chance of getting her back. She'd proved the past three years that she didn't need him. Hell, that she did even better on her own.

"Neil," his sister rushed up to join them now. "Is Elise okay?"

He shrugged. "I don't know. That's why I have to go."

Her brow furrowed. "Why didn't you go with her?"

Because she hadn't wanted him to...

"I—I..."

"Do you want me to drive you?" she asked.

"Then we can take your report on the ride," Carpenter added.

He shook his head. "No. I need my vehicle. And I

didn't see anything." He turned back to Jordana. "Ask your other brother. The one you asked to follow me and didn't think to inform me about."

She glanced around. "Where is Ty?"

"I think he took off after the hit-and-run driver," Neil said.

"You think that's all this was?" Reese asked. "An accident? Someone who had too much to drink that nearly struck her?"

"No. It was the same guy I saw in her condo."

"I thought you didn't get a good look at him," Jordana said, her eyes narrowed with suspicion.

"I didn't—not with the hoodie pulled around his face, but it was the same guy." He was certain of it. Now he just had to be certain that Elise was truly all right. "Talk to Ty. I have to go."

He only hoped that when he got to the hospital he wouldn't be too late.

That Elise hadn't lost their child…

LILLY PACED THE ambulance bay, but even as fast as she walked, she couldn't escape the fear that gripped her. Fear for Neil, for Elise and for the grandchild she was going to have—as long as Elise hadn't been hurt too badly.

*Poor Elise…*

"The EMT said she'd been struck by a car?" she asked for confirmation from the ER resident who leaned against the wall behind her, smoking.

Why would a health professional neglect his own

health? She resisted the urge to lecture, barely, reminding herself that she wasn't this young man's mother.

The guy nodded. "Yeah, hit-and-run."

Her stomach flipped, making her feel as nauseated as if she was pregnant, too. The explosion and now this.

What was going on? Why was someone after Neil and Elise? Or was the mayor the real target?

"Only a female was injured?" she asked.

The guy nodded.

"Was she alone?"

He shrugged. "I don't know," he replied, irritation sharpening his voice. "I wasn't there."

Now she really wanted to lecture him about common courtesy as well as his severely lacking bedside manner. And as part of the training and development team at the hospital, that was her place. But before she could open her mouth to make any comment, the ambulance sped into the bay.

The young resident finally moved, tossing down his cigarette before helping the EMTs open the back doors. Lilly, despite all her years of nursing experience, froze for a moment. It didn't matter that Elise was no longer her daughter-in-law; she loved that young woman like she was one of her daughters.

And the baby...

She sucked in a breath as the EMTs pulled out the gurney, and along with the resident, wheeled Elise toward the open doors to the emergency room. Lilly rushed along beside it. "Are you all right?"

Tears trailed down Elise's cheeks, and she shook her head.

Lilly glanced toward the paramedics. "How badly is she hurt?"

"She says she's fine," the female EMT remarked. "She's just worried about her pregnancy."

"She's pregnant?" the resident asked.

"Not more than four weeks," Lilly replied.

"First trimester," the resident murmured, then directed his attention toward the EMTs. "Any signs of miscarriage?"

"No bleeding and she has no pain," one of the EMTs replied. "She doesn't have any cuts or even apparent bruising. Looks like she was damn lucky."

"A car ran her down, though," Lilly reminded them.

"I jumped," Elise said. "I jumped out of the way— onto another car. It hit that one and knocked me off onto the sidewalk." Lying on the gurney, she wrapped her arms around her stomach, as if trying to hold the baby inside her.

And Lilly's heart broke at the fear and loss on the young woman's face. She reached out and squeezed one of Elise's arms. "You're going to be fine," she said. "And that's all that matters."

Elise shook her head. "Your son doesn't think so. To him, the baby is all that matters."

Lilly gasped. Neil could be such an idiot. What had he said? What had he done?

"I don't want him in the exam room," Elise said. "Don't let him in." She reached out and grasped Lilly's arm now, her grip reassuringly strong but that might have been the strength of the desperation on her face. She reminded Lilly, "You told me to do what I want. I don't want him in there."

"Okay..." Lilly said and swallowed hard. "Will it be all right if I check on you?"

Elise grasped her arm more tightly. "I want you with me." More tears rolled down her face. "If it's okay with you."

Lilly knew how hard it was for Elise to ask for help. She was as strong and fiercely independent as every one of Lilly's biological children. "I want to be there."

The resident glanced at her as she ran alongside the gurney. Once they'd rolled Elise into an open bay of the ER, he asked, "You got this? You'll get her ready for exam?"

She nodded. "Of course." She waited until he and the paramedics stepped out before she pulled the curtain closed. Then she helped Elise out of her dress and into a gown.

The EMTs had not done a very thorough evaluation of Elise. Bruises were already beginning to darken the skin on the young woman's shoulder, hip and back.

Her heart aching over the injuries, she murmured, "You're going to be sore tomorrow."

It was clear that Elise was hurting already, though. Emotionally.

Without waiting for the resident's orders, Lilly dragged over the ultrasound machine. She wanted to check on her grandchild nearly as much as Elise wanted her to, but before she could even turn on the machine, the resident stepped back into the area.

"I thought you said she was only a month along," he said. "You're not going to be able to tell if she miscarried with that."

"Dr. Thiel did a transvaginal ultrasound when Ms. Willis was in the ER last night."

"Last night?" the resident asked. "What's going on?" He examined Elise now, finding the bruises the paramedic had missed. "Is a partner abusing you?"

At the thought of her son harming the woman he obviously still loved, Lilly gasped.

But Elise's lips curved into a slight smile of amusement. "No. I'm in danger, though."

"There are women's shelters—"

"Not that way," Elise assured him. "Somebody is trying to kill me."

"Yes, and you need to report him—"

"I would," Elise interjected. "If I had a clue who it was. Can you please just check, like the other doctor did, to see if that weird little bubble shows up yet?"

The doctor's brow creased with confusion. Either he was struggling to believe she didn't know who hurt her, or he didn't follow what she was talking about.

"The gestational sac," Lilly said. "That's what she wants to see." She wasn't the only one.

But before the doctor had a chance to comply with Elise's request, another nurse pulled the curtain aside to say, "Lilly, your son's here and he's trying to come back—"

"No!" Elise said.

"Is he the one?" the doctor asked. "The one who's hurting you?"

Elise shook her head. "Not like that…"

Not like that. But he was hurting her. And Lilly hated that—hated that Neil couldn't make things right between them again. But she knew why.

He was too damn much like his father.

"I'll handle it," Lilly assured her former daughter-in-law, and she headed out to the waiting room where Neil was yelling at a nervous security guard. Her son appeared to be fine except for the anger flushing his face and making his eyes glow brightly.

"I want to see my wife!" he shouted. "The ambulance just brought her in. I need to be with her!"

"You should have thought about that before you divorced her," Lilly admonished him.

Neil's mouth fell open as if Lilly had slapped him. Maybe she should have—not now but when he'd made such a stupid decision. But she'd never been one of those mothers who meddled in her children's lives. With the mistakes she'd made, she'd never felt qualified to give out advice.

"Mom?" Neil finally remarked questioningly, as if he wasn't sure he recognized her.

She drew in a deep breath to calm herself; she was nearly as angry as he was, as he'd been. Now he just stood there, waiting, as if expecting the worst.

"Is she right?" Lilly asked. "Is the baby all you care about?"

The color faded from his face now, leaving it starkly white. "Is that what she thinks?"

"What else would she think after what you did." She shook her head. "You screwed up once with her. She must have given you a second chance or you wouldn't have conceived that baby in the first place, but you're obviously messing that up, too." She'd never been as disappointed in one of her children as she was now.

"I didn't run her down," Neil said, as if she was blaming him for that.

Then she realized he was blaming himself. Her anger drained away, and she approached him, hugging him tightly. "I know. You would never hurt her physically." No matter what the ER resident might suspect now. "But emotionally, you have to be more careful. Elise isn't as tough as she wants everyone to think she is."

Lilly knew because she was the same way herself. She had never been as strong as she'd wanted to be. She'd once been very, very weak.

Tears stung her eyes, but she blinked them back. She couldn't fix what she'd done. But there was still time for Neil—if he was careful.

"Be patient for once," she told him. "Don't fight to get your way like you've always done." As a triplet, he'd probably felt like he'd had to, but as a husband...

But he wasn't a husband anymore.

"She doesn't want me back there, does she?" Neil asked, his shoulders slumping.

Her mother's heart ached for him, but she was

also a nurse with a patient that was very special to her. "No."

"Can you tell me if she mis—"

"No," she said. "Wait for Elise." She hugged him again and then stepped back and repeated the advice she should have given him a couple of years ago, before the divorce. "Wait for Elise."

It was what he should have done last time but hadn't. Would he take her advice? Or would he once again push too hard and lose the woman he loved?

Of course—with someone trying to kill her—he might lose Elise another way—a way in which he would never be able to get her back.

SHE WAS HEARTBROKEN. But she wasn't heartless.

Not long after Lilly left to get rid of her son, Elise called another nurse over to allow him to see her and their child. She stared so intently at the ultrasound screen, at that little bubble that was the developing baby, that she didn't notice the curtain had been opened...until she heard Neil's gasp.

She turned toward him, and the look on his face... The longing, the love, as he stared at that screen. She probably stared at him the same way—with the same love and longing. If only he had ever looked at her like that. While love for him overwhelmed her, she also felt a pang of jealousy, of regret.

A few years ago she hadn't understood why he'd wanted so badly to start their family, especially as they'd still been getting their practice going at the time. But now she knew how much it meant to him to be a father. How much the baby meant to him.

"That thing," she said, pointing toward the bubble. The doctor had removed the ultrasound wand but had left the image up on the screen—at her request. "That's what they call the gestational sac. It's still there, so the baby is still there, too."

He nodded and turned his attention to her then. "What about you? Are you all right?"

"Yes," she said. But it was a lie.

"Elise, I don't know why you're upset with me."

That was the problem; he had no idea.

"I'm sorry that I wasn't there when that SUV came after you," he said. "I was talking to Ty, and I—I shouldn't have let him distract me. I should have been protecting you. I promise that I'll do that now…if you'll come home with me. I'll take care of you now."

"No." She shook her head. "I can't stay with you." Because it would only make it harder for her to leave again once their would-be killer was caught.

# *Chapter Seventeen*

Neil couldn't stop staring at Elise as she studied the ultrasound image. He had no idea what she was looking at. There were only fuzzy bubbles on the screen. But he could easily determine that the look on Elise's face was a combination of concern and love.

She loved their baby already. Would she ever love him again? Or had he completely blown it with her?

The young doctor who'd joined them seconds ago looked at Neil with suspicion. "A car really almost ran her over?" he asked.

Neil nodded. "But she jumped out of the way before it hit her."

The doctor's eyes narrowed, but he remarked, "That must have been frightening. Did they catch the guy?"

"I hope so," he said.

Had Ty caught him? He hoped like hell that he had, that this was all over, but then he knew that Elise would insist on returning to her condo despite its current messy state. And a pang of regret struck him. He silently cursed his own selfishness.

"If you'll be safe, you can go home," the doctor told her.

"I'll make sure she is," Neil vowed.

The doctor spared him a skeptical glance before turning back to Elise. "You're going to be sore tomorrow. I would prescribe painkillers if you weren't pregnant."

"I'll be fine," Elise assured him, with her hand sliding protectively over her stomach.

"You can ice the bruises," he advised, "and take low-dose aspirin as needed."

"Thank you, Doctor," she said.

The resident pulled the curtain aside and slipped out of the space, leaving them alone together.

Elise kept staring at that screen. She wouldn't look at him, hadn't looked at him since he had first joined her in the ER.

"Why are you so angry with me?" he asked.

She shook her head. "I'm not. I'm just..." She sighed. "I'm tired, Neil."

"Then let me take you home," he urged.

She shook her head again.

"You can't go back to your condo," he said. "It isn't safe."

"Maybe they caught him," she said hopefully. "My phone's been ringing, but I haven't picked it up."

It had probably been Detective Carpenter either calling to question her or update her. She was the mayor, so the police department was more likely to keep her apprised of the investigation than they were him.

He sighed. "I hope he was caught." He didn't want them or anyone else in danger because of this maniac—even if it meant she would be able to return to her condo. "But even if they have, your place is a mess. You need rest. Stay with me tonight."

She uttered a heavy sigh and nodded. "Just for tonight."

The tension inside him didn't ease any. He wanted her home with him, but not just for one night.

"Elise! Elise!"

Neil shouted her name, panic in his voice. The panic drew her to the top of the steps. "I'm up here," she called down to him.

He appeared at the foot of the staircase, her bags clutched in his hands. "Why?"

"I'm sleeping up here," she informed him.

"But the doctor said you would be sore," he reminded her. "You should be on the main floor—in our bedroom."

"Yours," she reminded him. "It's your bedroom." And she'd already spent too much time in it recently.

"Elise—"

"The doctor said I need rest," she interrupted. "So stop arguing with me and let me go to sleep."

He snapped his mouth shut and headed up the stairs with her bags. And she nearly laughed. It had to be killing him not to argue with her. But before he'd started calling for her, she'd heard him arguing with someone else. So maybe he'd gotten his fix for the night.

"Who were you talking to a little bit ago?" she asked. And had he been on the phone or had someone been at the door? She hadn't heard the doorbell, but the person could have intercepted him when he'd gone outside to retrieve the suitcases from her vehicle.

"It sounded like a female," she added, and heat flushed her face as she realized she sounded like a jealous wife. Since she was no longer his wife, she had no right to that jealousy—not even because she was carrying his child.

That night…

And last night…

Those had been aberrations. Errors in judgment. Because—despite his proposals—he had to know that they wouldn't be able to sustain a relationship, let alone a marriage. They'd already failed once. Why try again?

Elise wanted more for her child than she had. Two parents would be nice. But that didn't mean she had to be married to the baby's father—just that he had to be involved.

Would he?

Or would he be the kind of father he'd had? Always working and never around? That was one of the reasons she'd wanted to wait before starting their family. She hadn't wanted to be solely responsible for raising the baby like her mother had been, like Lilly had essentially been, despite having Fitz as a husband.

Neil remained silent as he carried her bags into the guest room, and she realized he was reluctant to tell her who he'd been talking to. Was he seeing someone?

Last month—when they'd succumbed to passion—
he'd told her no. But that had been four weeks ago. A
lot could have happened since then.

He lifted her suitcases onto the dresser then turned
back toward her. "It was Jordana."

"You were arguing with her," she said. "So I
guess they didn't find the person who tried to run
me down."

He shook his head. "And she wanted to interview
you. That's why she showed up here, but I told her it
would have to wait until you had some sleep."

"It would be a waste of her time anyway," Elise
said. "I didn't see him. I didn't even see the vehicle.
The first thing I saw were the lights when they came
on bright, blinding me." She shuddered as she remembered the fear, being frozen for a moment before
finally moving. She'd thought she was going to die.

Strong arms closed around her as Neil pulled her
into an embrace. Maybe he'd meant it to be comforting, but when their bodies touched, hers reacted to
the closeness of his. Her skin tingled, and her pulse
quickened.

She wanted to link her arms around his neck and
pull his head down for her kiss. She wanted to be
with him—completely—with him inside her, filling
her. But even then, she wouldn't be truly complete…
because there would always be the ache yawning inside her as her heart yearned for his love—his unconditional love.

She stepped back out of his loose embrace. "I'm
really tired," she murmured.

She really was and not just because of the long, exhausting day she'd had. She was tired of wanting something she would never have.

And even if he claimed to love her, she would never trust it. Not after their divorce.

They needed to find out whoever was after them, so that the threat against them was over and that they could figure out how to manage the future, raising a child together without being together.

But first they had to make sure they had a future, that the man trying to kill them was identified and brought to justice.

JORDANA SHOOK HER HEAD, disgusted with her brother's stubbornness. "You'd think he would want to do everything possible to try to find out who the hell is after him and Elise," she muttered at Neil's closed front door.

But she knew better than to continue arguing with the consummate arguer. So she walked away from the house to where her partner leaned against the passenger's side of their unmarked car.

"He won't let us interview her?" Reese asked, then covered his mouth as a yawn escaped with his question.

"I know it's late," Jordana said. Or early, actually as the sky was already beginning to lighten with dawn's approach. "But he's being overprotective."

"Says the woman who enlisted the security expert to follow them around," Reese teased.

She snorted derisively. "A lot of good that did me."

"Hey!" Ty exclaimed in protest of her complaint. He leaned against the side of his truck, which was parked in front of the Braxville PD vehicle. "Once I got to town, which unfortunately was after he tried confronting the intruder at Elise's place, I was with Neil, protecting him—just like you asked me to."

"I know. I know." Jordana sighed. "I'm just worried about him."

"I'm more worried about Elise," Ty said.

She tensed. "Why? You think she's the real target?"

"I think if something happens to her, it'll kill Neil," Ty said. "So keeping her safe should probably be our first priority."

"Too damn bad you didn't catch the guy who tried running her down."

"I got you a plate number," Ty said defensively.

Too defensively.

Jordana knew that he was pissed at himself for not catching the guy.

"The license plate number of a vehicle reported stolen earlier today," Reese said. "It doesn't lead us anywhere."

"We'll figure out who's trying to kill them," Jordana said.

They had to…

"You're sure it's not Dex?" Ty asked.

After the guy had shot him, it was no wonder Ty would harbor a grudge against him. Jordana wasn't happy with their father's business partner, either.

She shook her head, though. "Neil and Elise think

it's probably something to do with the time they were in practice together."

"They actually agreed on something?" Ty asked.

Jordana chuckled. "Yeah."

"You want me to protect both of them from this would-be killer?" Ty asked. "But the real question is who's going to protect them from each other?"

## Chapter Eighteen

Despite not having a case and refusing to take on any new clients, Neil had spent the entire day in the office, going through old files. Mostly he'd packed up the ones on which he'd worked with Elise. And he'd remembered how it had been to work with her, to live with her, to make love with her.

That was all he'd spent the previous night imagining…while he'd slept alone in their bed and she'd spent the night in the guest room upstairs. Hopefully she'd gotten some rest—because he sure as hell hadn't.

Which, unfortunately, hadn't done anything for his temper. So when he arrived at City Hall to pick up Elise at the end of what had seemed like an interminably long day, he was in no mood to confront slimy Jeremy again. But as Neil was heading toward Elise's office, Jeremy was leaving it. The guy, with his slicked-back blond hair and phony tan, pulled her door shut and stood in front of it, as if barring Neil entrance to it. To her…

Neil furrowed his brow and stared at the other

man. "What are you doing, Jerry?" he asked, impatient to get the man out of his way and to get Elise home—where she would be safe.

Elise thought she was safe here because of the security at City Hall, and Neil's detective sister and security brother had concurred. But he wasn't as convinced, mostly because of her deputy mayor.

"What are *you* doing?" Jeremy asked. "You divorced her. Why don't you leave her the hell alone?"

"Why don't you mind your own damn business?" Neil asked.

"Elise is my business," Jeremy insisted.

Neil snorted. "I'm sure you'd like to think that, but you're delusional if you think you're anything more to her than her deputy mayor."

"I'm her friend," Jeremy said. "A friend who's worried that you're putting her in danger."

"I'm trying to keep her safe," Neil said in his defense, though doubt niggled at him. Was he the reason she was in danger?

Jeremy snorted now. "If you really wanted to keep her safe, you would stay the hell away from her. You and your family has been involved in every bad thing to happen to Braxville over the past several months." He snorted again. "Hell, probably years. Who knows what the health department's going to find out about your father's business?"

Nerves tightened Neil's stomach. What was going to be discovered in the investigation? He'd been wondering that himself. But he was almost afraid of what the truth might be.

Of how involved his father was in everything.

"Markus Dexter had been his business partner for years," Jeremy continued. "How the hell could he not know the man's a killer?"

"Alleged killer," Neil said, the lawyer in him automatically making the correction.

"Yeah, because innocent men flee to avoid prosecution," Jeremy scoffed.

Neil sighed. "I'm not saying he's innocent. I just don't think he's the one going after Elise."

"So you're saying the attempts on her life have nothing to do with you?" Jeremy asked, his voice thick with disgust.

Neil wished he could say that, but he shook his head. "I don't know, Jeremy," he admitted. "Maybe these attempts on our lives have been made by someone who's frustrated that no matter how much he wants Elise, he'll never be able to have her—that she will always belong with me instead. You know how some stalkers get. If they can't have the object of their affection, no one else can."

Jeremy's face flushed, and his eyes bulged with fury. "I don't know what the hell you're insinuating."

"You know exactly what I'm insinuating," Neil said. That was why Jeremy was so damn mad—that Neil knew exactly how the man felt about his boss and that it was futile for him to have those feelings.

"You're a son of a bitch!" Jeremy hurled the insult at him and then stepped closer, as if he was about to hurl his fists, as well.

Ty might have thought he didn't need to trail Neil

inside City Hall—that the security would eliminate any threat to his and Elise's safety. But Neil wasn't so damn sure...

Jeremy was bigger than he was, like the intruder at Elise's condo. And like the intruder, he was also fast. He swung his fist before Neil even had a chance to duck. The blow knocked him back and released his fury. He came back swinging.

WEARY FROM ANOTHER sleepless night, Elise hadn't jumped up from her desk when she first heard the heated confrontation between the two men outside her office door. She had little energy to deal with a show of male testosterone.

But when the insults began, she rose from her chair and headed around her desk. She'd just pulled open the door when the first fist landed—squarely on Neil's square jaw. Neil, being Neil, couldn't walk away from a fight. So he swung back, knocking Jeremy toward her. She stepped back, out of the way, as he struck the door jamb near her.

"Oh my God, Elise!" Neil exclaimed. "Did he hit you?"

"I didn't hit her," Jeremy said. "You almost did."

"Did I?" Neil asked with concern.

"No, I'm fine," she said, but it had been too close for her comfort. Fury erupted. "But what the hell is wrong with the two of you?"

She glanced from one to the other. Neil's face had gone pale but for a slight red mark on one cheek, while Jeremy's eye was already swelling, and for once his slickly gelled blond hair was mussed.

"I'm sorry, Elise." Jeremy was the first to apologize. "But this guy wasn't ever good for you, and now he and his troublesome family are going to get you killed. I can't just stand by and say nothing when you're in danger."

Neil cursed, and the color rushed back into his face. But he didn't argue now.

"I appreciate your concern, Jeremy," she said with sincerity. She was actually impressed that he'd taken on Neil like he had. She hadn't believed he had the guts. "But I don't believe Neil or his family is at fault for the recent attempts on my life."

At least not solely. She had probably had some part in it, too, from back when they'd shared their practice. She wasn't about to share that with Jeremy, though. While she was impressed with his show of bravery, she still didn't entirely trust him. He enjoyed talking to the press a little too much, and she didn't want to give him fodder for the media. It was bad enough she'd had to dodge them on her way into the office again that morning.

Apparently they had police radio scanners and had heard about her being nearly run down the night before. After the explosion the night before that, most had suspected—rightfully—that the hit-and-run had been no accident, either.

If Jeremy had been responsible for those nonaccidents, though, why would he blame and attack Neil?

Just to deflect suspicion? While she knew he was ambitious, she doubted he was that diabolical.

But then he was a politician.

So was she, though. But she was much too straightforward to be diabolical, no matter what her former father-in-law believed of her.

"How can you not think he or his family have anything to do with the attempts on your life?" Jeremy asked, clearly dumbfounded and maybe even a little disappointed with her.

"I know them better than you do," she pointed out.

"I know that they're going to hurt you," Jeremy said. "If not physically, then politically. Nobody's going to vote for anybody that has anything to do with a Colton. You even risk a recall if you continue to associate with them."

A recall…

Had he started the process? Getting her recalled so that he could take her job?

Bristling with defensiveness, Neil interjected, "You don't know—"

"Stop!" She tightened her grip on his arm, tempted to shake some sense—or at least some patience—into him. But that was something she'd never been able to get from him: patience.

"How can you not think he's capable of violence?" Jeremy asked.

She smiled at the irony, while Neil bristled even more.

"You threw the first punch!"

"I was protecting her," Jeremy said in his defense.

Elise's patience ran out now. "Enough! Jeremy, I appreciate your concern, but you need to let me handle my own life." She pointed toward the door.

"I just want to make sure you have a life," Jeremy said, but he headed to the door, as if realizing she wasn't going to listen to him in regard to Neil.

She hoped he didn't take it personally. She rarely listened to herself when it came to Neil…or she wouldn't be pregnant right now. She wouldn't be staying with him in the house they'd designed together. But because she was pregnant—and in danger—she would stay with him until they discovered who was after them.

"I thought he'd never leave," Neil murmured.

She turned toward him and shook her head in disgust. "What the hell is wrong with you?"

"What do you mean?" Neil asked. "He started it."

"Because he was protecting me," she said. "What's your excuse?"

"I'm protecting you, too," Neil insisted.

She snorted. "You weren't protecting me, then. You two were acting like a couple little boys posturing on the playground. And I felt like your mom having to break you apart."

His mouth curved into a slight, sexy grin. "That's good practice for you, then," he said. "In case we have a son."

Her heart warmed. A son…

She wouldn't care if they had a boy or a girl, though. She just wanted the baby to be healthy. "Girls can fight, too," she reminded him.

He chuckled. "You don't have to tell me," he said. "I have sisters." His grin slipped away. "I don't want this child to be an only child. I'd like for him to have sisters and brothers, Elise. Please won't you just accept—"

She reached out and pressed her fingers over his lips. "No. You promised you'd stop pressuring me."

"Elise…" He sighed, and his breath brushed across her fingertips, making her skin tingle.

She wanted to say yes, but she could only do that if she truly believed that Neil loved her—just her. And she would never believe that now.

"Is it because you're worried about what Jeremy brought up?" he asked, his lips moving against her skin.

She pulled her hand away from his mouth, from his damn handsome face. "What?"

"A recall. The Coltons hurting your career."

She snorted again. "No. I'm not worried about that. And I'm not worried about this baby being an only child. I'm an only child," she reminded him. "And I think I turned out fine. I'm not brawling in City Hall like you are. So maybe having siblings to fight with isn't all you think it is."

"That's not the reason I was fighting with Jeremy. I have had my suspicions about your deputy mayor for a while now," he replied.

She had, too, but she wasn't about to admit that to Neil. "I thought we both agreed that whoever is after us must have something to do with a case we worked on together."

He shrugged. "That makes the most sense."

"So we're going to the office to look through those now?" she asked.

He shook his head. "I packed them up and have them with me. We can go through them at home."

Home…

She swallowed a groan. She was going to start thinking of it that way again, too, if she kept going back there with him. They had to find and stop the person trying to kill them, so that she could go back to her condo. So that she could get the distance from Neil that she so desperately needed, or she might just accept his proposal.

HE HAD TO be careful now—because he wasn't the only one watching them. There was the man in the truck, the man who had come close to catching him the night before. He'd ditched that stolen SUV, though, and had rented a vehicle.

He wasn't going to try to run them down again… or even off the road. They'd driven separately to their offices this morning, and while Colton had joined her at City Hall and walked her to the parking garage, they'd driven separately back to his house. It was there that they were together—in one place—and it was there that he would take them out.

Together…

# Chapter Nineteen

A dark shadow fell across Neil as he stepped into the foyer of his house. Only faint light shone from the glass of the front door, filtering through the branches of the tree leaning against it.

"No deliveries," Ty admonished him. "That just gives this damn stalker of yours an opportunity to make another attempt on your lives."

"It's just a Christmas tree," Neil said as he pulled open the front door. The tree fell against him, nearly knocking him down, the way Jeremy nearly had Elise when Neil had struck the man earlier. Guilt and regret weighed on him as heavily as the tree did.

He shouldn't have lost his temper like that. Shouldn't have risked Elise getting hurt.

Ty inspected the tree, then helped Neil carry it into the house. Elise, after changing into an oversize sweater and leggings, stood on the staircase. Once the tree cleared the foyer, she rushed to close the front door.

That was the only reason she was here, he reminded himself, for the security. She wasn't here because she was coming home to stay. No matter how many times he asked her, she kept turning him down.

Was it possible that whatever she'd felt for him once was gone? But then why make love with him last month?

Elise was more in control than he was. She didn't indulge in casual encounters. She was too busy and too public a figure to take the risk. He needed to ask her more about that night. But not now...

Not with Ty in the house, helping him stand up the tree in the great room. "So you think it's safe?" Neil teased his brother.

Ty sighed. "Nothing about this assignment is safe."

"For you?" Neil asked. His brother had always been tough and fearless.

"For you," Ty said, and he nodded his head in the direction of Elise who was in the kitchen.

Elise was the greatest danger to Neil—to his heart, which she'd already broken once. He was willing to trust her with it again, though, if she would give him the chance.

"I'm safe, right?" Neil asked. "With your protection?"

"I can't watch you twenty-four seven," Ty said.

And he had his own life, his own love. Neil understood that. And he could see, much to his disgust, that his brother was so in love that it had made him goofy.

"I think Jordana overreacted bringing you into it," he said.

"I'm not sure she's reacting enough," Ty said.

"You and the mayor, especially, need police protection around the clock until this killer is caught."

When Elise had first become mayor, she had turned down having a personal protection detail. Maybe she hadn't wanted the city to pay for it; maybe she hadn't wanted anyone to know everywhere she went and whom she saw, like him.

Ty pushed a hand through his hair. "But I need to be with Ashley." He grinned at just the thought of his new girlfriend. "So I'm going to call Jordana to bring in police protection."

Neil felt a pang of jealousy. Love was so simple for Ty—disgustingly simple. "You can go right now," Neil urged him. "We're inside. We're safe."

Ty narrowed his eyes and studied his face. "You're going to stay inside? You won't let anyone else in?"

"I'm not an idiot," Neil said. And he hated how often he had to remind his older siblings of that fact.

Ty glanced at Elise again.

Was that why his family doubted his judgment? Because he'd divorced her? He couldn't blame them over that; it was the stupidest mistake he'd ever made.

But he'd really believed that they would never agree on one of the things that mattered most to him: family. And he hadn't wanted to wind up like his parents—with that chilly indifference between them.

He should have known then that he would never be able to be indifferent to Elise. He would always want her—even when she infuriated him. Maybe most when she infuriated him. He sighed.

And Ty chuckled. "Yeah, right, you know…"

Unfortunately he did. "I'll be careful," he promised his brother. "Go home to Ashley."

Ty's grin widened. "I'll make sure the police protection is on its way then head out."

"Thanks for coming to help," Neil said. Then he hugged his brother, maybe a little too tightly given he was still healing from his gunshot wound.

Ty let out a grunt as he patted his back. "Stay safe." He waved at Elise. "You, too."

She smiled at her ex-brother-in-law. "Thank you, Ty," she said. "Are you sure you won't stay for dinner?"

Ty shook his head. "Hopefully I can get home in time to eat with Ashley," he said, hurrying toward the front door.

As he opened and closed it behind himself, a chill ran down Neil's spine. Maybe it was just that a cold wind had blown in from outside. Or maybe it was unease with being alone.

But Jordana would send over protection, of course. They would be safe.

From whoever was trying to kill them.

Neil wasn't safe from Elise, though, not with him wanting her as much as he did. "You didn't have to cook," he told her as he joined her in the kitchen, where she was chopping up vegetables on a cutting board next to the stainless steel stove. She'd picked out the white cabinets, marble countertops and the fancy appliances, which he'd teased her about since she hadn't been very domestic back when they'd married.

After tossing the vegetables into a pan in which

slices of chicken sizzled, she turned toward him and smiled. And as always, warmth flooded his heart.

"Don't worry," she said. "My cooking's gotten better since our divorce. I'm not going to poison you." She turned back to the stove and murmured, "At least not accidentally."

He chuckled. "I hope you're joking."

"I am," she said, her smile gone as she turned serious. "We're in enough danger. The stir-fry will be done in a little while. After we eat, we can start going through our old records."

Neil sighed. "I went through some of them today." He wanted a break now, a break from thinking about the past, so that he could focus on the future—a future he wanted to share with her and their baby. "How about we decorate the tree first? It looks so bare with nothing on it."

"It will survive," she said.

She obviously wasn't as convinced that they would.

"You teased me about not having any decorations up yet," he reminded her. "Pot…"

She smiled again, making that warmth flood his heart once again. "Calling me a hypocrite?"

"We'll need to get used to decorating for the holidays—with the baby coming," Neil persisted.

She sighed. "We'll be decorating separately, Neil. Not together."

"Why won't you even consider marrying me again?" he asked, hurt that she wasn't at all tempted to accept his proposal. "Don't you have any feelings at all for me anymore?"

SHE HAD TOO many feelings for him. That was why she couldn't trust him with her heart again—not after he'd already broken it once.

"I once asked you that question," she reminded him as she blinked away the tears stinging her eyes.

She didn't dare look at his face, so she focused on the frying pan. The food was done, but she was reluctant to remove it from the burner. A low growl of hunger emanated from her stomach, though. And she knew she had to eat—for the baby.

That was the only reason she was here in this house, with its high-tech security system. For her child.

For the child who was all Neil had ever wanted. He hadn't wanted her. She nearly reminded him of that, but she was too proud to let herself sound that pathetic. At least to him...

She'd already admitted as much to his mother. But that had been in a weak moment. And she trusted Lilly Colton. In her, she'd found a kindred spirit more so than she had in her mother. But in raising this child alone, she was going to be more like her mother now—in the one way she'd vowed to never become her. But her mother had had no choice about being a single parent. Elise was choosing this over being with someone who didn't love her.

"And I told you that I would always love you," Neil insisted.

A cry burned the back of her throat, but she forced it out as a laugh. "You always divorce the people you love?"

"You know why I asked for the divorce."

"Asked?" She laughed again. If he'd asked, she would have told him no, just like she'd told him no to starting a family at that time.

But he'd replied that no time would ever be good for her. And maybe he'd been right. Because now, with someone trying to kill them, was not a good time.

"You know I didn't want to become my parents," he said, his brow furrowing.

"We'd be even more like them if we got married now," she said. "We'd be sticking together just for the sake of the kid—which is probably the same thing they've done, sticking together for the sake of all of you."

Neil sighed and pushed one of his hands through his thick, short hair. "Well, we're all grown up now, and they're still together."

She shrugged. "I can't explain your parents' marriage." Any more than she could explain hers. "I just know that I don't want it. Not for me. Not for you and especially not for this baby."

Neil's broad shoulders slumped as if he'd finally accepted defeat. And maybe he had because he nodded. Then he helped her set the table—well, the granite island—with plates and silverware. They ate together as they had so many times before, except that he hadn't cooked it and she hadn't picked up takeout.

"This is good," he said as he cleaned off his plate and reached for seconds.

She laughed. "You don't have to sound so damn

surprised. See, our kid won't starve." She patted her stomach. Maybe she was finally getting over the nausea because she didn't feel sick now. At least not physically.

Emotionally, she wasn't sure she would ever get over Neil. And now they would share a child...

Better that they share a child than an enemy, though. "You started on the files," she prodded him when he'd gone curiously silent. "Anybody stick out to you?"

He sighed. "Everybody who didn't get away with their crimes."

She chuckled. "So a lot of somebodies."

"You know a lot of clients weren't happy if the deal we got them involved serving any jail time," he said. "So I forwarded those names to Jordana to check out which ones might have been paroled recently."

"Hopefully, there won't be many of them," she said. And then this would be over soon. "Unfortunately, they aren't the only unhappy ones in our old cases."

His brow furrowed as he stared at her. "I know you weren't crazy about practicing criminal law."

She smiled at how foolish she'd once been. "When I chose criminal law, I believed I'd have all these innocent clients to represent."

Neil grimaced. "Didn't turn out that way."

"Nothing turned out like I thought it would back in law school," she ruefully admitted. Most especially them...

"I'm sorry," Neil murmured. "I know I disappointed you."

"We disappointed each other," she said. "But I actually wasn't talking about my being unhappy. I was talking about the victims' families."

Neil groaned. "A lot of them were unhappy. Some of the suspects' families, too. I might be giving Jordana a very long list."

"Let's clear away these dishes," she said, "and start going through those files."

Neil glanced wistfully at that bare tree. "You sure you don't want to take a moment and do some decorating?"

She wanted to—badly. She wanted to turn on the Christmas music and dance around that tree like they had their first Christmas together. She wanted Neil—the way she'd had him that night, wearing nothing but the glow of those twinkling lights, as they'd made love over and over again.

If only they'd been able to restrict their passion to lovemaking and not to arguing.

But she knew they were too much alike to ever cohabitate amicably, and she didn't want to raise a child in an atmosphere of constant arguments. That would be even worse than the silent indifference with which Neil's parents treated each other.

"We really need to get a complete list of potential suspects to Jordana," Elise said.

Neil nodded. "I know..."

Perhaps they had finally found the one thing they

could easily agree on: they needed to find out who the hell was trying to kill them.

TY ACHED TO see Ashley again, but he was still reluctant to leave, even after the police car showed up to take over protection duty. Nevertheless, that car with its lights and *Braxville PD* emblazoned on it was probably more protection than he was. Sitting there on the street, in front of his brother's house, it was a visible deterrent to whoever was after them.

Accepting that they would be safe, Ty drove away, but doubts niggled at him yet. Was he doing the right thing? Would his brother and Elise be safe?

# Chapter Twenty

She was so damn sexy. Black-framed reading glasses had slid down her nose like that oversize sweater had slipped off one shoulder. While she'd been studying their old case files, he'd been studying her.

She wasn't very far along in her pregnancy, but she had that famous glow that pregnant women were rumored to get. She seemed to radiate energy and life and beauty. And just watching her stole his breath away.

She glanced up and caught him staring. She arched one dark blond brow above the black frames in a quizzical expression. "What?"

He had to clear his throat, clear the desire from it, before replying with a question of his own, "Do you ever miss it?"

Furrows formed in her forehead, beneath a golden tress of hair. "Miss what?"

Them. He missed her so damn much, missed working with her, being with her...

"Our practice," he said.

"I told you that criminal law was not what I

thought it was going to be," she reminded him. Then she sighed. "And it was never our practice. It was always yours." She glanced around the dark-paneled office. "Everything always felt like it was more yours than mine. This town. This house. Your family…" She shrugged. "I never really belonged."

Her admission stunned him. "You regret moving here with me after we graduated law school?"

She shook her head. "I didn't want to go back to Detroit. And I didn't want to stay in Boston." She shrugged. "But I just now feel like I've made my own life here."

Was that why she kept refusing his proposals?

"I would say that the town is more yours than mine now, Madam Mayor," he said. "Especially with how my family is being perceived."

She reached out then and ran her fingertips along his cheek. "Don't let Jeremy get to you."

He'd forgotten about his skirmish with her deputy mayor until she touched the slightly swollen area on his cheek. But it didn't hurt. It tingled instead from her touch. "Jeremy isn't the only one who's wondering what my father knew about his partner and why so many of the construction company employees have gotten sick."

Elise's fingertips slid along his cheek to the short beard on his jaw. He kept it for her, because she'd always loved running her fingers over it. "I'm sorry," she murmured.

"Me, too," he said. "I just hope my dad…" He

shook his head, unable to even put into words his fears for his father.

"I know," she said.

And she did.

Despite her own tense relationship with his father, she'd always been supportive of his.

Her fingers slipped away from his face, and she leaned back in the chair behind his desk, putting some distance between them. He sat in a chair on the side of it, close but not close enough.

He sighed, trying to shake off the tension inside him. But that tension wasn't just from his fears about his family or his and Elise's safety.

He was tense with desire for her. He wanted her so badly that his body ached. Though tempted, he didn't reach for her but instead for the legal pad on the desktop. They'd taken turns scribbling down names from the files—clients who'd wanted lighter sentences in the deals they'd negotiated. Victims' families who'd expressed outrage because they'd considered those sentences much too light.

"This is a long list," he said. "I should get it to Jordana so she and Reese can start working on it— see who's been released, where some of these people might have been last night and the night of the explosion."

She nodded. "Good idea."

He called his sister and read off the names to her.

"Wow," Jordana replied. "And I thought I had a lot of enemies."

"We might be overreacting," Neil admitted. "But

we didn't want to miss anyone, which is why I think you should add Elise's deputy mayor to the list."

"Neil!" Elise exclaimed.

Jordana chuckled. "Just because you don't like him?"

"Let's say he has an unhealthy obsession with Elise."

Jordana chuckled again. "I would say he's not the only one."

He couldn't deny it. He'd been obsessed with his ex-wife since the moment he'd caught her looking at him in that law school lecture hall. She was so beautiful, so smart, so damn independent.

He'd never met anyone who challenged, infuriated or intrigued him as much as Elise did. And he had a feeling that he never would.

"LET'S DECORATE THE TREE," Elise suggested. To get them out of the office. To get Neil's mind off his family drama. And her mind off him and how badly she wanted to kiss him.

When she'd run her fingertips along his beard, she'd wanted to lean closer, to brush her mouth over his. But she'd controlled the urge, not wanting to lead him on or to make him think that she might accept his proposal.

She also hadn't wanted to lead herself on…to believing that he might still love her. If he ever really had.

Maybe she had been as delusional about his feelings for her as she'd been about practicing criminal law. But she wasn't the naive girl she'd once been, not anymore. She jumped up from the chair behind the desk and headed out of the office, which was just off the foyer.

She glanced out the glass of the front door and breathed a sigh of relief at the sight of a police vehicle parked at the curb. They were safe here.

And maybe Jordana would be able to quickly figure out which of the many suspects on their list was responsible for the attempts on their lives. Then Elise would be able to return to her life.

For now she returned to the great room and stared up at the tree that Neil and his brother had set up near the fireplace. He took a little longer to join her, his arms full of the large plastic bins he must have brought out of the storage closet near the garage.

"Are you sure you want to decorate?" Neil asked her as he dropped the bins near the tree. "You're not still feeling all bah humbug?"

"Oh, I am," she said as she pulled a cover off the bin on top of the pile. She lifted out a silver ornament and studied it before putting it back inside the plastic tote. "I just don't want to think about that list you gave your sister."

"Jeremy?"

She shook her head. "Jeremy wouldn't hurt me..." She wished she could say the same for Neil. But she couldn't, and that was why she couldn't trust him with her heart again.

Neil touched his cheek, which she'd touched just

a few minutes earlier. "He had no problem hurting me," he said.

"Poor baby," she teased him.

"You never offered to kiss it and make it better," he said. "That's what mothers are supposed to do."

"I'm not your mother," she said.

"No, you're not," he said. "But your kisses have always made everything better." His blue eyes twinkled with amusement as he flirted with her.

"Neil…" Temptation tugged at her, making her pulse quicken. Flirting with him was exciting, too exciting for her resist. So she stepped closer to him, rose on tiptoe and brushed her lips across his cheek.

But he quickly turned his head, and his mouth covered hers as he kissed her. Really kissed her.

Now her pulse raced as passion overwhelmed her. Why was she so weak when it came to Neil? She wanted to blame the pregnancy hormones, but if she hadn't been so irresistibly drawn to him, she wouldn't have been pregnant in the first place.

She slid her arms around his neck, clinging to him as his lips nibbled at hers. His tongue swiped across her bottom one, and she opened her mouth. He deepened the kiss, stealing her breath away as her heart hammered with desire.

He was such a good kisser. Always had been.

But then Neil was good at everything he did. Always had been…

Except marriage. Neither of them had been very good at it. They had been good at making love, though.

Wanting him too much to push him away, Elise

clutched him closer and kissed him as deeply as he kissed her, tangling her tongue with his, nibbling at his lips.

He groaned and pulled back. "I don't want to stop. Do you?"

She shook her head. "No, I want you." So damn much...

His brow furrowed for a moment and he murmured, "I wish..." But then he shook off whatever maudlin thought had crossed his mind and swung her up in his arms.

She giggled and clutched his shoulders. "Hey, I'm getting too heavy for you to carry me."

"You're not even showing yet," he said. "You're light as a feather."

She laughed at his lie. She was curvy and soft, but she was happy with herself. And Neil had never seemed to have any complaints about her body.

After carrying her into the master bedroom, he quickly undressed her, pulling her sweater over her head and pushing down her leggings. When she stood before him wearing only thin bits of lace and satin, his breath escaped in a gasp. "You're so beautiful."

He'd always made her feel that way. A smile tugged at her lips, and she reached behind herself to unclasp her bra and let it drop to the floor.

He groaned.

Then she pushed down her panties. And he groaned again, more deeply.

"You're killing me," he said.

She flinched, momentarily reminded that someone was trying to do just that. Kill Neil…

And her…

She couldn't imagine a world without him in it. She couldn't imagine being without him. So she reached out now, pulling at his zippers and buttons until he stood before her naked. He was perfect—in every way. All toned muscles, soft hair and sleek skin.

Her body throbbed with desire. She reached for him, but he stepped back and shook his head.

"I want you too much," he said. "If you touch me…"

She understood; that was how she wanted him— too much. Too much for her to have any control. Any resistance, any common sense…or she wouldn't be here, with him.

"I want to please you first," he said. He kissed her again, just lightly brushing his lips across hers before lowering his head. He kissed her neck, which always made her crazy with passion.

She clutched at his shoulders, trying to pull him closer. "You're pleasing me," she moaned.

Then he moved his head lower, to her breasts. He touched the tip of his tongue to one of her nipples, and her legs nearly folded beneath her as she shuddered with pleasure.

"You've always been so responsive," he said.

But she was even more so now, to his touch, to just the sight of him.

She'd never wanted anyone the way she'd wanted Neil. But now it was more than want—it was need.

She needed him inside her, needed to feel them move as one. She stepped back, toward the bed, and dragged him down with her. His weight settled heavily on her for just a moment before he rolled to his side.

"We have to be careful," he said.

"I'm not going to break," she assured him.

"Of the baby…"

A pang of disappointment struck her. Of course because of the baby. The baby was all he truly cared about.

While she knew that in her heart and in her head, her body had other ideas—other needs. And Neil satisfied those needs as his hands and mouth touched her everywhere. He pleased her—over and over again.

She called out his name and shuddered with release. And finally he moved, flopping onto his back, and pulled her astride him. She guided his erection inside her before settling onto him. He filled her— as he always had, filling the emptiness inside her.

But she wasn't empty anymore. She had a life growing inside her. A life they'd made together.

Neil gripped her hips, and she flinched as he found the bruise. He gasped and jerked his hand away. "I'm sorry. So sorry."

She wasn't sure what he was apologizing for—not now, not when he felt so damn good inside her. She forgot about her hip, about his not loving her, and she focused only on the pleasure he gave her. Neil moved his hands from her hips to her breasts, cupping them in his hands. He slid his thumbs across her nipples, and she cried out as she came.

But she kept moving, kept going for more, and another, more intense orgasm overwhelmed her.

Neil tensed and growled before his body shuddered as he came, too. Then he melted into the mattress, as boneless as she felt as she collapsed onto his chest.

He closed his arms around her, holding her close.

She could feel his heart hammering beneath her cheek. Could hear him panting for breath.

Then she heard something else—the trill of the doorbell. "Ty told you no more deliveries," she reminded him.

"I'm not having anything delivered." He'd tensed again. "But I should see who it is."

Panic flashed through her, and she clung to him as he rolled her to her side. "Don't go."

He chuckled. "I would love nothing more than to stay in this bed with you, but it could be Jordana. Maybe she got a lead off that list of names I gave her."

"That fast?" Elise asked doubtfully. "She's good but she's not that good."

He chuckled. "I won't tell her you said that."

Regretfully Elise watched as he covered up his gorgeous body, pulling on his jeans and sweater. But regret wasn't the only feeling plaguing her. She reached out and grasped his hand. "Don't go…"

The doorbell buzzed again. Whoever was waiting was getting impatient.

"Jordana knows the code," she said. "Your whole family does." She hadn't been happy when he'd given it to them after they'd first moved into their house.

An only child, she hadn't been used to siblings just dropping by whenever they wanted to visit.

It wasn't a Colton ringing that bell.

So who was it?

"The killer isn't going to come up and ring the bell," Neil assured her.

But she wasn't as convinced. "I don't know."

THE LIST OF names that Neil had given her both overwhelmed and frightened Jordana. With her partner's help, she would whittle down the suspects. But in the meantime, she had to make sure that her brother and her ex-sister-in-law stayed safe.

She understood why Ty had needed a break, why he'd gone back to Wichita. Since Elise was the mayor, Braxville PD should be protecting her anyway. But still…

Jordana would have felt better if Ty had remained on the job. But Braxville PD had good officers.

She was good.

Still, she felt compelled to reach out to the officer posted outside Neil's house. First she tried the radio, but there was no response. Then she called dispatch, and the operator confirmed her fears. He hadn't checked in since arriving at the house.

Maybe he'd just fallen asleep. But her gut, and the instincts that had kept her alive while she'd been in the service, warned her that something else had happened to the officer.

Or somebody else had happened to him.

Had hurt him so that he hadn't been able to call out for help.

# *Chapter Twenty-One*

*Answer the damn door!*

He probably didn't have much time before some-one came to check on the officer. Or radioed him.

Even now, standing at the front door of Colton's custom-built house, he heard something from inside the patrol car. Was the officer waking up?

No. Not with as hard a blow as he'd got.

Maybe he would never wake up. That wouldn't be such a bad thing. In case he'd seen his face. Had he seen him? He'd been careful to lure him from his vehicle with the whole staged flat-tire drama. And he'd acted old and feeble so the officer stepped out to help him.

When the young man had gotten close enough, the tire iron had changed from a tool to a weapon and knocked him out. Blood spattered the pavement and the side of the rented vehicle. The tire was changed now. And so was the officer.

And so was he. He wore the young man's uni-form…although it was a little tight, a little too tight. But Colton wouldn't have time to notice.

Because the tire iron had been replaced with the young officer's service revolver.

He had to get Colton to open the damn door, though. He had to get inside before he started firing so that neither of them had the chance to escape this time.

Impatience nagging at him, he pressed the bell again. Soon...

Soon he would get inside that damn house...and the lawyers would finally get what they deserved: death.

THE DOORBELL BUZZED AGAIN, making Neil wonder why his visitor was so damn impatient. Thinking maybe Elise was right to be concerned, he pulled out his cell phone. There was a camera at the front door, but before he opened the security app for the camera, he noticed a text from his sister.

Can't reach officer stationed at your house. I'm on my way. Don't do anything until I get there.

The text hadn't been sent long enough ago for his sister to be the one at the door. So Neil opened the security app. The man ringing the bell had his head down, face turned away, but his uniform was clearly visible, if a little ill fitting. The officer was at his door.

So why hadn't he checked in with Braxville PD? As a criminal attorney, Neil knew all officers carried radioes on them, usually fastened to their shirt collars for easy communication. Most officers were equipped with body cams as well, which was partly the reason why Neil urged his clients to take plea deals instead of risking trials.

The uneasiness that Elise must have felt crept over Neil now, raising the short hairs on the nape of his neck. Something was off.

Could the officer be the one after them? Maybe he and Elise had gotten too good a deal for someone the cop had arrested.

They hadn't included the arresting officers of their clients on that list they'd given his sister.

Elise must have dressed quickly, because she caught up with him before he made it to the hall. She clutched his arm with one hand and her phone with the other. "Don't open the door!" she said. "Jordana sent a message."

His sister had apparently texted them both. Maybe because she hadn't trusted him to do nothing while he waited for her.

"I know," Neil said. "But it's the officer at the door." He showed the image on his phone to Elise.

Her brow furrowed as she studied his screen. "I don't know…"

"It is the officer," he insisted. "That's a Braxville PD uniform."

"Then why hasn't he answered your sister's calls?" Elise asked. "Just wait for her."

But the doorbell rang again. How many more times would the person ring before just forcing his way inside? The security system was good, but it wasn't foolproof.

As they watched the cell phone screen, the officer pulled out his weapon and pointed it toward the door. If he shattered the glass, he would be able to reach inside and turn the dead bolt. He and his gun would be able to get to them. And while the alarm would go off, police would not arrive immediately.

Maybe not in time to save them…

"I have a gun," Neil said. "It's in the safe, in the den."

Elise shook her head. "That's too close to the front door. If that isn't really an officer and he starts shooting through the glass…"

But Neil had to do something. He couldn't just cower inside his house while he waited for help to arrive. He had to make sure that his wife—*ex-wife*—and their unborn baby stayed safe.

"I bet it's the officer," Neil said, but it wasn't a bet of which he was sure enough to wager their lives. "I'll be perfectly safe. But just in case…"

"What?"

"Go to the garage, get in the SUV, and if you hear anything, get the hell out of here."

She shook her head. "No. I am not leaving you alone in here. Come with me. Leave with me."

But then the person would hear the garage door open and would be waiting for them.

Neil had to distract him. So, as he watched that screen and saw the man's finger move along the barrel of his gun, he called out, "I'm coming!"

"You can't!" she exclaimed. "You have to wait for Jordana. She should be here soon."

Not soon enough. Not with the person already at his door pointing the gun at the glass…

If it was truly just the Braxville officer in a too-tight uniform, why would he have his weapon drawn and pointing at the house he was supposed to be protecting?

Neil sighed and shook his head as realization dawned. "He probably thinks something's happened to us because we haven't answered the door yet. We're just being paranoid."

"Cautious," Elise said. "We're being cautious."

Neil wanted to err on the side of caution, as well. "So go, get in the SUV."

"I don't have my purse or keys," she said. "They're upstairs."

"Mine are in the console of the vehicle, it's unlocked. Get in it and start it up," he advised her. Getting impatient himself, he gently shoved her toward the kitchen from which led the hall toward the service door of the garage. "Go!"

"Neil—"

"Go!"

He expected her to keep arguing, but instead she headed toward that door. Then he realized what she was doing—she was going to try to distract their visitor from the front door…just as he'd wanted to distract the person from her. "Damn it!" he called out.

She was going to get herself killed.

He was going to get himself killed—if she didn't act fast. Her heart pounding with fear for the man she loved, Elise ran to the garage and hit the switch for the garage door. The sound of it opening would distract their visitor from the front door.

But she hadn't realized that it would attract him to the garage before she even had a chance to jump in the SUV and start the engine. Within seconds of the garage door rising up to the ceiling, she had confirmation that they weren't just being paranoid about the officer.

And that he wasn't an officer…

Because shots rang out.

Like when the headlights had blinded her, she momentarily froze before she could even pull open the driver's door. She would have gotten hit for certain if something—or somebody—hadn't pushed her forward in front of Neil's vehicle and then knocked her to the ground. She recognized the shape and hardness of Neil's body as he covered hers with his.

She felt his heart pounding fast and heavily against her back, his breath panting in her ear. He was as scared as she was.

She had tried to stop him from putting himself in danger, but her misguided effort had put him in more peril. Glass from the SUV rained down on them, falling in her hair that was spread around her head.

Neil's hands covered her face to protect her from the glass, so she couldn't see much even though she turned her head. And she couldn't hear much, her ears ringing from the gunshot blasts.

Then silence fell. Neil's hands moved slightly. She could see more now—of the concrete floor and the undercarriage of Neil's vehicle and the black shoes on the other side of it.

But those shoes moved, as the shooter headed closer to them.

There was no way they would be able to avoid getting shot. In trying to save Neil, Elise was going to get him and herself killed.

# *Chapter Twenty-Two*

If only he'd retrieved his gun from his safe…

But there hadn't been time. If he hadn't acted when he had, Elise would already be dead. He wouldn't be able to protect her when he was dead, which probably could happen soon.

The gunfire stopped, but he heard the scrape of shoes against concrete as the shooter walked around the back of the SUV. Neil pulled Elise up, just enough to scoot her forward around the front of his SUV to the passenger's side. She must have been hit because he felt something wet against his hand. He'd tried to save her from getting hurt, but he must have been too late. She was alive, though, her body trembling against his.

He crouched low, keeping beneath the already shattered windows. And held his breath…

Then he heard the sirens. They wailed loudly as emergency vehicles approached. Those black shoes moved quickly now, running out of the garage and away from the house.

Neil released the breath he'd been holding. "Are you okay?" he asked Elise.

"I don't know."

"Did you get hit?" he asked as he stepped back and looked at her face. It was pale with fear except for a slight scrape on one cheek. He had done that, when he'd knocked her to the ground.

Her clothes were wrinkled, too, but that might have been from when he'd pulled them off earlier. He couldn't see any blood on her. So maybe that wetness he'd felt earlier had been tears.

Her eyes were dry now, though, and wide. "Is he gone?" she asked in a nervous whisper.

"I think so."

He raised his head to try to see which direction the man had gone. He couldn't get away—not again. He had to be stopped.

"Stay here," he told Elise as he leaned her against the passenger's side of the SUV. But before he could take more than a few steps, Elise grasped his arm and he flinched with pain.

"You're bleeding!" she exclaimed and jerked her hand from his wound.

He glanced down at his forearm, where blood saturated the torn sleeve of his sweater and trailed down his hand. "It doesn't hurt," he said.

But letting their assailant go, that would hurt.

"I'm fine," he insisted, and once free of her grasp, hurried out of the garage. The patrol car was still parked at the curb. The pseudo officer hadn't taken it.

So what had happened to the real officer?

Dread gripping his stomach, Neil started toward the cruiser. Before he could approach it, another police vehicle, lights flashing, pulled up next to it. It wasn't marked as clearly as the cruiser. But for the light on the dash and the government license plate, it might not have been real—just like the officer hadn't been real.

His sister jumped out of the passenger's side of this one, and there was no way anyone could impersonate Jordana, not even his other sisters. She was one of a kind and as tough as they came—until she saw that he was bleeding.

"Neil!" she yelled his name, her voice cracking with emotion. "Oh my God, are you okay?"

"No," Elise answered for him. "He's been shot."

Neil shook his head. "No, it's just a scratch." But he couldn't be certain what had scratched him. A bullet or some of the broken glass.

"What the hell happened?" Reese Carpenter asked the question as he jumped out of the driver's side. "We were coming over here to check on you and got the report of shots fired." He glanced into the garage and whistled. "Looks like the vehicle got the worst of it."

"I warned you to sit tight until we got here," Jordana said. "You have to stop putting yourself in danger and let me handle this."

"It was your officer at the door," Neil said. "With his gun drawn."

Jordana glanced toward the patrol car and shook her head. "No..." She pointed at Reese, who drew his weapon like she drew hers and they approached the

parked vehicle. Once she got close enough to look inside, she cursed. "We need an ambulance," she called
out before she even opened the back door. When she
did, she reached inside and leaned over a limp body.

"Is he okay?" Neil asked with alarm.

"Unconscious," Jordana replied.

"But breathing," Reese added with an audible sigh
of relief.

"Thank God," Neil murmured.

The police officer wasn't dead, and hopefully he
wasn't hurt too badly. A pang of guilt struck him that
the man had been hurt protecting them, though. Com-
pounding the guilt was relief that it hadn't been Ty
who'd been hurt. But maybe his brother would have
caught whoever had knocked out the officer.

Jordana must have been thinking the same thing
because she murmured, "Too bad Ty left."

"We don't know that he would have been able
to protect us," Neil said. He might have gotten hurt
worse than the officer was. Neil wasn't sure that anyone would be able to protect them.

ELISE COULDN'T STOP SHAKING. Why the hell had she
been so stupid? She could have gotten herself and
Neil killed. She wasn't any more rational than he was.
Which made it just too damn dangerous for them to
stay together.

"You need to go to the hospital," she said when the
ambulance arrived.

He shook his head. "The officer is hurt far worse than I am."

The young man had regained consciousness, but it was clear that he was in pain. Neil was, too, wincing every time he brushed his bleeding arm against something.

"Your wound hasn't stopped bleeding," she said, pointing out the small pool of blood forming on the driveway beneath his hand that dangled at his side. "You have to get stitches."

"She's right," Jordana agreed, but the ambulance was already speeding away, lights and sirens going, behind a police escort.

"Was he able to tell you anything?" Neil asked his sister, pointing toward the departing ambulance.

She sighed. "He got conned. Guy pulled up on the street with a flat tire, acted like he was struggling with it. When Officer Lester walked over to help, the man hit him with the tire iron, knocking him out."

"Was the officer able to give you a description?" Neil asked.

She shook her head. "Sunglasses and hat pulled so low that he couldn't say what color his hair or eyes were. And with him crouching next to the car, he couldn't even tell how tall he was."

"What about the car? Was he able to describe it?"

Jordana shrugged. "What does it matter? I doubt it belonged to him. He probably stole that one, too. What can you two tell me about the guy? What did you see?"

Anger gripped Elise, anger at the lunatic who'd tried to kill them and anger at herself for putting them in danger. "I didn't see anything," she said. "But his damn shoes…"

"I showed you my phone with the video from the security camera at the front door," Neil reminded her.

She shook her head. "I didn't have my glasses on."

"What did you see on that video?" Jordana asked her brother.

Neil shook his head. "Not much," he admitted. "He kept his face turned away from the front door."

"So he either knew about the security camera or he didn't want you to recognize him before you'd opened the door," Jordana surmised.

"So we might know who he is," Elise said. "He's not just some hired hitman, then."

"If he was a professional, you would probably already be dead," Jordana said.

And Elise couldn't argue that; they'd had too many close calls.

"Did you notice anything else about him?" the detective asked.

"The uniform was too tight on him," Neil said.

"So he's bigger than Officer Lester," Jordana said.

"I wish I could tell you more," Neil said with a groan over his frustration. Then he raised his arm, probably to push his hand through, his hair, and a grimace of pain contorted his handsome face.

Concern grasped Elise's heart. "You need a doctor to look at that wound."

"Yes, I'll take you to the hospital," Jordana said. "And you can send Yvette the video. Maybe she can use her crime tech skills to find something else that might help us identify this guy."

Elise let out a soft sigh of relief that his sister was also pushing him to seek treatment. And while he was gone, she intended to pack up her stuff and head somewhere—anywhere—else. It was too dangerous for them to be together.

It was too much temptation for their assailant to try to take them both out at the same time. And it was too much temptation for Elise to fall into Neil's bed and back in love with him.

YVETTE REWOUND THE footage and watched it again, watching as the man pulled the gun and pointed it toward the glass in Neil's front door. Despite the uniform he wore, he wasn't there to check on Yvette's brother and the mayor. He was there to kill them.

"Come on, come on," she murmured. "Turn toward the camera. Look at me…"

But he kept his face turned away from the front door, showing only his profile. Who the hell was he?

She rewound again…to when he started walking up toward the house. Something about his walk…

It was vaguely familiar.

Uncle Shep…

A smile curved her lips as she thought of her favorite family member. Of course, it wasn't him in that uniform with the gun. But the way this man carried himself reminded her of her dad's brother.

"You look pleased with yourself," Jordana remarked as she joined her in the tech lab. "You found something?"

Yvette pointed at the screen. "Who does that walk remind you of?"

"Military bearing," Jordana remarked.

Of course she would recognize it. Like Uncle Shep, she had served, too.

"I'll ask Neil which of his former clients might have been in the military," Jordana said.

"Is he okay?" Yvette asked, concern for her brother gripping her. Ty had been shot last month, and now someone was trying to kill Neil.

"Physically, yes," Jordana said. "He just needed a few stitches for a cut on his arm."

"Emotionally, I can understand why he'd be upset," Yvette said. "Someone's trying to kill him."

"He's pissed about that," Jordana said. "But I'm more worried how he's going to react to finding out Elise is gone."

Yvette gasped with horror. "What? The killer got to her? She's dead?"

"Not dead," Jordana quickly assured her. "She just doesn't want to stay with Neil anymore."

"I'm surprised she agreed to stay with him at all," Yvette said.

"They still love each other," Jordana said.

"Then why won't she stay with him?" Yvette asked.

She did not understand why people in love acted so

damn crazy. She wanted no part of that; she wanted only to focus on her work. She could make a difference with it—do some good now.

"I suspect that's why she won't stay with him," Jordana said. "She also thinks they'll be safer if they're not together. She's probably right. But Neil won't see it that way…"

"And it doesn't mean that their assailant won't still get to both of them…"

The man had been bold enough to take down a cop and risk getting caught on the security video. He wasn't going to give up.

## Chapter Twenty-Three

She was gone.

Neil knew it the minute he walked in the door. When she'd refused to go to the hospital with him, he'd realized she was planning to pack up and leave him.

Just like she had three years ago.

That time it had been his fault. His impatience spurring him on to give her an ultimatum. He should have been more patient this time. He should have stopped pressuring her to accept his proposal.

He reached for his phone to call her, to beg her to come back, but then he noticed the text she had sent him.

We're safer apart than together.

She was probably right. But he didn't care if his life was in more danger when he was with her. He cared only about keeping her and their unborn baby safe.

The cell vibrated, startling him. Jordana.

"Did you find something?" he asked anxiously. They had to catch this person.

"We think the guy might have a military background," she said.

"Because of the bomb?"

"Possibly," she said. "But even just the way he walked up to the door."

Neil hadn't seen that part of the video. He'd been preoccupied—with Elise. He couldn't imagine sleeping in that bed now without her. He didn't know how he'd managed to get used to sleeping alone the past few years, but he didn't want to get used to it again.

"He reminded Yvette of Uncle Shep," Jordana continued, her voice warming as she spoke of their uncle.

While the career Navy man hadn't been around much when they were growing up, he had made an impact on all of their lives. He was such a good man. An honorable man.

Neil wished he could say the same, with all confidence, of his father. But he just wasn't sure anymore...

"I'll look through the case files again," Neil told his sister.

"Not tonight," Jordana said.

"She wants to go home to Clint and not be interrupted," Yvette called out from the background of wherever his sisters were.

Jordana continued as if her little sister hadn't interrupted her, "Get some rest. It's late. Let me know tomorrow if you remember any clients with a military background."

Clients...

Maybe he'd had a couple of them, men who'd struggled after returning from combat. But he didn't remember any of them threatening him or Elise. Something else flitted through his mind, though.

*He'll get what's coming to him.*

"Did you already fall asleep?" Jordana asked.

"No." He doubted he was going to be able to sleep at all.

"You're safe, you know," she said.

"It's not me I'm worried about," he admitted.

"I know. There's a patrol car parked outside both your homes," she said. "And after what happened to Officer Lester, they're going to be extra vigilant. Braxville PD wants this guy as much as you do."

"Officer Lester is going to be okay," he reminded her. The other Braxville PD personnel gathered in the waiting room had confirmed that their comrade had a concussion but was expected to recover.

"I know," Jordana said. "It's just that we now know exactly how dangerous this guy is."

"I already knew that," Neil said, letting the irony slip into his voice. But he had learned something new and not just about the guy's military background; he'd learned exactly how determined the man was to kill him and Elise.

So determined that he wasn't likely to give up until he'd been caught or until he was dead.

"Be careful," Jordana told him. Needlessly.

The minute their call ended, Neil headed into the den. He opened the safe in the wall behind his desk and pulled out the gun he should have had on him earlier. Maybe then this would have been over already.

He had the gun for protection.

What did Elise have…besides that patrol car?

ELISE WAS TIRED and not just from her recent sleepless nights, not even from growing the baby inside her. She was exhausted from clearing away enough of the destruction in her condo so that she could sleep. While she was no neat freak, the chaos was unsettling. But the chaos wasn't just inside her condo; it was inside her heart and her head, as well.

She'd wanted to go to the hospital with Neil, like he'd beseeched her. She'd wanted to hold his hand while he got the stitches he'd obviously needed to stop the bleeding. She'd wanted to return to their home with him and to their bed and to pretend they'd never gotten divorced.

That it had all been a bad dream.

But that wasn't possible. Elise was too much of a realist, and she knew that reality would come crashing down around her if they tried to make a go of it just for the baby's sake.

Her cell phone, sitting on the nightstand next to her bed, vibrated. Already knowing who it was, she reached for it, accepted the call and said, "I'm not coming back to your house. This is for the best."

"It's not," Neil said. "You know what would be best. For all of us."

"Neil…"

"But I'm not going to pressure you," he said. "I just want to make sure you're safe."

"There's a police car parked in my driveway," she assured him. And if she wanted, as mayor, she could use city funds to hire additional security. She just didn't want to do that, didn't want that to be necessary. She wanted their would-be killer caught soon.

"There's one here, too," he said.

She had no doubt that his sister would have made certain he was protected, just as she'd made certain he'd received stitches, too.

"Are you okay?" she asked.

"No."

"I thought it was just a cut," she said.

"It is just a cut," he said. "I was talking about your not being here with—"

"Stop," she interjected. "Or I'm going to hang up on you." That was what she should have done when he'd divorced her—stopped having any contact with him. But they had promised to be civil and to work together on the loose ends from their former business and personal relationships.

"I have another reason for calling," he said. "Jordana and Yvette think the person after us might be military."

"Because of the bomb? Can't anybody make one of those off YouTube videos nowadays?"

"I think it was more to do with the way he walked, according to them," he said. "And the bomb was more complicated than something someone without any experience could have made."

"Oh, then that makes sense," she murmured in agreement. "And that leaves out Jeremy."

Neil cursed as if he was really disappointed, but then he begrudgingly admitted, "I didn't think it was him on the security footage. Jeremy doesn't ever hide from cameras. He seeks them out."

She chuckled. She should have been happy to rule out her deputy mayor, but she found herself suggesting, "He could have hired someone to get rid of us."

"No, this feels too personal," Neil said.

"But then wouldn't we have figured out who it was by now?" she asked. Her head was beginning to pound with exhaustion and with frustration. How could they not have any idea who was after them?

"It's been a few years since we practiced together," he said. "It's understandable that while we might remember the clients, we could have forgotten other people associated with those cases. I keep thinking it might be a victim's family member."

Her skin chilled as she remembered someone shouting out in the courtroom after the judge had accepted their plea deal and sentence recommendation.

*He'll get what's coming to him.*

"There was someone," she murmured. "A dad or a brother of a woman who died."

"Dad," Neil said. "It was her dad. He wanted his daughter's husband sentenced to death, and instead he got a light sentence for manslaughter."

"Our client wasn't happy with the sentence, either," Elise remembered. "He kept claiming he was innocent." She'd hoped he was, but she hadn't been convinced, and neither would the jury have been. If she'd truly believed he was innocent, she would have told him to reject the plea. It had been more than fair... unless the murder had been premeditated, like the victim's family had believed.

"But we pointed out that the prosecution had enough evidence for a conviction," Neil said, "so he accepted the deal for manslaughter."

"Nobody was happy with that case," she agreed. Just thinking of it, of that poor woman's death, unsettled her. Had it been a heat-of-the-moment, almost-accidental death like Neil had convinced the prosecutor it must have been?

"I'll call Jordana back," he said, then chuckled.

"What?"

"I'm not supposed to disturb her tonight, though."

"Don't, then," she said. "It's late. Let her get some sleep."

"Will you?" he asked.

"I'm exhausted," she admitted.

"But will you be able to sleep?" he asked. "I won't. Not without you."

Temptation pulled at her. She would like nothing more than to lie in his arms, with her head on his chest, in the bed they'd once shared. But she couldn't trust him with her heart again. Not when it still hadn't healed from the last time he'd broken it and not when she knew he only wanted to be with her again because she was pregnant. If she'd lost the baby that first night he'd found out, the night of the explosion, he never would have proposed in the first place.

Needing all of her energy to fight the temptation to go back to him, to that house, she didn't argue. She simply hung up her phone.

*Damn it.*

How could he have fired so many shots and missed them? Well, he'd missed her. Colton had gone to the hospital, but he'd been released—and driven home by a police officer.

Police officers were stationed at both their places now. He wouldn't be able to get to them like he needed to. He wouldn't be able to finish them first like he'd planned.

He would have to go on to his next target.

But he'd be back…

Eventually their security would slip up or they would, and he would end their miserable lives like he should have years ago.

## Chapter Twenty-Four

Neil studied the man as he walked toward them. He was tall and leanly muscled, with a certain bearing that commanded attention even across the crowded restaurant. "So that's the military walk?" he asked his sisters.

"Yup," Jordana confirmed and she jumped up to greet the man. Instead of saluting him, as Neil half expected she might, she hugged him.

Yvette hugged him next, and the man clasped her a little more tightly than he had Jordana. But that might have been just because she wasn't armed like their older sister. Once he released Yvette, he clasped Neil's proffered hand tightly.

"It's so good to have you home, Uncle Shep," Jordana said, gushing.

Uncle Shep pushed up the bill of his ball cap a little, and his brown eyes warmed with affection. "Glad to be home." He looked at each of them for a long moment before narrowing his eyes slightly and asking, "Why do I think you didn't ask me to meet you here just for breakfast?"

La Dolce Vita probably hadn't been the smartest place to meet at all—not with how Megan Chase kept glaring at them. Her husband had worked for Colton Construction…before he'd gotten sick. So very sick.

Neil ignored the proprietress's scowl and focused on his uncle. "I need your help, Uncle Shep," he admitted.

Uncle Shep nodded. "I heard about somebody going after you and the mayor. I'm happy to help out anyway I can." He slid into the booth next to Yvette.

The three of them filled him in on everything that had happened and shared the security footage and information on the bomb with him.

"I'd say your assailant definitely has some military training," he agreed.

Yvette and Jordana nodded in agreement of his conclusion. Before they could say anymore, their cell phones rang. "We have to leave," Jordana said.

"Duty calls," Yvette agreed.

Neil's heart jumped in his chest. "Elise? Has something happened to Elise?"

"No, not at all," Jordana assured him. "Her protection detail assured me she is safe at City Hall as we speak."

"This has nothing to do with you," Yvette assured him. "I have a robbery scene to process."

"And for me to investigate," Jordana added with a smile.

After more hugs for Uncle Shep, they left. Neil reached for his cup of coffee, and his hand shook slightly in reaction to his fear that something might have happened to Elise.

"You're really worried," Uncle Shep remarked.

He nodded. "This guy just keeps coming for us."

"Any idea who?"

"We've narrowed it down to a former client and maybe his victim's family. When we first started our practice we represented a man, Seth Costner, accused of murdering his wife, Leah. He claims he didn't do it, but there were enough witnesses and circumstantial evidence for the DA to get a conviction. We got him a deal instead."

"Didn't he think it was a deal?" Uncle Shep asked.

Neil shook his head. "He swears he was innocent."

"You didn't believe him?"

Neil shrugged. "I don't know. His wife's family sure didn't, and they thought he should have gotten the death penalty. Her dad, Walter Shultz, yelled out in court that he was going to get what's coming to him."

"Has he?" Shep asked.

"We're checking to see if he's been paroled."

"He might be in danger if he has," Shep said. "Or he might be who's coming after you."

"I don't think Seth had any military training, though."

"Let me check," Shep murmured as he pulled out his cell phone. He didn't make his call in the diner, though. He stepped outside instead.

No longer hungry or thirsty, Neil dropped some money on the table to pay his and his sisters' bill and joined his uncle outside, where a patrol car was parked at the curb. His security detail.

With his uncle present, he doubted he needed additional backup. Despite his recent retirement from the Navy, Shep was in great shape and maybe not so retired that he didn't still have connections.

Neil couldn't overhear much of the conversation, with his uncle keeping his voice to a gruff whisper. But it wasn't long before Shep disconnected the call and said, "I don't think Seth Costner is your man."

"Damn," Neil said. "I thought it was a good lead."

"It is," Shep replied. "Because I think it's Costner's former father-in-law who's going after you. Walter Shultz has the military experience with explosives, and as an excavator he still has access to explosives."

"So he could be making more damn bombs as we speak," Neil murmured. More bombs that he could be planting to kill him and Elise.

He needed to check on her—personally—to make sure she really was safe. But first he had to know, "How did you find all that out so quickly?"

Uncle Shep flashed his quick grin. "I have my ways."

"I thought you retired your ways," Neil said.

The grin turned slightly sheepish. "I still have connections. And I have some experience investigating."

"In the Navy?"

"Navy Intelligence," Shep admitted.

"Oh…" That made so much sense now. "Jordana takes after you so much."

"Yvette, too," Shep said. "With the investigating…"

Neil nodded. "Hopefully they can use those skills to track down Walter Shultz." Before he built another bomb. Before he tried to hurt him or Elise again.

"They will," Shep assured him. "You need to let them do their jobs."

Neil groaned. "Please don't tell me to stay out of it. I can't—not when there are so many lives in danger. Mine, Elise's and our…"

Shep tilted his head and peered at Neil. "Your what?" he asked.

Neil hadn't shared their news with any of their family. And his mother wouldn't have, either, since she was fanatical about those privacy laws. He could have told his family, but he'd wanted to wait…until Elise had agreed to marry him again. He doubted that was ever going to happen, though.

So he told his uncle, "Our unborn baby's."

"Elise is pregnant?" Shep asked, his brown eyes wide with surprise.

Neil nodded. "Yes, and it's mine." In case his uncle wondered.

Shep chuckled. "Of course it is. You two might be divorced, but I don't think there will ever be anyone else for either of you."

"Not for me," Neil confirmed. "But Elise refuses to give me another chance." He'd screwed up too damn badly when he'd asked for the divorce.

Uncle Shep squeezed his shoulder. "Don't give up. A love like that…" he cleared his throat "…like yours is worth fighting for. Don't give up, Neil, or you'll spend the rest of your life regretting it."

He'd already spent the past three years regretting the divorce.

"And be careful," Uncle Shep cautioned, "so that you have a long life to spend with the woman you love and the child you've created."

Emotion choked Neil at his uncle's words, and he could only nod in agreement. His uncle had always been a confirmed bachelor, but now it sounded like that hadn't been his choice. And that he regretted not fighting for the woman he'd loved.

Neil had already spent too much time dwelling on regrets. He was going to make sure that he didn't have cause for any more.

HE HADN'T BEEN LYING. With the dark circles beneath his eyes and his mussed hair, Neil looked as if he hadn't slept at all last night. But Elise doubted that it was for the reason he'd claimed on the phone the previous evening—because she hadn't been in his arms, in his bed. There was no place she would have rather been…if he loved her.

If only he loved her…

He hadn't even spoken to her yet. Since walking into her office, he'd been on his cell with one of his sisters. He paced the small confines of her office, his handsome face tense as he listened.

Exhausted just from watching him, she leaned back in her chair. She already knew what he must have learned. The minute he disconnected his call, she said, "Seth Costner was paroled last week."

He nodded. "Even earlier than the deal we made for him."

"Good behavior is the reason his parole officer gave me," she said. "He also said that he's still proclaiming his innocence."

Neil sighed. "I don't know what to believe about that, but it's clear that his father-in-law holds him responsible for his daughter's murder."

"Manslaughter," Elise murmured. An accident. That was what Seth had claimed it was. His father-in-law had insisted it had been planned, that the couple had been fighting nonstop. "And how is it clear that his father-in-law still holds him responsible? Has he gone after him?"

"I don't know about Seth, but I think Walter Shultz is who's gone after us. Uncle Shep confirmed he's former military, with experience in explosives and current access to them."

She was glad she was sitting down, since her legs started shaking. "That's why you told Carmen not to allow any packages up here." When she'd overheard him talking to her assistant, she'd figured he was worried about explosives.

He nodded. "We have to be extra careful until this guy is caught."

Even after he was caught, she had to be extra careful so she didn't fall back in love with her ex-husband. "Are Jordana and Reese looking for him?"

He nodded. "But they haven't tracked him down yet. They're looking for Seth, too. Does his parole officer know where he is?"

She glanced down at the paper on her desk, at the address his parole officer had given her. She'd intended to call Jordana and give her the information. But she hadn't had a chance before Neil entered.

He stepped closer to her desk and picked up the slip of paper. "Is this it?" he asked.

"You need to give that to your sister," she said. "That's what I was going to do."

"It's more important that she focus on finding Shultz," Neil said. "I can stop by Seth's and warn him that his ex-father-in-law might be gunning for him like he's been gunning for us."

Her legs were shaking even more now, but she jumped up from her chair anyway. "No!" she exclaimed. "You need to stay away from him."

"It's not him," Neil insisted. "It's Shultz."

"And Shultz could be going after him right now," she said. "And you could walk right into the middle of a bad situation if you go see him."

"He needs to be warned," Neil insisted.

"I'll call his parole officer back," she said. "I'll have him warn him."

"Seth might also have some idea where Shultz could be," Neil said. "I need to talk to him myself."

"No, you don't need to—you want to," she said. "You want to put yourself in danger."

"I want to put an end to the danger," he insisted. "I want to make sure you're safe."

"Me? Or the baby?" she asked.

His brow furrowed. "What do you mean? Both of you, of course."

If only she could be certain of that.

"All of us," he said. "Seth, too."

"That's not your job," she said. "Leave that to the police to handle."

"What if we were wrong?" he asked. "What if he was innocent?"

"Then he'd be as mad at us as Walter Shultz is," she said. And she wouldn't blame him. "But he didn't have to take the deal. He could have taken his chances with a trial."

Neil nodded. "He could have, but we strongly warned him against doing that. And I need to strongly warn him now about his father-in-law."

"He probably already knows," she said. It might have been too late for Seth. She didn't want it to be too late for Neil, too. "Don't go!" She grasped his arm, holding onto him so he wouldn't leave.

"I'm doing this for us," he insisted. "And to protect you."

"I don't need your protection," she replied. She needed his love. But she was too proud to admit it and too damn mad at him for not listening.

He groaned with frustration of his own. "I know you're fierce and independent and think you can take care of yourself. But it's not just you anymore. You're carrying my baby. And I will do whatever necessary to protect you both!" He pulled from her grasp and headed out of her office.

She could have chased him, but she knew he wasn't going to stop for her. He was too damn stubborn. So she went back to the pad on her desk, from which she'd torn off the first sheet of paper. She ran the edge of a pencil over the page and the address stood out in white.

Her hand shaking, she punched in Jordana's number.

"Elise, everything okay?" the detective asked.

"No," she replied and filled the young woman in on what her brother was doing.

Jordana cursed. "He has a car following him. I'll make sure they stick close and don't let him get in any trouble."

"What about you?" Elise asked. "Can you get to him before he makes it to that address?"

Jordana cursed again. "No. Reese and I are out of town—where we were told Walter Shultz was working. But he's not at the job site."

Which meant that he could be with Seth, which meant that Neil would be too late to save him. What about Neil? Would the officers following him be able to protect him?

Jordana wouldn't be able to make it any time soon to the address Elise had given her, but Elise might be able to—just probably not in time to save Neil if Shultz was there, though. But she couldn't wait in her office until she knew what had happened.

She had to go there, too, had to check on the man she loved, the father of her baby. If the police officers weren't able to protect him, what would she tell her child about his or her father?

That the man had given up his life to protect theirs…

MAYBE HE SHOULD have started here, with Seth. But his intention had been to frame the killer for the murders of his lawyers. Seth wouldn't have lived to accept another plea deal, though. Walter would have made certain of that. Seth would have had a horrible accident—like the one he'd claimed Leah had had.

But her death had been no accident. It had been murder. Not manslaughter, like his slimy lawyers had convinced the prosecutor and the judge it was.

"I didn't do it, Walt," Seth whined from where he lay on the scuffed hardwood floor.

Walter had knocked him down the minute Seth Costner had walked into the old Costner family cabin. He hadn't known he was there because Walter had parked his vehicle over a mile away. He could use Seth's to leave here once he was done, once Seth was done. Blood trickled from the corner of the weasel's thin lips, and Walter's knuckles stung. So he kicked him instead, driving his steel-toed boots into his former son-in-law's ribs.

Seth cried out in pain. "Stop. Please stop."

Fury rushed through Walter, nearly blinding him. "Is that what Leah did? Did she beg you to stop?"

"It wasn't like that, Walt," he insisted. "I didn't see her in the garage. I accidentally ran her over..."

"Shut up!" Walt raged. "The coroner said her injuries were inconsistent with a vehicle—more like a fist. You beat her to death just like I'm going to beat you to death."

Seth whimpered and tried crawling across the

floor. He wasn't going to get far—at least not alive. And if he tried to run…

Well, Walt still had the gun from the other night. And this time he wasn't going to miss. But before he could drag Seth back, a noise drew his attention to the window. The crunch of gravel as a car slowly approached the cabin.

Who the hell had chosen to visit an ex-con now? Then he recognized the man behind the wheel and grinned. At least one of the lawyers had showed up.

## Chapter Twenty-Five

Neil had lost the patrol car that had been following him. He'd done it inadvertently, though. Maybe—because there were so many white sedans like the one he'd rented—they'd lost him in traffic. He hadn't realized they weren't there until he'd turned onto the gravel road leading to the cabin that Seth Costner had listed with the parole office as his current address. Full of deep ruts, it appeared the road wasn't well maintained and probably not often traveled.

But then Seth had only been released the week before, so he'd not been staying at the cabin very long. He must have inherited the property when his parents died while he was in prison.

It was possible he still harbored resentment toward Neil for encouraging him to accept the plea deal. But Neil was less concerned about Seth hurting him than he was about Walter Shultz hurting all of them.

Did Walter know where Seth was staying? Had he known about the cabin?

The house Seth had lived in with his wife, Leah, had belonged to his former father-in-law, just as Seth had also worked for the man. Walter Shultz had been a highly controlling man. He'd also been composed, but for that one outburst he'd made in the courtroom after sentencing.

He'd been furious about the manslaughter sentence. How must he have felt over Seth being released early due to good behavior? Maybe Seth was already dead.

As he turned onto the drive leading to the cabin, Neil noticed a plume of smoke rising above the trees, and when he drew closer, he saw it above the chimney sticking out of the roof the cabin. Someone had recently started the fire in the hearth, so Seth might still be here.

And with only one vehicle parked in the drive, it was probably just Seth.

Neil stopped his car behind Seth's battered pickup, which he'd probably inherited along with the cabin. Then he reached into the glove compartment for the gun he'd taken from his safe the night before. He wasn't taking the risk Elise thought he was.

He was prepared this time. Not that he wanted to use it, but thanks to his father and his uncle, he knew how to shoot. He even occasionally visited the shooting range with Jordana and Ty.

He had never pointed a weapon at a real person, though. Just a target. But if he had to use the gun, he would, because he wasn't just defending himself now; he was defending his family. The family he'd wanted for so long.

So why wouldn't Elise accept his proposal and make them a family again?

Suddenly, realization dawned on him like a slap upside the head. God, he wished now that she had slapped him—instead of getting that look on her face that she'd gotten every time he proposed or talked about the baby.

She thought that was all he wanted.

That all he cared about was the baby she carried...

His ears buzzed as he remembered his mother saying something like that to him, in the waiting room after the hit and run, but he'd been so worried about Elise that he hadn't fully understood what they'd both meant.

Elise didn't think he loved her. How the hell could she, after he'd divorced her just because she'd wanted to wait before having kids?

How could he have been so stupid?

Shaking his head in self-disgust, he stepped out of his car. At once, a gun barrel pressed to the back of his head, and he realized just how blind he'd been. He hadn't even noticed the man sneaking out of the house and up on his vehicle.

"Nice of you to join us, lawyer," Walter Shultz said.

"Us?" God, he hadn't somehow gotten to Elise and then beat him here, had he?

"I presume you've come by to talk to your client," Shultz said. "You better talk fast, because I'm not sure how much longer he's going to last."

Seth wasn't dead yet. But, apparently, he was dying.

And once he was dead, Neil had no doubt that he would be next. He couldn't die, though, not without making sure that Elise knew how much he loved her, how much he had always loved her.

"WHAT DO YOU mean you lost him?" Jordana exclaimed, her voice rattling her cell phone with the frustration and fear gripping her. "You're supposed to be sticking close to him. Too close to lose him."

Oh, God, Elise had been right; Neil was going to get himself killed.

"This is where he was headed," she said, reading off the address that Elise had given her. "And I hope like hell you're closer than we are."

Reese pressed harder on the accelerator as he steered around slower-moving vehicles. Hell, everything on the freeway was moving slower than they were as he raced past them, lights and sirens flashing. "You don't even know that Shultz is there," Reese said. "You might be worried about nothing."

Every instinct she possessed screamed out in protest. "It's not nothing. Shultz wasn't where he told his office manager he'd be. He has a reason for that, a reason for being somewhere else."

"With Seth Costner?" Reese asked. "With the man who murdered his daughter?"

"Exactly," she said.

Reese groaned. "You think he's killing him."

And she shared Elise's fear that her brother was walking blindly into the middle of that murder to his own. "I don't know if he would set up a bomb or just shoot him."

"Do we need to send out a bomb squad?" Reese asked. "A sniper?"

She would…if she thought any of them would arrive in time to save her brother. But she didn't even believe that she was going to arrive in time to save Neil.

ELISE WAS A good driver, but she'd never taken a defensive driving class or participated in a car chase. So instead of driving herself to the address the parole officer had given her, she'd climbed into the back seat of the patrol car parked outside City Hall. And when the unit following Neil radioed in that they'd lost him, she was damn glad that she had her protection duty.

Not just for her protection but also so that they could maybe save Neil, as well. Of course he didn't believe that he was in serious danger from Seth Costner. He just wanted to warn the parolee that his father-in-law might want to kill him.

Elise was pretty sure that Seth was already aware of how Walter Shultz felt about him. What she hadn't realized was how the man might have felt about her and Neil.

Was he really the one who'd tried to kill them?

"Are you all right, Mayor Willis?" one of the officers asked her through the metal screen separating the front of the car from the back. Since the young officer had been hurt outside Neil's house, two officers were now assigned to each of them.

Two hadn't been enough for Neil, though, since he'd lost them. What the hell had he been thinking?

Of the baby, probably.

She slid her palm over her stomach, and something fluttered inside her. Maybe it was just nerves, but she wondered if it could be the baby moving restlessly, also worried about his father. Would they ever meet?

Even before getting pregnant, she'd worried about becoming a single parent like her mother. She'd feared that her baby might be abandoned like she had been. She shouldn't have suspected that Neil, who'd wanted a family of his own so badly, would ignore his child. But now she knew that while he might not do it willingly, he might still abandon him or her.

"Mayor?" the officer called out to her.

She was bouncing around on the back seat as the car traveled down a gravel road with deep ruts in it. Grasping the armrest, she assured the officer, "I'm fine."

"Is this it? The right address?" the driver asked, voice doubtful.

She glanced at the piece of paper with the numbers and letters standing out in relief against the gray pencil lead. "I—I think so."

She couldn't be entirely sure, though, that the four wasn't a nine or maybe a seven. Not that it could have made much difference. There weren't many houses out here. In fact all she'd seen was trees dusted with snow on either side of the road and now on either side of the driveway down which they traveled.

Finally a gap widened between the trees, revealing a small cabin nearly obscured by the two vehicles parked in front of it. "There's someone here."

And from the sticker on the back bumper, it was clear one of the vehicles was a rental. Neil had had to rent one while his vehicle was being repaired from being shot up in the garage the night before.

"Yes," she said. "This has to be the right place." As the officers stepped out of the police cruiser, she reached for her door handle. But it didn't budge. She would have to wait for them to let her out.

But before they could, gunshots rang out.

Now she had no doubt: Neil was here. Or he had been...

Was he dead now?

## Chapter Twenty-Six

As the gun blasted, Neil flinched, bracing himself for the bullet to strike. The barrel had been pressed against his head for so long, but then the police car had pulled into the driveway. And Walter Shultz had reacted, turning his gun toward the window...toward Elise.

Because somehow Neil knew she was in that car, that she'd brought along her security detail to stop him from putting himself in danger. From impatiently rushing into a situation without thinking of the consequences.

He'd done that too many times. The worst time had been when he'd told Elise he'd wanted a divorce. He hadn't thought that through, hadn't imagined what it would be like to live without her.

And he didn't want to find out now, either. So when Walter turned that gun toward the window, Neil reacted. He jumped the former soldier and wrestled him for the weapon.

While Walter was older than him, like Uncle Shep,

he was still in great shape. Strong and more than that, crazed with rage and determination.

He'd nearly killed his former son-in-law, or so Neil had thought when Walter had escorted him, with the gun barrel pressed to the back of his head, into the cabin. Seth had been lying on the floor, bleeding from his nose and mouth. Unconscious.

Or so Neil had believed.

But as he rolled around on the floor with Walter, struggling to hold the gun barrel away from his face, he heard something other than the gun going off. He heard shoes scraping against the scuffed hardwood floor. Then something struck Walter's back. It didn't knock him out; he remained conscious, his eyes full of rage as he stared at Neil. But his grip loosened enough on the gun that Neil was able to take control of it and finally direct the barrel toward Walter.

"Stop," he warned him. "I will shoot you..."

He would do whatever was necessary to keep Elise safe and to be able to see her again.

Walter must not have believed him, though, because he reached again for the gun. Before Neil could pull the trigger, more noise erupted inside the cabin. Wood splintered as the door was kicked open, and the police officers rushed into the one-room cabin, their weapons drawn.

"Put it down, put it down!" they yelled at him.

"I'm Neil Colton," he identified himself.

He wasn't sure if the officer believed him or not, as the man took the gun from his hand while the other officer helped Walter up from the floor. Handcuffs snapped around Walter's wrists, though, while the other officer merely helped Neil to his feet, asking, "Are you okay?"

He nodded but peered around him to where Seth had slipped back to the floor. "He needs an ambulance, though." Walter had nearly killed his former son-in-law before Neil had even stepped inside the cabin. But he somehow felt responsible.

Had he gotten Seth too good a deal? Had justice not been served as Walter maintained? The older man kept shouting, "Let him die! Let him die!" His voice cracked with sobs, but he continued, "He shouldn't be alive when my sweet Leah is dead. None of you should."

"I didn't do it," Seth murmured from the floor.

But Neil still couldn't be certain. There had been so much evidence to indicate otherwise. Walter, obviously, had been convinced—so convinced that he'd tried to deliver his own form of justice.

To Seth and to Neil and Elise...

"What about the mayor?" Neil asked the officer. "Is she with you? Is she okay?"

The officer nodded. "Probably just pissed that we left her locked in the back of the car."

"Thank you," Neil said. They had protected her while he'd just put her in danger over and over again.

It was no wonder that she kept turning down his proposal. Not only didn't she trust that he loved her, she didn't trust that he could take care of her.

He understood. If not for Seth rallying enough

to hit Walter, he might have gotten shot or worse. Killed...

He shuddered in reaction to the close call he'd just had. He'd had too damn many of them lately.

"Are you sure you're all right?" the officer asked.

No. He wasn't—because now that he'd realized why Elise kept turning down his proposal, he wasn't sure what he would ever be able to do to make her change her mind.

ELISE HAD BEEN home for hours, but she still couldn't stop shaking, couldn't stop reliving those moments she'd heard the gunshots and believed Neil was dead.

That she would never see him again...

But when she could have seen him again, she'd refused. Her fear, her emotions, had been too raw for her to trust herself. The minute he'd walked out of the cabin looking just a little mussed but overall healthy, she'd pleaded with another officer to drive her home.

Since she was the mayor, he'd been quick to agree—quick enough that Neil hadn't had time to stop her from leaving. But would he have tried?

She wondered now, since she'd been home for a while and he hadn't called, hadn't even texted. Was he mad at her for leaving?

Did he think she didn't care about him?

Because she cared—too damn much. She couldn't handle him putting himself in danger again. She just couldn't handle him.

Hunger, for which she liked to blame the baby, had finally taken her mind off what had happened, and she busied herself in the kitchen. After eating a bowl of chili she'd made and leaving the rest of the pot to simmer on low on a stove burner, she whipped together and rolled out some dough for Christmas cookies. It was not the first batch she'd made. While she considered before Thanksgiving too early to start decorating for Christmas, she never considered it too early to start baking for Christmas.

Her mom had taught her to cook and bake, but it wasn't something Elise had often done when she was married. She hadn't ever wanted to be a traditional wife who gave up or back-burnered her career to support her husband and take care of the children.

That was why she'd wanted to wait to start their family—until she'd established herself in Braxville. Until she was more than Neil Colton's wife and business partner.

She'd done that. She was the mayor.

And soon she would be a mother.

She wasn't sure she ever wanted to be a wife again, though—that she would ever be willing to risk her heart. Wadding up the leftover cookie dough, she popped it into her mouth just as the doorbell rang.

She'd left the crime scene earlier without giving a statement, so it could have been Jordana or Detective Carpenter following up with her. Leaving the stove and the oven on, she headed toward the door. The police interview would not take long; she hadn't seen anything. And she'd only heard that shot.

She flinched now as she relived that moment when fear that Neil was dead had slapped her like a physical blow. Her face might have still been in a grimace when she opened the door because the first question fired at her was, "Are you okay?"

Jordana wasn't the Colton who asked it, though. Neil stood outside her door. Then, uninvited, he stepped inside and closed the door behind himself. His hair was damp; maybe it was raining outside. Or maybe he'd recently showered…

The thought of which had an image popping into her mind, of him naked, water sluicing over his lean muscles.

"Elise?" He reached out for her, but she stepped back.

If he touched her, she wouldn't be able to resist him, not when she wanted him so damn much.

He flinched now. "I'm sorry," he said. "I won't."

"Won't what?" she asked. Make her want him? That wasn't possible.

"I won't push you," he said.

She snorted. "Of course not. You'd be worried about hurting the baby." The flash of jealousy she felt for her own child embarrassed and disgusted her. So she turned to head back toward her kitchen and the cookies she'd left in the oven.

He followed her but more slowly than she'd ever seen him move. As she took the cookie sheet from the oven, she studied his face. Dark circles rimmed those beautiful blue eyes of his, and his usually neatly clipped reddish beard was longer than usual.

"Are you okay?" she asked.

He shook his head.

And she gasped with concern. "I didn't think you were hurt." If she had, she wouldn't have left the scene.

"That's why you took off?" Neil asked. "It wasn't because…" He drew in a deep breath as if bracing himself for whatever he was going to say.

She held up a hand to stave off another proposal. "Now is not the time to bring up marriage."

"I wasn't going to," he said. "In fact, I'm taking back my proposal."

Skeptical, she narrowed her eyes and studied his handsome, exhausted face. "You are? Really?"

He nodded. "I realize what a fool I've been, Elise."

She sucked in a breath now, her heart and her pride stinging. "So wanting to marry me is foolish."

"You must think so, too, or you would have said yes," he murmured. "You wouldn't be getting so angry every time I propose. I figured that was why you had one of the police officers drive you away from the cabin. You were angry with me."

"I still am," she admitted. "You put your life in danger over and over again."

"I was a fool," he said, more easily now. "I'm lucky I didn't get killed or get you killed."

"What about Seth?" she asked. "Is Costner going to be okay?"

He nodded. "Yes. He's really beat up and still professing his innocence."

"Do you believe him?" she asked.

He shrugged. "I don't want to believe I convinced an innocent man to serve prison time."

"There was so much evidence," she reminded him.

"Too much," he said. "I lean more toward his guilt, but I suspect it was in the heat of the moment, not premeditated."

"So he served the correct sentence." She was glad of that; she would have hated to send an innocent man to prison, as well. Keeping the innocent free had been the reason she'd wanted to go into criminal law. Unfortunately, more of the guilty had wanted their representation than the innocent.

"I'm going to be more careful when I take on clients from now on," he said.

"And wives?" she quipped. "Since you've rescinded your proposal."

"You were never going to accept," he said. "I realized that, too, when I understood what a fool I've been. I realized that you're never going to trust me."

She sucked in another breath. "What happened in that cabin?" she asked. "How did you come to so many revelations? Did you get hit over the head? Near-death?"

Maybe he had been seriously hurt. She stepped closer to him and noticed the blood smeared on his hand. It might not have been his, but it looked fresh, like it was trickling down his arm as it had after the shooting in the garage. She gasped. "You're bleeding!"

He glanced down at his arm as if just noticing it. "That cut must have opened up again."

"How?" she asked.

"When I was wrestling with Shultz over the gun."

She closed her eyes as emotion overwhelmed her. She had come so close to losing him forever. But he wasn't hers. He hadn't been hers since the divorce.

"I'm sorry," he said. "I'm sorry I put myself in that position and worried you."

"What would I tell our child?" she wondered. "What would I say about his or her father if the baby is born after you're dead?"

His lips curved into a slight grin. "I imagine you could say a lot of things about what an idiot I've been."

"You're one of the smartest people I know," she said. Once she'd gotten to know him, she'd fallen even harder for his intelligence and wit than she had for his good looks.

"But I do stupid things," he said. "The stupidest thing I've ever done was divorce you."

A pang struck her heart. "Neil…"

He held up a hand now. "I'm not going to pressure you for anything anymore," he assured her. "I was a fool to pressure you to have kids right away."

"That's why you divorced me…" And since he was being so honest, she felt like she should be, too. "Because I wasn't enough for you."

"Oh, God, Elise, I was afraid that's what you were thinking," he said. "When I was having all these revelations, I realized you must think the only reason I want to marry you again is because of the baby."

"It is," she said. And she was certain. Too certain for him to convince her otherwise, not that she expected him to try.

He closed his eyes now, as if reeling from the same emotions rushing over her. "It's not. I wanted to marry you again the minute I divorced you. Hell, I never really wanted to divorce you."

"You just wanted me to have a baby before I was ready," she said. "And if you loved me, really loved me, you wouldn't have pressured me."

"I did really love you," he insisted. "But I was also impatient and selfish and wanted what I wanted when I wanted it."

"Did? Was? You've changed?" she challenged him.

His lips curved into that grin. "I will," he promised. "That's why I rescinded my proposal—to prove it. I won't pressure you anymore."

She touched her stomach, which was full of the chili and the cookies. "Because you're getting what you want, the baby you want."

"I want a family," Neil said. "That's what I wanted then and what I want now. I wanted a real family— with love and affection between the parents and time and attention given freely to the children."

A pang struck her heart. "Neil…"

She'd always envied his childhood, how he'd had the big, boisterous family. But she hadn't been part of that family for very long before realizing that his parents really weren't happy together, and their tense relationship must have affected all the kids. Neil more than she'd realized.

"I'm sorry," she said.

He shook his head. "You had it far worse than I did," he said. "Being just you and your mom."

But now she wondered. Sure, her mother had had to work hard, menial jobs to support them, but Elise had never had any doubt that she was loved. And since it had been just the two of them, there had been nothing but love.

"I hadn't wanted to wind up like your parents, either," she admitted. "That's why I didn't fight the divorce. I didn't want there to be that cold resentment between us."

He shivered and nodded. "Me, neither. That was why I filed, but I'd hoped you'd change your mind. And I'm sorry for that—for trying to manipulate you to get what I wanted."

"I wanted a family, too," she said. "I just wanted to wait to find myself and to forge my career. I didn't want to have to make the sacrifices my mother made."

"I know," he said. "And I wish I'd been patient."

She chuckled. "That's just not you."

"It will be," he promised. "I won't pressure you ever again."

She narrowed her eyes and studied his handsome face again. "Is this a manipulation to get what you want? To get me to accept your proposal?"

He sighed. "I deserve that…after the things I've done. But no, I rescinded my proposal and I won't ask again."

"Then what do you want, Neil?"

He shook his head. "It doesn't matter what I want. I want to know what you want. Do you want me to leave you alone?"

That was the last thing she wanted. But she wasn't

ready yet to admit it. She wasn't sure if she believed in his turnaround, and she worried that she might never completely trust him.

"You're bleeding on my floor. I want you to go the doctor and have your arm stitched back up," she said.

He nodded and turned as if heading toward the door. That easily? Without an argument?

"Neil?"

He turned back, his eyes bright with hope. "Is there something else you want, Elise?"

Him. But not now, not when he was hurt and exhausted and she wasn't sure this was real or just brought on by his close call.

"Time," she said. "I want time to think…" Time to trust.

He nodded. "Let me know when you want to see me again."

"What about our standing dinner?" she asked.

"You still want to do that?"

Every month she looked forward to meeting up, to talking and arguing and entertaining each other over a meal. And last month they'd made a baby.

"Yes. I'm not angry with you," she assured him.

"You just don't trust me," he stated as a fact.

Maybe he knew her better than she'd realized. Of course, that had been one of his revelations—that she didn't trust him.

"Not yet," she admitted, then warned him, "and maybe not ever."

He flinched. "I deserve that. I made a lot of mistakes, but if you'll give me a chance, date me, I'll prove to you that I can be patient, that I can put your needs first."

He'd always done that in the bedroom. Maybe it was possible that he could do it in other aspects of their lives.

She drew in a shaky breath and nodded. "It's a date, then."

"Friday night?"

She nodded and waited for him to close the distance between them, to kiss her. But he turned away again and headed toward the door.

And a curious mixture of disappointment and hope coursed through her. Could it be different this time? Could they actually make it work if they tried again?

She was afraid to hope that it was—afraid of being devastated again like she'd been when he'd divorced her. But she owed it to herself and to their unborn baby to give him a chance to prove it to her. To prove that he understood and loved her...

"YOUR SON IS in the ER again," a young nurse informed Lilly, making her heart flip with fear.

She hurried from the empty training room down to the bustling emergency room. Where was he? What had happened now? She'd thought it was all over—that the person trying to kill him and Elise had been caught. When she found which ER unit he'd been assigned, she jerked open the curtain to see him, to see how badly he was hurt.

Again.

A resident leaned over Neil's arm, stitching up a

small wound. "Your son is giving me a lot of practice," the young woman said with a chuckle.

Lilly couldn't laugh with her, not over this. "Too much practice."

"It's over, Mom," Neil assured her. "The guy that was after us is in jail now."

"I know," she said. "Jordana told me."

He winced, and she doubted it was because of the needle piercing his skin. This resident would have made certain he was numb before she started stitching. "I'm sorry," he said. "I should have called you and Dad."

It was her turn to wince now. She hadn't told Fitz yet. Maybe Jordana had called him, too, though.

She glanced around the waiting room. "Is Elise here?"

He shook his head. "She wasn't hurt."

"That's good," she said. "But I thought that maybe you two were back together. I was hoping that she'd come to Christmas dinner with you."

"I was hoping that, too," he said. "But we're not back together."

Lilly stepped closer and squeezed his free hand. "I'm sorry. I know how much you love her." And how much he was going to need her and not just for the holidays, but for support to deal with everything that was about to be revealed.

Too many secrets had been kept for too damn long...

"I do love her," Neil said. "But she doesn't trust my love anymore. And I'm not going to convince her by pressuring her. I'm going to show her that I love her by giving her what she needs. Patience."

The resident emitted a wistful sigh. And Lilly smiled in approval. "Good. She loves you, too. She'll come around." Or maybe all those damn secrets would push her farther away from Neil and the Coltons.

As the mayor, Elise couldn't subject herself to the scandal that was becoming their lives.

Neil squeezed Lilly's hand as if he suspected she had doubts. "She will," he said, but he sounded as if he was trying to convince himself as much as he was her.

She pondered telling Neil the truth now, so that he would have a chance to do the right thing for Elise and for her career. But one of the secrets, the worst one, wasn't hers to tell.

## Chapter Twenty-Seven

Maybe it was the candlelight. Maybe it was the pregnancy, but Elise was glowing. Just radiant.

She raised her hand to her face and touched her mouth. "Do I have something in my teeth?" she asked. "Or did I dribble on my chin?"

Too overwhelmed with her beauty to speak, he just shook his head.

"What is it?" she asked. "You're staring."

"You're beautiful," he murmured in awe.

Her green eyes narrowed, and she stared at him. "Are you trying to manipulate me again?"

A pang struck his heart—of regret and despair. "You're never going to trust me," he said. It didn't matter how slow he went, how little pressure he exerted. "You're never going to accept my proposal."

"You rescinded it," she reminded him. With—*was that*—a trace of disappointment?

If she was disappointed, maybe she had been more tempted to accept than he'd realized. Or he was just grasping at straws.

But Elise was the one grasping the straw in a tall

glass. Closing her eyes, she took a long draw and moaned in delight.

And his body tightened with desire. She was so damn beautiful, so sensual...even more so now that she was glowing. It wasn't fair. How could he be patient when it was killing him not to touch her, to taste her?

She swiped her tongue across her bottom lip. "You sure you don't want to try this shake?" she asked. "Eggnog. It's so good."

He wanted to taste it but not through the straw. He wanted to taste it on her lips, on her tongue...in her mouth. "Elise..." He cleared the desire from his throat. "I'm not an eggnog fan."

"You don't know what you're missing."

But he knew all too well. He was missing her. He'd been missing her since she'd moved out of their house, and not just since the other night but since he'd done the stupidest thing he'd ever done: filed for divorce.

But he couldn't tell her that—it would be manipulative. So he pushed aside how much he wanted her, how much he ached to be with her again. And he asked about her running the city and even about Jeremy and he told her about the practice, about his new client—the single mom going after her kids' father for back child support.

"It's not criminal," she remarked.

"No, it is," he insisted. "It's criminal that he's not helping her raise their kids—not physically and not financially." But Neil was going to make certain that he helped—whether the man wanted to or not. "I hope that's not why you were nervous about having kids with me, because you thought I might take off like your dad did."

She flinched and pushed away her shake, as if she suddenly felt queasy.

He did, his stomach clenching with dread that she'd had such doubts about him.

"I just wanted to wait until I was sure of *me*," she said.

"You can be sure of me, too," he said. "Sure that I love you for you. Always have. Always will. From the first moment I saw you."

She giggled. "Staring at you…you caught me staring…"

"Like you just caught me," he said. "You're so beautiful. Believe that. Believe how amazing you are. How smart, how sexy, how…" Desire choked him, making his voice trail off.

Elise's beautiful eyes glistened with tears, and she jumped up from her chair and rushed toward the exit.

Neil groaned. He'd done it again. While he was just being honest about how he felt about her, she must have considered it another manipulation to push her into what he wanted. So he resisted his impulse to chase her out of the restaurant. They'd met there, each driving their recently repaired vehicles, so she could drive herself home.

Once he'd paid the bill and left the restaurant, he resisted the urge to drive to her condo to apologize to her. She would probably construe that as pushing her again.

He needed to give Elise space, but staying away from her was so damn hard.

Especially now when he realized what a fool he'd been and how much he wanted—*needed*—to be with her—forever. While he wouldn't let himself go to her house, he didn't want to go home, either—to that empty house they'd been supposed to share.

But where else could he go? To his parents'? To his siblings'? It wasn't as if any of them was going to give him the sympathy or encouragement he wanted. Most either thought he was a fool for divorcing Elise, or, in his father's case, a fool for marrying her in the first place.

The family Christmas party was soon, so he would see them all then. But he would be attending alone…

He hadn't even had the chance to ask Elise to join him for the celebration. Not that she probably would have accepted anyway. And he couldn't blame her—after all the mistakes he'd made.

It didn't matter how long he drove around town or whom he went to see, he wasn't going to be thinking of anyone but Elise, of anything but how badly he'd screwed up. So he might as well go home.

Not that it had felt like a home since she'd moved out. He should have sold it then. But he'd really believed they'd get back together, that she would move back in.

Maybe it was time to accept reality. She was never going to trust him. She couldn't even trust that he was telling the truth when he complimented her.

The garage door opened as the SUV neared it, and

he pulled inside the recently cleaned space. All the glass was gone now, his vehicle repaired. So everything was back to the way that it had been before Walter Shultz had come after them—everything but him.

He was different. He only wished Elise could see that.

The minute he stepped inside the house, he felt something was different about it. It didn't feel empty...like he'd dreaded it would, like it had for the past few years.

But was that a good thing or a bad thing?

Had someone gotten inside while he'd been gone?

The alarm wasn't going off, but a lot of people knew his security code. One of them could have gotten in without setting off the alarm.

His pulse quickened with excitement. Not fear.

Walter Shultz was in jail and had been denied bail. He couldn't get out. Not that Neil couldn't have another enemy...

As he walked through the mudroom to the kitchen, he noticed a strange multicolored glow. Then he heard the music playing softly, charmingly...

Christmas music.

Christmas lights.

As he walked past the island in the kitchen, he noticed the tray of cookies sitting on it. And a smile curved his lips and his pulse pounded now with excitement, with anticipation.

When he stepped into the great room, Elise raised her hands with an ornament dangling from one finger. "Don't shoot," she said. "I'm not here to hurt you."

"I'm the one who keeps hurting you," he said, his heart heavy with regret for all the mistakes he'd made. "I'm sorry I sent you running out of the restaurant."

She shook her head. "I was just overwhelmed…"

"And I didn't mean to do that," he said. "I didn't mean to pressure you."

"I know…"

But did she? Did she know how much he loved her?

Afraid to give in to hope, he had to ask, "Why are you here?"

She pointed toward the tree. "We never finished decorating."

He stepped closer and repeated, "Why are you here, Elise?"

ELISE DREW IN a deep breath to settle the nerves fluttering around in her stomach. Then she realized she wasn't nervous. Not at all…

Because she trusted Neil and, more important, she trusted his love.

Maybe the fluttering in her stomach was the baby, then. Maybe worrying about losing him or her these past few weeks had made her more sensitive to his or her movements.

Or maybe she'd eaten too much at dinner and too many Christmas cookies since then.

"Elise?" Neil prodded her. "Why are you here?"

She smiled at him, at the tension on his handsome face. He looked nervous.

She was not, as she dropped to her knees in front

of him. "You rescinded your proposal, so I'm offering mine."

His brow furrowed with confusion. "What?"

"Will you marry me, Neil Colton?"

"You're proposing to me?" he asked, his voice gruff.

She nodded. "You said you wouldn't propose to me again."

"Not until you were ready," he said.

"I'm ready," she said.

He shook his head. "This is too soon. I promised I wasn't going to pressure you. I was going to give you time."

"You did," she said.

He snorted. "Barely a week."

"You gave me three years," she said. "Three years to find out who I am without you."

His lips curved into a slight smile. "The mayor. You're pretty damn powerful."

She nodded. "Yes, I am. I'm not going to lose myself this time."

"You didn't lose yourself last time, Elise," he said.

"No, I didn't," she said. "And I survived when we were apart."

His brow furrowed again. "So why are you proposing, then? Is this because you don't want to be a single parent?"

Shock gripped her; she was stunned that he had the same doubts about her love that she'd had about his. Until tonight, when she'd seen how he'd stared at her.

And she'd remembered that he'd always looked at her that way—with love.

"Whether we're married or not, I would never be a single parent when you're the father of this baby," she said. "I know that you would never abandon a child the way my father abandoned me. You are too good a man to ever do that. You're such a good man, Neil Colton, that you put your life on the line for me and for our baby and even for Seth Costner when you have no idea if he's guilty or innocent. I love you."

His breath shuddered out in a ragged sigh of relief. And he dropped to his knees in front of her. "And I love you, Elise. I always have and I always will, and I hope you believe that."

"I do…"

"Will you say that again as soon as we can get down to City Hall and make this official?"

"Are you accepting my proposal?" she asked.

"Hell yes," he said, and he lowered his mouth to hers.

She kissed him back with all the passion and love she felt for him. He groaned and murmured her name, and his hands shook a little as he fumbled to undress her and him…until they were naked but for the glow of the multicolored lights on their skin.

Neil pushed her gently back onto the rug and he showed her how much he loved her by giving her more pleasure than she'd thought it was possible to experience. And she wondered how she had ever doubted his feelings even during and after the divorce. Because she could feel his love for her as fiercely as she felt hers for him.

"I love you," she cried out as another orgasm shuddered through her body. Then he was inside her, filling her as completely as he always had. They moved together, in sync, finding the rhythm that led to another release for her and one for him that had him shouting her name and his love for her.

Then he held her closely as if he never intended to let her go. But it didn't matter; she had no intention of going anywhere. She was right where she wanted to be—in his arms.

SEATED AT THE head of the dining room table, Fitz Colton usually felt like a king surveying his empire. That was what his family felt like to him—something he'd built, like he'd built so many other things. Since last Christmas his empire had grown, and many more people sat around the long table. Significant others of his kids. His brother…

But this Christmas, he didn't feel like a king sitting on his throne; he felt more as if he was seated in the witness chair during a trial—his.

Maybe that was because there were two lawyers at his table now. His son Neil but also Neil's once-again wife, Elise. Even though she was now the mayor, or maybe because of it, Elise scrutinized him with an unsettling intensity. She knew something was up.

But how could she not, with everything that had happened in Braxville over the past several months?

Some of it had been terrible, like that maniac trying to kill her and Neil. Some had been wonderful, like the fact that she was pregnant with his first grandchild. He smiled at her, and her eyes widened for a moment with surprise before she smiled back.

A tinkling of glass drew his attention to the other side of the table across from Elise and Neil. Bridgette lightly struck her wine goblet with a fork. "I have an announcement to make," she said. Then she reached for Luke Walker's hand.

Fitz still wasn't entirely sure how his daughter had fallen for the owner of the local hardware store, but she had rented an apartment from him. And like his father, who'd worked for Fitz, Luke was a damn nice guy. Good looking, too, with his light brown hair and green eyes.

"We have an announcement to make." Bridgette held up their joined hands and a diamond sparkled on hers. "We're engaged!"

Cheers and shouts rang out around the table as they had moments earlier, when Neil and Elise had announced their happy news.

This news didn't make him as happy as the baby news had. But then he hadn't quite forgiven Bridgette for her investigation shutting down his business. "So who's moving?" Fitz asked the couple.

Bridgette smiled. "Me. I'll be working out of the field office in Wichita and commuting from Braxville."

"We'll be building a house soon," Luke added.

"I would have offered to build it for you," Fitz said, "like I did Neil and Elise's—if you hadn't opened that investigation and shut down my company."

"Stop it!" Lilly yelled as she jumped up from her chair at the other end of the long table. "Stop it!"

Shame gripped him, and he knew she was right. It was time.

"Stop blaming Bridgette or Elise or the previous mayor or even Dex for what you did…" she said, and tears began to stream down her face. "Tell them the truth."

"I—I thought we were going to wait until after the holidays," he reminded her of the promise he'd extracted from her when he'd finally told her the truth.

She shook her head and a tendril of deep red hair slipped free of the knot she'd bound it in and trailed down her face like the tears. "I didn't agree to that. Now is the time…when we're all together."

While he stared at his wife of so many years, the rest of the family were all staring at him as if they already knew. Maybe they did or at least suspected.

"What is it, Dad?" Neil asked.

Fitz expelled a shaky sigh and cleared his throat. "I might know why my former employees have gotten sick," he admitted.

Bridgette gasped, and Luke slid his arm around her, holding her close. One of those employees who'd gotten sick was Luke's father.

"Twenty-five years ago the company was struggling," he said. He gestured around the table. "We were struggling. With all you kids and all the expenses, I couldn't afford to lose the business, so I cut some corners."

"What kind of corners?" Bridgette asked.

"I bought some construction materials from overseas," he replied. "Materials that weren't subjected to the same guidelines and inspections as the materials here…"

Bridgette understood more than the rest of them, because she clasped a hand over her mouth, as if to hold back another gasp or a cry.

"I wouldn't have used them if I'd thought they would make people sick," he said. He hadn't wanted anyone to get hurt, but he could see that he had hurt not just his employees but his family, as well.

Especially his family.

He closed his eyes as shame overwhelmed him. A strong hand grabbed his shoulder, squeezing. He opened his eyes, expecting to find Shep offering him comfort. If only Shep had helped him with the business instead of joining the Navy…

But it wasn't Shep standing over him. It was Neil.

"You need to make a full confession to the authorities," Neil said. "I'll go with you. I'll represent you."

Fitz sucked in a breath of shock. "I—I'm not ready."

It was bad enough that his family knew. If everyone else learned the truth…

"It's going to come out," Elise said.

Now he didn't give a damn that she carried his grandchild; he glared at her. "I thought I could trust you—now that you're a Colton again."

"I'm still Mayor Willis," she reminded him. "And I have a duty to protect this town. Do I need to shut down the mall, Fitz?"

He groaned and turned toward Bridgette.

"What was it, Dad?" she asked. "What kind of materials did you bring in?"

"Treated lumber."

She gasped. "Arsenic…that's what's getting everybody." She turned toward her fiancé. "I'm sorry…"

"It's not your fault," Fitz said. "It's not any of your faults. I brought in Dex and I thought he would help, but he was all talk and empty promises. And I had to figure out how to keep those promises or lose the business." Instead two people had lost their lives, and so many more had gotten sick. He knew now that what he'd done was wrong. "I can't undo it," he said. "I can't go back and change the past. What will it matter if we wait another week?"

"I'm shutting down the mall," Elise murmured.

"We already checked it once," Bridgette said. "The levels weren't too high. Most of the wood would have been covered up. We'll see what we need to do."

His family was going to work together to make right what he'd ruined. Fitz saw that now as his children all began to talk at once, to each other and to the new loves in their lives. Only Lilly didn't speak to him; she spoke to his brother instead. She couldn't even look at him anymore.

Fitz accepted then what he had known for a while. His life as he knew it was over. Nothing would ever be the same.

* * * * *

# COMING SOON!

We really hope you enjoyed reading this book.
If you're looking for more romance, be sure to
head to the shops when new books are
available on

## Thursday 12th November

To see which titles are coming soon, please visit
**millsandboon.co.uk/nextmonth**

MILLS & BOON

# MILLS & BOON

## THE HEART OF ROMANCE

## A ROMANCE FOR EVERY KIND OF READER

**MODERN**

Prepare to be swept off your feet by sophisticated, sexy and seductive heroes, in some of the world's most glamourous and romantic locations, where power and passion collide.
**8 stories per month.**

**HISTORICAL**

Escape with historical heroes from time gone by. Whether your passion is for wicked Regency Rakes, muscled Vikings or rugged Highlanders, awaken the romance of the past.
**6 stories per month.**

**MEDICAL**

Set your pulse racing with dedicated, delectable doctors in the high-pressure world of medicine, where emotions run high and passion, comfort and love are the best medicine.
**6 stories per month.**

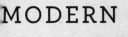

Celebrate true love with tender stories of heartfelt romance, from the rush of falling in love to the joy a new baby can bring, and a focus on the emotional heart of a relationship.
**8 stories per month.**

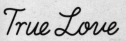

Indulge in secrets and scandal, intense drama and plenty of sizzling hot action with powerful and passionate heroes who have it all: wealth, status, good looks...everything but the right woman.
**6 stories per month.**

**HEROES**

Experience all the excitement of a gripping thriller, with an intense romance at its heart. Resourceful, true-to-life women and strong, fearless men face danger and desire - a killer combination!
**8 stories per month.**

**DARE**

Sensual love stories featuring smart, sassy heroines you'd want as a best friend, and compelling intense heroes who are worthy of them.
**4 stories per month.**

To see which titles are coming soon, please visit

## millsandboon.co.uk/nextmonth

# JOIN US ON SOCIAL MEDIA!

Stay up to date with our latest releases, author news and gossip, special offers and discounts, and all the behind-the-scenes action from Mills & Boon...

 millsandboon

 millsandboonuk

 millsandboon

*It might just be true love...*